DEATH STONE

RUBY JEAN JENSEN

Gayle Jensen Foster

RING OF DEATH

It was in front of her now, a tall and slender black figure that seemed bent forward slightly in the middle so that its head came down toward her. And there were arms now, and large hands, like a man's hands, and just for an instant it seemed she could see its eyes. Then a sharp pain in her hand drew her attention downward, and she sank to the floor. Red and blue and green fire shot from the ring, thin, streaming, piercing the air, reaching toward her face.

And she knew. It was the ring. Somehow, it had something to do with the black thing.

She got to her feet and ran down the bedroom hall to the bathroom, and the whisper became a sound that filled her head and the hall, roaring as if she were in a huge, dark cave, echoing back at her, coming in hisses and commands, one word tumbling over the next so that she understood only the gist of what was being said to her.

Kill ... kill ... kill ... Clare ... kill ... pets ... pets ... kill pets ... Clare Greta fell into the bathroom and locked the door, and then realized she had shut herself into a room without light. She leaned her cheek against the door and breathed heavily for a moment and then she stood up and screamed, "NOOO!"

First printing: October 1989 Printed in the United States of America

Published by: Gayle J. Foster, Carrollton, Texas

Library of Congress Control Number: 2020909519

Cover art: SelfPubBookCovers.com / RLSather

My continuing thanks for the guidance of my agent, Marcia Amsterdam, and my editor, Leslie Gelbman.

"In the night-time it glows like fire, for it is red and emits rays; and if you look at it, it smites your eyes with a thousand gleams. And this light within it is a spirit of mysterious power, for it absorbs to itself everything in its neighborhood." Quoted from Man, Myth and Magic

❀ Created with Vellum

PROLOGUE

YOU KILLED ... you murdered an old woman for this ... a ring?

No ... no! ... I hate you ... I didn't!

There's blood. Blood on the stone. Here ... keep it ... and be damned ... damned ...

No! I didn't! He ... he did ... he! He gave it to me ...

There's blood on your hands, damn you to hell ...

The hand struck her face again and again, and she tasted blood in her mouth, a sweetish, sickening, thick substance. Red. She tasted the color red. And as the hand struck her head again, she saw colors behind her eyes, flashing like neons on a downtown street, blurred behind a sheet of tears that was like rain, falling and blending with the red and with the greens, blues, and reds of the neons.

YOU'LL BE SORRY, she screamed, lashing back. You'll be sorry!

There came an added strength, another blow that knocked her backward. The colors blurred to gray. She fell to the floor, the flashes of light behind her eyes gone, as if the rain had grown heavier and had now obscured the flashing neons.

Arms picked her up and carried her.

Then she was falling, forever, into a dark place where there was no light at all. She kept falling and falling and falling ...

CHAPTER 1

Greta, at age nine, was six months younger than her cousin Derek. He had been her companion and playmate all her life. Their houses were separated by two wide yards and a narrow citrus grove, and their mothers were sisters. As Greta crawled through the tall grass that was left to weeds and natural growth at the rear of the houses, her hair blended and was lost within it, both the color of ripe wheat. She was making a pathway through the grass, and a few feet away, his own hair blending, moved Derek, though she couldn't see him. They were African lions and they were hiding from the great white hunters, Derek's fourteen-year-old brother, Kenny, and his friend, Calvin. They were working on their jeep, which actually was a bicycle; and it didn't matter at all that neither Kenny nor Calvin even knew they were in the tall, brown grass. They were cruel hunters, with long guns and sharp knives, and they killed lions.

"They're coming," Derek hissed, in the low growl of one lion warning another. "Run. Keep low."

Greta lowered her head until her chin grazed the ground, and crawled faster through the grass, blinded by its thickness. She butted the obstacle in the grass with her forehead, a hard blow, and jerked up involuntarily, crying out, "Ouch!" '

"Hey!" Derek warned, his head coming up to glare at her.

Over the top of the grass she could see they were in the old orchard, surrounded by almond trees whose bark was rough and whose limbs were unpruned and twisted. They had gone farther into the edge of the orchard than they ever had before. Behind them half the length of a city block were their houses, shaded and half concealed by trees; and in the alleyway in between, Kenny was bent over his bicycle. Calvin sat on the ground, his own bike a few feet away. They didn't know Greta and Derek were anywhere around, nor did they care. Greta's eyes swept the neighborhood. In a row with Derek's house and hers was the older, larger house of their grandfather, the original farmhouse. And behind it all the interesting old farm buildings were clustered, no longer used.

No one was in sight other than the two boys.

"What are you doing?" Derek demanded. "Get down! The hunters will see you. Wanna get your head blown off?"

Greta rubbed her forehead and felt the small swell of a knot. She lowered her head and peered at the object in the grass. It looked like a curving metal wall, with a wooden top. Altogether, it was only half as tall as the grass.

"Hey, Derek, look here. What's this?" She sat up, parting the grass. There was directly in her path a thick plank lid of some sort, sitting on rusted metal that was built in a circle no wider than the top of a small table.

Derek came toward her, on his hands and knees, his eyes just skimming the top of the grass. His crew cut looked as stiff as clipped grass, as if it had been mowed. Greta almost giggled as she glanced at him, but her forehead throbbed and dampened her amusement. She rubbed the low swell of the bump. In all the years they had crawled through the tall, uncut grass, they had never come upon this, whatever it was. And then she noticed they were in off-limits territory. They had made their pathways deeper into the orchard than ever before. Hadn't they always heard: Stay in the yards. Don't go back into the old orchards. Don't go in the barns. Don't go in the sheds. There were so many places they weren't supposed to play because, their mothers said, it wasn't safe. Why wasn't it safe? That was just one of the things mothers said that didn't make sense, that had no real reason behind it. Unless, of course, they had meant that something like this might happen, and one of them would crack his forehead against rusty metal tucked down into the cover of the grass.

Derek sat up beside her and helped push the grass back from the wood lid. He picked at a piece of the wood and it came away in his fingers, rotten, soft. He began working at that board, nailed to the others by a cross plank, and the board came loose.

With her head close to his, Greta cautioned, "Derek, don't. Mama wouldn't want you to do that. What is it?"

"I don't know." He pulled another board off and leaned over the metal wall and peered in. Greta tried to push her head in beside his so she could see too, but there wasn't room.

"What is it?" she demanded. "Is it a pipe?" A big pipe, she amended, looking at its circumference. A yard wide, as her mother would say, as she measured cloth.

"Hey!" Derek called into the opening, and his voice echoed back deeply from somewhere below. With eyes rounded, he looked over his shoulder at Greta. "It's a well!"

"A well!"

Greta shouldered him away, gripped the curved, rusty metal in her hands, and peered into the dark interior. Darkness, eerie and deep, came up to meet her. Cold air rose and covered her face like wintertime. She shuddered and didn't resist when Derek shoved her aside.

With both hands he began tearing at the lid. "Help me," he said. "You lift that side."

Greta moved around to the other side of the metal pipe that stuck six inches up out of the ground, and gripped the heavy lid. Grunting, she lifted. Across the lid she saw Derek's face turning red and twisted as he applied strength. The lid began to move. They twisted it sideways and the bolt that had been holding it pulled free of the softened wood. The lid slid off beneath their hands and the top of the well was opened to the air. Together they looked in, each gripping the metal edge, their heads close.

It seemed, just for a flash, that she glimpsed the reflection of water far below, but she couldn't be sure. The cool air rushed upward against her face, and she felt suddenly uncomfortable, as if she were going to pitch head forward into the long, dark, deep hole. She drew back. Derek looked up at her, his face shining, with the look in his eyes that meant he had thought of something really fun to do.

"It's got water! Let's go fishing."

"Fishing!" she cried scornfully, but Derek was already on his feet. "Is there fish down there?"

"Sure there's fish down there," Derek called back over his shoulder as he began rushing through the grass toward the lawn shed behind his house. Greta followed him.

"There is not! Fish don't live in wells."

"They do too. Especially when it's connected to the ocean."

"The ocean?" Greta looked over her shoulder, but the well was hidden by the tall grass that grew in the orchard as well as the empty spaces between the alley and the orchard.

"Sure, the ocean," Derek said with great enthusiasm as he stumbled through the obstructing grass, trying to run but unable to. "That's why it's so cold down there. The water comes from Alaska. From the North Pole, even. I'm going to get my dad's fishing gear."

"Hey, you better not!"

Greta caught up with him at the edge of the lawn, then she had to run to keep up. They crossed behind the citrus grove and into the mowed backyard of Derek's house. He stopped and looked around. Greta looked around, too. Not even Kenny and Calvin were in sight now.

"You stand guard," Derek ordered, and slipped into the shed.

Greta stood on the grass just off the worn path that led from the shed to various points in the rear yard of Derek's house, and watched for any sign of movement. Two thick-leafed orange trees obscured the back door of his house, and the kitchen windows where Aunt Alyne might be. The corner of the house stuck out toward the driveway and the garage, but there was no window at the point that was visible.

Farther over, just across a vine-covered wall, was the white exterior of Grandfather's house. She could see the sloping roof of his back screen porch and the steep rise of the roof above the attic, and she could see windows where Grandfather's housekeeper, Miss Reade, might be, hidden behind the lace curtains. But Greta spent only a moment looking at the windows. Miss Reade was a nice lady who gave them milk and cookies on the screened porch sometimes, on those occasions they wandered into Grandfather's backyard, usually by accident. She was soft and round and wore dresses and aprons instead of slacks and blouses, and she never, never wore shorts. Once Greta had asked her mother why Miss Reade never wore shorts, even on the hottest days, and her mother had laughed and said, "She'd be fired if she did." So Greta supposed that meant that Grandfather wouldn't like it.

Grandfather himself was a somewhat fearsome figure. He was extremely tall, even though he bent forward over a cane when he walked, and he had hair as white as cotton that he kept brushed back from his forehead. It never slipped and fell forward like Kenny's or William's, or like Derek's had before his new crew cut. It always waved back, as if it were freshly dampened and combed.

Greta didn't see her grandfather very often. She didn't think he liked kids a lot, though sometimes when he was out on his front porch, he would call Derek and her to him and he would touch their heads and there would come into his eyes a misty look that made them vague and distant.

Derek came out of the shed, head first, as if it were disembodied. He looked cautiously in all directions before the rest of him followed, holding his dad's best fishing rod behind him.

"Is it safe?" he inquired.

"All clear," she answered.

"Okay, let's see. We got to get there without Kenny and Calvin seeing us. William's gone over to Rudy's today. We don't have to worry about him. Shh! Wait!"

A door slammed, then the voice of Stephanie, Greta's sixteen-year-old sister, drifted to them. "Okay, Mom", she called to the house as she moved into sight on the walk beyond the citrus grove, only her long, tanned legs showing beneath the thick, green leaves of the grove. "Okay, okay. I promise! I'll be back by five."

Greta watched the legs move out of sight beyond shrubs in her own yard next door.

"All clear now?" Derek asked, ready to scoot back into the shed.

"All clear," Greta said, looking for Kenny and Calvin as she led the way around back of the shed to the unpaved alley that ran behind the three houses.

"Let's go this way," Derek said, running past her into the orchard. "Bend down so they won't see us."

Greta followed, bent, her back only slightly higher than the grass that had grown very tall during the summer. She had meant to tell Derek that they weren't supposed to go into the orchard, but of course he knew that. And hadn't they just come out of the orchard where they had found the well? This was land that had belonged to a large farm that once was owned by Grandfather's father, so her mother had told her. But other people owned part of it now, and there were rumors that someday there would be houses here, just as there were houses all along the road back into town. Besides, her mother said, you never knew who might be in the orchard. When she was a child, it was old bums, and perhaps there were still old bums in the orchards. Greta raised her head, but saw nothing that looked like it might be an old bum. She wasn't exactly sure what bums were supposed to look like, but she had an image in her mind of a dark, mysterious, bent figure in a heavy cape, someone who looked out through beady eyes. A stranger. Bums were synonymous with strangers who were never, never supposed to be talked to.

"Is it all clear?" Derek asked.

Greta looked over her shoulder. Kenny and Calvin were still in the bare alley, still bent over the bicycle. Near them was the old dog, Buster, a blue heeler, who followed Kenny wherever he went so long as he was allowed. But he never barked at Derek or Greta, he only barked at strangers.

"All clear," Greta said.

"Good." Derek sat down in the grass at the edge of the open well and looked at Greta. He admitted, "I forgot bait."

Greta knelt in the grass and looked at the bare hook on the end of the line. It was cruel and sharp, with claw-like projections. Poor fish, she thought. If a fish bit the hook, it would never be free again.

"What are you going to do with the fish?" she asked.

Derek twisted his mouth sideways and looked off into the grass. "Eat it," he said, clearly thinking of something else.

"I don't want you to eat it," Greta cried. "I don't want you to kill a fish!"

"I won't kill it," Derek said with contempt, looking at her as if she'd lost her mind. "I'll just ..."

"Throw it back? Uncle Ross says he throws them back lots of times."

"Sure, I know. I went fishing with him this summer."

"I know that," Greta said pointedly as she leaned to look again into the well. How very well she knew that Derek had gone away for a week's fishing with his dad and Kenny and his other brother, William. It had been lonesome here, with no one but Stephanie, who was no company at all, no fun, and their mothers, and of course Grandfather, who didn't really count as a companion anyway.

Derek elbowed her aside and she moved willingly. The cold air was still wafting up from the deep, black hole, and she could see nothing down the pipe but the dwindling, rusting walls, lost in the darkness. She shuddered again and Derek noticed.

"Chicken," he said, grinning. But then he was suddenly serious as he let out the fishing line into the hole. "I'm going to fish anyway, even without bait. Some fish will bite an empty hook, you know."

"Why?"

"Because it's shiny."

Greta peered over the edge of the metal and saw the line trembling as the hook went out of sight. "It doesn't look shiny to me."

"It will to the fish."

"I really don't think there could be any fish down there."

Derek concentrated on letting out the fishing line, ignoring her. "Gosh, it's deep," he said in a suddenly muted, awed tone.

Together they leaned over the edge of the pipe, looking down, but the line dwindled to nothing in the darkness that was so close to the top of the pipe they could have reached down and touched it. Greta pulled back hurriedly, but Derek stayed looking over as he let out more line.

He looked at Greta and his eyes were round as moons, staring at her the way they always did when he was surprised or scared or something. "There!" he whispered. "Look. The hook hit the water."

He pointed to the line and the way, for a moment, it leaned against the side of the pipe, as if folding upon itself. But then, slowly, it straightened.

"See, I told you!" Derek whispered excitedly. "There's water down there." He jiggled the rod up and down, tightening the line, relaxing it.

"What are you doing?" Greta asked.

"I'm fishing, silly, what else?"

"Is that how you fish?"

"Sure."

She had only Derek's word for it. Her own dad, Philip, was an accountant, if that had anything to do with fishermen. Anyway, he didn't go fishing. On his vacation he liked to go to Las Vegas.

Derek began to wind the reel. It made a soft noise, almost like a mouse squeak, against a whispered background.

Greta leaned forward cautiously, looking over the dark edge. "Did you catch something?"

"I don't know. You have to reel in once in a while and look. Get it?"

"Sure."

She moved back again, suddenly visualizing the eyes of a large fish moving silently up the walls of the well, coming face to face with her.

The hook came in sight and Greta stared. For a long, breathless moment, Derek stared too. Both of them were silent. Something small and round hung on the hook. Slowly Derek reached out, as if he were going to remove it from the hook, but instead he caught hold of the line above the hook and pulled it toward them.

It looked like a ring, darkened with something like moss, concealing the stone. Water dripped from the moss, striking the edge of the pipe and making a soft sound that seemed to echo back from the depths of the well.

They spoke simultaneously in lowered, excited voices. "It's a ring!" And Derek added, "A man's ring."

"It could be a girl's," Greta said, trying to peer through the slimy green stuff that strung down from it.

With the tail of his pullover knit he cleaned the ring superficially, uncovering a round, polished stone, red, surrounded by a setting of gold.

"Gosh," he breathed. "A pirate's ring, I bet."

Greta leaned closer, her hands flat on the ground, and watched him try to clean it. Icky stuff stuck to the depressions in the carving of the gold and made a black circle around the stone. Yet the stone turned to fire for a moment when he turned it, as if something had exploded deep within it. Greta jerked back, but Derek seemed not to notice.

"Golly," he breathed again.

Then suddenly he thrust it toward her, and she put her palms together, like a cradle, to receive it.

Derek was leaning into the well again, not even looking to see if he had dropped the ring into Greta's hands.

"Treasures!" he cried. "There's treasures down there. A big treasure chest, I bet. Somebody dropped it in a long time ago, the pirates, and when it hit bottom the lid flew open. A thousand years ago. I'm going to fish for more." He grabbed up the fishing line and began letting the hook down into the narrow, black hole.

Greta cleaned the ring. Bits of dark scum made the gold look black in places where figures had been carved. The gold encircled the ring, making it look larger than it was. The tiny figures looked like birds. No ... maybe ... bats? And there were vines with leaves, or something like that.

"I'll have to have some soap and water," she muttered.

"I'll give my mom a diamond necklace," Derek cried with great enthusiasm. "And my dad a dagger with jewels set in the handle."

Greta put the ring on her largest finger, but the stone slid around to hang beneath. She would have to pad it, but that would be easily done with tape. She'd seen her sister fix a ring like that not many weeks ago, when some boy gave her his class ring. Stephanie was still wearing it, Greta thought. She turned her hand, looking at the stone. The light from the cloudy day brought out a fiery shine that increased as she rubbed her fingers over the top of the smooth, red stone. On the surface it looked deep red, so dark it was almost black. But coming through, in sharp little shafts, was the red fire, rising and receding as she turned the ring to catch the best light.

She loved it.

She had to have it.

"Can I have it, Derek?"

"No. I'll give it to my dad."

"Please, Derek, oh, please! I'll give you ... anything. My next week allowance?"

Derek hardly paused. "No."

"Derek! Please. It's mine. You can have my whole piggy bank with all that's in it. Okay? Okay, Derek?"

He glanced toward the ring. "It's too big for you."

"I can fix it. Like Steph fixed her ring that the guy gave her. She put adhesive tape on it."

Derek shrugged, which, as Greta well knew, could mean almost anything. Sometimes it meant he was weakening, and sometimes it meant for her to shut up.

"Derek? *Please?*"

"And your knife? The one you found on the school yard? With the pearl handle."

Greta frowned, looking at the ring. She turned it, watching it change from dark, blood red to bright crimson. She sighed.

"Well, okay."

Derek nodded, leaning over the well, staring into the hole. "You can have it then."

Greta smiled. Her tongue licked the corner of her lips in satisfaction. Then suddenly Derek sat back and was pulling on the line again.

"I hit bottom," he cried. "Maybe I got something really neat. I think I got something."

"Is it heavy?" The ring, its stone warm against her palm, was kind of heavy.

"No," he admitted. "But ..."

She tightened her hand over the ring, the stone pressed inward against her palm. She got on her knees again, her hands on the ground, and peered over the edge.

A soft rush of wind whispered through the grass, moving it as if a huge hand had brushed across it. Greta shivered. She heard the beginning sprinkles of rain, but the almond tree they were sitting under kept the rain away. It pecked the leaves above, little noises that blended with the soft brushing of the fishing line against the pipe.

The line was rising. The hook came in sight, and there was something attached; but it didn't look like treasures or jewels or anything from a treasure chest. It was dark and limp, and black water dripped from it back into the well.

She was only vaguely aware of footsteps in the grass behind them, of someone coming to stand and watch.

Derek lifted the hook slowly into the air. The thing hanging on it was about the size of a man's handkerchief. It was mostly covered with the same dark, greenish slime that had covered the ring.

Derek shook it, slinging water back on Greta. But she didn't notice. Figures on the torn scrap became visible in the light, almost obscured beneath the blackish scum that covered it, and Greta realized it was a piece of cloth, that once it had roses or some other small flower.

"Hey!" a voice said from behind and above. "What's that? What're you doing? Derek? Greta? Does Mom know you're out here in these weeds? What if you get snake bit?"

Greta and Derek whirled, looking up at the two tall young figures that hovered almost threateningly over them. Kenny and Calvin. Behind them, his tail wagging, was old Buster.

"What're you guys doing?" Kenny demanded. "What is that place?"

Kenny and Calvin crowded in against the pipe, forcing Greta and Derek back. Kenny took the fishing rod away from Derek, at the same time peering down into the open pipe.

"What're you doing with Dad's rod and reel? What the hell have you done to his line, Derek? You got it all unwound. Don't you know Dad's fishing gear is off limits? Why didn't you use your own? You got a brand new rod last summer. Hey, what is that? What's down there?"

"Looks like a well to me," Calvin said.

Their heads came together over the well, Calvin's dark hair falling forward and contrasting with the light brown of Kenny's for a moment as their foreheads touched. Calvin had dark, soft fuzz on his upper lip and at two spots on his chin, and at times, like now, his voice was deep and low.

"Jesus Christ," Kenny muttered, and then whistled through his teeth as he drew back and reached for the limp, dripping thing that was attached to the sharp hook.

Greta frowned at Kenny. He was not usually into swearing, and she thought it sounded strange coming from him. She clasped her hand, holding the stone of the ring tightly against her palm, suddenly glad the ring was so large the stone turned inward where it was easily hidden. She knew at this moment, in the deepest part of her being, that what she was doing was wrong, that she should give Kenny the ring. But she couldn't give it up. It was against the rational part of her will that she was hiding it, as if something cold and dark and evil were in the pretty stone and was pulling her to its will.

Kenny removed the ragged piece of material from the hook and made a sound of distaste as his fingers worked it into a flattened leaf on his hands. He looked up into his buddy's eyes and they whistled softly together.

"A piece of dress or shirt," said Calvin.

"There's something down there, all right," Kenny said. "I wonder if it could be a body? A *dead* person? Derek, how long have you known this was here? How did ..."

But Derek began scrambling up from the ground, running before he was fully on his feet, going like a small animal, with his hands and his feet pushing him along at first, into the thick, tall brown grass.

Not treasures, but a body. A dead person.

Greta followed him, the tall grass holding her back, so that it seemed someone had grabbed her and was keeping her from running. From the corner of her eye she saw a dark shadow running beside her, and thought of it as her own. She felt as if she were in a nightmare, trying to run but unable to, as if something were pulling her backward to throw her into the deep, dark hole of the well to lie in the stagnant water with the bones and the rotted flesh of the body.

When at last she reached the alley, and felt the rain grow heavier on her head, she realized there was no sun to throw a shadow.

She ran on, sensing something behind that kept pace with her.

CHAPTER 2

ALYNE STOOD over the sinks in the island in the center of her kitchen cleaning vegetables. In the top rack of the steamer she placed broccoli and cauliflower. Then, in the small center sink of the triple sink arrangement, she began to scrub carrots. She sighed and changed position, putting most of her weight on one leg.

She had spent her day doing the same thing she always did. First, the beds and laundry. Each one of her three boys had to make up his own bed and straighten up his room, but she always went in after they were gone to school or out to play and smoothed the beds to suit herself. If they ever realized she had redone their work, they hadn't let on to her. If she knew boys, and she thought she did, they didn't have the foggiest that anyone had been in their rooms but themselves. After the bed smoothing and the couple of loads of laundry, she had gone shopping, partly because she needed fresh vegetables for dinner, and partly because it was her recreation. At the snack bar in the supermarket she had treated herself to a soft drink and a doughnut. She had felt properly guilty for an appropriate length of time, and then promised herself she would cut back on calories tonight. At the checkout stand she had bought a magazine.

Home again, she relaxed and read part of the magazine with the radio on her favorite station of easy listening music. Then when she got up an hour later, she switched the station to rock and roll, music to help her feel young and agile again. She sighed. Young and agile again? She was only thirty-eight. Only, she told herself pointedly, because thirty-eight didn't seem young. It didn't feel young. And from the viewpoint of her oldest son, Kenny, it was definitely not young. But her father was now eighty-three, and to him it was ridiculously young. All a matter of perspective. And energy. Of which she didn't have much at the moment. Today being Saturday and the boys home from school, she'd had to prepare lunch in the midst of her other daily doings. Ross, her husband, had worked most of the day, as he so often did. He worked longer hours and more days since he received his promotion to Managing Engineer at the factory, so the promotion sometimes seemed more of a curse than a blessing. He was turning into a workaholic. He was happy with life the way it was and she should be too, but sometimes she envied her younger sister, Clare, with her job and her totally different lifestyle.

She glanced up and out the wide windows at the rear of the kitchen just in time to catch a glimpse of Derek and Greta flashing out of sight beyond the corner of the house. She paused, arrested by something beyond, a movement in the orchard.

She dried her hands on the towel that lay on the counter, and walked around to the dining area of the kitchen where she could look out the back windows. She saw nothing out of the ordinary. Rain was dampening the walk that curved left from the patio to the back door of the garage. The narrow, unpaved service road that lay behind her house, her sister's house, and her father's house, looked dark, the usually brown dirt dampened with the light rain. Beyond the road was a strip of land given over to grass that hadn't been cut in a while, probably not since last year, if then. And beyond the grass was the old almond orchard, now looking deprived of light, as if it were a medieval forest.

But there was something too still now about the scene, as if something were missing. She concentrated on it, and saw nothing out of place.

The garage, separate from the house, was to her left. A garden shed was behind that, though not directly behind. A path ran from the garden shed to the garage, for some reason, grass trampled down by bicycle tires, probably. A rack beside the garage held five bicycles, one for each of them. To her right she could see the wall that separated the old, big house her father owned from her own yard, a good-sized lot given to her at her marriage. And to her left was the row of fruit trees and grape vines that separated her yard and Clare's.

Nothing moved, except a bird at the feeder.

Alyne went back to the sink and put the rest of the vegetables into the steamer and put it on the stove. It was two hours until dinner time. She set the burner on low. At least that part of the dinner was finished.

She sensed movement in the backyard again and turned, and this time she saw Kenny and Calvin coming toward the house, across the grass. They had a fast, purposeful walk that made her watch them as they came up onto the patio and toward the sliding doors. Something had happened that Kenny was going to report. She knew her sons, and she suspected that whatever it was involved Derek. It usually did. Poor Derek, he hardly got a chance to misbehave because if Kenny weren't reporting on him, then Willy was. This afternoon, though, Willy had gone over to Lenny's or Rudy's house to play.

Kenny was holding something between his finger and thumb, Alyne saw, as if it were distasteful. But he was bringing it into the kitchen, like an offering to her. She automatically put her hands behind her back. She'd had these offerings ever since Kenny learned to walk thirteen years ago.

"What is it?" she asked, as soon as the boys stepped into the house, leaving the door open behind them.

"You're not going to believe this, Mom," Kenny said. Alyne nodded in agreement, but he wasn't looking at her. The thing in his hand was dripping a growing little pool of dark liquid onto her clean, white tile. "But this came out of an old well back in the edge of the orchard, and you know what?"

Calvin burst out, as if he couldn't stay quiet, "There's a body down there!"

Kenny said, almost at the same time, "This looks like a piece of material to us. What do you think, Mom?" And he thrust it at her.

Alyne drew back, frowning down at the dripping cloth in his hands. He gave it another jab toward her, and she automatically put her hands out for it though she shrank inwardly in revulsion. Now the slimy and rotted piece of fabric lay on her hands, and she saw tiny rosebuds on a curling stem with little green-black leaves. The rosebuds were blue, the background white. She knew this suddenly with an unpleasant sensation of breathlessness, though there were no colors left in this piece of material. It was all brown and blotched and dripping slime. But for a moment she had seen the blue of the flowers, the green of the leaves, and the white background as if it were not soiled and discolored. She wanted to jerk her hands back and drop this thing, as if it had seared her skin; but she couldn't do anything but stare at it.

She was surrounded by darkness and fear, and she knew something was wrong. She glimpsed movement and felt her helplessness. A memory stirred, far back, a flash of white, with blue rosebuds ... so wrong. Rosebuds weren't blue, they were red or white or pink or yellow. Never blue. It was wrong, all wrong. Something ... was smothering her.

She turned quickly and dropped the damp, ragged bit of material on the white counter beside the sink; then she washed her hands, leaning over the backside of the counter, reaching beneath the spewing faucet. Her heart was beating so fast she could feel it through her body. Was she going to have a fatal heart attack at age thirty-eight? As her mother had at thirty-six? She waited until her heart slowed. Behind her, Calvin and Kenny were talking excitedly, telling something about how they had found Derek and Greta fishing in the well and using Dad's favorite fishing rod.

Well? What well?

She suddenly felt angry.

"What are you talking about, Kenny? Slow down." She drew a long breath and turned, leaning back against the counter. "What well?"

"It's out there in the edge of the orchard."

"It had a plank lid on it," Calvin added.

"It's a pipe, a big pipe, rusted. Come and see."

She didn't want to, but she had no choice. She had never been allowed to play in or near the orchard, nor had her own children. They were not to go beyond the alley road at the rear of the yards. It was the same rule that she and Clare had grown up with. Back in those days, when they rode their bicycles along the alley road, the big house, their home, was the only house on this side of the street. A few old farm buildings stood back in the edges of the old orchards, and that was all. Across the road was a similar home that belonged to Mrs. Crossover; but most of its land had been sold off too, and new houses had been built over the years. She wanted to leave things the way they were, before Kenny had brought in the piece of fabric. She wanted to go back just five minutes and push away this feeling that had settled in and over her.

She followed them out into the backyard. Rain fell very lightly, and she had not thought to bring something to cover her hair. It didn't matter. What mattered was this other thing.

"You know you kids aren't supposed to go into the orchard ..." She stopped. Why weren't they supposed to play there? Why weren't she and Clare allowed to play there? If there had ever been a reason, she had forgotten. Maybe it was because of the well.

She followed Kenny and Calvin through the tall grass and to the trampled area beneath the outer limbs of rough-barked old trees. The sight of the rusted metal pipe startled her, its gaping, open top filled with the blackness of depth.

It looked frightening and dangerous, and she instinctively grasped the sleeves of both Kenny and Calvin and pulled them back.

"My God," she cried. "A kid could fall in that!" And then, the horror of the piece of material struck her. "Oh, my God! Do you suppose ... ?"

The boys were talking excitedly at the same time. Both of them pulled forward out of her grasp and looked down into the well. She stared at the black hole, feeling as if she stood on the edge of the world, with nothing beyond but the void of forever.

"I didn't know that was there!"

The plank lid was propped against the opposite side of the well, and she felt another horror as she realized what must have happened today, as she listened to Kenny and Calvin tell again how they had found Derek and Greta fishing in this open, hideous pipe. They could have fallen in.

"I don't think so, Mom," Kenny said, and she realized she had spoken her fears aloud. "A kid could fall in, but he'd have to lean over it, I think. Do you suppose some little kid did that once a long time ago?"

"Maybe not so long ago," Calvin said.

"But it had a lid on it," Kenny mused, his mouth pursed.

"The lid might have been pushed over, like it is now."

Kenny bent down, dangerously close to the open well. "No," he said, pointing to a part of the lid. "See, this is freshly torn. I think Derek and Greta took it off. You know them. What one can't think to do, the other one does. They oughta be grounded for a month. No television, no playtime together. They're destructive, Mom!"

She had to go closer to the well. She didn't want to, but she had to. She put her hand on Kenny's shoulder and pulled him back, and then she leaned forward.

A rush of air struck her face, and it was a frigid, stale air, as if it came from a root cellar, or a cave. Visibility was almost zero. She could see over the sides of the rusted pipe down a few feet, and then the darkness took over. And the silence.

Old clothes, she thought. And said aloud, "Somebody tried to fill it in, maybe, and threw junk down there. Trash. Old clothes. That's all it is." It was a relief to hear it spoken, if only by herself. She felt like a small child that had been comforted.

"But, Mom," Kenny complained. "It might not be, either. Don't you think we should call the police?"

"We probably should cover it up again. In fact, we must cover it up again." She tugged on the lid and found it heavy and unyielding. "How could two little kids get this off the top? It's heavy."

"Mom."

"What, Kenny?"

She hadn't meant to sound so impatient and cross, but on the other hand she didn't feel like apologizing. She struggled with the lid and found it coming apart as she pulled, plank separating from plank. But she couldn't leave this horrible hole uncovered.

"Mom! We ought to call the police."

"Well, for God's sake, Kenny, I don't know why. It's an unused well that somebody tried to fill in ..." She stopped, biting her lower lip. This was land that might belong to her father, she supposed, part of the old farm that had belonged to his father. She didn't know the actual lines of ownership, where Papa's land ended and the neighbors' to the north began. Whatever, a new lid was going to be needed. This one was rotten as old paper—or cloth.

Her hands felt slimy and dirty, and she pulled back and wiped them on her slacks, something she would have yelled at the boys for doing.

"There's a body down there, I just know it."

"There are old clothes down there!"

"But, Mom, what if you're wrong?"

"You go ask your grandfather. He'll probably tell you it's been filled in with trash."

She saw the blackness, the dark and the cold reaching up from the depths of the pipe, and she heard the soft whisper of rain in the grass and on the leaves of the trees. The rain was becoming heavier, and she put her hand to her hair; but there was only slight dampness. She moved back from the hole in the ground, the old lid only half covering it. "What are you going to do, Mom?"

"Well, it's a dangerous place, with no lid to speak of. We'll go talk to Papa about it."

She picked her way through the damp grass back to the alley road, and then walked along the narrow road to the wall that surrounded the backyard of her father's house.

Vines grew thickly on the wall, so that it looked like a wall of vegetation.

He was an old-fashioned father, already near the half-century mark when she and Clare were born. He had always insisted that they call him Papa, never Dad or Daddy; heaven forbid that they should call him Daddy. So it was only fitting that the grandchildren call him Grandfather, not Grandpa, or Pawpaw or any of the babyish names that most grandfathers preferred. He was an imposing figure, even now in his eighties. He was still tall and straight, standing well over six feet; and though he was thinner now than he used to be, he still had the wide, straight shoulders that she had always associated with strength and power.

But he had weaknesses too, if partiality could be called a weakness. It was as if he could deeply love only a certain number of people; the rest he tolerated. Clare was his favorite. She was his baby, for one thing; but he had loved her better, Alyne always thought, because she was the pretty one. Didn't people always love the pretty one?

Yet when the grandchildren were born, he had not chosen the pretty one. Greta was far prettier than Stephanie, in Alyne's opinion, but Papa loved his firstborn grandchild, Stephanie. Coming second in his affections was Kenny. But the other three children were little more than nuisances, and she kept them away from his yard as well as she could.

She led the way up the walk from the gate that led out into the alley. The upper windows of the tall house looked out into treetops, and the first floor porches reached into the shade beneath them. Papa was surrounded by shade. He lived in a world of shade. The yard was filled with pathways and shrubs and trees. A driveway came straight in from the street to a garage near the back of the lot, but it was a narrow driveway, and the garage had been built for one car only. Papa's last new car, a 77 Buick, took up the space in the garage, and Miss Reade, the woman who had been his housekeeper for many years now, was forced to park her car beneath the trees. In Papa's day families didn't have two cars. In Papa's day the woman didn't need a car.

Alyne's life followed Papa's beliefs in what a woman's life should be, except for that second car. She had lived at home until she married, and then she had accepted land from her father on which to build her house. And then she had stayed at home and taken care of the children. Even with all that, Clare, who had followed the rules only to building her house where he wanted it, was still his favorite.

The boys came quietly behind Alyne. She opened the screen door on the back porch and crossed the squeaky wood floor to the kitchen. She knocked lightly, even as she opened the kitchen door and looked in. Marvelous smells of something sweet baking permeated the warm air.

The kitchen hadn't changed in all her lifetime. The linoleum was not quite as bright as it used to be, and the room seemed smaller and darker than it once had; but the only difference was that Anne Reade had put up new curtains a decade or so ago, and there was occasionally a new cloth on the table. Never plastic. Papa tolerated no plastic tablecloths on his table.

A light burned in the work area of the kitchen, and Anne greeted her with a smile and a motion of her hand to enter. She was the epitome of the old-time mother, though she had never been married or had a child that Alyne knew of. Papa was her child. She fussed over him as much as he allowed. She was a woman of medium height, but of slightly above average weight. She wore housedresses and aprons around the house, and dressed in suits or neat dresses when she went shopping or took her employer out for a drive. Her hair was neat; and although she was in her fifties, or perhaps even her sixties, there were no gray strands among the rich brown. She never wore makeup. But her spectacles had rhinestones in the upper corners, something that had always struck Alyne as being flamboyant, especially for Miss Reade.

"Hello Alyne, hello boys. You're just in time for fresh-baked cookies, boys. Sit down. Your grandfather is resting at the moment."

"I'd like to talk to him a few minutes, Anne. What time will he be up?"

Anne tilted her head sideways like a bird in the grass looking for a worm, but she was listening to sounds that meant something only to herself. She said, "He must be up now. Just a minute." She motioned toward the cabinet where cookies were cooling on a sheet of waxed paper. "Help yourself, Kenny and Calvin. You, too, Alyne." Kenny went to look on the waxed paper. "Hey," he said, helping himself with both hands. "These are snickerdoodles. My favorite. Anne makes great snickerdoodles. How come you don't bake them anymore, Mom?"

Calvin joined Kenny, and Alyne was tempted. But then she remembered. Sugar cookies, such as the ample snickerdoodles, have at least one hundred calories, and if she were going to keep her calorie count down to a thousand for the day, and if she wanted to eat a satisfying dinner, she'd better not add cookies. Remember the doughnut?

"Nobody can eat just one," she said, and broke off a half piece for herself. Tomorrow, she'd count calories.

"So who's going to eat just one?"

The buzzer on the stove timer went off, and Alyne stopped it and opened the oven door. A large cookie sheet filled with browning cookies sat on the middle rack. Alyne put on the oven mitt and removed the cookie sheet. She had finished scraping the hot cookies onto wax paper when Anne came back into the kitchen.

"Thanks, Alyne. Your father's awake from his nap. He'll be in the parlor."

They went through the hall to the front room. Just before she entered the door to the parlor, she cast a severe look at Calvin and Kenny. Her son interpreted her look correctly and stuffed the last bite of cookie into his mouth.

"Wipe those crumbs off. You could have stayed in the kitchen with Miss Reade."

Kenny shook his head and used his sleeve to wipe his mouth. Alyne frowned at him.

"Don't you have a handkerchief?"

Kenny shook his head and tucked his shirt into his pants. As soon as the boys looked presentable, Alyne opened the door to the parlor.

Papa was already seated in the brown leather chair that did not match the rest of the parlor furniture. The chair was in front of the windows that looked out toward the driveway and the street. Behind the chair stood a floor lamp with a swan neck and a glass shade. Alyne had no idea how old it was. It had stood beside that chair all her life, but both the chair and the lamp had occupied the small dark office hallway down the hall until the past ten years or so when Papa had moved it into the parlor. A table beside the chair was filled with magazines, newspapers, a magnifying glass, and a small tray with medicines and a pitcher of water. Alyne doubted that he ever took the medicines. Anne dragged him out for a physical once a year, and the doctor always gave him something for his heart, but Anne complained that she couldn't get Jonah to cooperate.

He sat with his cane between his knees, his hands folded over the curved top of the cane. His hair was thick and looked as if it had been brushed. It was as white as if it had always been his natural color. She could hardly remember that once her father's hair was dark. His eyebrows had grown over the years like shrubs, and now hung above his eyes like brush piles. The dark brown of his eyes was unblemished.

He spoke to the boys and motioned toward the love seat. They sat down. Only in Grandfather's house did Kenny sit still. He always looked uncomfortable. Calvin looked even more tense, his eyes roaming the cluttered room without turning his head. This was probably the first time Calvin had been in Kenny's grandfather's house, though Alyne had seen him on the front porch in summer evenings when he went out to sit in the porch swing.

"Papa, the children have uncovered an old well in the orchard. I ..."

"What?" He almost spat the word, leaning farther forward over his cane. "What the hell are you kids doing out in the orchard? You know better than that." His gaze left the boys and settled on Alyne. "What's happened to discipline? Don't you keep your children under control anymore, Alyne?"

"Well ..."

"That old well is off limits. None of your children are allowed to play close to it."

Alyne listened to him in astonishment. He was talking as if she knew all about the well.

"I didn't even know it was there, Papa."

"Of course you did. You and Clare were not allowed to go past the alley road because of that well."

"Is that why? Honestly, I guess I had just forgotten it."

Kenny said, "Derek and Greta were fishing in it."

"Fishing! In the well? How did they get the lid off?" He seemed more curious now than angry. He sat back in his chair, his eyes pinning Kenny to the love seat.

Alyne said, "The old lid was rotten, Papa. It probably wasn't difficult to get off. The thing is, Papa, there seems to be some old clothes down the well. I thought perhaps you might have filled it in to a certain depth."

Jonah had grown still and contemplative. He shook his head. "No, it's never been filled in that I know of. But with the newcomers on the other side of the orchard, who can tell? Some of them might have thrown something in." Newcomers. Alyne almost smiled. The houses built on the street beyond the orchard had been there, for the most part, since she was a child, or earlier.

"They fished up a piece of somebody's clothes," Kenny said. "I think there might be a body down there, Grandfather. Don't you think we should call the police?"

Jonah gazed steadily at Kenny, but there was a thoughtful look in his eyes. Or perhaps a faraway look, as if he were trying to decipher a problem.

"Of course there's no body down there," he said, blinking, his voice sounding normal, his gaze sharpening. "What would a body be doing in the well? That's the trouble with children. They can make something out of nothing." Anne Reade appeared in the doorway, leaning in, an apologetic grin on her round face. She was carrying a tray with cookies and a glass of milk.

"Can I get the rest of you a glass of milk?" she asked as she came on into the room and put the tray down on a cleared spot on the table.

"No thanks," Alyne said, rising. "I have dinner cooking, and I'd better get back to it. Come on, boys."

Jonah thumped his cane against the floor. "You tell those children of yours to stay away from that well. And you see to it, Alyne, that it's covered."

"What was it for, Papa?" Alyne asked.

"Water, of course. Years ago, before your time. When my father built here, they had to use well water. But it went out of use back in my youth, and has been covered ever since. A new well was drilled here in the backyard, and the pump put in. Then, in later years, the city water was piped through. That old well hasn't been used since I was Kenny's age, and it wasn't much good then. It's not extremely deep. Thirty or forty feet, perhaps, with only a few feet of water. Not good water. Cover it up, fill it in if you want. Keep the young ones out of the orchard. Leave it alone. Forget it." Alyne left her father looking at the glass of milk Anne was trying to get him to drink. He was willing to eat the cookies, but she had poured too much milk into the glass. Didn't she ever make coffee any more, Jonah wanted to know.

They went out the way they had come, into the alley and back toward the house next door.

"Call the police, Mom," Kenny urged, excitement in his voice once again. "You heard him yourself. Nobody ever filled in the well. There's got to be a body down there."

Calvin said, "Fell in, I bet you."

"Naw. How could they put the lid back on after they fell?"

Alyne asked, "How do you know the lid was on? If, as you said, Derek and Greta were the ones who found it, maybe the lid was already off. Where are those kids, anyway?"

"I don't know. They ran, like the brats they are."

"That's no way to talk about them, Kenny."

"Well, it's true. What about the police, Mom?"

Alyne opened the sliding doors into her kitchen. The steaming vegetables didn't give off the aroma that Anne's snickerdoodles had, but it was good to be back in her own bright familiar home. She put her hands to her damp hair and fluffed it, running her fingers through the short curls she had so carefully combed out this morning.

"Do what you want to, Kenny," she said.

"Hey, right!" Kenny slapped Calvin on the shoulder. "Let's go to the phone in the den, Cal."

GRETA WRAPPED a strip of adhesive tape around the backside of the ring and then tried it on her ring finger. It was still too loose. She took it off and laid it on the vanity beside the bathroom sink. She was alone in the house. Stephanie was gone, she knew, and her mom was evidently gone also, in her car. She didn't leave notes or anything the way Aunt Alyne did. When Greta's mother decided to leave, she just left. If anybody had been in the house, Greta would have locked the bathroom door, because she didn't want anyone to see the ring. She'd wear it to school, just to make the kids jealous, but at home she'd turn it so that the set was hidden in her hand. If Stephanie saw it, she'd want it for sure. And their dad would make Greta give it to her.

She put another strip of tape on the ring and tried it on again. It fit.

There were footsteps in the hall suddenly, too near the door for Greta to slam it shut and lock it. She was expecting to see Stephanie's or Mom's face look in at her, but it was Derek instead. His hair was all mashed, as if he'd just pulled off a cap, which he never wore. His eyes were bright and round, just the way they'd been when she had separated from him earlier, when they were trying to keep from being seen.

"Hey, Greta, come on!" He grabbed at her arm.

She pulled back. "Why? Where?"

"You'll never guess." He gave her only two seconds, and then he was telling her. "It's the police. Somebody called the police. Come on, let's see what they find."

Greta ran with him out of the bedroom hall through the kitchen to the patio. Her house was built a lot like his, and they were equally at home in both. They crowded through the sliding doors together, then Greta had to turn back to close the screen so the neighborhood pets wouldn't just walk in.

The police car was parked in the alley behind Derek's house, and

Kenny and Calvin were walking through the grass toward the well with a tall, handsome man in uniform.

Greta stopped.

She could see the top of the pipe, the rusted brown metal rising out of the trampled grass. She felt the cold that was rising out of the dark depths as if she were leaning forward into the well.

She wanted to cry out, 'No, don't look in. Cover it. Cover it and leave it alone.'

She felt surrounded by the darkness, helpless within it. Invisible. Unseen even by Derek. Beyond help.

K-iii-lll.

At first it seemed the word was in her mind, and then it came again, a low, strange hissing sound. A whisper. She turned her head and looked behind her to see the whisperer, but there was no one.

Killl ... go killl ... pets ... pets ... k-iii-lll ...

She put her hands over her ears and squeezed her eyes shut.

Pets? Kenny's dog, Buster? Grandfather's canary, Yellow Bird? Her own kitty, Snowball?

Kill them?

"No, no, no," she cried, but no one heard her.

CHAPTER 3

Detective Sergeant Conrad Donally stood in the grass a few feet from the well. Two patrol cars and his own car were parked in the alley a few yards away. Pulled up into the grass was the van used by the rescue unit. They were getting serious about the well because part of a body had been brought up. It was lying on a canvas on the grass and looked like the bones of what once had been a human leg.

The police had answered the call a few days ago, but it was not until this morning that serious work had begun on the old well. The property belonged to Betsy and Lawford Sallingse, who had bought it from the Pattison farm estate more than forty years ago. Their property line was just six feet beyond the well. From that point, the land belonged to Jonah Pattison. The Sallingses knew the well was there, but hadn't even thought of it in years, they said.

Conrad hung around partly because this was his neighborhood. He had grown up in a house across the street just beyond the Crossover place. All of the homes out in this area had been part of small farms, and some not so small. The Pattison farm had been the big one in the neighborhood, now cut down to perhaps four acres in all, including the home of Clare and Alyne. His own home had been a seven-acre place, back in the days before his parents sold it. They had moved to town; and then when he grew up and got married, he had bought back the house and one acre of land.

Whoever this was in the well might have been known by him once, and it gave him chills just to think about it.

Although, it was too early yet to speculate.

The rescue unit had resorted to sending their smallest member down into the well. A tackle unit fixed to a truck had slowly and carefully let the slender man, who was the size of a teenager, down into the well head first. It was the only way. He was carrying a light on his helmet, and his voice, calling back up periodically, sounded as if he were deep in a barrel.

"About thirty feet, I'd say," he yelled back. And then, "Here it is. Hold it."

The man closest to the well waved a hand signal at the man in the truck, and the winch stopped with a cessation of the loud squeaking of the cables.

The activities had drawn a crowd of sorts. Some of them Conrad recognized. He had gone to the same school with Alyne Pattison, whose name was now Kerwin, though he was a few grades ahead of her. She stood off to one side, a worried look on her face, her arms folded closely across her breasts, hands gripping her upper arms. She looked in pain, or cold perhaps, although it was a warm day. Sun shone through the outer branches of the old, rough-barked trees, spotting the grass, touching the hair of the men who worked over the well.

Most of the crowd was made up of kids and dogs. Conrad counted at least four dogs, none of them on leashes, though the number tended to vary. They didn't stand around gazing and speculating like the kids. The leash law extended to this area, Conrad knew. His own dog was enclosed by a backyard fence and taken out only on a leash. But he didn't feel like making an issue of it. In fact, he rather hoped the dogcatcher didn't happen out into the area to see what was going on.

The kids looked more excited than anyone else. There were seven or eight young teenagers, most of them boys. But like the dogs, their number grew or lessened, depending on factors Conrad only peripherally considered. He had seen the kids around the neighborhood, but wasn't sure just who they belonged to. One of them, a boy about twelve, looked enough like Alyne, with dimpled face and rich, thick, light brown hair, that he had to be her son. Another, older, slimmer, better looking, seemed also to belong to Alyne, because of the way he occasionally went to her and filled her in on what was happening.

Conrad moved about, going deeper into the grass, parting it with his foot, looking at the ground as if the crime were recent. He saw a few ants, and one beetle. Crime? He wasn't sure yet if it had been a crime, yet one had to wonder how a body came to be down the well if it hadn't been put there by someone else. Of course it could have fallen in, but who in the neighborhood had ever reported anyone missing? These were puzzles that would be looked into later. First things first. They didn't even know the approximate age or sex of the victim yet, or how long ago it had happened.

The winch was working again, pulling up the rescue worker. The sound of it spread through the orchard, a scream of metal, of one rusted object rubbing against another. Conrad felt it in the back of his head and neck and shrank from it. He turned to see that Alyne was walking back from the alley, going into her yard. But instead of going on to the house, she stopped again, her face pulled into a crumpled bed of seriousness or discomfort. She stared toward the old brown pipe that protruded above the trampled grass.

Conrad went back to the well and joined the men who were waiting. The rescue man crawled out of his harness. The bones on the canvas now had increased to the major bones of a body. A skull was there, with strands of hair still clinging. Bits of cloth hung to part of the bones, especially the body frame. Surprisingly, much of the skeleton was intact. A hand was gone, but the other was still there, with only a couple of fingers missing. The skeleton seemed to Conrad to be female, though he was no expert. In fact, during his years in police work he had seen only one skeleton before, and that had belonged to a man drowned in the river and who was not found for seven years. His body had become partly covered by sand and wedged in beneath tree roots. It had been a gruesome discovery.

"Do we need a diver down there?" one of the men asked.

"No. The water's only about three feet deep. I was able to reach to the bottom of the well. It felt like packed dirt, like the water was just standing water, with no fresh input. I picked up everything I felt."

A wet and dripping bag was emptied onto the canvas. Small bones joined rotted pieces of fabric, of web-like materials that no longer had any color. The only intact object looked like a small leather pouch, its drawstring still tightly closed.

Edward Taylor, captain of the rescue squad, rested on his knees at the side of the canvas, and pulled on the top of the pouch. It fell apart in his hands, the material softened and now useless. Conrad heard a muttered word, scarcely more than a grunt, pass his lips. Jewelry spilled out. Rings, bracelets, brooches. They had turned dark, as if a growth of slime coated it all. The crowd pushed closer to see what had silenced the men around the canvas.

MILTON CROSSOVER EASED UNOBTRUSIVELY into the crowd beneath the edge of the orchard. At age sixty-seven, he had grown to be built more like his mother than his father, the years having shortened him from his tallest height of five feet seven; and now he was scarcely noticeable among the young teenage boys who tried to get a better look at what was on the canvas beside the old well.

Milton peered over the shoulder of the boy in front of him. He had lived all his life in the neighborhood, in the farmhouse across the road, which was now heavily shaded and hidden by trees and shrubbery that had been allowed to grow undisturbed. He had lived behind that screen of vegetation like a mole in its tunnel, leaving it only as was necessary for work or for what shopping he needed. All his life he had lived across the street, and now it was like coming into a foreign land, the well a gaping reminder of youth lost. The trees of the forest-like orchard, it too untended and overgrown far more so than his own yard, looked strange and dangerous. He stared past the faces that surrounded him, into the muttering, moving collection of uniformed and plain-clothes men who had dug into the well, and was aware suddenly of only one thing. A piece of sodden leather lay torn apart, or eased apart by time and decay, and spilling from it was a small arrangement of jewelry.

He saw the brooch.

A thick hand brushed across it and left a diamond gleaming. Milton stared, unable to move his eyes until suddenly they seemed to be jerked by something beyond his own will to the disjointed bones that lay on the canvas. The skull was facing him, as if grinning a hideous greeting. Hello, Milton. Surprise, surprise. Hair, as darkened and thickly coated with greenish-black slime as the jewelry, clung obscenely to the back of the skull. Where was the hair that had grown on the top of the head? Where was the ribbon that had tied it back?

Milton felt suddenly sick to his stomach. He turned and pushed his way out of the small crowd of teenage boys and girls, and sucked into his open mouth the fresh air that seeped through the limbs of the almond trees. Had anyone seen him? Were they watching him now? He turned and looked back, but only Alyne stood in the alley road, and her eyes were toward the well, like the eyes of all the others. Milton stumbled through the grass, feeling it tangle around his feet and legs like vines in a medieval forest. He wished he hadn't come. What had possessed him to come here? He was not the type of person to follow a crowd.

He put his hand against his throat, trying to hold back the demanding need to vomit. His stomach had gotten sensitive over the years, so that now he was like his mother had been. The medicine cabinet was filled with various antacids, just as it had been when she was alive. Just as his figure now looked enough like hers so that he could have worn one of her dresses, one of those thirty-six dresses that still hung in the closet of her room so far as he knew. So, too, his stomach was repeating the trials of hers. Like a curse, she had become him, as if to say, you'll never be rid of me, Milton, because you are me.

"Hello, Mr. Crossover."

With a mouse-like cry, Milton jerked back. The voice was the voice of a child, the only kind of humanity that Milton felt comfortable with. And it was a familiar voice, but it seemed to have come out of thin air.

"Here I am, Mr. Crossover."

He looked up. She lay on the limb above him like a cat. A golden, wheat-like curl hung past her face, like the tail of a monkey. Beyond her Milton saw the blue-jean legs of someone else.

"Hi, Mr. Crossover," the other voice said, and the face became visible among the leaves of the tree like a monkey in a tree puzzle.

Milton's nausea receded. He felt a tremulous smile of relief quiver at the corners of his lips. "Hello, children. What are you doing up in the tree?"

The girl, Greta, said, "We're watching them get the skeleton out of the well."

"We were the ones who found it, did you know that?" asked Derek, his voice filled with the excitement that seemed to belong only to the very young. "We went fishing in the well, and do you know what?"

Milton saw a hand stretch down from the tree and open in front of his face. Lights flashed toward his eyes, blues, reds, greens, white lights so thin and so rapid he thought something had exploded silently in her palm. What kind of dangerous toy was this? Not even the children could be trusted.

Milton threw his arm up to protect his eyes.

"Do you know what?", one voice said—the boy, Milton thought, while the girl burst in, "He found this, and he gave it to me."

They dropped out of the tree, one after the other, right in front of him.

He was startled to find how much they had grown lately. How long had it been since he had stood this close to them? Six months? They seemed tall now, and in some way threatening. Milton stepped back. Yet they followed, crowding closely against him, their voices lowering.

"I fished it out of the well. And a piece of cloth."

The little girl said, "But it's okay if I keep it, isn't it, Mister Crossover? You won't tell, will you?"

"No, no, of course not. Yes, I suppose it's fine—if you keep it ... yes ... excuse me, children. I really have to go. I have to go ..."

What were they talking about? He had to get away from them.

Milton, it's the most beautiful thing I've ever seen. Can I have it, Milton? You won't tell anybody, will you?

He hurried on. Behind him the voice of the boy was still telling him how he had brought up a piece of material on the fish hook. Milton was almost running, his upper body rushing ahead of his feet as he went through the yard by Alyne's house and out into the street in front. Sunlight slanted long and unclouded on the surface of the street and he ran from it, toward the shielding shade hovering over the front gate to his house.

CONRAD HADN'T NOTICED the little man in the crowd until he saw him hurrying away. Not quite running, he looked as though he was about to fall forward, his arms jerking out for balance, his legs too unused to running to get him away fast enough. The two kids who had dropped out of the tree beside Milton followed him a short way and then dropped back to return to the edge of the drifting groups of young area residents, who could see that things were about to be wrapped up at the well for awhile. The sun was sinking low, dropping behind the trees to the west, leaving the light beneath the orchard pale and shadowing fast.

Conrad went back to stand near the County Coroner, who straightened with a hand to his back as if he were pressing the kinks out of a rusted chain.

"Just off the top of my head I'd say it's female, five-four or so. A girl ... it was, anyway, a teenage girl, fifteen, sixteen, and she's been dead for twenty-five to thirty-five years."

Conrad stared at the arrangements of disjointed bones on the canvas, as if they might somehow come together and give him a picture. Twenty-five to thirty-five years put the death back to the years when he had lived here as a kid growing up. In fact, twenty-five years ago was when, at age fifteen, he had moved with his folks uptown, when they had bought their little store on East Forty-second. So the girl went into the well sometime between his own age of five and fifteen. Or, according to Sam Preston, who, so far as Conrad was concerned, was always right, the girl died, or was killed, at that time. Her body could have been put into the well years later. He began listening to the conversations around him again.

"How the hell can I tell what she died from? There's a skull fracture, nothing massive that I can see. No broken arm or leg. Looks like there might be a greenstick fracture right here on this here femur ..." He picked up the right leg, which was surprisingly intact, even to the main bones of the foot. The left leg was separated at the knee, with the lower bone and attached foot lying to one side, like a puzzle that hasn't been put together. "But that could've been done when she fell down the well. So could have the skull fracture."

"Or was thrown down," a voice muttered.

"Load it up. Take it in for a thorough examination. Send it to the State Medical Examiner. I've got to get back to work."

Sam Preston was the county coroner, and owner of the most prestigious and the oldest funeral home. When he was on duty with a funeral, he was soft-spoken and serious. When he was out on a job for the county, he was loud and half-angry, as if the very sight of death, especially violent death, made him furious. Conrad wondered why he kept putting his name on the ballot for County Coroner when he hated the job so much. He could see why he had become a funeral director. He had inherited the business. Sam acted like a man who all his life had allowed himself to be forced into work he hated. He was a short, heavy-set man, with a jowly face and permanently lowered eyebrows that just missed being in a perpetual frown. He took a last look at the pitiful pile of bones and shook his head.

"Wrap it up. Send it off. Bring it back to me and I'll bury her. Somebody must have cared sometime. It's a goddamned shame that when we die we can't at least have a tear shed over us."

He went away muttering, and the men from homicide began loading up their find. One of the uniformed men waved his arms at the small crowd of kids who had hung around, dispersing them. They wandered away in twos and threes, looking over their shoulders. He saw Alyne go into her house. Down at the end of the private road behind the houses, the brick wall of Alyne's father's house blocked whatever view the old man might have had. If he had come out of his yard in the two days that work had been going on at the well, Conrad hadn't seen him.

Conrad checked his notebook. Unnamed female, fifteen, give a year or two in either direction, dead twenty-five to thirty-five years. One slight fracture in her thigh. Broken, perhaps, when she was put into the well.

A girl that age wouldn't have fallen in accidentally. Was there a missing report filed at that time? He'd ask the chief if he could have the job of looking into the girl-in-the-well case. Since he had lived here at the time of her death, he might be able to come up with something that none of the other guys would be interested enough to delve into. They had recent missing persons and death reports to deal with. A quarter of a century ago would seem not really worth the trouble now.

Conrad wondered if someone had gotten away with murder. If so, was that someone a person who had lived in this neighborhood, or possibly someone who still lived here?

His thoughts went instantly to Milton Crossover, and his scared-rabbit reaction to the skeleton on the canvas.

Another thought intruded sharply upon the first. Milton's mother had been murdered thirty-three years ago. He remembered the time period because at the time of the murder he had been seven years old, and he had gone through a series of nightmares about a hooded man coming at him with a scythe. Exactly why he had chosen a scythe for the murder weapon he didn't know. He also had no memory as to exactly how Mrs. Crossover was killed. He only remembered the time. It had been during the summer, just before he started second grade.

Thirty-three years ago. Was there a connection?

"HEY, YOU," Kenny said, his voice squeaking comically the way it sometimes did now. Ordinarily, Greta and Derek would have giggled, and Kenny would have turned red in the face and chased them and caught them each by the collar and bumped their heads together; but this evening neither Greta nor Derek so much as smiled. They both looked at Kenny.

"Hey, you," he said again, and jerked his thumb over his shoulder. "Mom says for you to come in now. It's getting dark."

They stood together in the grass, watching the police and rescue squad cars load up and leave, one by one, while behind them the grass looked mashed into the ground, as if a huge animal had made its bed there.

"It's not dark," Derek said.

"She said it's getting dark. Come on. And you, Greta, you go home."

Derek shrugged. Greta heard him draw a deep breath. She had known him all her life, and knew him better than anyone else on earth, and the long, deep sighs meant he was tired and sleepy and willing to go in and end the day. Greta watched him follow Kenny, tall skinny Kenny, whose voice was changing, as her mother had told her, the way boys' voices do when they reach a certain age. It was something like menstruation in a girl, she had been told. It had something to do with not being a kid anymore, and being on the way to an adult. Like a bug that changes from one thing to another? Her sister had gone through the change already, she knew, although Stephanie didn't know she knew. She had heard it all, through slightly open doors.

Humph. Greta snorted through her nose and followed the last car out of the orchard. The shadows left behind were growing deeper and longer. She stopped at the edges of the trees and looked and listened. Somewhere on the other side of the orchard, where there was another street and other acreages and houses, there was also a pond. And frogs sang in it as evening deepened, getting louder and louder, all pitches of voices from bullfrogs to little peepers. In front of her, from one of the yards in her own neighborhood, a mockingbird sang, as if it were coming morning instead of night. She loved all these sounds.

From farther down the street two dogs barked, one with a fine voice, and one bigger, deeper bark, like the dog in a cartoon. Bark ... bark ... yipe, yipe. A car drifted out onto the street and picked up speed. The sounds softened. There was a faint drifting of music from somewhere, now here, now gone. Voices might have come from real people in a house nearby, like Aunt Alyne's house, or might have been on the television at Grandfather's house. Sometimes he had his television so loud she could hear it clear over the wall that surrounded the back and sides of his yard. She thought he might have built that wall to keep her and Derek out, but Aunt Alyne said no, he had built it a long time ago, when she and Clare were just little girls. So maybe he had built it to keep them in. Anyway, it was there, covered now in vines, like a fortress around an old castle.

She thought of Yellow Bird and the terrible whisper she had heard behind her. She blinked the memory away and turned. She had put it out of her mind before and she could again. She didn't want to think about it anymore. She didn't want to be scared by the whisper anymore.

She was alone, but she could see her own house, just on the other side of the narrow grove of trees that separated her mom's house from Aunt Alyne's; and she could see that it was still dark. Her mom hadn't come into the kitchen yet to turn on lights that would shine in a welcome streak out onto the back patio and yard, the way the light shone out now from Aunt Alyne's kitchen.

mmmm ... kill ... mummmm

Greta whirled, every hair on her body rising in sudden surprise and icy fear. The whisper, again. She had thought she was alone, but the whisper had come sharp and definite at her shoulder. Who was doing it? Who was playing tricks on her?

The trees behind her threw long, darkening shadows all around, and the aisles between the trees went on and on into darkness like many long, narrow tunnels.

No one stood near her, yet she had heard the whisper ... the same terrible, hissing, mumbling whisper that she hadn't quite understood. Someone had said something about kill—or killing—they had said something about ... something. First it was pets, now ... ? She searched for it in her mind as she searched the orchard with her eyes.

She saw no one, yet the icy fear did not leave her. She turned slowly in a circle, expecting to see somewhere in the maze of leaves and dark limbs the evil face of the person who had whispered to her to ... kill. She wished herself across the alley and into the safety of her own backyard, but she was afraid to move. It was behind her, she knew, somewhere in the shadows of the orchard.

The top of the well gaped open, black and deep, but there were stakes driven into the ground and a rope stretching from stake to stake to keep people out until a lid could be made. Now she thought the whisper might have come from the well.

Staring at that dark circle of rusted pipe, she began slowly to back toward the alley.

Listen to me ... mmmummm ... ki ... ill ... pets ... pets ... p-p ... a ... pe ... ts ...

Greta gasped and whirled. It was behind her again, just over her shoulder, and it seemed for just an instant that her brain, not her ears, received the message, and it was horrible. And then a searing pain scraped down her arm, and she saw welts rising there, and blood beading to the surface. She screamed and began to cry.

Silence answered her. The frogs grew still for just a moment, and the mockingbird hushed. But the voices in the house of her cousins continued, closed into the warmth of their own world.

Alone in the growing dark, Greta ran down the alley toward home, running from the phantom whisper and the invisible nail that had slashed her arm.

She stopped, seeing the shadows and the gate. She had come the wrong way and was at her grandfather's back gate. The latch had been turned and the gate stood open halfway, as if inviting her in.

The walk was almost dark now, the heavy shadows of the trees moving upon it like phantoms. Greta entered, going slowly along to the screen door of the back porch, as if pulled by the canary whose cage she saw hanging in the kitchen beyond the porch. Anne, Grandfather's housekeeper, sometimes brought Yellow Bird into the kitchen, and the cage would hang there, waiting to be cleaned, and the voice of the canary would carry through the open doors and over the wall and into Greta's yard. She had always loved to look at Yellow Bird, had wanted to touch those silky, golden feathers. But Grandfather didn't want Yellow Bird bothered. Mama had said to stay away from the bird. Birds don't like to have their feathers touched.

No one was in the kitchen, and Greta stood silently on the threshold. Yellow Bird was still. She was not even on her perch. Where was she?

Greta moved closer, her breath held.

She looked into the cage.

Yellow Bird lay on the bottom of the cage, her neck pulled back and twisted into an awkward, still torture of death.

Greta stared, both hands crushed against her mouth.

Had she killed Yellow Bird?

Had she killed her without knowing when she did it?

She turned and ran, but her fear stayed with her.

CHAPTER 4

Greta stood in the hall bathroom with the door locked and all the lights on bright. The long row of bulbs over the vanity glared into the room, as well as the small light over the tub and shower, the one in the cubicle where the toilet was, and the one in the center of the room. She looked over her shoulder for shadowed corners, and found none, yet she did not feel she was alone. Something had lurked just behind her, watching her with no sympathy for the cut on her arm, stared at her beyond the blur of tears through which Greta sought to see its face. She bent over the sink and let cold water rinse down over the shallow cut on her arm, rushing away the little swells of blood that stood along the cut like red beads on a string.

The cold water hurt, and Greta gave vent to her tears for a few more minutes as she stood holding her arm. No one came to her. The house had been filled with shadows and cold, it seemed to her, when she rushed through the kitchen and into the bedroom hall. She had called for her mama, but not even Stephanie had answered.

The pain receded, and she used a soft towel to wipe the tears from her face and the bloody water from her arm. She stared at it. The cut reached from her elbow to her wrist, a long, curving, narrow cut that looked as if it had been made by the point of a knife. Or a very sharp, long fingernail.

Shuddering, her face screwed up into a grimace of pain and fear and loneliness, she drew a long line of pink ointment down the scratch. It felt cool and soothing.

She wished Stephanie would come home. Anything was better than being in the house alone. And where was Snowball, her cat? She needed company, someone to cuddle close, to hug and comfort her.

She unlocked the door and looked out into a dark hall, and realized she hadn't turned on the lights when she burst into the house. Now she was faced with darkness. She was afraid, for the first time in her life, to go into the hall. But she was afraid to stay in the bathroom too. She needed someone.

With her head past the door, yet still in protection of the light, she called timorously, "Kitty, kitty? Snowball?"

There was an answering meow from the direction of the front of the house, from the window seat in the living room, probably, where the cat liked to sleep on the cushions. Then Greta saw the small white body, a blur of white on the floor, as the cat came into the hall and toward the bathroom. Greta leaned down, holding out her hands, ready to pick the fluffy white cat up and hug her tightly, the way she had done all the years of the cat's life, ever since Greta herself was a little girl of three. The cat's tail waved in the air like a banner or a flag, high and fluffy, and then the cat reached the dwindling edge of light that flowed from the door into the hall. She stopped, her blue eyes fastened on something behind Greta in the bathroom.

Suddenly the stance of the cat changed. Her back arched, and her tail and legs stiffened. She spat, growling three times, and then she whirled and ran, yeowling like a cat in the wild.

A light snapped on in the hall, and Greta's mother stepped through a doorway. The light glistened on her shoulder-length blond hair, and she was dressed in a lightweight suit, the kind she wore to work. Greta rushed toward her.

"What's wrong with the cat?" Clare asked, taking Greta by the shoulders and holding her back from the encircling, tight hug Greta was trying to give her. "What did you do to Snowball?"

"Nothing."

"Then what is it?" Clare pushed Greta away and walked down the hall to the brightly lighted bathroom. She looked in, the puzzled expression on her face relaxing. She started turning out lights, leaving on only the dim light on the wall beside the door.

"I don't know!" Tears came to Greta's eyes again.

"You must have done something to scare her like that. I haven't seen her act like that since she met that strange dog on the back patio."

"I didn't do it."

Clare turned and looked down at Greta, then she took her hand and looked closely at her arm. "Good Lord, girl, how did you do this?"

"I ... I don't know."

"Well, I know. You got scratched by a limb in the orchard, didn't you? You were probably climbing trees again."

Greta sighed. Someone was whispering at my shoulder saying something about kill—telling me to kill. And then ... then I went to Grandfather's ... and Yellow Bird was dead. No. She couldn't tell. There were no words to explain to her mother the feelings she had, about the whispers she heard so clearly at times and only half heard at others, no way to tell about the sudden pain on her arm and seeing the cut appear as if by magic. About the bird ... about not remembering. Grownups never believed kids very often anyway. It's your imagination, they said. You've seen this on a show, on video, on television. You've heard this on one of your crazy tapes, that awful stuff you call music. You've mixed reality with fantasy. Greta hardly believed it herself. Maybe Mama was right, and she had scratched her arm on a limb. She had done it before, once, when she fell out of a tree she and Derek were playing in. On the way down, she had scratched her arm. But it hadn't hurt like this.

Maybe Yellow Bird ... was only resting.

Her mother was going ahead of her toward the kitchen, and Greta hurried to stay close to her. Yet even then she felt the other ... the presence that followed so closely behind her.

ALYNE WOKE, moving restlessly in her bed, helplessly trying to escape from the dream. She lay still staring at the ceiling, trying to recall the dream. Only one thing in it remained with her, the piece of material, the skirt of a dress? Clearly she had seen, and still saw, the white background, and the tiny blue rosebuds that seemed to stand out on the material as if flocked. She felt tense with trying to remember something just beneath her consciousness.

A few feet away in his twin bed her husband Ross slept deeply. Between them on a cherry wood table glowed the numerals 11:20 on a digital clock. So early for such a vivid dream. She had gone to bed less than an hour ago. She must have fallen instantly asleep and gone right into the dream about the dress. Was it a dress? It was almost as if she had seen it herself at one time in her life.

The girl who had worn the blue rosebud material died at least twenty-five years ago, she had heard them say, perhaps thirty-five years ago. There was no one in her memory who could have fit the vague description of the girl in the well.

The mental picture opened behind her closed eyes as if she were seeing a film. She saw the back of a dress that was small at the waist with a tied bow, the ends hanging down into the folds of the full-circle skirt. The girl who wore it was walking, her hips swaying, the skirt of the dress moving in a rhythmic swing, the folds swishing left, right, left. Long, light red hair hung down over the shoulders of the dress, and the girl stooped and went through a green barrier and disappeared. Alyne saw the leaves tremble after the girl had disappeared beyond them. At first it seemed the girl was gone, but then Alyne, small and agile, was crawling beneath the green barrier and lying on her stomach on damp, cool ground. Beyond she saw the white walls of a building, and against it stood a man and the girl in the white dress with the blue rosebuds, so pretty and bright. There was a blue ribbon in the girl's hair, she now saw. But the faces of both the girl and the man were hidden from her.

Alyne lay straight and tense in her bed, her hands gripping the sides of the mattress, her eyes open and staring at the faint outlines of the ceiling light fixture.

A memory ... it had been a memory ... of herself, very young, and the girl in the white, printed dress. A tall young girl with long, pale red hair and wearing a blue ribbon. Not a dream, but a memory, triggered perhaps by the dream.

Or was it all only part of the dream she'd had? Had her imagination been so stimulated by the occurrences at the old well that she was now making up a person to fit the image?

She got out of bed, moving quietly to avoid disturbing Ross. She went out into the hall, closing the bedroom door behind her. A night light burned in the hallway, and all three doors of the boys' bedrooms were open. Their rooms were clustered at the end of the hall, with the master bedroom at the front. She could hear the heavy breathing of William. It wasn't quite a snore, but she suspected it would be someday in his future. He'd probably snore like his grandfather, who could wake a household on a stormy night.

In the kitchen she finally turned on lights, but then she went out onto the patio and stood in the cool air. The dog came up from somewhere in the dark backyard and put his nose in her hand. Street lights from the front made streaks through the darkness, shining at the corner of the house onto the grass and dispersing again to darkness out back by the alley road. The trees in the orchard were black, uneven lines against the paler, star-studded sky.

She had known the girl.

It wasn't just a dream; it had been a memory. And she felt uneasy, as if something corroding had entered her peaceful life. Who was the girl? Why, at such a young age, had she been following the girl? Who was this unknown person that had once been part of her life? Or was she only adding to a dream brought on by this terrible thing that once had happened? If it had been a memory, where was the shrubbery or the hedge ... yes, a hedge ... she had crawled under?

She walked around the house. Many of the older places along the street had hedges. The first house beyond Clare's had a hedge across the front of the yard and down one side. And across the street and a few yards back toward town, almost across from her own house, was the Crossover place, and the tall, carefully maintained hedge had hidden the front yard there for as long as she could remember.

She stood on her front walk and looked at the Crossover house. A light burned in an upstairs room, muted behind drawn curtains. The house's front porch, which extended around three sides of the front wing, was dark. But the street light on the corner shone on the dark hedges, where only a white gate created a gap.

Was it that hedge through which the girl had gone and beneath which she had crawled? Was it that house, around on the side where the porches ended, that the girl had stood with the man?

With Milton Crossover?

She felt the wind touch her bare arms and realized she had come out of the house without her robe. She went back around the house to the patio, the dog at her side. In the kitchen she looked for something to eat, then decided food would not calm her. She closed the patio doors and locked them, and turned out the lights and went back to bed.

She stared at the ceiling fixture then as the memory receded and became part of a dream again, as it must have been in the beginning. She realized how terrible it must be never to be quite sure if you're fantasizing, if what you see and hear is real or unreal.

• • •

THE REPORT WAS BACK. Jane Doe was fourteen or fifteen years old at the time of her death, which occurred approximately thirty-three years ago. Sam Preston, the coroner, had been very close with his figures, as he usually was. Of course, the twenty-five years was somewhat off, but the thirty-five was close enough. It wasn't likely the state's medical examiner was very wrong. So Sergeant Conrad Donally set it down as reasonably accurate.

He had asked to be assigned to the case and it was given to him. None of the others were very interested. The trail had long been cold, and it wasn't likely anything could be learned. And certainly if the girl had been murdered, the killer wouldn't be found.

"He's probably dead by now himself," the chief said, sitting behind his desk, the swivel chair leaned back to its last spring, one heavy knee jutting out to one side while the ankle rested on the other knee. He lit a strong-smelling cigar and puffed it to glowing. Smoke trailed up, polluting the air. The chief gazed calmly through the smoke at Conrad. "Since we don't have too much going right now anyway, you might as well do what you can. File a report and stick it away in the computer. What else can you do? If the girl died thirty-odd years ago, you don't think anybody is going to step forward and admit they threw her down the well to keep from paying for a decent burial, do you? Or if she was running through the orchard—if the orchard was there then—and stepped into the well ..."

"Why wasn't she reported missing? She was murdered, Chief."

The chief of police shrugged. "Maybe." He pulled out a mouthful of smoke and blew it toward the ceiling. "Did you check the files for missing persons?"

"Of course. Thirty-three years ago, and two years on each side."

"You found nothing."

"That's right."

The chief shrugged, then with his chair squeaking loudly, he leaned forward over the littered desk and began to move papers about. "Well, do what you can. File it away. If something fresh comes up, you'll have to drop the old thing. What about that jewelry?"

"I'm looking."

The chief nodded. "Okay."

Okay from the chief meant dismissal. Conrad left the small, smoky office and went out to his own desk, which was tucked back into a cubicle just like the dozen others in the long room. The old-time folder, which he had requested, had been laid on his desk, and he sat down and started going through it.

The murder of Sally Crossover, age seventy, occurred on August 12, thirty-three years ago this coming summer. She lived alone with her son, Milton, who was at that time thirty-four years old. He had come home from his job as bookkeeper at First Federal Bank at his usual time of five-thirty to find his mother in her upstairs bedroom bludgeoned to death. She lay on the floor at the foot of her bed. The death instrument had been a poker from the downstairs fireplace, and the killer, never found, had stolen a leather pouch of jewelry.

Conrad's heartbeat speeded. The description could have fit the jewelry that had been found in the well. One bracelet of rubies and diamonds, worth three hundred dollars. Three brooches, one set with yellow stones of little value, and another, a cameo. The jewelry had been partly described by her son, Milton. He wasn't certain of the kind of jewelry most of it was. He thought it might be valuable, but he didn't know.

A report from the jeweler who had appraised the pieces found in the well set the value at about one thousand dollars. The only really good piece had been the bracelet, the jeweler said.

Conrad stuck the descriptions in his pocket and went out to his car. Milton Crossover would now be sixty-seven years old, and most likely retired. Conrad remembered noticing that whenever he happened to be home, especially on a warm day, he could catch glimpses of Milton working in his yard.

Conrad drove out toward the edge of town, past his own white farm-style house, past the hedge that surrounded one side, the back, and the front of the Crossover place. Across the street the lawns of Alyne and Clare stretched to the sidewalk. Conrad pulled into the narrow driveway at the side of Milton's house. He sat for a minute listening to the sounds of this almost rural area, where once the older houses had been farmhouses.

He realized he was being watched, and he turned to see Milton standing at the corner of the porch that wrapped around the front of the house. He had pruning shears in his hands.

When Milton saw that Conrad was aware of his scrutiny, he smiled and came forward. A Truman Capote type of man, with roundness his major feature, he was almost bald now, and he wore a hat woven loosely of some thin fiber.

"Good morning, Sergeant Donally," Milton said. "You must be lost.

This is the first time in the several years you've lived next door that you've driven into my driveway. What can I do for you?"

Conrad got out of the car. Although he had spoken to Milton a few times, he hadn't been sure Milton even knew who he was. His yard was as secluded as any yard in the neighborhood and didn't yield to talking over a neighborly fence.

Conrad leaned against the car fender. "Had you heard about the body in the well, Mr. Crossover?"

"Call me Milton, please. When I hear Mister, I feel like I'm back at work, and I'd just as soon not hear it. Yes, about the well. Yes, I expect most people around heard of it."

"Do you think you'd be able to identify your mother's jewelry? I think it's the jewelry found in a leather pouch in the well. I wonder if you've got time to come down to the station with me?"

Milton looked over his shoulder, as if searching for some reason to keep him from going with Conrad.

"It will only take an hour or so, Milton. It's beginning to look as if the death of the girl might in some way be tied to the murder of your mother. I'm pretty sure it's the same jewelry you reported missing."

Milton put down his pruning shears on the porch. One of the three cats that wandered casually about came and sniffed the shears, and then lay down near them and stretched lazily.

Milton reached over and rubbed the long, bluish fur. "I'll be right back, dears," he said.

On the way to the station, they talked mostly about the weather, and a bit about how the old neighborhood had changed. Conrad wondered exactly how to phrase the questions he wanted to ask, and came up with nothing. How does a person drag up something that must have been very painful? The man's alibi had checked out. He had been at work at four-thirty, which was the approximate time of death. He had never been a suspect.

Conrad parked his car in front of the station and led the way past a group of teenagers who were sitting on the low wall listening to a heavy-metal band on tape. He and Milton went up stone steps and past the twin trees that had been planted a few years ago to make the police station look more inviting.

Telephones were ringing noisily, and Milton looked pained by the racket as he followed Conrad back to the cubicle. Conrad saw that the man's soft face made him look almost feminine, as if the years had created a sexless person in him.

Conrad watched Milton's face as he spread the jewels out on the top of the desk. The jeweler had cleaned them up so they sparkled and gleamed in the overhead lights, a small collection of trinkets that meant more to the owner than to anyone else. Conrad hated to think that a life had been taken because of these jewels, but lives were taken daily for much less. It was a world where both animal and human life was cheap, easily replaced.

Milton said nothing. He seemed to be taking a long time studying the jewelry, and Conrad saw no change in his expression, though his eyes were downcast, as if he were taking as long as he could to hide them from Conrad.

"Do you recognize any of these?" Conrad urged.

Milton shrugged. "It's been so long ... she had brooches, it's true." He picked up the bracelet. "And this ... was hers, I'm sure."

"This jewelry fits the description of the jewelry you said was missing when your mother was killed."

Milton drew his hand back. "Then I guess it's hers." He sat back in his chair and folded his hands together in his lap. "Could we go now?"

"Sure. I'll make arrangements to have this jewelry returned to you. It'll take a while to get through the red tape."

"Of course. It doesn't matter." Milton got up and led the way down the aisle between the cubicles and the desks into the open room at the front of the station house. He was hurrying, Conrad saw, looking somewhat like a big Easter rabbit with his upper body leading the way. He slowed when he reached the open air and drew a deep sigh.

Conrad understood. He always sighed like that when he reached his house after a day or night's work. Even now that his house was always empty, except for his dog waiting in the backyard.

On the drive back, Conrad talked about the town. "When I was a boy of fifteen, we moved from our little farm on the edge of town, where I live now, to downtown. Now, the edge of town is about five miles farther on. Maybe more. It keeps spreading."

Milton was quiet, staring straight ahead, as if he could hardly wait to get out of the car. Conrad hated to disappoint him, but it wasn't going to be that easy. When he pulled into the driveway he shut off the engine, and Milton cast a glance at him that clearly questioned why he just didn't go on now that he had his information. The jewelry was his mother's. So?

"I need to ask you some questions, Milton," Conrad said, putting his window down and leaning an elbow on the door. Milton sat with one foot out of the car. He hesitated, opened his mouth, closed it again.

"According to the information gathered thirty-three years ago when your mother was killed, you could tell them nothing to help identify the killer or killers. There were indications that suggested two people might be involved, that the killer might have been known by Mrs. Crossover." Milton's mouth opened again, and then snapped shut like the mouth of a snapping turtle. It stayed shut. A light sparked in his eyes, made up perhaps of anger or fear. Strange, negative emotions were hard to read, to differentiate in some people.

Conrad said, "The murder took place in her bedroom upstairs. She was wearing a robe, which seems to me meant she must have known the killer."

"Mother always wore robes around the house. They were more comfortable, she said. She dressed only when she left the house. She had a closetful of leisure robes and muumuus. They were very stylish in those days."

"I see. But she was upstairs in her room, and there were no signs of a struggle. The report claims that someone must have struck her from behind as she sat at her dressing table. With a poker they had brought up from the fireplace downstairs. Which made the murder premeditated."

A nerve in Milton's cheek twitched rapidly. He stared straight ahead.

There was a thump on the hood of the car that made Conrad jump. One of the cats came walking along the hood to the window where it peered in at them and opened its mouth in a silent meow. It was large, blue-gray, with long fur.

Milton smiled faintly. "That's Charlie. He likes to sit on cars. I have to watch that he doesn't ride off on strange cars that park outside on the street. Cars don't park there often, but when they do Charlie likes to take a ride."

Charlie had left paw prints all along the once shiny hood of the car, but Conrad didn't really mind. A cat print was better than some of the things one might find on the hood. Charlie chose a comfortable spot in a little patch of sunshine and lay down.

The conversation had been lost. Conrad couldn't remember exactly what he had been leading up to.

"I need to ask you if you remember seeing a girl about five-four, with long hair—we're not sure of the color—age fourteen, fifteen, maybe sixteen, in the neighborhood at that time."

"No. That question was never asked me."

"I realize it might not have been. There's no mention of anyone being questioned except the closest neighbors. There was never a suspect, was there?"

"No. People wandered around in those days just like they do now. Drifters from the inner city came out into the rural areas now and then and committed crimes. Somebody probably saw Mother wearing her bracelet or one of the brooches and thought it might be valuable, followed her home, and went in and killed her for them when she was alone. I never doubted but that was what happened."

"Except now we know that isn't what happened, right?" Conrad asked.

Milton jerked his head around and stared at Conrad. "What?"

Conrad frowned. Had the finding of the girl, with the jewels, meant nothing to him? As if he weren't able now, after all these years, to change what to him was the reality of the murder of his mother?

"The killer did not take the jewels, didn't want them. Or they wouldn't have been thrown into the well."

"Maybe the killer was the girl, and she accidentally stepped into the well! Of course, that was what it must have been. You can't see that?" Milton blinked rapidly.

"Then who put the lid on the well?"

"That's very simple. The owner. He probably came along and found the lid off and simply replaced it, without knowing that someone had fallen in."

So Milton had been thinking about the girl. About how she might have fallen into the well.

"You don't think the girl was a second murder whose body was thrown into the well?"

Milton's mouth hung open. His eyes darted sideways, toward the cat. He closed his mouth. "But ..." He licked his lower lip.

Conrad watched him closely and saw emotions that had been hidden back at the police station. But they were emotions he couldn't read. Not yet.

"You're sure the girl was not a neighborhood girl, Milton?"

Milton shook his head. "There were girls here, teenage girls, just as there are now. I remember there was a Whitaker family had some girls. I don't know, I might have seen her. How can I tell? I don't know what she looked like, do I?"

"No, I guess you don't. Well, if you think of a girl who disappeared at that time, whose description might fit the dead girl, let me know."

"Sure, I'll do that."

Milton got out of the car, gathered Charlie off the hood, and went through the side gate to the yard with the cat in his arms. He didn't look back at the car.

Conrad backed the car out into the street and spent a few minutes making notations in his notebook about his conversation with Milton. It all boiled down to a very few words. Milton did not remember the girl.

The street was fairly quiet. School was in progress, and the bicycles that usually could be seen drifting along the street were parked in racks at various garages. Cars passed by occasionally, most of them driven by housewives. Clouds drifted overhead, signaling the time of year past summer and not quite into the rainy season.

Conrad parked the car against the curb in front of Jonah Pattison's big two-story farmhouse. The trees around the house were as old as, or even older than, the house, and hovered around it like umbrellas. There was scarcely a spot of sunshine big enough for a cat to lie down in. The house had a front porch that reached across the entire front, and at one end was a porch swing. Conrad had often stopped over in the evening when he saw Jonah out on the swing, just long enough to pass the time of day and discuss the weather. He had known the man he called Mr. Pattison all his life, and during his own bicycle riding days had once been sent home by him for riding down the private lane behind the house. The kids in the neighborhood had pretty much left the old man alone.

There was no one on the porch today. Conrad went up the steps, heard the creak of a board, and felt it give slightly beneath his weight. He crossed the porch and knocked on the door. There was in the door an inset of stained glass, oval in shape, just as there was in the Crossover house, but nothing was visible beyond it. He found the button of an old-fashioned doorbell, pressed it, and heard a ding-dong somewhere deep in the house.

A few minutes later footsteps came along an inner hall, and the door opened. When Anne Reade saw him she smiled and pulled the door open. He had seen her enough to know her name and her face, but that was all.

"I'm on official business, Miss Reade. I need to talk to Mr. Pattison, if he's up to it."

"I'm sure he is. He just came back from his morning walk and is having a cup of coffee. Just go on into the parlor. He's a bit depressed today. His canary, Yellow Bird, died. But please don't mention it. Mr. Pattison doesn't like anyone to suspect he might have a weak spot. He wouldn't appreciate my telling you this. I'll bring you coffee."

"No, please, no coffee. I'm sorry about his bird, but I won't say anything. Just for the record, Miss Reade, how long have you lived in the neighborhood?"

"Oh, twenty years or so. I came when the girls were teenagers. Their mother died years before, and Mr. Pattison had one or two housekeepers before I came."

"Do you know who they were?"

"No, I don't."

"Anne," a strong voice called from beyond the open door of the parlor. "Bring the young man in."

Conrad entered the room and saw the old man sitting straight and tall in his chair, leaning slightly forward against the cane between his knees.

"Good morning, Conrad. You're out on official business, you say? It must be about the bones in the well. I've been wondering when you'd come around asking questions. It's taken longer than I expected. What're you up to these days?"

"Not much, sir. Mostly work."

"Sit down, anywhere. Anne, bring coffee."

"He said he didn't want any."

"No, thanks. I can't stay but a couple of minutes. How are you these days, sir?"

"Just like always. People keep expecting me to become paralyzed or something, the way they act. What is it you want to know? How the girl got down the well? That I can't tell you. That well was drilled, or dug, by my father when he was a young landowner here, and it was covered properly all these years. I never saw the lid off after I was a youngster of twelve or thirteen. It was a heavy lid, but I understand my two grandchildren, the youngest two, got it off and were fishing in it, of all things. You never can tell what tads that age will think to do. It's a wonder they didn't fall in too. I never let my own children play close to it, and my grandchildren were not allowed to play close to it, either. But the parents these days are far more lax than the parents in my day!"

Conrad listened to the changes that had come to the neighborhood, to the changes in people themselves. He listened politely about the changes that had come in government. But the subject was drifting too far astray, and finally he had to interrupt.

"I need to know, sir, if you remember a girl in the neighborhood, around thirty-three years ago when Mrs. Crossover was murdered, who might fit the description we have."

Mr. Pattison raised one long hand whose skin looked as if it had been stretched and allowed to fall back into hundreds of small wrinkles, whose nails were long and coarse and darkened. He rubbed his nose and stared thoughtfully at the opposite wall.

"I've been thinking about that. A family lived down the road. It's a street now, but then it was a farm road. They had the farm down at the corner. They had a grape vineyard. Name was Whitaker. They had two or three children. I often saw groups of girls walking past, who lived down that way somewhere. What kind of description do you have?"

"Five-four. Weight difficult to tell. Average, probably, around one-fifteen to one-twenty. Hair long. Color unknown, but light, straight. White girl, Caucasian."

"What color did you say her hair was?" He leaned forward, squinting slightly, as if he had trouble hearing.

"We're not sure. A rather medium texture, straight, long, probably, which could have been almost any color. Fair, maybe. Straight, not curly."

"And you think she was here at the approximate time of the Crossover killing?"

"Yes. The jewelry found with her has been identified as the jewelry stolen from Mrs. Crossover."

Mr. Pattison leaned more heavily on the cane, his eyes staring brightly and steadily at Conrad. "You don't say."

"Yes, sir."

Jonah Pattison shook his head slowly and leaned back into his chair. He suddenly looked tired, his face sagging more than before, his hands, clasping the head of the cane, looking more shriveled, the fingers longer and more like claws. How cruel age could be, Conrad found himself thinking. Why couldn't life just go on smoothly and comfortably until the end, and then the end slip in gently and easily during sleep? Conrad got up. The old man had an excellent memory and had told him about the way things used to be, but he obviously couldn't help with the identification of the girl.

"Anne, you don't remember this girl, do you?" Jonah Pattison asked unexpectedly, causing Conrad to stop and look back.

Anne Reade, who had risen from her chair to follow Conrad to the door, looked back also.

"I wasn't here then, Mr. Pattison."

The old man laughed. "That's right. I get to thinking you've been around here forever, Anne."

She laughed with him, and Conrad left the house feeling just a bit lighter of mind than when he had entered.

CHAPTER 5

ALYNE SAW CONRAD COMING. She had been out sweeping the small stoop at the front of the house when he drove into Milton's driveway and sat for a few minutes with Milton in the car. And she had seen him later going up the walk to her father's porch. He wasn't in uniform, but there was something official about the way he moved about, and she knew he wasn't just stopping by to say hello.

She opened the door before he could ring the bell. He was a tall, thin man, who looked much the same as he had years ago when, as a little girl riding the school bus, she'd had a crush on the older boy. And when he had moved away she'd been heartbroken for a few weeks. For years then she wondered what had happened to him.

She had grown up and married a man who looked enough like Conrad Donally to be his brother, except Ross had darker hair and a square jaw, while Conrad Donally had an oval face, brown hair, and straight expressive eyebrows that made him look as if he were asking questions all the time. He had gotten into the right work, she guessed. All he had to do was look at a person and that person would know a question was about to be asked.

"Hello, Conrad," she said, feeling a little shy, the way she had when she was nine years old and he'd smiled at her. When he moved back to the neighborhood a few years ago she had been oddly pleased. He was married then, of course, and she'd seen his wife a few times, never to speak to or become acquainted with. Then a few years later his wife had left, and she read about them in the list of divorces printed monthly in the newspaper. There were no children that she knew of.

"Alyne. How are you?"

"Fine." She stood in the doorway, leaving him on the stoop. Sunshine drifted across him as the clouds above moved. "You're here about the ... the body?"

"Yes. You anticipated me, I see, just like your dad did."

"Uh-huh. That's father, not dad. Never dad. Can you imagine ever calling Jonah Pattison, Dad?"

Conrad smiled. "No, I can't. But I thought you did."

"Oh, he was okay. In fact, he was a great father. Strict, but good, anyway. Clare and I always knew he'd take care of us."

"That's a lot more than some kids get."

"I know."

"You must have been how old when Mrs. Crossover was killed? Do you remember that murder?"

"Barely. Or maybe I just remember hearing about it. I can't say I actually remember it happening. I was ... I'm not sure. Just when was it?"

'Thirty-three years ago in August."

"Then I was five. Clare was three."

"Some memories go back that far, some don't."

Alyne felt the frown of bewilderment touch her face and quickly smoothed it away. She didn't want to talk to Conrad about her dreams, about the dream that might be a memory. She hadn't been able to get her mind on anything else the past couple of days, the memory, or the dream, just beyond her reach, so that she was beginning to feel as if she had existed in another life and was almost able to recall it.

"Mine doesn't seem to," she said, "except I can remember my third birthday party. Mama and Papa took me to a park where there were ponies. I can remember riding a spotted pony. And I can remember the cake and candles later, and the number three. It's interesting how memory develops, isn't it? Just fragments at first."

"Yes. What about the girl?"

"The one in the well, of course. What did you find out about her?"

"She was young, but almost grown. Her bones had started to close off, so that she couldn't have been more than an inch taller, the medical examiner said. She might have been anywhere from fourteen to sixteen or seventeen, so she's being called fifteen. She had long, straight hair. And, oh yes, she was a Caucasian."

"You were here then, weren't you, Conrad? How old were you at the time of the murders?"

"Murders?"

Alyne shrugged. "Well. Weren't they? Both? Do you really think a girl that old would have accidentally fallen into the well? It isn't that wide, and it probably wasn't uncovered. It seems to me that she must have been killed and her body put there." Alyne crossed her arms over her chest and hugged, shuddering visibly. "And to think I lived only a few hundred yards from that well at the time."

AND THERE WAS A BIG GIRL, *and I followed her, beneath the hedges of a yard. And she wore a full-skirted dress with little blue rosebuds on a white background.*

"AND?" Conrad encouraged, as if she had started to speak aloud.

Alyne realized she had been staring across the road at Milton's closed house. The blinds were almost always drawn there, those which were visible through the trees.

"You talked to Mr. Crossover. Did he remember this girl?"

"No, not specifically. He said there were a number of teenage girls in the neighborhood around that time. The Whitakers, who live down at the corner had some daughters."

"Oh, yes, I remember them. Pretty girls, with black hair and blue eyes and incredibly white skin. They rode the school bus. I remember when I was ten I wanted to grow up to look like Rose Whitaker."

They both laughed. Conrad said, "I remember her too. She got married when she was a senior in high school."

"And her younger sister, Grace ... didn't something happen to her? I think she died when she was in her twenties."

"That's possible ... always frail, wasn't she?"

Alyne said impulsively, almost without realizing she was going to say it, "Sometimes it seems I can see a girl wearing a dress with blue rosebuds. But it's so much like a dream that I can't be sure. Seeing that dirty little scrap of material from the well was such a, well, not a shock maybe, but such a weird experience, that I started dreaming about it right away. So now I don't know if I really saw something, or someone wearing it, or if it's my imagination working overtime."

Someday she might tell him the rest, the part about the girl going through the hedges and then being sharply displayed against a white wall, with a faceless man beside her. A white wall that, in her mind at least, might be the outside wall of the Crossover house. But if Milton Crossover said he did not remember such a girl, it could be she was wrong. Milton Crossover had never had a girl in his life that she knew of. The consensus in the neighborhood was the man was slightly effeminate, perhaps wholly homosexual. Or, it would seem nonsexual. He stayed at home, with his cats and his pruning shears. Sometimes he came onto the outside of the hedges and pruned there, and mowed the grass there, and carried on brief conversations with whatever kids happened to be out on the street. She had seen him talking to Derek and Greta a few times, but when she asked them what he said, they said, "Nothing."

Still, since the body in the well was discovered, she was more aware of the house across the street than she had ever been before. She was aware at night that his blinds were drawn and the lights upstairs did not go out until very late. Last night it was two-thirty. The night before, three. She found herself wondering what he did, and her feelings put mysterious, sinister actions beyond those drawn blinds. Yet in the morning light she felt ridiculous. Why was she looking? Almost spying on the quiet, gentle man across the street. At least she had always assumed he was gentle. But now it was as if deep in her mind she had convicted him of the murder of the girl, if not of his mother too.

Conrad had gone down the steps, but he turned back suddenly. "Actually, we think the girl was murdered. The examination showed a trauma to the head, an almost invisible fracture, as if she had been struck extremely hard and repeatedly, not by a sharp instrument. A hand, maybe. A fist. So I think you're right, Alyne. It was a double homicide. But no girl her age, or any age, was reported missing that summer."

He went on, and Alyne watched him go. He hadn't said it all. He hadn't said, "And someone in this neighborhood remembers that girl. Someone killed her."

MILTON WATCHED the policeman from behind the protection of his curtains. The tall, brown-haired young man seemed to be moving leisurely from door to door like a Bible salesman, or like a neighborhood resident visiting. Alyne had not invited him into the house, but had stood outside, her arms folded, talking with him. And he saw her eyes on his house, and then the policeman had turned and looked straight at him, it seemed. Although he knew he could not be seen, still he instinctively drew back and pressed himself against the wall.

When he looked again, they were gone. The door was closed. He had to move the curtain before he saw Donally getting into his car. As he watched, the Sergeant drove slowly on west, and he knew he was going to the Whitaker's.

Why had he mentioned the Whitakers? And why hadn't he mentioned the ring? Where was it?

He dropped the curtain, checked the door to be sure it was locked, and went down the hall to the staircase. The house was dark, as he liked it. As his mother never had liked it. He remembered the light she had insisted upon, all the blinds open, the curtains pulled back and secured in their ties. Perhaps at that time he had liked light, though there weren't many things his mother liked that he had liked too. He wondered if it were that way with other sons and daughters. Were sons and daughters that much different from their parents, or was there some deep-seated hostility inborn? A wedge that grew and grew until the feeling was of repugnance? His mother had ordered him about, he recalled, as if he were perpetually ten years old. He could remember her furious words still, as if the walls had caught them and played them back at him.

'You're being a fool, Milton. This is ridiculous. She's only a child. I've wondered when you would show your real self. You have hidden it from me all these years, haven't you, Milton? Why can't you be interested in a woman your own age? Why can't you act like a man, and marry and have your own children? Then you will see what it is I'm talking about. I'm getting so I don't trust you to be alone anymore. How can I take my cruises, if I can't trust you?'

He put his hands over his ears to drown out her voice, and the harangue drifted to silence. Almost to silence. It followed him, a whisper, an echo of a whisper, as he went up the stairs and along the dark hall to the big bedroom at the front.

From the circle of keys at his belt he chose one and inserted it into the door. It had been a long time since his mother's room had been opened, and the door hinges squealed, causing him to shrink into his shoulders. He pushed the door back and waited.

A strong smell of age rushed out of the room. A sliver of light came in around a blind that was hanging slightly crooked, and sharply etched its way along the floral carpet on the floor, touching the huge stain that was now dark brown, almost black. The blood had never been cleaned up. He had simply closed the door and locked it, as soon as the police gave him permission. Thirty-three years ago in August he had locked this door.

He went into the room slowly, walking on his toes as if the blood were still sticky and the carpet fibers filled with it, like water in sand. He had to cross the large splattered stain to get to the dressing table where she kept her diary. The police had never seen the diary because it was in a secret drawer, and he hadn't told them about the drawer. She also kept her jewelry in that drawer. But the police didn't know that either.

Only he had known that.

He sat down on the vanity bench where she had sat so many times in her life, where she had played with her makeup and her perfumes and her jewelry. She had been a vain woman. Even at seventy she had made up her face as if she were twenty years old. And she had looked beautiful, he had to admit, and at one time he had been very proud of her. Then she had taken the trip to the Middle East and had brought back things. Among them the ring.

From among the keys he chose a small one, and he pulled out the center drawer and reached behind it. He had to feel for the key hole, and at first the small key did not seem to fit anymore. Then it slipped into the slot and he turned it. The lock snapped open. He pulled out the small, shallow drawer and placed it carefully on top of the vanity. The mirror reflected his movements and the contents of the open drawer. Nothing was in it now but the diary. The part he wanted was one of the last notations.

'Home again, and what a lovely trip, although I must say I would hate to live in some of the places I saw. I did get some interesting jewelry, one especially is fascinating, and has a history that is supposed to be—cursed? Except, of course, I don't believe in jewels or gems having powers. This one is a red stone, though it isn't a ruby, the vendor said, nor a garnet. He wasn't sure what it was—I might take it and have an authentic jeweler tell me what it is—this one, at any rate, is said to glow like fire, and indeed it does, at times, very eerily, I must say. And it is said to affect everything and everyone who touches or owns it, in some strong way, sometimes good, sometimes evil. I wonder if the vendor could have embroidered the facts some? I really doubt that it has such powers. However, it does glow sometimes. Last night I woke up to see a faint light, and it was, I do believe, the ring. Ah, but that is the good part of my trip. The bad part is Milton, what he was doing—God only knows—while I was gone. I think that boy is going out of his mind! I do believe he thinks himself in love with that little '

The diary ended at that point. Perhaps he had entered her bedroom at that point, or perhaps something else had happened. Anyway, she had never written another word, and she had put the diary back into the drawer and locked it away.

He had hoped for a better description of the ring. He remembered it, though, as vividly as he remembered her last words to him. She had kissed him goodbye that morning, and he had smelled her perfume and the powder on her cheek. She had patted his shoulder with the hand that wore the ring. "Do be a good boy, Milton," she had said, "and go on to work. Well talk about this later." Still treating him like a ten-year-old. He could see her hair yet, white with a blue tint, raised into a pompadour on her head, tucked into a bun at the back. She was a beautiful woman, made quite rich by three husbands who had died and left her everything, the first one his father. She still had a small waist, though she wore caftans and muumuus and robes and rarely showed it unless she dressed to go out.

And the ring was on her finger that morning. Not her ring finger. It was too large for that. She had worn it on her second finger, and it caught the light in an almost magical way and released it in long rays, darting like slivers of broken glass. It was diamond cut, he remembered, and set in a unique framework of dark gold. There had been figures, he thought, carved into the gold, but he wasn't sure of that. He wondered if he should mention the ring to Conrad Donally.

His mother's voice came at him again from the walls, and he could see her holding out the ring for him to look at. He could hear her amused laughter. *It is supposed to absorb the souls of those who possess it. What do you think that means, Milton?*

THROUGHOUT THE DAY, when she grew tired of classroom work and the teacher wasn't watching her, Greta peeked at the stone of the ring. She held it in her hand, a large, square red stone with little lights of yellow, green, and blue, like lights from twinkling stars. She'd have to tell Derek about that. She'd have to remember to tell him that the ring was warm and felt almost hot into the palm of her hand like a lump of real fire, or like coals on the hearth. Except it didn't burn her. She could just feel it, warm and comforting.

She almost showed it to her playmates, first to Dorrey, then to Janet; but something stopped her. Janet would want it, she knew. Janet was like that. She wanted everything you had. She'd try to trade at first, and when that didn't work she'd start begging just to wear it for awhile. And when she got it, she'd say you'd given it to her.

Sometimes Greta didn't like Janet much at all. Still, she was fun to play with, and no matter how fast Greta ran, Janet was always right behind. She and Janet and Dorrey had been playing together at school since kindergarten, but she didn't quite trust either one of them with her best secrets.

During last class, when she was supposed to be reading quietly, Greta propped up her book and opened her palm against it. Lights overhead in the schoolroom reflected in the jewel as if it were made of mirror; and though she held her hand very still, she could see the lights moving, turning to blue and yellow and brilliant white. She wondered if the red jewel were a rare diamond, or if rubies sparkled like diamonds.

Suddenly the teacher was behind her, and Greta closed her hand swiftly over the jewel. She held her breath, sensing Miss Hunter looking over her shoulder. But a moment later the teacher moved on slowly, going on down the aisle.

Greta didn't see Derek until she was already seated on the school bus. Sometimes he sat with her, but more often lately he didn't. She looked around and saw him sitting with Lydia from the fourth grade. He wasn't even looking at Greta, and she felt a sting of jealousy. Why was he sitting with Lydia?

An arm reached suddenly over the crowded seat behind and grabbed her wrist, and the familiar high-low voice of Kenny growled at her.

"What's that you got, Greta? Where'd you get that ring?" She closed her hand tightly over the ring, realizing too late that in turning to look through the crowded school bus for Derek, she had forgotten to keep the ring hidden. Kenny was leaning over her now, using both of his hands to pry hers open. She squealed loudly enough to get the attention of the bus driver, but at the same time the bus roared forward, pulling into the traffic, and the driver was too busy to hear her.

"Cut it out, Kenny! Stop it!"

"Let me see that! Did you take that from the stuff in the well?"

"It's mine! I found it. It's mine."

"Let me see it, Greta. I only want to see it. I promise."

"No!"

Kenny leaned over her, his arms pressing against both sides of her head, and forced her hand up. His fingers dug into her hand, prying her fingers open. Greta screamed again, her voice mingling with the yells and cries of all the rest of the kids. But suddenly the school bus jolted to a halt.

The driver turned around, his jaw set the way it was when he'd had enough of the yelling and screaming.

"Cool it!" he shouted, his voice rising above all the others and creating a sudden silence throughout the bus. "All right, you big kids, can't you pick on somebody your own size? Get back in your seat there, Ken Kerwin! Leave the little girl alone."

Kenny reluctantly moved back, releasing Greta's hand. But he whispered in her ear, "I saw what you've got, Greta, and the police are going to want it. You'd better give it up."

"Down!" the driver shouted again. "All of you. Not one more word, do you hear, until you're out this door. I've had it up to here with you!"

The bus idled a minute more, the only sound now. Kids sat still, looking straight ahead. Somewhere in the back of the bus came a soft giggle. Then the driver turned around, put the bus into gear again, and pulled back into the traffic.

The bus made dozens of stops before it reached the stop where Greta and her cousins would unload, along with some other kids who lived down some of the side streets; and Greta made plans to dash for protection from Kenny. She would like to play with Derek, but if she did, Kenny would be sure to catch her. The only other thing she could do would be to run into her house, hide the ring, and then go play with Derek, but she couldn't bear the thought of taking off the ring.

She watched for her own stop anxiously, stretching up in her seat, her books in her arms, ready to run. Her mother wouldn't be home yet, she knew, and certainly not her dad. Stephanie might, but lots of afternoons now she stopped at the mall to shop or to hang around with her friends. On her sixteenth birthday their dad had given her a new car, and so Stephanie didn't ride the bus anymore. Also, she was in a different school. So was Kenny, for that matter, but since only one bus came out this way, he had to ride it too.

The road curved, and the trees grew thicker and taller, the houses farther apart. The bus made the stop just prior to Greta's stop, and she grew even more tense. She glanced back at Kenny, hoping he had forgotten. But his eyes were pinned on her, his eyebrows lowered the way they were when he was getting really mad. She and Derek often played that Kenny was the Great White Hunter or the Pirate or the K.G.B. man, and at this moment he was the Pirate, ready to make her give up her treasures. She saw him ease forward on his seat.

The door closed, the bus moved on. They passed three more houses.

They passed Grandfather's big house back in all its trees, and then the bus began slowing, pulling over to the curb. It stopped in front of Aunt Alyne's house, and the door began to slide open. Greta ran forward and saw from the corner of her eye that Kenny had stumbled over some kid's feet. She pulled up more energy from somewhere deep in her belly and spurted down the aisle and out the door, leaping from the second step way out into the grass between the sidewalk and the curb. She heard the driver yell, "Careful!" but she didn't look back. She ran across the sidewalk, across the grass, through the triple line of trees that separated her yard from Aunt Alyne's, from Derek's and William's and Kenny's, getting her key ready in her hand as she ran.

The key went in and she turned it. The door opened. Kenny came around the corner of the house, leaped onto the patio and was just reaching for her when she slipped into the house and slammed the door shut. He yelled in pain, she wasn't sure what from. Maybe she had caught his finger in the door. But she didn't stop even to look through the glass to see. She hurried on into the quiet of her house, to her bedroom where she shut the door, and then brought over her desk chair and propped it under the knob, just in case. Then she sat down on her bed and puffed weakly to regain her strength and her breath. She heard Kenny pounding on the door at the back of the house. Then silence.

A few moments later the doorbell rang. Greta sat still. It might be Derek, but more likely it was Kenny, like the wolf still trying to get into the Three Little Pigs' house.

The house grew quiet. She let a long while go by, and then she got up and went from window to window through the house looking for Kenny. He'd probably be hiding just outside the door, waiting for her. She wondered what she'd do about tomorrow. She had to go to school. Her folks would never let her get by with a stomach ache as an excuse.

She had no choice but to hide her ring. But not yet. Not tonight. She loved it, and she wanted to keep it tucked warmly into her palm always.

Kenny caught Derek by the back of the neck the first time they were out of sight of their mother, and waltzed him down the hall to the bedrooms.

"All right, Derek," he growled in Derek's ear, pushing his brother's face against the wall. "That was a ring Greta had. You got it outta the well, didn't you? Confess or I'll wring it out of you. I don't want to have to tell on you, and I'll give you and Greta the chance to take it to the police yourselves."

Derek couldn't talk. Kenny's hand wasn't really tight, but it seemed to be choking the life out of him. He knew just where to put his fingers on Derek's neck to cut off his ability to breathe, to talk, even to think. Sometimes it seemed like Kenny could paralyze him all over just by getting hold of him around the neck. He struck out against the wall with his hands, reached back, and tried to hit Kenny, but Kenny merely stretched back out of his way. Derek heard the rumble of his giggle. It sounded like the man on the old sitcom reruns he'd been watching. Gildersleeve? Something like that. And the sound of that giggle, coming from Kenny, made him furious. It meant he wasn't entirely serious. But if Derek tattled to his mom or dad later, Kenny would only tell about the ring, and all Mom or Dad would do would be to scold Kenny a little, and make Derek and Greta take the ring to the police.

Derek saw another figure come into the hall. A shadow moved across the floor. Was it Mom? No, it was William.

"What'd Derek do now?" William asked. He was eating a cookie. One hand carried more.

Derek held his breath. Was Kenny going to tell?

"I don't know yet," Kenny said. "That's what I'm trying to find out."

William stood a moment longer. "What'd you do, Derek?"

"Nothing!"

Kenny gave him a little shake, and William went on into his room. Derek heard him say, "Forget it." That was William. He minded his own business. He never tried to be like Mom or Dad or a teacher or a child care specialist.

"Better tell me," Kenny hissed in his ear. "Where'd she get that ring?"

Derek gave a sudden twist and freed himself.

"Tell!" Kenny demanded.

"None of your business!" Derek shouted. "Bug off! You chicken shit!"

"Boys! What's going on back there?"

Their mother's voice. Now Derek was about to get in trouble because of what he'd called Kenny, and she didn't know the half of it.

"Nothing, Mom," Kenny called, and Alyne's face, just for a moment visible at the end of the hall, withdrew. Kenny knotted his fist threateningly and waved it in front of Derek's eyes.

Derek drew a long breath. He was sorry, but Greta was going to lose her ring. Kenny would take it away from her, and there was nothing he could do about it. If he told his mother, she'd make him hand it over to the police too, so Greta was going to lose no matter what he did now. He thought swiftly. He'd wait until Kenny took it away from Greta, and then he'd tell his mom about it and she'd make Kenny give it to the police. They'd think he was the one who took it from the jewelry in the well. Derek turned, his back against the wall.

"What're you grinning about?" Kenny demanded, suspicion entering his eyes.

"Nothing." Derek sobered, and with effort kept the smile off his face. "You win. I fished it out of the well and I gave it to Greta."

"You fished it out of the well," Kenny repeated, his mouth curling in a grin of incredulity. "You expect me to believe that story? Next you're going to be telling me you fished up a forty-pound salmon."

Derek shrugged. "You can believe it or not, I don't care. That's where it came from, anyway." He dared to slip past Kenny and walk casually away.

"You got it out of the jewelry that was in the pouch, didn't you?"

"How could I do that? The police had it."

Kenny was walking down the hall with him, like a buddy. His hand touched Derek's shoulder companionably. "Where did you get it, no shit?"

"I told you. You didn't believe me."

"You fished it out of the well."

"Yeah. First it, then the piece of cloth."

"Really."

"Yalp, really."

Kenny caught him again just before they came to the swinging door into the kitchen and held him. He lowered his face to Derek's ear. "Well, listen to this. You'd better tell Greta she's got to take it to the police, or to Mom or Dad, or Aunt Clare and Phillip, or somebody, because what you're doing is wrong. I'll give you three days, and if you haven't done it by then I'll have to tell on you, or take it myself and turn it in. Hear me, Derek?"

Then Kenny walked away, going on into the kitchen and talking to Mom just like he always did.

GRETA HAD NEVER BEEN SO glad to see Stephanie. Through the window she saw the small car come rushing around the corner into the drive and slide to a stop near the garage. It was a yellow car, and it looked good with

Stephanie's dark brown hair. She got out of the car, reached back in, and began gathering up an armload of books. Greta ran out to meet her.

"Hi," Stephanie said in answer to her greeting.

"Can I help carry the books?" Greta walked along beside her, pausing to cast a glance toward the trees that separated her yard from Kenny's. She expected to see his face somewhere there among the foliage, and felt she would have if she'd had longer to search.

"No, just open the door. Is Dad home yet?"

Stephanie always asked about Dad. He was the one she loved most in all the world, and she was the one he loved. Sometimes it was like Greta and Mom just weren't around.

"No."

"Mom here?"

"No,"

"Crap," Stephanie said. "I suppose that means dinner will be late. And I have band practice tonight."

Greta opened the sliding door on the patio and stood aside as Stephanie entered. The cat came from around the house to rub against Stephanie's leg, and she stooped to touch her nose to the cat's and croon some baby words. Though she called the cat to follow, it ran off the patio again and faded into the shrubbery. Looking at it, Greta had a feeling that it ran because of her. It left her with a lonely, rejected feeling, a sad coldness. She followed Stephanie.

"I have to study," Stephanie said. "Why don't you start dinner?"

"What'll I do?"

"I don't know. Scrub four potatoes and put them in the microwave for a few minutes. And don't forget to prick them like you forgot the last time, or you'll be washing exploded potatoes off the oven."

Greta groaned. Baked potatoes. All the time baked potatoes. Stephanie was a vegetarian, and had been since she'd learned last year how cattle and hogs and lambs are slaughtered—rounded crying into pens and rushed down corridors toward men with large knives ready to slash their throats. She had cried for days, Greta remembered, and she hadn't touched meat since, not even a hot-dog, which she used to like better than anything. Chicken and fish were living things that were slaughtered too, and Stephanie had even stopped going shopping with their mother because she didn't want to see the packages of chicken so openly displayed. "Barbarians, that's what we are," Stephanie had said, and Greta remembered it so well because she said it so often. "We're as bad as the South Koreans eating dogs."

Yuk.

Greta didn't feel like eating anything. She wanted to go out and play with Derek, but she didn't dare leave the house. Not until Kenny forgot about the ring.

Greta turned her cupped palm and looked at the ring, and for an instant the ring was like a square, shining bubble of blood in her hand, swelling out beneath her finger, heavy and thick and red. She closed her hand over it again. How could it change its looks so fast? At school it had gleamed, shooting out little lights like a diamond. And now it was heavy and thick and dark red.

Tomorrow she would hide it in her special box, the little metal box with the birds and flowers painted on the lid, and there it would lie with such treasures as the empty bluebird egg she'd found on the grass last year, and the little sea-shells she'd got at the beach. There were a lot of things in that box. A lock of Derek's hair when he got his crew cut, and a lock of her own hair, which Derek had snipped for her. Then they'd gotten into the spirit of collecting and had taken locks from Buster's fur and Snowball's. She also had in the box a braid made of grass that looked like a snake. And buttons she'd found, and snail shells. Once Stephanie had seen the box, and her whole face had curled up in disgust. "Yeow!" she had cried, and went to their dad and told him, "Do you know what kind of crap Greta is saving?" And she had told him about the stuff she had glimpsed. But that time their dad surprised both of them and he'd only laughed.

Greta turned on the television just because she didn't know what else to do, but she was walking circles in the floor in front of it when the back door opened and her dad came in.

She never looked at him without feeling a rush of pride. She thought him handsome and exciting and very wise. He was the best dad in the world, and she wanted him to love her the way he did Stephanie; but it was a deep-seated, very subtle longing that she was hardly aware of. She wanted to look like him. She wanted hair that glistened, dark and wavy, and eyes as blue. But none of his features were hers that she could see, although she had heard Grandfather say once that she looked like Phillip. She had liked her grandfather better since then.

"Where is everybody?" Phillip asked.

"Stephanie's studying, and Mom's not home yet."

Phillip went toward the hallway, taking off his suit coat and loosening his tie all at the same time. Greta went back and stretched out on the floor in front of the television. Phillip was an accountant and assistant manager of the Jim Dean's Menswear downtown, and sometimes on Saturdays they all went down and had lunch with him. It was a big thrill, the only thing she liked doing better than just wearing her old jeans and playing with Derek.

She muted the television and heard her dad's and sister's voices. She turned the television back up and watched the figures move on the screen.

The show had just finished when the back door opened again and Clare came in. She threw her jacket and purse on the end of the counter, kicked off her shoes, and came on into the family room barefoot. She flopped down into her chair, which was just across a small lamp table from Dad's chair, and stared for a moment at the television screen. Greta watched her, waiting. Mom didn't like to be talked to for a few minutes after she got home from work. She was still staring at the set when Phillip came in and touched her lightly on the shoulder, then sat in his chair and unfolded the newspaper he had gotten off the front porch.

Greta turned back to watching television. Her family was home now, and she waited for the warmth of security to fall over her like a warm blanket, the way it always did. But her eyes kept straying to the window, toward Kenny's house, and she was more aware of the lump of the ring on her palm than she had ever been before.

SOMETIMES IT SEEMED she was dreaming, and at other times it seemed real. Greta was trying to run. She saw herself visualizing the running in her brain, and she felt her legs stretching, stretching, slowly, her need to run so great that her body seemed mired in a strange, thick atmosphere. Her need to run so exceeded her ability to move, that she willed it in her brain, and knew she was dreaming. But she must run, run, to escape whatever it was that had followed her, even if the running were only in her dream, in her mind. She felt her legs try to move, and then they were moving, and she was running with long, sweeping steps through the air. But the landscape beneath her was not moving, and she gasped in a terrible, silent scream as she felt herself falling. She knew she was in a narrow, dark tunnel that had no bottom, and she was falling, falling.

But she was dreaming and this she knew in her mind, and so she willed herself again to run, to reach up and stop falling, and move her legs ... move her feet ...

She rose from the bed and her feet moved forward, the carpet soft and deep beneath her bare toes. She came to the door, which stood halfway open, and she pushed it back, all the way to the wall. She walked through, her legs awkward and heavy, and she walked down the hall out into the night.

KENNY WOKE and lay still staring at the window. It was dark outside, the street light too far away to light the yard on the bedroom side of the house. The night was quiet, so quiet everything in the world might have been dead. But something had awakened him.

He pushed back his covers and got out of bed and went to the window. The blind was pulled to within a foot of the sill, and he kneeled on the floor so he could look under it. He pressed his face to the glass. Gradually the night seemed less dark. He could see the corner of the garage and the front of the shed. Its white walls seemed almost to contain a ghostly phosphorescence in the dark. Beyond the shed he saw the alley, lighter than the surrounding area. Lighter than the orchard beyond, which looked black. It seemed he could see the yellow ribbon the police had stretched around the well. Although the lid had been replaced and a truck had even come and dumped a load of rocks into it, the yellow ribbon had been put back up again. Just why he didn't know, because they had gotten all the clues they were ever going to get. Especially now that rocks had filled it in.

He saw a movement in the backyard. A small figure had stepped out of the grove of citrus trees between his yard and Aunt Clare's, and now stood in the streak of light from the street light beyond. It stood still, as still as if it weren't real, and then it moved again, closer.

Greta? He glanced at the dial on the clock. What was Greta doing out in the yard at three-thirty in the a.m.? Which was, in his mind, nighttime, not morning.

It was Greta, all right. She was wearing white or light blue or pink, pajamas or nightgown, and he could even see the long ringlet down over her shoulder like a tube. She must be crazy, coming out at three o'clock in the night. Asking for trouble.

He left his room and went out onto the back patio. He stopped on the corner and looked at his cousin. She was no more than twenty feet away now. He could see her clearly enough to know positively that it was Greta. And she was acting odd.

A sliver of unease moved over his shoulders. He stepped off the patio and went slowly through the grass, feeling on his bare feet the dampness of dew or light rain that had fallen since bedtime.

"Greta?" he asked softly, testing.

She didn't answer. She stood very still now, her arms straight down at her sides. And he knew suddenly, and with a sense of eeriness beyond any he had ever felt before, that she was not aware of what she was doing. She was asleep.

He moved closer hesitantly. What was it you weren't supposed to do with a sleepwalker? Wake them up? Terrible things happened when they were awakened, but he didn't know what they were. He didn't want to do anything that would cause any hurt to Greta. She was just a dumb little kid, and ought not to be out here at this time of night. Where would she have gone if he hadn't seen her? Would she ever believe tomorrow that he had saved her life maybe? Naw, she'd never believe that.

He approached nearer. She was no more than six feet away now, her pale little face staring right through him. He saw she had her eyes wide open, and he lifted his hand to wave it in front of her face, to test her, to make sure she wasn't up to something weird. It was then he saw the other ...

Just behind her stood another figure, concealed in the shadows of the trees.

Kenny paused, his hand in the air.

The other figure looked dark and shapeless. Taller than Greta, taller than himself, and somehow almost formless, as if the soft edges were indefinite, fading into the black shadows beneath the trees.

Mr. Crossover? Milton Crossover?

What was he doing out here? Had he seen Greta too, and had he come to ... *whatever*? Kenny had a feeling the figure behind Greta was not there for her protection. He stepped forward.

"Hey, look ..."

He had started to say, *Hey, look here, what are you doing?* But his tongue stuck to the roof of his mouth and a terrible heart-clogging fear entered his body, seeming to radiate out from the black and shapeless form behind Greta. It had moved forward like a cloud, a black cloud fallen to the earth or risen from a hole in the ground. It moved without seeming to move at all, so that suddenly it was closer, and Kenny could see it wasn't a real figure but only a black shadow of one that seemed human.

He saw hands reach out from it. Incredibly, in his suddenly heightened senses, he could see fingers on the hands, and he watched them spread. At the last moment, thinking only of escape, he tried to run. It seemed then he was caught in a dream where his legs wouldn't move, and it seemed he was falling, falling, down a deep, dark tunnel, and he could feel the sides of it, rough and metallic and rusted, scrape his arms and legs and face like fire.

Then for a moment reality touched him and gave him a clear picture of Greta, now above him. She was still staring, but her face was turned downward, toward him.

Slowly she was opening her mouth in a wide, silent scream.

Kenny knew something dark and terrible had invaded their lives.

Pain exploded in his head, and lights came at him, brilliant, broken, arrow straight. He wanted to shout at Greta to drop it—*Drop it ... Throw it away*—but he couldn't move or speak and the bullets of glassy colors turned to black.

CHAPTER 6

Greta was struggling through a painful rebirth, and her new world was filled with darkness and cold fear. The fear was the worst, all reality as she had known it gone. The fear rose from deep within her, consumed her, was her. She had no identity outside her fear. Gradually her eyes saw figures within the total lack of light that had filled her brain. She saw the shapes of leaves, individuals, clusters, limbs filled with leaves. Their edges became light, slowly, and she even saw the tiny hairy spikes at the edges of the leaves. And in front of her was the corner of a house, and other buildings, their roofs outlined against tall, dark trees, and against the sky. But she didn't know where she was.

Sound reached her, but rather than sensing it, hearing it, she felt it. It raged inside her, erupting like a volcano of cold ash on a distant and unknown planet. Then the sound became a part of the exterior darkness and thundered against her ears. Something was lying on the ground at her feet, and it became visible in the dark. She had known it was there. Something within her had known. And she knew why it was there. She had killed someone.

Suddenly the world changed, and she saw herself standing beneath the outer leaves of a citrus tree, the orange, or the lemon. She saw the light lying in streaks along the grass, coming from the street lamp down the block. The dark cold still surrounded her, and the fear rose like vomit with each gushing scream.

Figures were running toward her. Lights came on in the house and made pathways through the dark. White frosting on black grass. She saw Aunt Alyne pulling on her robe as she came. She saw Uncle Ross and William. William stopped on the patio, the light from the kitchen shining out around him. She looked down.

It was Kenny ... it was Kenny she had killed.

Somebody picked her up, and she smelled her daddy's cologne. His hand pressed her head against his chest. She heard her screams turn to gasps and sobs, and her voice began making sounds and, finally, words.

"Kenny ... Kenny ... I ... didn't ... mean ... I didn't want to ..."

"Hush, hush, baby." That was her mother's voice, soothing but edged with a strange roughness, as if in a minute she too would scream. Behind her in the dark, as her dad carried her back through the citrus grove, she heard Aunt Alyne's voice cry out. She was calling Kenny's name, over and over, and then she was crying, loudly, saying no, no, no.

They put her back into her bed, and her mother sat with her, her cool hand on Greta's forehead. Greta stared into the light, unwilling to let it go, unable to forget the awful darkness, the total lack of light in the world she had awakened from.

Where had she been? The space was narrow and rough and cold, so very, very cold. She thought of the well. It was like the well, that long, deep pipe, that cold, dark place. So she stared into the light, absorbing it into herself. Once her mother put a cool hand across her eyes, as if to shield her, but Greta pushed it away, twisted from beneath it in a sudden and terrible panic. She couldn't let the light go.

A doctor came to see her. It was not her pediatrician, but a younger man she had never seen before. He had fine brown hair and a face that didn't look much older than Kenny's. Smiling, he sat down on the side of her bed and stuck the ends of a stethoscope in his ears. He put the cold end of it against her chest, then, still smiling, he removed it from her chest and from his ears, and hung it around his neck like a big wishbone necklace.

"How're you doing, Greta?" His hand was warm and smooth. Her mother had moved aside, and Greta could see her from the corner of her vision standing against the wall at the head of the bed as if she were there to watch every move the young doctor made.

Greta tried to answer him, but found her throat was hurting. She licked her lips and nodded her head. Her voice came sounding like a voice out of a cartoon.

"Kenny-y?"

The doctor's smile didn't waver. "Can you tell us what happened?"

"I ... killed him."

She became aware of other people in the room. A tall man stood in the doorway, but he wasn't totally unfamiliar. She had seen him at the well when they had brought up the bones, and she had seen him across his fence just down the street. One day she and Derek had ridden their bikes out onto the street and farther back toward town than they were supposed to, and they had ridden up onto the sidewalk to get out of the way of a car. The man had been mowing his yard, and he had shut off the mower and watched them; and then he had told them they shouldn't be out on the street, that they should ride in the alley behind their houses until they were a few years older. She didn't know his name, but she guessed he knew hers.

"What makes you think you killed him, Greta?"

"I ..." She thought hard, trying to remember, and her throat constricted and the cold and dark swam over her again, like black water in a deep well. The doctor put his hand on her chest and patted.

"Here, here, you're all right, Greta. Greta?"

She focused her eyes on him. The light was behind his head now, making a halo around it like the pictures of Jesus. She concentrated on the light and the kindness she saw in his face. He was like Jesus, that distant king she had heard about in Sunday school. The Son of God. The son that God had sent to earth to save people from their sins. The son that God had allowed to be hanged until death on a cross. Why had God done that? If God could do anything, why had he made people that sinned in the first place? She thought it might be a game God was playing, using the people like chess pieces. Daddy and Stephanie spent lots of time playing chess, especially on rainy days in the winter time, and she sometimes watched. It was a game, but a very serious game. Was that what God had done? Was doing? Playing a serious game with the people and animals on earth? And why had he made the thing ... the terrible cold, the awful nightmare that was all she remembered of the *thing* ... whatever it was ... that had made her kill Kenny?

She felt molten tears sting her eyes like acid and run tickling down her cheeks. With the backs of her hands she wiped them away.

"I don't know," she wept. "I don't know. I don't know."

"Tell us what you were doing in the yard, Greta," the Jesus man said.

"I don't know! I don't know!"

"Do you remember meeting Kenny?"

"No. I don't remember. He was on the ground. I killed him."

"Did you hit him with something, Greta?"

"No! No! I didn't do that."

"Did someone else?"

"No! No, it was ... I don't remember."

"You didn't kill Kenny, Greta." The voice was gentle and comforting.

"I didn't?" Hope rose in her, a tiny flame, as if she might wake now from this nightmare and find that her world had gone back to the way it was last week, before she and Derek found the well. She half-raised onto an elbow, staring at the face of the doctor, at the halo of light around his head. "Is Kenny alive?"

For just a moment too long there was silence in the room. No one answered her. She dropped back onto the bed, feeling scared and very weak. And she knew. Kenny was dead.

Someone handed the doctor a glass of water, and suddenly there was a small capsule in his hand and he was putting it to her lips. "This will make you feel better," he said.

They dimmed the lights and left the room, and Greta saw her door was closed now, and even her mother was gone. Her eyes grew droopy as she gazed from one familiar object to another—her dresser across the room with the little twin blue lamps, and the ceramic pitcher in the matching bowl. On the wall on each side of the dresser were the little shelves she had helped her mother pick out, and sitting on one shelf was a blue glass bird, and on the other was a little pot with dried flowers, and a smaller blue glass bird.

In the corner of the room was the stuffed-animal hammock, filled with teddy bears, fuzzy dogs and cats, and creatures that were a mixture of all. One of them had a nose like an elephant, and a tail like a bunny rabbit. She remembered getting it for her fifth birthday. It had been a present from Derek. He had picked it out himself, he said, and so it was one of her favorite stuffed animals. Another one had horns and a funny nose with big fluffy pink nostrils. It was supposed to be a cow, she guessed.

Slowly she became aware that she was not alone in her room, and that her room was not the safe, warm place it had been. She turned her head to the left, looking toward the window, and the corner to the left of the head of her bed. And she saw it, filling the lower part of the corner, black and formless like a thick shadow, like her nightmare, her fears, come to live with her forever.

• • •

SERGEANT CONRAD DONALLY wanted to put his arms around Alyne and comfort her. What worse thing was there than losing a child, a son? Having no son at all was preferable. He had more or less watched Kenny grow up. He had seen the tow-headed youngster riding his bike when he was the age of the youngest boy, the age of the little girl, Greta, who thought she had killed Kenny. He had seen him grow tall and handsome, and had seen him walking in the mall lately with a couple of girls, his buddy, Calvin, and other young teenagers on their way to becoming adults.

Now this kid would never grow up, and the image of him lying twisted on the grass, his face contorted into a terrible grimace of pain, or fear, his eyes staring upward, would stay with him forever. He hurt for the parents, and for the brothers who had seen him there, so helpless in his death.

The coroner hadn't been able to tell them much. The boy had no visible marks outside of an abrasion at the edge of his hair that looked as if he had received one hard blow to the head. It shouldn't have been enough to kill him, Sam Preston said, and Conrad felt Sam knew as much about what caused death in an individual as the State Medical Examiner did. But nevertheless, the report would have to come from the State Medical Examiner.

In the days it took for the body to be returned for burial and for the report to come in, Conrad went through the growing file that started with the murder of Sally Crossover. For years that file had been inactive, and then the bones of the girl in the well had made a nebulous connection by way of the missing jewelry. And following upon that came the strange death of Kenny Kerwin.

He sat in his cubicle and put together what he had. Nobody in the neighborhood remembered a girl who might have fit the description of the girl in the well. He had yet to get in touch with the two Whitaker girls. He had put in a call to both and had been unable to reach them.

The medical report on Kenny Kerwin came in three days after his death, with cause of death listed as a massive brain hemorrhage, from a blow to the head. Or, since the blow had seemed not severe enough to cause such internal damage, could it have been caused by a weakness in an artery or vein, a genetic weakness?

He had asked Sam these questions, and Sam had said, "Sometimes we can only guess at the cause of death, but you may be right."

The thing was, while Conrad couldn't bear thinking that Greta had struck Kenny with something hard enough to make the bloody cut on his forehead, even if she did it still should not have caused his death.

Conrad stared at the thin wall of the cubicle and thought of having to take this news to Alyne. So the death probably had been caused, although it seemed incredible, from that blow to the head. According to the report. But who had struck him? And where was the weapon? The little girl had kept crying that she had killed Kenny. Was there truth in that after all? Conrad didn't think so.

The weather was appropriately dreary, dark clouds hanging low, and a drizzling rain falling just enough to keep the windshield wipers activated. He drove slowly, reluctant to carry this news to Alyne and the rest of the family. He thought about the death site—the murder site, in fact—that mown area of grass between the trees that separated Alyne's house from Clare's. A strip of grass that was perhaps twenty feet wide, where the street light filtered through the trees and laid down slivers of light that did little to dispense the dark. She had been standing there, wailing, weeping, sometimes screaming, when he had arrived on the scene, and the body of the boy was on the grass at her feet. Alyne was holding Kenny, cradling him in her arms. But the thing was, had anyone really looked for a weapon? It had seemed beyond reason that the little girl would have struck Kenny. He was taller, heavier. She would have had to stretch in order to hit him with anything, even a quite long weapon. But no weapon had been found that he knew of. There was nothing in the report. Freshly mown grass, the report had said, was the site of the death.

The street was quiet. He pulled in and parked at the curb in front of Alyne's house, and went up to the front door and rang the bell. He stood waiting. He looked across the street at the glistening hedges that surrounded Milton Crossover's house. Rain obscured the setting even more. As was the case most of the time, there was no sign of life or movement. He wondered what Milton did, all alone, on days like these. On winter days when there was so much rain, such darkness. He saw no light on in any of the windows.

Just beyond Milton's yard was his own. There the hedge ended and a yard of grass began, surrounded by the metal fence with the old-fashioned fancy ironwork that had been around the yard all his life. His house was hidden behind the trees in Milton's yard and in his own, as was the house across the street from his. Jonah Pattison's big old rambling farmhouse.

The door opened. Alyne's face looked as if it were veiled, behind the screen of the outer door. At first she acted as if she didn't even know him. She looked through the screen without speaking. Her face was thinner, as if she had lost a lot of weight in the past few days. Her hair was hanging loose around her face, dropping against the shadowed cheekbones. The sadness in her eyes made his chest hurt. He wanted to hold her, again, just as he had wanted to the night she was moaning over the body of her son. This was a feeling he shouldn't have been having. She was happily married, so far as he knew. At least she had been until recently, when it seemed the world was being turned inside out, upside down.

"Alyne, I have the report from the medical examiner. Kenny's body has been sent to the mortuary. I guess you were notified about that?"

She nodded, then she opened the door and stood back. "Come in. We're in the family room. I haven't sent the boys back to school yet. Ross has gone back to work." She went ahead of him down a carpeted hall to a door at the rear. "Ross will always go back to work," she said, her voice soft and low, but holding for just an inflection a touch of bitterness. "It's good that he can. It keeps his mind occupied. My work ... it's home and family. And ..."

She opened the door into a large combined room at the back. On the left was a stone fireplace in the corner, with sofas and chairs and a television that was turned on low. Straight ahead was a dining area with a breakfront filled with colorful dishes, a round dining table, a braided rug on the tile floor beneath it. Farther on was a nine-foot section of glass and doors opening out onto a patio. To the right was a kitchen, bright and cheerful, with its own smaller table, as well as a bar. He had never been in Alyne's house before. She liked things made of straw, he saw, and she liked color and texture and pottery. It was a warm place, visually, yet he felt a strange coldness, a darkness that was not dispelled by the wide windows and doors.

The two boys were close to the television, which was playing via a VCR some kind of animated movie. The older boy, William, had brown hair and a round, almost plump face. The other one was small with blond hair and lighter eyes. The hair would change as he grew older, but it would never be the rich brown of his brother. Both boys looked at him, but neither spoke nor smiled. He didn't expect them to, nor, it seemed, did their mother. She pulled out a chair at the dining table, and he sat down. He shouldn't, he reminded himself. He should have just stopped at the front door and told her what the report amounted to and gone on.

"Would you like some coffee?"

He wanted to say yes, but he shook his head. When she sat down in another of the chairs, he asked her, "How are you getting along?"

She shrugged and nodded, her eyes lowered. "It's like a severe physical pain. There are moments when you feel nothing. Then it comes back again. I guess it will go on being this way. Kenny was here. He was a big part of my life. And now he's gone. And yet, how can he be gone when he was part of my existence, my reality?" She reached up and rubbed the back of her neck. "What killed him then?"

"He had a brain hemorrhage. There might have been a weak artery or blood vessel. But there was also a blow to his head."

She looked up sharply. "Who hit him? With what? Not Greta! But she was there, wasn't she? What did she see?"

"As you know, she was hysterical. Incoherent. I don't think she saw anything. I think she found him."

"But who could have hurt him? Who would have? *Why?*"

She sounded on the verge of hysteria. He saw surprise in her eyes and a sudden desperation, as if she had to know. He wondered if they would ever know.

"That's what I'm going to try to find out," he said. He had learned from experience that the members of a family in which one person had died accidentally or otherwise suddenly, were somewhat comforted if they knew the authorities were working on finding a reason why. The why was an important factor in putting grief to rest with the victim. Alyne reached over and grasped Conrad's wrist pleadingly.

"Please, please do."

"Yes, I will."

As he left, he wondered why he had committed himself in that way on a death that didn't look as if it would ever be solved. In that way it was like the death of Mrs. Crossover thirty-three years ago and the death of the girl, which must have occurred at the same time. And there were other similarities. Mrs. Crossover had died of a severe blow to the head, and so might have the girl. Also, Kenny. In Mrs. Crossover's case there had been many blows, perhaps as many as twenty, and the weapon was a poker.

He had asked permission to look at the yard again, and Alyne said yes. He asked her if anyone had cleaned up the yard, and she said no. He saw, in walking through the grass, that it hadn't been mown recently. The grass was a couple of inches higher than most lawns.

He stood on the spot where the boy had died and looked around. The trees were just a few feet away. He could see beneath them to Clare's house where Greta had exited by the back door. It had to have been the back door because the front door had been looked.

He turned his attention to the grass, looking for a limb, a rock, anything. There was nothing. Of course it could have been picked up the very night it happened, and also others of the police had looked for the weapon that night.

There was one other choice. A human hand. A fist. But it would have had to be incredibly strong. And so, it had never even been considered.

Greta's memory of what had happened hadn't disclosed anything along that line. She couldn't remember how she had gotten into the yard, the report said. Suddenly she was there, Kenny was on the ground at her feet. And she had killed him. What made her think that? She didn't know.

She had become almost hysterical and the questioning had been dropped.

He got into his car and started the engine, and he found his mind connecting the three murders, as if they had happened within weeks of one another. In order to find out who had killed Kenny, did he have to go back and find out who had killed Mrs. Crossover?

That was as unreasonable as a human fist having struck the blow to Kenny's head. But he found himself driving on down the street, passing other houses along the way, farther apart now as the rural took over. On the corner, where the road turned left, he took a right-hand swing into the driveway of the old Whitaker place. The long lane was lined on both sides by English walnut trees, the old kind that were not grafted on black walnut. They were as tall and spreading as some of the old oak trees and sheltered the lane entirely.

The house was old, but it had been redone, remodeled and bricked on the outside. There was a chain link fence completely surrounding the house and yard, leaving the garage outside the fence on two sides. Two tail-wagging dogs came to the gate to greet him. A bell rattled when he opened the gate, and Mrs. Whitaker came out onto the small screened porch.

"Hello, Sergeant Donally. This is a coincidence. I was just thinking about calling you. Won't you come in?"

He went into the shelter of the porch, but didn't accept her invitation to come on into the kitchen for coffee. They stood on the porch, Mrs. Whitaker hugging her arms. She was wearing a housedress and apron, and he saw a spot of flour on the tip of her nose.

"I've been thinking and thinking, and couldn't come up with a thing. About the girl you asked about. But then this morning when I woke up, I remembered. There was a girl in the neighborhood, a strange girl, the year my own daughter, the oldest, was fifteen. I don't remember her name, but she was quite tall and mature for her age, and she had long, straight, reddish hair. Her hair was quite beautiful, as I remember it, and she was fair skinned with a few freckles. She was here at the house once or twice, and didn't seem to fit in really well with the other girls. I don't remember her name, who she was, where she lived or anything."

Conrad felt the excitement, as subtle as a butterfly lighting on a source of nectar. But these feelings sometimes had a way of turning out to be false leads. "Your daughter was fifteen, you say?"

"Yes. So that would make it precisely thirty-three years ago. It was summertime. School was out. Estie is forty-eight now. I called, and she was out. But I left a message for her to call you about this. I gave her your name and number. You'll be hearing from her sometime soon."

They talked about her three daughters. One had passed away at the age of twenty-seven, a cancer victim, and Mrs. Whitaker's eyes misted and she looked away from him, toward a horizon in the distant blue of her mind. It never stops hurting, she told him. When you lose a child, it's forever. He thought of Alyne and the fresh savagery of her pain, and the forever ahead of her.

"MAMA?" Derek asked. "Can I go play with Greta?"

Greta. Usually Greta was in her house at least once a day, sometimes many more times than once. Alyne thought of her niece and wondered if she had been going to school these days, when she had kept her own two sons home because of their brother's death. They would not go back to school until the day after the funeral. But she had not seen Greta since the day it happened. Stephanie had come to see her, to weep with her, several times, and Clare had brought food; but now she remembered her own negligence. She hadn't even asked how Greta was. She had been so crushed by her own loss, by the impossible knowledge that Kenny was gone forever, that it was like being isolated from all but anguish. With Greta's name in the air between her and Derek, she saw her again as she stood in her pajamas at the crumpled body of her son, and her screams echoed in Alyne's memory. "I killed Kenny!" she had screamed. Why did she think she had killed Kenny? Why did Alyne feel that Greta was, in some way, more responsible than anyone else in the world? Greta was her niece, and she loved her. Greta had always been almost like her own. She couldn't have killed Kenny. But why did she say she had?

"Yes, Derek," she said. "Go on over and play, and if Greta's alone, ask her if she wants to come over here."

DEREK WENT out the patio doors. A light rain was in the air like mist, and the clouds rolled overhead as if the sky had fallen during the past three days that he hadn't been outside. It was like it had been the time Mama got sick, that winter she'd had the flu. Like something had been put around him, chains or something, holding him, so that he didn't feel like doing anything but just lying around in front of the television with his coloring books, his comics and transformers, just something to keep his hands and eyes busy while he waited. It had been that way this time, like he was waiting for Kenny to get well and come back into the family with the rest of them.

He hadn't thought he would ever miss Kenny. Kenny had always been nothing but a big brother, there to make his life miserable. Squeezing the back of his neck until he hollered, pulling his ears until he hollered, telling him he couldn't do anything he wanted to do, keeping an eye on him like some invisible camera that watched every move he made. But now with Kenny gone the world seemed duller and darker, as if the clouds had lowered just because Kenny wasn't there to hold them away.

He remembered exactly the spot where Kenny had lain. The grass didn't look as if a foot had ever stepped upon it, or as if a body had lain twisted the way Kenny's had. Derek stopped and stared at the spot. It stood out as if it were marked with white paint and a sign that said, *Kenny died here*. For a few moments Derek stared at it, and then he turned and ran, across the grass and beneath the low branches of the citrus trees, pushing them out of his way, feeling the cold drops of water shake off from them and roll down the back of his neck.

He came out on Greta's side of the trees and stopped, looking at the brick wall of her house. Blinds were drawn at the bedroom windows, and draperies covered the big windows at the front. It was like something sleeping, all its eyes shut.

He heard a movement behind him, something coming beneath the trees and through the damp grass. With his heart pumping suddenly, he whirled. But it was only the dog, Buster, and Derek bent to hug the smelly, wet-tongued old friend. His eyes looked older now than they had when he had followed at Kenny's heels. He was really Kenny's dog, always had been. He had been a puppy a long time before Derek was born, and Derek had always known that Buster belonged to Kenny.

The old, fading eyes looked sadly up into Derek's and the dog whined, as if to ask, Where's Kenny? Why hasn't he been bringing my feed and water? William had taken over that job. Would it be Derek's next?

Derek pushed the thought away, denying it, as if it predicted William's death. Although he had never played much with William, not as much as he played with Greta, still he couldn't imagine life without William. He was the easy brother to be around, the friend, if he needed a friend outside of Greta.

He went to the back of Greta's house and knocked on the door. But the house seemed empty, isolated by the citrus trees on one side and a line of taller trees and a fence on the other. From the back patio he could see the trees of the almond orchard and the alley road. He could see the corner of the shed in his own backyard and the bicycle rack at the back of his folks' garage.

Had Greta gone to school?

He put his face to the glass, his hands on each side to shade the light to make a tunnel of vision, and peered into the kitchen. He could see right on through to the hallway that led to the front of the house, and he could see to the right where there was a wall and a door that opened into the family room. But all he saw were things that didn't move, inanimate objects, the things on the cabinet, the chairs at the table, the telephone on the table in the darkened central hall. With a long sigh he pulled back. Even if Greta had gone to school she'd be home by now. He could see the clock on the kitchen wall, and it was later than four, which meant Greta should be home. Had her mom picked her up at school today because it was a special day?

Derek went around the corner of the house and crossed the walk that led out to the driveway. He went up the steps to the front door and put his finger on the doorbell and held it down. Beyond the wall he heard its ringing.

He began to feel that someone or something was watching him. The small porch roof kept the rain off his head, and there was no one out walking. Even the cats and dogs that usually lay on porches were gone now, back into their houses or somewhere in shelter. Derek took his finger off the doorbell and turned slowly, looking into the trees, the shrubs, and finally across the street. Mr. Crossover's house looked even more abandoned than Greta's, with the thick green hedge all across the front and the shadows beneath the long porches. Mr. Crossover's house was more in front of his own than Greta's, and his view was oblique; but through the trees he saw a window that wasn't covered by a blind or a curtain, and in the darkness behind the glass he thought he saw a movement. He stared at the window for a few minutes, then he leaped off the porch and went back through the wet grass toward his own house. He stopped in the trees and looked back at the blinded windows.

He knew suddenly that Greta was in the house.

Greta had never hidden from him before. Why was she hiding from him now?

CHAPTER 7

From the day Stephanie was born Clare had ceased being number one in Phillip's life. Neither Phillip nor Stephanie ever knew what that had taken away from Clare. A day so proud and so joyous as the day of Stephanie's birth had become one of hurt and confusion. Phillip, so handsome, so young, his dark hair falling over his forehead in wayward curls, his dark blue eyes sparkling with pride, had come to her and, even without asking how she was, began to tell her what a beautiful baby Stephanie was.

They were both twenty years old, Phillip just a few weeks older than Clare. They had held hands before the birth. Phillip had looked as if he were in as much pain as she was. He definitely was as filled with fear as she. He had kept asking if she were all right. He had lost the golden tan of his skin, that natural cast of old gold that looked so great on him, that contrasted so deeply with the pale peaches and cream of hers. He was so worried that it had brought out her maternal instinct and helped her to feel older and wiser, and she had comforted him. Then she had been taken away to the delivery room. And when she came out her world had changed.

They had met in their freshman year of high school. They were thirteen. He was from Eastside Grammar School, while she was from Sunnyside, a west-side school. She had fallen in love for the first and last time the moment she saw that beautiful face. He gave her a brilliant smile, and then in the classroom he had taken the seat right behind hers. A week later they were holding hands on the school ground when no one watched. At school gatherings and parties they paired off, and when they were fifteen they started dating. Neither of them had ever seriously dated anyone else. For a while Phillip had gone out with various other girls, but he always came back to her. And she had waited. A few times she had gone out with other guys too, but she had been bored to death and wondered all the time who Phillip was with.

Finally, her papa had given in and allowed her to date Phillip exclusively. She would never forget that day. At age seventeen she already knew that all she wanted out of life was to be with Phillip. Nothing else mattered. They were married when they were nineteen, and ten months later Stephanie was born.

Papa's gift to them, when he finally accepted the marriage, was the house and the land it stood on. As he had also given the first house to Alyne. Until their house was built, when Stephanie was five, Clare and Phillip had lived in an apartment downtown. Phillip had worked full-time and gone to college as well, until he was sufficiently educated to get the job as accountant and assistant manager of the men's store. She had worked too, leaving the baby in the home of a woman who for a while was like a grandmother to Stephanie, though Phillip had never wanted her to work. "The baby needs you," he used to say, until he realized he was only wasting his breath. He didn't know the resentment that made her feel. What about herself? Why did it always have to be what Stephanie needed?

When she became pregnant with her second child, she thought it might change things. Now, with two children, his love would be more divided, and it might somehow reinstate her to the number one spot in his life. But it was as if another child had not been born. Greta was not ignored by Phillip, but she definitely took place number two, crowding in there with herself. But Greta had always been number two or three and didn't know the difference. Greta was able to take care of herself.

But now, lying awake beside Phillip, as she so often did, hearing his light snores, the house quiet and dark, Clare heard strange sounds beginning somewhere, as if they might be part of the walls or the attic. It seemed she heard whisperings and small cries. Since Kenny's death Greta had been different. She had been so quiet, so withdrawn. It was not like Greta at all. It was not like Greta to have dreams, nightmares, in which she made those sounds of whisperings and cries.

Lying beside Phillip, unable to sleep, Clare's mind drifted back to its old problems, as if thinking about her yearning for Phillip's love was going to give it to her. As if thinking about Stephanie's soon going away to college would at last give her Phillip's undivided attention.

Not even the death of Kenny had kept her mind from this old groove, this tiresome old obsession that Phillip probably didn't know existed.

The sound of the cries down the hall, in the walls or the attic, brought her attention to them as if someone had knocked on the door. It didn't really sound like Greta.

She got out of bed and stood for a moment in the shadows looking toward the open door and the pale light in the hall where a night light cast its own shadows. The cries had stopped. Was Greta sleeping, dreaming? Since the night her screams had drawn them all outside to see her standing stiff and terrified at Kenny's side, Greta had made little sounds in her sleep, cries, moans. Or so, at least, it seemed. Perhaps it was Stephanie. Kenny had been as close to Stephanie as Derek was to Greta. The two had been playmates when they were younger, even though Stephanie was two years older than Kenny. Only in the last two years had they grown apart. Stephanie had grown up suddenly, it seemed, and had become even more Phillip's closest ally.

The cries came again, too young to be Stephanie, too childish, the voice thin and distant, the cry trailing away to a faint moan that brought eerie chills up Clare's neck, icy fingers into her hair and over her scalp. She moved on before she lost the nerve to go at all. Before she let herself believe it was neither of her girls, but something else that had entered her house. A foreign thing—a horror new to her, to their lives.

She went into the hall and passed the closed door of Stephanie's room. Stephanie always kept her door closed, since she was about fourteen. It had been a barrier to everyone except Phillip and a few of her closest friends, of whom she didn't really have a lot. Stephanie could be snobbish and sarcastic, really a disagreeable person at times. But when Clare once tried to talk it over with Phillip, he had looked at her as if she'd gone crazy. His face had turned uglier than she'd ever seen it. "What the hell are you talking about, Clare?" he had asked, his tone of voice successfully letting her know there was no way he would ever agree with her. And it was true that with Phillip the girl was always sweet and easy to talk to. But couldn't he hear how Stephanie talked to Greta? To her? Even to some of her friends? No, he was deaf and blind where Stephanie was concerned, and happily unobservant in all other ways too.

Clare stood still again, feeling the familiar hall somehow an unfamiliar territory suddenly, as if during all the years she had lived here, she had not actually seen it in reality, hadn't seen the dangers here. The wallpaper was still gold and green, with flocked leaves and trailing vines. The old grandfather clock down in the broader foyer at the front of the house still ticked in long, slow tick-tocks. Dim light swelled out from the little lamp on the table, just as it always did. And the chair beside the table still had its needlepoint seat. But there was a quality in the hall that had never been so strong as now, though as she stood there she realized the feeling wasn't entirely new, as if it had been coming on for several days and nights now and was only getting stronger.

The silence seemed pregnant with the quality of ... change?

She listened for the sound of the cries, the moans, and heard nothing but the slow, deep tick of the clock. Farther on along the hall, opposite the guest room, Greta's door stood partway open. The area beyond was totally dark, a black nothing upon which the door opened, like a narrow, vertical cave.

She didn't want to go in there, she realized, though she knew her child was there. She was afraid. Unreasonably, unaccountably afraid.

Greta was not in danger, she told herself. Greta was sleeping.

She started back to her bed, where Phillip could be beside her, when the sound of whispering reached her ears. She stopped. The whispers drifted away and were replaced by the moans again, the soft little cries.

Greta ... Greta's room. Clare had to go to her.

Without further hesitation she went down the hall and pushed wide open the door to Greta's room. The darkness was still too complete to reveal anything but the ghostly white sheets of the bed, the side of the mattress. Clare slipped her hand inside the wall and flicked the light switch.

The overhead light came on, the room in stark outline beneath the sixty-watt bulb in the pink light fixture. Greta was turned with her face toward the wall, her body pulled up into a knot that looked tight and uncomfortable. She had pulled the cover over her head so she was more just a bulge beneath the blanket than she was actually visible. But the thing that stopped Clare and made her stare was the thing in the corner beyond—the almost thing, the dark place, the thick shadow that the light did not at first dispel. It was like something was squatting there, an enormous black shadow thrown onto the wall between Greta's bed and the corner. But as Clare watched it, the wallpaper, the corner, became visible, so that she was left blinking at an empty wall, in which she saw only the figures on the wallpaper, the geometric greens, blues, and reds, and the teddy bed hanging high in the corner, filled with so many stuffed animals that some of them looked like they might fall out at any time.

Was it the teddy bed that had thrown the shadow? Had there been a shadow at all?

Greta was quiet again. Clare could not even hear her breathe.

With a sudden lurch of fear she went to the bed and put her hand on the lump that was Greta's head beneath the blanket. If Kenny could die so suddenly with a blood vessel bursting in his brain, couldn't Greta? Perhaps it was a genetic defect, a weakness never known about before. Phillip had said that was what it must have been with Kenny. A blood vessel with weak walls, just waiting all these years like a deadly, tiny balloon in his brain, ready to burst at any time. The abrasion, the broken skin, Phillip said, was probably caused when he fell.

Greta's head was warm. Clare felt weak, as if her legs were going to drop her helplessly to the floor. She pulled the tightly tucked blanket out from under Greta's head and then pried her small, tight fingers away from it. Greta was wet with perspiration. She moved, turning onto her back, her face in a frown, her lips parting in one of the eerie moans that had brought Clare out of her bed. Greta faced the light in the ceiling now, her eyes squeezed tightly shut. She drew a long breath and turned onto her right side, now facing the door.

The teddy bed in the corner moved.

Clare's eyes jerked toward it, and she stood, frozen. A stuffed animal with horns seemed to be hanging even farther out, its head below the woven hammock. It had moved, and yet it could not have. Clare stared at it, the whole bed, secured to the wall at three points, and then she watched as the horned animal tilted farther forward and fell to the floor. It seemed to fall in slow motion, in time with her heart, that heavy thud of fear in her chest.

She swallowed. She was the one who had decorated this room, who had seen the ad in the magazine for the teddy bed and thought to herself what a cute way to get all those stuffed animals under control. She had tried to talk Greta into giving a bunch of them away, but Greta refused. So Clare had bought the teddy bed, a woven hammock, and had hung it herself. If it had moved, it surely was not because something stood in the corner beneath it, something that had remained dark for just a few moments after the light went on and then faded to blend in with the corner less visibly, it was only because the horned cow, or whatever it was, had been in the process of falling out. Gravity had taken over, that was all. The bottom of the teddy bed had not been touched.

She went around the foot of the bed, picked up the little pink and blue creation with the horns and floppy ears, the red tongue, and the shiny black eyes, and tossed it onto the very top of the pile in the teddy bed.

She looked back at Greta from the doorway and saw her face had relaxed. She was no longer frowning. Like most nine-year-olds, she had the sleeping face of an angel, of the baby she had been only a few years ago. Clare smiled faintly.

Clare went back to bed and fell asleep almost immediately.

"Do I have to go, Mama?" Greta asked.

Clare hesitated. She was dressed in a black suit with a white blouse and a little black hat with a veil. Greta thought she was beautiful. Her eyes looked strange though, behind the veil, darker than they should have been. As mysterious as a princess from some faraway land. Standing not far away, looking at her, was Stephanie, wearing a suit too, and white gloves. But her shining dark brown hair was uncovered, and her face unveiled. Phillip was coming out of the bedroom hall, adjusting his tie. His hair was like Stephanie's, dark and shining.

"You're nine years old now, Greta, and this is your cousin's funeral," Clare said. "I think you should go."

But she wasn't sure. Greta could see her giving in, and Greta let her misery show on her face. She saw her dad stop and stare at her, but this time she didn't care if he did see her being ugly.

"I don't want to go, Mom. I don't want to see him dead." She had seen him dead, she guessed. But it was like a dream, like one of the hundreds of terrible dreams she'd been having lately. Kenny crumpled on the ground, and then the ground turning into a deep hole beneath him and Kenny falling, falling, soon out of sight in the deep, black hole. And his cries ... oh, Lord, his cries. They haunted her day and night. All she wanted to do was huddle in her room, in the corner, beneath the teddy bed, and put her head down on her knees, her knees sharp against her eyes, and try to shut out the light. And the dreams. Or whatever they were.

Clare looked at Phillip. "What do you think ... ?"

Stephanie said, "Of course she should go. Derek is going. What will Aunt Alyne think if Greta doesn't go?"

Clare looked at Stephanie. "Are you sure Derek is going?"

Phillip passed them, finishing the adjusting of his tie. "Stephanie is right," he said.

Clare watched him go out toward the kitchen. He would get the car out and be ready to go. Stephanie shrugged and followed Phillip.

"Of course Derek is going. Natural intelligence would tell you that."

Clare muttered, loudly enough for Greta to hear, although she'd been talking to herself. "Well, I don't have all that much natural intelligence, I guess, because I'm not so sure." She picked up the hall phone and began to dial.

Sometimes, it seemed lately to Greta, Mama didn't like Stephanie very well. But at the moment she was too anxious to let her mind dwell on it. Behind her back she crossed her fingers and hugged into her palm for good luck the fat jewel of the ring. Please, don't make me go to the funeral.

Clare listened into the phone but didn't speak, and Greta felt her chances slip away. Clare looked at her with a small, sympathetic smile, reached over and patted her with her gloved hand. She hung up the phone.

"You look so pretty in your blue dress," she said. "Aunt Alyne is already gone. Derek is gone too, or he would have answered the phone. I'm sorry sugar, but you have to go too."

They went out of the house with Clare's arm across Greta's shoulders.

"I understand how you feel," she said. "When I was just a year older than you are, my mother died. She died in the hospital, and I had never seen a dead person before either, and I didn't want to see my mother dead. It's very hard to lose your mother. Especially when you're only ten years old. I didn't want to go to the funeral. I wanted to remember her the way I'd last seen her, but Alyne wanted to go, and she wanted to stay with her. She didn't want to come home."

"She wanted to be buried too?" Greta cried, looking up at Clare's veiled face incredulously.

"No, not buried. Or perhaps in a way buried with her, so to speak, because she was so unhappy at losing our dear, sweet mother. She didn't want to leave her there in the cemetery. But of course she had to. And I had to go, which I hadn't wanted to. So you see, even though we were sisters, we had this completely opposite reaction to our mother's death."

Greta walked beside Clare down the path to the driveway and the car, where Phillip and Stephanie sat waiting. She thought about what her mother had said, rolled it swiftly around in her mind searching for parallel meanings, for something that applied to herself.

"You mean like even though Derek and I are cousins, maybe he wanted to go to Kenny's funeral?"

Clare looked down at Greta as if her mind had wandered far off. Phillip reached over and pushed open the car door, and Clare put her hand on it.

"Something like that," she said.

Greta got into the car and sat in the seat behind her mother. They always took the same places in the car if the four of them went, with Stephanie behind Phillip, Greta behind Clare, and in the past, when it mattered, Greta had sometimes fussed to change places with Stephanie, but without result. Today, it didn't matter.

They drove down the boulevard that was tree-lined, that had a strip down the center between the streets that were filled with colorful flowers, now glistening under the soft mist that tilled the air. The flowers were called chrysanthemums, or just plain mums, Clare had told Greta last week or the week before, when Greta had gone shopping with her. They were in all colors.

"Those are mums," Greta said, looking out her window, seeking to break the depressing silence in the car.

Stephanie said, "Only part of them are mums. The browns, yellows, and golds. The others are something else. Mums are never blue. Asters, I think."

Greta said nothing, but the silence was broken.

They parked in the chapel parking lot, where it looked at first as if all the places were filled. Greta saw a line of young people going into the chapel doors, boys and girls Kenny's age. She began to tremble and tightened her hand over the ring. It felt hot in her palm, the way it sometimes did, and the cut edges seemed sharper than usual. She looked down at her hand and it seemed she could see light coming through her fingers, as if she had her hand cupped over a small flashlight. She dared not open her palm to see, because Stephanie was just a few steps behind her. She pulled her fist in against her full skirt, tucking it into one of the folds. Clare put her hand on Greta's shoulder, guiding her along toward the open doors of the chapel. Greta glanced back. Phillip was coming with Stephanie, just a few paces behind. Both of them were looking straight ahead, their faces like masks, so smooth and yet so stern, or maybe as Stephanie would say, composed.

The chapel was full, but there was a special room to one side for the family, and they went in there and took seats behind Aunt Alyne, Uncle Ross, William, and Grandfather. William's face looked spotted white and red, and his full lips had almost disappeared into the tightness of his mouth. He had been crying, Greta could see by the wet red of his eyes, a lot, a long time. She stared at him, his hurt a deep pain within her. She had never seen William anything but carefree and easy going before. Nothing had ever bothered him, it seemed. And it hurt to see him looking so sad. At the end of the row sat Derek, looking small in his dark suit. He didn't look back at her, and Greta wondered miserably if he hated her now, now that she thought she might have killed his brother, even though the doctor said she didn't.

She looked around. Miss Reade sat in the back row. The room was small, but filled with straight chairs with thin, padded seats. There was a wide door on the right, with a curtain pulled partway across. Beyond the curtain Greta could see a huge arrangement of flowers and the end of the gray and white coffin. The lid was raised, and a veil hung down from the top. The room looked like a flower shop, with a coffin sitting on display in the center of the flowers. Fragrances drifted through the air, sweet, almost stifling, as if it came in invisible layers. She heard someone weeping and saw Aunt Alyne bow her head.

A man in a black suit, walking so softly he made no sound, came and opened the curtain wider, and Greta could see a man standing behind a kind of pulpit; he had a Bible, and in the total silence of the chapel he began to talk. Greta wanted to ask Clare who he was, but she dared make no sound.

The man talked about Kenny's activities in school and about his friends, and the year he was born. He told things such as Kenny winning the poster award one year. Greta hadn't known that. The Kenny she was hearing about, so helpful, so good, didn't sound like the Kenny she had known. She was sorry he was dead, she was sorry she had not liked him, but the Kenny the minister talked about was kind and sweet and never mean.

They said she didn't really kill him, but Greta looked at her cupped hand with the light shining through her fingers, and knew she had. She had somehow opened up the hole in the ground for him. She was afraid. She was terrified that she would open up that terrible hole for someone else. The whispers kept coming in her ears, from just behind her head, so often, when she thought she was alone. And sometimes she wondered if they came from within her head.

She realized the preacher had stopped and a group of singers was singing a hymn. Then there was silence except for piped organ music, so soft in the background, and the sound of many feet on the thickly carpeted floors.

She watched as people came up the aisle and went by the coffin, stopping briefly to look in on Kenny. She began to dread her turn. She wanted to reach over and clutch her mother's hand and beg to be excused, but she couldn't move.

Then the man in black was beckoning to Uncle Ross, and the family rose to go into the big room of the chapel and see the full length of the coffin. Clare's hands were on Greta's shoulders, pushing her gently along. When they came close to the coffin, Greta shut her eyes. But still she saw him, lying pale and still, with his hands folded on the chest of his neat suit, his face so composed. She even glimpsed the touch of pale color on his lips and cheeks.

Her eyes flew open and she stared at him.

He wasn't dead.

His cheeks were healthy and pink, and his lips pink and full, just like always. Kenny wasn't dead!

She jerked away from Clare and looked hurriedly from face to face. Aunt Alyne was weeping hard, and Uncle Ross had his arm around her, his own face crumpled and tears running down his cheeks. William looked more plump, his cheeks somehow blown out. A drop of moisture oozed from the side of his mouth, and Greta was afraid he would start screaming. Derek was standing back, off the area at the front, almost in the aisle. He looked terrified, white and scared, more than Greta had ever seen him. Grandfather walked up to the coffin, leaning heavily on his cane. He was more bent today, and Miss Reade hurried to stand close to him and link her arm with his. Stephanie stood sedately beside her dad, and he put his arm around her waist and turned her toward the door.

Greta heard her own voice cry out, "Kenny's not dead!"

Slowly, it seemed, as if in slow motion, they all turned and looked at her, shock white on their faces. They stared at Greta as if she were a stranger they had never seen before, a horrible newcomer who didn't belong in their group. Grandfather's face looked angry, his heavy eyebrows lowered like roofs above his eyes.

"But he's not!" Greta cried again. "Can't you see? Dead people are gray and white, and Kenny isn't that way! Kenny has *apples* in his cheeks!"

She looked desperately from face to face. Wasn't that what Grandfather himself always said when he saw her? "You must be a healthy girl," he'd say. "You've got apples in your cheeks."

Greta repeated, anxiety making her voice shrill, *"He's got apples in his cheeks!"* How great to find that Kenny wasn't dead after all! How great, how lovely! He was going to wake up and sit up and climb out of the coffin and yell, "Surprise!"

It was just another of his jokes, one of his tricks that he played on her and Derek. She knew dead people were gray and white and terrible looking because she had seen them on television and on video horror shows. Couldn't these people see that Kenny was not dead?

Grandfather lifted his cane and pointed it at her. His cheeks shook even before he spoke.

"Get that child out of here! *Get ... her ... out!"*

One of the men in black took Greta's hand and drew her down the aisle toward the doors at the front. She began to cry, to try to twist her arm out of his grasp. He leaned over her.

"It's going to be all right," he said. "Just come out into the foyer."

She allowed him to lead her through the doors. He closed them and then, leaning down toward her, as if he had difficulty seeing her, he said, "That's makeup, dear child. Makeup."

Makeup? What did he mean?

And then she knew.

She stared at the man open-mouthed. It was just like Stephanie sitting at her dressing table putting on mascara and spreading rouge onto her cheeks, blending it with her fingers until it looked like ... apples.

She felt her legs give and almost collapsed. But she held herself up. They hated her now, her whole family hated her. If she fell and had to be carried out, they would hate her more. She held her head high and walked through the outer doors and toward the car.

CHAPTER 8

THE PHONE CALL came while Conrad was preparing his dinner. He had gone to Kenny Kerwin's funeral and felt as dragged out emotionally as if the boy had been a close relative. It was always hard to see a funeral, but especially hard when the victim was young, with his life gone. The only kind death seemed to be that of a person or animal very, very old, who had lost the ability to enjoy life. Then, death was a blessing. In a world where death was a necessity, why couldn't it have a better connotation? Why must it always be a horror? It was the not knowing, he guessed, not knowing what, if anything, lay on the other side.

He picked up the phone.

"Sergeant Donally? This is Estie Whitaker. Used to be Whitaker, now Mayhewn. As you probably know, I live on the East Coast, and I don't get home real often anymore, but I do talk to Mother a lot, and she told me you were wanting to know about a girl I used to chum around with some."

Conrad felt the excitement building again, the anxiety that said he was on the edge of learning something that would clear up the mystery of who the girl in the well had been.

"You knew her then?"

"I knew a girl during the summer when I was fifteen who was with the rest of us kids just two or three times. She was quite tall and grownup, though she was only fourteen, a year younger than I was. She had long, reddish blond hair, very beautiful. Her name was something like Adriene. I'm almost sure it was Adriene."

Conrad grabbed a note pad and pencil out of the desk drawer. "And the last name?"

"That I don't remember. And I don't know where she lived. I was never in her house. I met her one day on the street. I and my sisters and some more kids were riding our bikes, and we came upon this girl just walking along. We stopped and talked to her a few minutes. She said her name was Adriene, or something very similar. I've been trying to get all this together since Mother told me that body had been found in the well, and you were searching the neighborhood trying to identify her. I was shocked. Just to think we lived so close to a tragedy like that! A body in the well? Could it possibly be her? Adriene?"

"Your description of her fits what little we know."

"I can't believe it. I wondered what happened to her."

"Did you know her very well?" He was afraid not. If she didn't even know where the girl lived.

"At that age we don't try to know people well, I guess. She was around quite a bit. She'd join us girls when we'd walk down to the river and go swimming. I felt sorry for her because she didn't even have a bathing suit. She had to swim in her dress. And when she got out, that one day I recall, she acted scared because her dress was wet. She stood in the hot sun letting it dry. We had to go home. Mother insisted that we not stay long at the river, but Adriene wouldn't go with us. She had to let her dress dry first."

"Was that the last time you saw her?" He visualized a young girl alone at the river, and perhaps some man finding her there, raping and killing her, and then dumping the body down the well. Hiding it forever.

Almost forever.

"No," Estie said. "No, she was around later, I'm sure. We walked together, and she came to our house once or twice for cookies and punch, or lemonade. Mom was always good to let us bring housefuls of kids. We always had a lot of company. And this girl ... I remember her as not really part of the group ... was sort of on the edge. I pulled her along, I guess, because I felt sorry for her."

"Would your sister remember anything about her family, where she lived, or anything like that?"

"No. I have already talked to her. She was younger, you see, ten at that time."

"Is there anyone else? One of your friends?"

He waited through the silence, tapping the pen softly against the pad, reaching over to rub his dog's ears. He always let his dog in when he came home, the only companion he'd had for a few years now. The house would have seemed dead and lonely without Mutt.

"The only one I remember who still lives in the neighborhood is Carla Summers. She's married, of course. More than once. I don't know her present name. But Mother might, or someone else who's lived there since the beginning of time. The Salingse's, the ones who bought that property with the well on it, might know more. Or some of their kids. Mr. Pattison, who owns the big old house in that area, who used to own the land, might know."

"Yes, I'll ask around."

"It's such a long time ago. Do you really think you could find the murderer now?"

"Probably not. It was probably done by a transient or a worker who's long gone, maybe even passed away. But I certainly appreciate your call."

He sat at the desk for several long minutes thinking. He was beginning to feel as if he lived in a web, that invisible strands stretched from one time in the past, from dozens of people, forward to now, holding tight with the sticky web the lives of others now, of deaths, perhaps even Kenny's. And yet it wasn't logical. It had to be a coincidence. Mutt whined, and Conrad rubbed both of the long, silky ears. Mutt had been a stray, a bedraggled little puppy standing in the rain that day six years ago when Conrad found him. He didn't know what background the dog had, what kind of parents, but he figured by looking at him that he was part something with short legs, like a dachshund or basset hound, and part something with long, silky fur, like a cocker spaniel. Whatever, he was unique, a mutt of beauty and good nature, and Conrad loved him. During the day or when he was gone anywhere, Mutt stayed in the yard, where he kept an eye on the neighborhood. But at night or when Conrad was home, Mutt came into the house and was a constant companion. Even when Conrad took a shower, Mutt came along into the bathroom and sat waiting, getting his long hair on the throw rug. Once a month a cleaning crew, consisting of two women who had started their own business, came out and vacuumed and dusted and mopped and otherwise made his house look good. The rest of the time, except for an occasional quick vacuuming, he lived in it like it was.

Conrad's dinner was actually a combination of lunch and supper. He had missed lunch, and the dinner hour was too far away. That was the only thing about living alone that struck him as at all convenient—he could fix his meals whenever he had the time or inclination. He heard the oven timer go off and went back to the kitchen to retrieve his potato. He split it open, and steam washed up into his face. He put a scoop of butter on it, opened a can of chili, stuck it in the microwave, and then went to feed Mutt. They ate together, Mutt on the floor not far away from the table.

The silence in the house was beginning to get to him. Usually when he came in, he turned on something, radio, television, anything that talked. Even after three years of living here alone, except for Mutt, who didn't talk a lot, he couldn't get used to the silence.

At the time of the divorce he had told himself that it was good they hadn't had kids to wrench apart. But he had only been kidding himself, trying to find something good out of a marriage that hadn't worked past the first six months. They had loved each other well enough, he thought now, but they had been two entirely different people, different backgrounds, and, what was more important, different ambitions. She wanted the best the world had to offer. She longed for excitement and faraway places. And she was beautiful enough to get all of it. She was the beauty queen of the small college where they had met, and while he saw that and fell in love with her looks, he had assumed it would not interfere with a normal married life, with a house in the country and kids and dogs and cats. But within months he had learned the painful way that his lovely bride was not about to ruin her figure with a baby.

"God!" she had screamed. "How could this have happened to me! I took my pill. I think I took my pill! Oh God, Con, do you think I missed my pill?"

He was overjoyed. His dreams were coming true. He had made the discovery that his old home, out at the west end of town, was up for sale, and he had made an offer and was planning to surprise her with it. Now she was pregnant, and his head was too far above the clouds to see anything beyond his own feelings. A week later she called him from the hospital. She'd had an abortion.

Nothing was right after that, even though the marriage lasted another few years. She had even moved into the country with him and had commuted to her job. Sometimes she spent the five work days in the city, coming home only for weekends. And finally she had started taking special assignment trips on the weekends. In her mid-thirties, she had been beautiful and sophisticated, a buyer for a dress shop, a world traveler. Then a few months after the divorce he had read where she'd married one of the upper-crust widowers, an older man who was rich enough to give her the kind of life she wanted. He had kept listening for news of her, and the thing that really got to him was the child, a boy, she'd had little more than a year after her remarriage. That had hurt like hell, and he always remembered his child, unwanted by her, destroyed almost before its heart had started beating.

He got up impatiently from the table and pushed his plate back. He tried not to think about her, because the bitterness covered him like a cloak, making him restless and with a smothered sensation. He had pleaded with her to marry him, and she had given in. He was older. He should have known at the time that a girl so beautiful would not be satisfied forever with the likes of him. He tended to be boring after awhile, and he knew it. Unless the lady liked to work in the yard and sit on the porch and watch the sun set, she wouldn't be content with him. And for that reason he hadn't let any of his brief romances linger on. Some of his dates had started bringing casseroles or baked things out to his house, but he had become very sensitive to differences by then, and he would notice that one of them didn't like dogs, for instance, and another couldn't care less for sunsets.

He went onto his back porch. The shrubs in the backyard looked dark with the mist that was still falling, but night was a long way off. He checked his watch. Only a few minutes past four.

He left Mutt in the backyard and went through the gate to his car. Something drew his eyes to the house next door, but there was no sign of Milton Crossover on the section of the porch that was visible beyond the trees and hedges. Conrad looked at each window in the upper floor, three of which he could see beyond tree branches, and saw the blinds drawn three-quarters of the way down, and lace curtains and darkness beneath the blinds. Yet he had been drawn to look at the house as if he were being stared at.

He got into his car and pulled out into the quiet street. He let the car drift slowly along, past the Jonah Pattison place, past Alyne's. He would like to go talk to Jonah again, but the old gentleman had just helped bury his oldest grandson.

Conrad checked out the older houses as he drove slowly down the street. Thirty-three years ago there had been five or six houses in the one-mile stretch where now there were dozens. He passed by the newer houses without a second look. At the corner, where the road angled left, another old farm house stood on acreage across from the Whitaker place. But there was a FOR SALE sign in the front yard, just as there was a year ago. And the family that lived there was young, with young children. He could see one on a tricycle, riding around on the big front porch.

Conrad turned right on a street that went through a subdivision built perhaps twenty years ago. The street was a shortcut to the road on which the Salingses lived; they owned the almond orchard and the old well. He had been to see them once at the beginning, but they hadn't been able to tell him anything. This time he wanted to know if any of their children might have known Adriene.

The elderly couple was sitting on their sun porch, a cheerful room on the driveway side of the house with windows around three sides. It was filled with potted plants, two bird cages with parakeets and a yellow canary, and fat, soft furniture. Mr. Salingse looked like a typical retired farmer, weathered and skinny but healthy, his clothes hanging on him loosely. His wife was plump and round and looked years younger, though she probably wasn't more than five or six years younger than her husband. The Salingses had bought their land from the Pattison farm fifty years ago, when they were first married. He knew this from his earlier visit. They had built the house, the barns, and replanted those orchard trees that needed replanting, and slowly had allowed the trees to take care of themselves. "At first," Mr. Salingse had told him, "we let people come in and pick for themselves, but they were ruining the trees. Then we leased the orchards, and that didn't work either. So now, much of the time, we just leave them alone. We keep thinking one of our sons might come back and want the land and trees."

They both got up to greet him. Mr. Salingse put aside his paper, and Mrs. Salingse asked him if he wanted coffee. He told her no, but he took the chair they offered, and he sat with them for awhile talking about the weather and the tragedy of the young boy's death.

"I don't recall ever seeing the boy," Mrs. Salingse said. "But sometimes I've heard him, I'm sure."

"You can hear the kids playing from here," Mr. Salingse offered. "Especially when their voices get loud. And the barking of the dogs."

"It's only a short distance through the trees to their alley."

"Three hundred yards, more or less."

"They've never bothered us. Never come on through the trees to our side."

"I'm still searching for information about the girl in the well. I've learned a few things about someone that might be her. The name Adriene, for one thing. And she was quite mature for her age, which one source, Estie Whitaker, tells me was fourteen. If it's the same girl. I have this feeling it is. I was wondering if your kids might have known her."

Mrs. Salingse looked thoughtful. "Thirty-three years?" Conrad remembered that when he had first talked to the Salingses he had been able to give only a vague time, twenty-five to thirty-five years ago.

"Yes," he said. "We found stolen jewelry in the well with the skeleton that makes us think the girl was killed approximately at the time of the murder and robbery of Mrs. Crossover. Her jewelry was found."

"Ah," Mrs. Salingse said. "And that was thirty-three years ago."

"Yes."

He saw the lady shudder. Mr. Salingse was staring at him with widened eyes, and the expression on his face was somehow different. The stare was too fixed, as if the old man were remembering, his eyes only accidentally fixed on Conrad.

"I remember that," Mrs. Salingse said. "What a horror. And right in our own neighborhood. I had a new baby. Our youngest son was only a few weeks old when that happened, and I was scared to death to stay in the house alone. Though I certainly didn't have anything worth stealing. Not like the jewelry, at any rate. Nothing that anyone would want."

Mr. Salingse let out a sigh and leaned back in his chair. Conrad hadn't noticed that the old man had been easing forward.

"Our children were too young to have known the girl. I don't remember a girl named Adriene, do you, Mother?"

She slowly shook her head. "Thirty-three years ago our oldest, a daughter, was ten years old. But we kept her close to home. I'm sure she wouldn't know. We'd been married a few years, you see, when we started our family." She shook her head again. "And you believe that this girl stole that jewelry of Mrs. Crossover's?"

"Either that, or ..."

Mr. Salingse said, "It doesn't make sense that anyone else stole it. But ... how'd she get in our old well?"

"She must have fallen in," Mrs. Salingse said.

"Could you tell me about the lid on the well, Mr. Salingse?"

"It was there when we bought the property. Jonah Pattison said the well was shallow, and had been closed since he was a boy. There was a heavy lid on it, the very same lid the youngsters took off."

"Was it ever left off the well?"

"No. Not that I know of."

"I just plumb forgot the well was there," Mrs. Salingse said. "So since the lid was on the well, she couldn't have fallen in."

"No," Mr. Salingse agreed. "She couldn't have."

Conrad got up and told the couple goodbye. He felt as if he were going round in circles. Who was left to ask? He could go to Jonah again, try to jog his memory. But what good would it do?

When he got into the car, a thought came to him. Any one of the men who had lived here thirty-three years ago was subject to suspicion. Mr. Salingse could have known the girl, for instance, and might have watched her from the edge of the orchard. And he might have killed the girl and put her body down the well.

"Naw," he said aloud, and drove back toward town, looking for a street to take him home. To try to fit a man like Salingse into the murderer's role was like trying to put a square plug into a round hole. Whoever had killed the girl—and Conrad was getting more positive all the time that it was murder—had also stolen the jewelry and killed Mrs. Crossover.

And yet that didn't make sense either. Something was wrong with every theory he'd had. And the same question kept rising in his mind. Why was the stolen jewelry in the well with the girl?

Mutt greeted him with the same enthusiasm with which he had greeted him two hours ago. Conrad paused to say a few words to the dog and to rub his ears. The mist had stopped for awhile, but the cloud cover was still heavy, and looked like it would last, maybe the rest of the winter. The day was losing light, shadows deep around the corners of the house and behind shrubbery. Across the road, lights were coming on in houses. Downstairs in Jonah Pattison's house a dim light shone out from behind pulled draperies, and in Alyne's house a light gleamed across the wet grass. Street lights had started to glow, and were growing brighter.

Conrad let himself into the house, and Mutt came in with him and then proceeded to shake the moisture off his fur. Conrad turned on lamps and the television.

He had just settled down and picked up the newspaper, determined to get his mind off the mystery of the jewels and the old murders, when Mutt leaped up and barked.

Against his will Conrad's heart took a plunge. He hadn't realized he was so edgy. He listened and heard nothing beyond a car going by on the street. But Mutt was staring toward the kitchen, his hackles stiff, a warning growl coming from his throat. Conrad muted the television and stood up.

A knock came on the back door, and Mutt rushed through the house barking wildly. They didn't have a lot of company. Conrad received most of his camaraderie downtown in gathering places with the men and women with whom he worked.

The knock didn't come again, as if the visitor had decided Mutt was too much to deal with and left. Some kid, Conrad was thinking, trying to sell a ticket to something or a box of cookies.

He opened the door to see Milton standing on the porch. The man's eyes were on the dog. Conrad laid his hand on the back of Mutt's head and told him to be quiet. The dog settled down only partway, his bark hushed to a low, rumbling growl.

"Come in, Milton. Mutt's all bluff. He'll settle down."

"No," Milton said in that effeminate manner, a fluttery nervousness that had always put Conrad off. "I just came to ask you something."

"Sure. Shoot."

"I remembered something. About my mother's jewelry. There's one piece missing." The man's pale eyes stared accusingly through the shadowy space at Conrad.

"Oh, yeah? Come on in and let me take a description of it. I need to get a pen and paper."

Milton came reluctantly through the door, and then stood in the kitchen, just barely within the room. From the desk Conrad brought writing equipment.

"It was a ring," Milton said. "A man's ring, or a very large and ornate lady's ring. I think a man's. It was in a setting of yellow gold, and had a diamond-cut red jewel."

"A ruby?"

"I don't know. Maybe not, maybe something like a garnet. But it was red. My mother had bought it somewhere in the Middle East on her last trip there."

Milton already had the screen door open behind him and was easing out.

"Is this all?" Conrad asked. "It wasn't among the jewelry that was listed as missing thirty-three years ago."

But Milton had gone, slipping away into the growing darkness, with

Mutt rushing after him, bristling, to see him out the gate into the driveway.

Conrad went out onto the porch and looked into the suddenly dark night. It struck him as decidedly odd that Milton should remember and mention a piece of jewelry now that he hadn't even mentioned at the time of his mother's death.

CHAPTER 9

In the darkness beneath her blanket Greta saw the light. Even with her eyes closed she knew the light had begun and was growing brighter. She opened her eyes. The light was coming through her fingers, through her cupped hand, shining through her skin and her flesh and her bones. It glowed red, filling her hand with a color like blood.

She threw her covers back and sat up. Her room was dark, totally without light, except for the light in her hand. Someone had closed her door after she went to bed, leaving her in the dark. But the red glow was like a small, terrible moon made of glowing blood, and Greta flung her hand out, opening it, spreading her fingers wide as if by that act she would rid herself of the deadly light.

The setting of the ring was like fire against her palm. The light it flashed out reached her face, the front of her pajamas, the small area around her in the bed. It glowed on the folded covers, turning the blue blanket a strange dark purple. She could feel the strange cold heat on her face.

She began wrenching at the ring, trying to pull it off. The tape she had wrapped round and round the band of the ring to make it tight enough to stay on her finger now seemed stuck to her skin. Moaning faintly, her voice too terrified to cry out, she struggled to jerk the ring off her finger. And the voice began, at her shoulder. The whispers ...

Mmmmpsssppp ... mmmbbbll ... no ... no ...

Greta whirled and scrambled backward down over her bed to the foot, and then whirled again. Because no matter what way she turned, the voice was there, over her shoulder, turning as she turned, talking, talking to her, telling her something she couldn't understand.

She covered her ears, and the voice silenced. The glow from the ring came around the side of her face and touched velvet fingers on her closed eyelids. Even with her eyes shut she could see it.

She opened her eyes and began again to try to take the ring off her finger. She succeeded in turning it slightly, but her finger seemed swollen or the ring had tightened.

No ... no ... keep the ring ... don't take it off ... no ... no ...

Greta shrank back against the head of her bed and tried to see the voice in the darkness. The red glow swelled out into the room and her fear grew into consuming terror. She heard the voice whispering, whispering, always just over her shoulder, and she jerked her head one way and the other seeking out the voice, and once she thought she saw it ... the black thing she had seen before, the thick cloud come to earth, the deep shadow, the eternal night, the piece of darkness that never went away. She thought she saw it, just over her shoulder, and then suddenly she was plunged into a world of light that made her blink and stare.

Stephanie was standing just inside her door scowling at her. Stephanie's hand was still on the light switch.

"What's the matter with you?" she asked. She stared at Greta, an expression of uneasiness crossing her face, her eyes. She blinked and her gaze went beyond Greta to the corner.

"Who were you talking to?" she asked Greta, and came on into the room. "What's the matter with you?"

Greta had been trying to speak, and at last she managed to say, "I ... I ... don't know." Her sister looked like an angel at this minute. She wanted to tell her how glad she was that she had opened the door and turned on the light, but her tongue was frozen again to the roof of her mouth, a big wad of useless cotton. She wanted a drink.

"Can ... I have a drink?"

Stephanie stared at her again. "Good Lord, get it yourself," she said, but then added, "Okay, just a minute." While Stephanie was gone, Greta looked toward the corner for the dark thing, the source of the voice, but it was not there. It was not always there, just some of the time. And at those times when it was gone, Greta wondered if it had been there at all. If maybe she had only dreamed it. Her dreams had been so bad and scary. Maybe she was being punished for Kenny's death. Even if it had not been her hand that reached out and struck the fatal blow to his head, as Mama had assured her it was not, still she had wished Kenny dead in the past, and so it was her fault.

They had talked, she and Derek, about their older sister and brother at times in the past, and wished they would go away. How much nicer life was when they were at camp in the summer. How cool, how great. Hadn't they talked about how much nicer life would be if they never came back? If they ran away? If, even, they died?

Greta shook her head, shook it as if that act might retract the thought. They hadn't meant it. She hadn't known that death meant they were gone forever, put in the ground in a silver coffin, and covered with soil and flowers.

But gone, gone ...

She was crying when Stephanie returned with the water. Tears ran freely down her cheeks and she shook her head back and forth, back and forth. She didn't see Stephanie with the water, didn't know she was there until her voice broke through Greta's anguish.

"What is *wrong* with you?" It was almost a cry itself, coming from Stephanie. Greta felt her sister's hand warm on her shoulders.

"I ... di-didn't mean it," she sobbed, looking through the tears at her sister's distorted face. It was like looking through a wavy glass, the tears blurring and displacing. "I didn't mean for Kenny to die. I didn't really want him to die. I didn't mean to kill him."

"*You* killed him? You didn't, Greta. Kenny died when a blood vessel burst in his brain."

Stephanie sat down on the bed beside Greta, her arm around Greta's back.

"Sometimes," she said, "little kids will blame themselves for things they didn't really do, just because of different reasons, like wishful thinking. You didn't have anything to do with it ... did you?"

Greta nodded her head vigorously. No one had believed her, not even Stephanie, until now. Now, she sensed, Stephanie was questioning that possibility, and she wanted to tell her. She gripped Stephanie's hand in hers and felt an answering response from her fingers as they closed lightly over Greta's.

"I hear a voice, Stephanie. It's right behind me. It whispers to me, and tells me things ... to kill, I think."

"A voice? But why does it tell you to kill?"

"I don't know. *I don't know.*" Greta's hands tightened on Stephanie's pleadingly. She looked up into her sister's face. She felt Stephanie's fingers straighten and pull against her. Stephanie was leaning back away from her now, easing away. Greta clung harder. "I'm afraid, Stephanie. Please help me. I'm afraid."

Stephanie smiled. "It's the experience, Greta. You were sleepwalking, right?"

Greta nodded. That was what they said she was doing, after she told them that she didn't know how she got into the yard where Kenny was. Sleepwalking. And every night when she went to bed she was afraid to go to sleep for fear it would happen again.

"You were sleepwalking, and that was clearly caused by the experience and trauma of the bones in the well. You saw them and, in a way, you found them. And the whispers? It's just more of the same thing. It's your subconscious. It's like a dream that's influenced by daily happenings, and when those happenings include such traumatic conditions as the death of someone close, your dreams become distorted and frightening. You were the first to see Kenny on the ground, and your inner mind has made you feel guilty. It's your mind's way of working out difficulties. One of these days it will go away, and you'll be just like you always were. Almost, at least. You'll get over it."

"Do you think so?" Greta whispered.

"Yes."

Stephanie extricated herself from Greta and put the glass of water in her hands. Greta drank, both hands holding the glass. She felt a nervous tremor up her spine into the back of her head, and she looked over her shoulder for the dark thing, but it wasn't there. Maybe Stephanie had made it go away.

"Would you like me to turn on this little dresser lamp for you?"

"Yes."

At the door Stephanie looked back once at Greta, then she turned out the overhead light and stepped out of the room, leaving the door partway open. Greta slid down into the bed. The little lamp on the dresser had beneath it an upside down cone of soft, yellow light, and Greta stared at it, drawn to it like a flower to the sun.

. . .

CLARE SHOWERED, a cap holding her hair back. Since she had let her hair grow long again, she didn't like to wash it every day. Every third day was often enough to get involved with all the curling wands and dryers and setting lotions. When she stepped out of the shower and removed the cap, she found it had leaked around her face and she had damp ringlets where the hair was supposed to be a smooth, wide wave. She slipped into lacy underclothes and checked her looks in the mirrors. She had gained two pounds, but it didn't really show. She wasn't much larger around the waist than Stephanie, who at sixteen was coming into her full glory of teenage figure. How she envied those upright breasts that needed no support. Having babies, the doctor had told her, will not ruin your breasts. But she hadn't believed him, and she was right. They sagged now, and nothing short of surgery was going to take the sag out. They also were bigger than Stephanie's, but of course Stephanie's would grow too, she supposed. Still, when she got on her blue robe and tied the sash at her waist, she looked good. She wasn't really unhappy with the way she looked. Most of the time. When the unhappiness became a dull aching depression, she found herself wandering the streets, the downtown area of bars. All she'd ever had to do was go into one of them for a few minutes, and almost like magic a dozen drinks would appear in front of her, from the men who sat around drinking and talking. If she stayed more than a few minutes, the men themselves would begin to drift over. It was an ego lift, one she tried not to indulge in too frequently. The smoke and the booze, she told herself, put wrinkles on delicate skins. The sun was more kind. An afternoon of swimming at a park pool was better, more relaxing. But lately she was becoming aware of her softening flesh, of her thighs not being quite so smooth and firm as Stephanie's. Last summer, when she'd gone to the same pool where Stephanie and her friends went, she had felt old and ugly.

She sat at the vanity in the bathroom and applied her makeup. She had just finished when Phillip came in, his pajamas wrinkled and twisted, his hair falling across his forehead like an adorable little boy's. He yawned, not bothering to cover his mouth. Clare smiled.

"Good morning."

He grunted an answer. She knew not to expect conversation from Phillip before he'd dressed and sat down with a cup of coffee. And as time went by and the sun rose higher, even then the conversation was thin and sporadic. They never talked anymore, it seemed. And she missed it.

"What would you like for breakfast?" she asked as he let his pajamas drop and stepped into the shower.

He grunted an answer she didn't hear. The water was already rushing down upon him, a suddenly deafening water spout, as she retrieved his pajamas from the floor and put them into the hamper. Why, she wondered, did she always have this job? She was beginning to resent a lot of little things like this.

On her way through the master bedroom she paused to straighten the bed, the blankets, and pull up the quilted bedspread that at night she folded back onto the cedar chest at the foot of the bed. She fluffed the pillows. She heard the shower turn off. From the closet on the right, Phillip's closet, she brought out a suit and laid it on the bed. And from the laundered shirts in the drawer she chose a pale blue, and took out the clips the laundry had inserted. She had always chosen Phillip's clothes. She wondered if Phillip noticed.

The hall was quiet, the girls' bathroom empty. She went on down the hall and saw that Stephanie had already gotten up and made her bed and was gone. Greta was still asleep. She pulled the blankets back, with Greta groaning and frowning and hanging onto them. She had at last to get Greta by the shoulders and pull her upright in bed.

"Wake up, Greta. School today. You don't want to be late for the bus."

Greta opened her eyes, blinked them widely twice, then crawled obediently out of the bed. It had been a couple of years since Clare had helped Greta dress, so she merely chose jeans and a sweat shirt from the drawer, and thought as she did how differently kids dressed for school now than when she was Greta's age. Papa would never have allowed his little girls to leave the house in anything but skirts.

She went to the kitchen to find Stephanie at the table with a bowl of cereal. A book was propped up in front of her, and Clare glanced at it just long enough to shudder. Molecular biology? It wasn't even a school book. Stephanie read this sort of thing for entertainment. Stephanie had been in special classes for gifted children for four years now and she would graduate from high school at the end of the semester. Invitations to colleges had come from all over the country, and the one she had chosen was a thousand miles away, although she and Phillip were still discussing it. He didn't want her to go so far away. "We'd never get to see you," he'd said a hundred times. "Sixteen is too young to go so far away from home." For once, Clare had spoken up for Stephanie's choice. She had said, "Sixteen is young for some girls, but Stephanie is perfectly capable of taking care of herself. She's not going to be persuaded by anybody to do anything wrong for her."

How true. Stephanie on drugs? It was almost as ludicrous as a pig smoking a pipe. There were times when Clare looked forward to Stephanie being a thousand miles away. Maybe she and Phillip could find each other again.

Coffee was perking on the stove in the old-fashioned metal pot that Phillip preferred. It had been his mother's coffee pot, and no one in the world could make coffee like his mother, he'd said a hundred times, except now Stephanie. He had taught her how.

"I made Dad's coffee," Stephanie said.

"Yes, I see."

Clare looked at the bread bin and saw nothing she wanted. Frozen doughnuts in the refrigerator grabbed her mind and held it, and after a few minutes of searching elsewhere for something half as attractive she gave in.

"You're eating doughnuts for breakfast?" her daughter said with disapproval heavy in her voice.

Clare wanted to say, Mind your own business. But she only sighed, helped herself to a cup of Phillip's coffee, and sat down.

Phillip came into the kitchen, his hair neatly back in a wave that would fall attractively out in an hour or so. Clare was glad he managed a men's store, not a women's. Though women came into the store too, but usually not without their husbands.

"Want an egg?" she asked Phillip.

"Where'd you get the doughnuts?"

Clare got up and took two more from the freezer and put them into the microwave.

"You two," Stephanie said. "Your nutrition will go to zero when I'm gone, I can see that. You're like a couple of children. You'll be eating junk food."

Clare smiled. At least the accusation made her and Phillip a couple, a pair, and she didn't feel at all insulted. Then Stephanie and Phillip began their usual morning conversation, about her school, his work, life, philosophy. Clare got up and went into the washroom off the kitchen and washed her hands.

When Clare returned to the kitchen, Stephanie was putting her cereal bowl into the dishwasher. Life was going on as usual in their house, while next door at Alyne's there was an empty place at the table, and Clare wondered if life would ever go on as usual again for her sister. But she couldn't bear to think of sad things, and she deliberately wrenched her mind back to the bearable. She had always been that way. She couldn't stand sad songs or sad stories. She didn't want to know about whales and dolphins beaching themselves, while here her daughter was going into the field of study that would enable her to help the animals of the world.

"My boss asked me if I wanted to work full-time," Clare said, but Phillip interrupted her before she'd quite finished to say something silly to Stephanie. They both laughed.

Greta came up behind Clare, and she turned to check her out, trying to keep the hot tears from overflowing and embarrassing her. Phillip didn't even know she'd said anything, she could see that, and he would think her babyish if she burst into tears.

Greta's small face was the face of a doll. Her hair was brushed back but was curling forward. Her pale blond hair was lovely, with natural curls hanging past her shoulders like little tubes and her lashes were long and tipped with gold. Her eyes reminded Clare of the eyes of a doll she'd had when she was a little girl, and which was probably still in Papa's attic. So perfectly blue. Almost glass-like in their purity, like the doll's.

"You're beautiful," Clare said, and kissed Greta's forehead lightly. She left a tiny smudge of lipstick and rubbed it off with her thumb. This was Greta's first day back at school since Kenny's death, but the lovely little face didn't show the enthusiasm it had shown a week ago.

"I don't want to go to school, Mama," Greta said softly. "Why can't I go with you?"

"With me? You never go with me to work, Greta."

"But I could. Couldn't I?"

"You'll be fine at school. You don't want to fall too far behind, or you'll never catch up."

Greta didn't argue or cry. She drank her milk, standing silent at the table, apart from Stephanie and Phillip. Then Stephanie was saying goodbye and gathering up the stack of books and going out the door, and a minute later Phillip followed.

Clare walked Greta to the front door and stood on the step watching as the little girl went down the walk to wait for the bus with Derek and William. She had reached the driveway when Clare stepped back into the entry and closed the door.

The house had a hollow, silent quality that she didn't like. Her part-time job didn't start until eleven o'clock, and she couldn't bear the thoughts of staying alone. She went to her bedroom and dressed. She'd go shopping or driving or maybe into one of the bars for a drink and some conversation with Rudy or Jake, whichever bartender she chose. Her boss hadn't offered her a full-time job. He knew she didn't really want that. She had only said so to see what Phillip's reaction would be.

Well, she'd found out.

MILTON WATCHED the little girl in the jeans and the yellow sweat shirt go down the sidewalk. She was carrying under one arm two or three thin books which were probably story books. A sliver of sunshine broke through the clouds and touched her hair, bringing out a brightness that made him stare a moment. Her hair had been bright too. Brighter even than the little girl Greta's. It had been like fire when the sun touched it. He hadn't allowed himself to think of her all these years, but lately ... since her bones had been uncovered, she had been on his mind. As obsessively as she had been before. Day and night, day and night.

He saw the little boys waiting. The one called Derek was twisting around, full of energy, a thin and stringy individual, with spikey blond hair cut in a flattop, but with a bang left that was sticking straight up in the air, like a banner over his face. What ridiculous hair styles the kids had these days, some of them. The other boy, older, heavier didn't waste energy hopping around. His darker hair was longer, brushed neatly back. The only ridiculous thing about it was the hair in the back, no wider than his finger, left hanging like a little tail.

Milton saw the girl had passed the row of citrus trees, and from the corner of his eye he saw that someone dressed in black, larger, taller, had joined her, and was walking just slightly behind her.

Then Milton's eyes jerked back to her, to the figure, the thing, walking so closely beside the girl, like a shadow, heavy and dark, like a funnel made of dust or cloud or fog. Upright, not stretched on the ground behind her, a shadow of her own making. But upright, just at her shoulder, like someone wearing a black cape that covered the head. Then the girl passed the citrus trees, and the sun shined down upon her again and the dark shadow was gone.

Milton squinted, as if he might be able to detect it visually, and the skin on his back tightened, the sensation going around him, enclosing him in a warning of fear. He stepped back beneath the protection of his porch, where the children were only partly visible beyond the vegetation.

Then he turned and almost ran into his house, locking the door behind him, drawing the blind. He leaned against the door breathing rapidly, the fear building instead of receding. He had seen that dark quality before. Just once. Thirty-three years ago.

CHAPTER 10

Alyne sat at the kitchen table, her hands cupping a glass of milk that was growing warm. Why had she poured this milk? She seldom drank milk. Yet she knew well enough why she had poured the milk. Three glasses. She had always poured three glasses of milk, from the time Derek was old enough to drink from a glass. One for Derek, one for William, and one ...

She hung her head and closed her eyes tightly. There was an almost constant pain behind her eyes, but no tears. The tears hadn't come easily even at his funeral. She was haunted by pain and emptiness instead, a feeling that the world had changed and another reality had taken over, and the old reality would never return.

She knew she should get up and get busy. She hadn't shopped in several days, and there were things she needed from the grocery store. She should clean, run the vacuum, dust, do laundry. The boys' hampers were full of jeans and shirts. Stay busy. She was needed by her surviving sons, and it was the only way to survive.

She got up and turned on the television. Phil Donahue was talking about something that made the audience laugh and applaud. Some social thing that nobody liked, but nobody could really do anything about. Still, the sound of voices in some way distracted her mind. She got busy cleaning the kitchen. She dragged out the upright Panasonic, plugged it in, and started vacuuming the kitchen carpet. Her brain was bombarded by noise, yet into her mind came a picture, sudden and shocking, a picture with the sensation of herself being small, invisible, hidden behind her own eyes and her own sharp awareness. Like a vivid dream, she saw the tall young girl, running, her skirt swinging around her knees. She saw the skirt, white with blue rosebuds.

... white, icy white ... with blue rosebuds ...

The vision was gone as swiftly as it had come, and she was in her kitchen again holding the handle of the vacuum cleaner, the noise from both the vacuum and the television beating in her ears. She felt weak with the memory of the vision. This time it had been no dream, although it had the clarity of some dreams, the kind that can be more real than reality.

She shut off the vacuum and left it standing in the center of the floor. She turned off the television. The house seemed then to throb with silence and emptiness, but her mind reached for the vision, and suddenly she knew something she had only guessed at. She had seen that girl.

She must have been very small. But she had no real knowledge of how far back a memory goes. She had been old enough to walk, certainly, because she had followed her. But where? Through bushes, if she could go by her earlier dreams, or memories, and that covered the whole area. Every yard in the neighborhood had bushes and shrubs that could have been the ones, but they could have long ago been removed.

Papa. Maybe he would know. He had phenomenal memory, as some sharp old people do. He was one of the lucky ones.

She got her sweater, looked out at the partly cloudy sky and decided against an umbrella. She went into the backyard and chose the alley road. The day was quiet. Not even a car passed on the street. Her eyes were drawn to the well, back in the grass that was still crushed. She had stood in her own yard and watched the gravel truck back into the edge of the orchard and dump a load of rocks and gravel into the well. And then a heavy lid had been put on the old pipe besides that. The girl's grave was filled in. It would never cause the death of another, or hold a victim of another murder, if that was what it was.

It was colder than she had thought, and her sweater seemed too thin suddenly. She pulled it tight around her breasts and held it. And realized she was afraid that her surfacing memories would take her farther on, to the end of the girl's life. Had she witnessed a killing?

No. No!

She could not have. If she had, how could it have not affected her life all these years? How could it have not lived in her memory? Something as traumatic as that.

No, she had only seen the girl. Once, maybe twice. She was sure of that. But so might her father have seen her, if she reminded him.

The shade was heavy along the alley, the tall treetops meeting, holding out sunshine and rain alike, and the shade continued as she went through the gate into her father's backyard. She passed the garden sheds and went up the walk to the back door. She knocked once on the screen door, but went on in without knocking again or waiting. By the time she reached the kitchen door, Miss Reade had opened it.

Her face held sympathy, and Alyne was afraid for a moment that Anne would hug her, then break down and start crying. She didn't feel she could stand that. She hadn't seen Anne since the funeral, but it was important to Alyne to try to act is if everything were normal, as if Kenny were in school with the other kids, the way he would have been. It helped her, she had learned, to pretend nothing had changed.

"How's everything today, Anne?" Alyne asked. "Papa up?"

"Oh, certainly." Anne gave in and patted Alyne's shoulder sympathetically, and her face crumpled. "Oh, Alyne. I just feel so bad about ... about Kenny."

"I know," Alyne said, wanting to get away from Anne. She wondered, how does one ever know how to treat someone who has lost a loved one? She sympathized with Miss Reade. She might feel that if she tried to pretend everything was normal, Alyne might be hurt. She couldn't have known Alyne's desperate struggle to accept. She didn't know that finally Alyne had realized she could not accept, she could only pretend. She put an arm around Anne's shoulder for a brief hug, then she stepped away. "You say Papa's up?"

"Certainly." Anne Reade wiped her eyes with a tissue from her pocket. "You know he was never a late sleeper. He gets up at the crack of dawn and goes out onto the porch to smoke his pipe. He's in his usual place in the front room."

"Thanks. I want to talk to him. You don't need to bring anything for me. I've had enough coffee. Food too."

She went slowly down the central hall, trying to place herself here when she was small, trying to go back in her memory. The wallpaper hadn't changed that she knew of, but her memory reached back only to her entrance to school. She could remember carrying her lunch box and hurrying down this hall when she was in the first grade. She was six then. Sometimes she carried a small paper sack. She could remember kissing her mother goodbye at the door, and then looking back at her from the sidewalk where she had waited for the bus. Her mother always stood on the front porch and watched until she had gotten on the bus.

But memories were vague from that first year. Her memories of Papa were rare. He was there, she knew, but her mother was the one who had remained in her memory. Her mother and her baby sister.

She passed the dark rise of the stairs and came into the wider foyer. The parlor door was on the right, and she entered to see her father sitting in his chair by the window, leaning back, his eyes closed. His cane was lying across the cluttered table at the side of his chair.

She paused, looking at him. His face had a dead look, pale and skeletal, and for the first time she wondered how it felt to lose your favorite grandson. As far as her papa was concerned he had only two grandchildren, this she knew. He had tolerated Kenny very well. He had adored Stephanie, had laughed at her attempts to walk, had brought her little gifts, had seemed to get a second run at life just because Stephanie, his first grandchild, the progeny of his favorite daughter, had been born. Then when Kenny was born he had seemed to enjoy the little boy, not as much as he did Stephanie, but enough that Alyne was pleased. It had been a joy to take her son over to see his grandfather. But then William was born, and Papa had shown no interest. When Derek was born, the infant might have belonged to a stranger. And the same with Greta. She supposed he couldn't help his preferences.

She hadn't really thought of her father during these days of losing her firstborn. And today he looked like death itself. She went quietly in and sat down in the wing chair to his left where the light came in at the front windows. Was he asleep?

He opened his eyes suddenly, and for a moment there was a wildness in his face, as if he had been not only startled but frightened. He stared at her as if for a moment he did not recognize her.

"Papa, I'm sorry," she said. "I didn't mean to startle you."

He sat forward and cleared his throat. He got his cane off the table and put it between his knees and leaned on it. Still, his face looked older than she'd ever seen it, and there were characteristics of old age about his face that she had never noticed before.

"You didn't startle me," he said gruffly, clearing his throat again. "I just didn't hear you come in."

"How are you doing, Papa?"

He nodded. "Well enough. How about you, Alyne?"

She was touched by his concern, and she felt her eyes burn with the awful tears that never came, and for a moment she was afraid that they would come now, bursting forth, all of them that had held back.

Papa said, sounding more like himself, "I saw the children got off on the school bus this morning, just like always. And I saw the neighbors are out, going on about their businesses. I think it would have been better if your youngsters had been more disciplined and stayed out of the orchard and off other people's property, the way they should have, and the skeleton of that poor creature had stayed where it was. I think the whole neighborhood would have been better off."

"Yes, maybe. But ..."

"I saw the young man, the police officer, leave in his car early this morning, going toward town. He's probably realized by now that all his questioning will not uncover something none of us ever knew anything about anyway. And I saw that Milton Crossover was out with his pruning shears again, working on that infernal hedge of his. I think he uses it as an excuse to spy on the neighborhood. I saw him on the porch watching the children get on the bus. I'd be careful of him if I were you. He's been odd all his life. His mother used to take these long trips and leave him alone for weeks and months at a time, when he was no older than Kenny."

His lips snapped shut and he was quiet, his eyes staring out the window.

"Papa, I remember her."

"What? Who?"

He had seemed to sort of lurch at her, and it surprised her so much that she drew back in her chair. He leaned with his folded hands on the cane, his eyebrows heavy over his direct eyes.

"The girl. In the white dress with the blue rosebuds. I remember her."

He frowned, as if he didn't know what she was talking about.

She tried to explain. "You knew that it was determined the bones in the well belonged to a girl fourteen to sixteen years old, and that she had been wearing something that was white background with small blue rosebuds?"

"Yes, yes, I knew that," he said impatiently. "But what do you mean, you remember her? What are you talking about, child?"

He hadn't called her child since her last quite serious mistake, a time when she was a teenager. And it made her feel like a child again. It was a harsh word, coming from Papa.

She found her lips dry. "I thought you might remember her too, if you really thought back."

He eased back in his chair. "What do you remember?" he asked, his voice suddenly mild, all vestiges of his former annoyance and impatience gone. He was going to try to listen to her, to talk to her. Maybe together they might bring the girl forth.

"Several times lately I've ... I thought at first I might be dreaming, but I'm sure now I actually saw her. I was very small, I don't know exactly how small. But I was following her. I remember seeing her skirt swing as she walked. I remember the material of the dress so clearly."

"What did she look like?"

"I don't know. It seemed to me she was quite tall, at least to me at that time she was tall. Conrad Donally, the police officer who lives across the street from you ..."

"I know! I know who he is. Conrad was one of the neighborhood boys until his folks moved away. Then he and his young wife came back and bought the old place and settled down there, I thought. But the wife was one of these modern young things that go off to a job every day, and sometimes she'd be gone all weekend. No children. She finally left, and I wasn't surprised. Conrad has lived over there by himself for the past three years or so."

Alyne listened, but her heart wasn't in it. She was waiting only for him to pause, so she could get back to the other.

"I keep expecting him to bring in another wife, but I guess he's had his fill of women. Modern women."

"Yes, Papa. The girl, Papa, I was wondering ..."

"I don't know what good it would serve to even try to find the girl. She should have just been left alone."

"I was wondering if you might have seen her. With your memory, Papa ..."

"Yes, yes. There were youngsters around, ever since I myself was a youngster. This neighborhood has always had its little group of children playing in people's yards and going up and down the road. It used to be by foot or bicycle. Now it's by automobile and motorcycle, as well as bicycles. Of course there were motorcycles in my day too, you understand, and I was just as bad as the rest to want one of my own. But my papa wouldn't have allowed it in a minute. When I wanted to go to the river to swim, I walked."

Alyne smiled wryly. "Well, so did I." They had a path to the river, she remembered, that had been there perhaps as long as the road had. It cut across a field and through the woods, and she and Clare had walked it many times.

She realized that her father would not be able to help her with the recognition of the girl. Perhaps she had been a visitor to the neighborhood, here only a brief time. Or perhaps she had been ... of course, she was a visitor.

A visitor? A visitor who had disappeared? And was never reported missing? It was possible, logical. The missing report would have been filed in another town, another state.

She sat a few minutes longer, listening to her father reminisce. He took her into the past, and she was willing to go. It took her away from the present and the pain of the death of her child. She listened to stories about her mother, about herself and Clare. Especially about Clare. And the perfect life that had existed before their mother's death. He didn't talk of his wife's death, and Alyne didn't ask. She knew there was something wrong with her mother's heart, but she didn't know exactly what.

But then her father was saying, "In these days, she would have been operated on. With all these heart bypasses."

She waited a few more minutes, but then she saw he was getting tired. Anne came peeking into the door with a tray. It held a glass of milk and a napkin with a pill on it.

"Excuse me. It's time for your pill, Jonah."

He didn't object or fuss at Anne the way he would have a week ago, and Alyne got up to go home.

She went out the front and down the sidewalk past her father's driveway and the edge of his front yard. She remembered Papa saying that Milton worked on his hedges just so he could spy on the neighborhood, and she looked toward his yard and house, but it looked as closed and isolated as always. She hardly ever saw Milton out in his yard. But then, she hardly ever looked for him.

She went up the front walk to her own door and found it locked. Of course, she had locked it after the boys left, just as she always did. She went down the driveway, but from there she could see beneath the rows of citrus trees to Clare's yard, and the place where Kenny had died.

She went into her kitchen area and stood beside the Panasonic. The house seemed too quiet, too empty. It had never seemed this way before, and she thought about turning on the radio or the television. But there was something that had come to her mind, brought back by the talk about her mother.

She had her mother's old picture album. One of them, at least. And there were some old pictures in it. Years ago she had gone into the attic, where her papa had put the albums, and had taken one. She had stolen it, you might say, but she had used the excuse that he didn't want them anyway.

She went into the den where the albums were stacked in a bookcase, like books, their leather spines dated. She had sat in here on the floor the day after Kenny died and looked at the pictures in what she thought of as his album. Kenny in the hospital shortly after birth. Kenny in his diapers, his little suits. Kenny as a toddler. She had albums on each of the boys, starting with pictures from the hospital on the day of birth.

She chose the old one that had no date and opened the draperies on the window for light. She sat on the window seat, where the cushions were soft, and opened the album.

She saw a young woman with fair hair, and a face as pretty as Clare's, standing with her arms around a tall stern man, handsome, older, his jaw line sharp and square, the dimple in his chin looking like a small blemish. His arm was around her mother's shoulder. The man only slightly looked like her father, but the name below the picture was definite. Jonah. They were standing in front of one of the old bulky cars of that day. The thirties or forties.

There were lots of pictures of people she didn't know. Then came the picture of herself and Clare. They were black and white pictures, and not very good for the most part. She saw little tow-headed girls, one of them, the younger, very pretty. It reminded her of Greta, except the blond hair was not so lushly curly as Greta's. There were several pictures of an older Jonah holding one little girl, with the larger girl standing at his knee. Very sober, very serious, all three of them, as if they were posing. Or as if they didn't want to pose. In all of the pictures it was the younger child, Clare, who sat on his lap. In none of the pictures did he have a hand on the older child. It was as if she stood forgotten beside him.

It hurt, even now. She hadn't wanted to remember how her father had ignored her in favor of Clare. Both of them would want to tell him something, but he would look at and listen only to Clare. She could recall her mother saying on several different occasions, "Alyne is trying to talk to you too, Jonah." So that by the time she was eleven years old she had stopped trying to talk to him. When her mother died, there was no one for her to talk to. Still, she and Clare had remained close. It had never been Clare's fault that their father really had only one daughter.

The pictures of the two girls became more recent, very few of them of the teenage years when there was no one to take the snapshots but themselves. She switched back to the younger years and began to look at details, at other faces in the background of casual snapshots. She saw the front porch of the big house looking much as it looked today, and the trees seemed just as tall and shading. On one picture there were pots of flowers on the porch.

She saw one picture taken at the river. There was a crowd of people, and one side of the picture had been cut off. It looked as if part of someone had been cut in half, leaving a portion of another. An arm, a young arm, a girl's arm, with part of a puffed sleeve. And then Alyne's heart nearly stopped.

She took the album closer to the light of the window and stared at the snapshot. It was in color, and there was a triangular piece of something, a white skirt, with touches of blue. Could it be?

Of course not.

She searched through the album for the piece that had been cut away from the side of the picture, but knew she would not find it. Whoever had cut it off would have thrown it away. And who would have done such a thing, and why? It was her mother's album. Almost all of the pictures were of other people, which meant it was her mother who had taken them. The picture at the river showed Clare, at about three, and another little girl with her back to the camera who must have been herself. Five? There were other people in the foreground. A girl smiling. An older couple.

Alyne turned it over and read the names. Genevieve, Charlie, Lawrence, Gladys, Doc, Clare, and Alyne. But one name was inked out.

She held it up to the light, trying to see the name that once had been written there, but nothing came through the solid line of ink. It was as if the rubbing out had been borne of anger, or some terrible emotion that she couldn't imagine her gentle mother ever having. But it was clear, someone had been cut out of the picture.

The telephone rang, a shrill bark that caused her to cry out. The snapshot fell from her fingers. She left the album open on the window seat and went to answer the phone.

It was one of her few friends, Rose Adler, with whom she had gone to school, wanting her to come out for lunch. Alyne decided impulsively to go.

Greta didn't feel like playing. The other kids rushed on away from her, headed for the playground. Some of them called to her, flung an arm out and waved her forward to join them. Everyone tried to be first on the monkey bars, the slides, the swings. Two of her best friends pushed away two others from the teeter-totter. Greta walked to one side of the playground and sat down on the cement slab that supported one of the drinking fountains, and from there she watched the school yard of kids at afternoon recess.

All day in school she hadn't been able to get her mind on her studies. Even reading, which she liked, especially the story that was now being read in class; but she hadn't heard half of it, and when it was Greta's turn to read, the teacher had told her almost in a scolding voice that she'd have to pay attention.

She had heard of people being depressed, and she wondered if that was what she had. Depression. Sometimes her mom got depressed, she knew, and sometimes she took pills for it. But not for long. The pills had made her feel crazy in the back of the head, she had told Phillip, and Greta overheard. And Greta's daddy said, "Why are you taking them then?" And he had acted as if Clare were doing something a little bit wrong. Greta leaned her chin in her cupped hand, her right hand, and the kids became a blur in front of her eyes. She kept her left hand, with the ring, clinched into a knot and out of sight between her knees.

Still, she could feel the ring tightening. She had tried again in class to take it off, working at it in secret beneath her desk, and she had noticed that her finger was swelling and changing color, turning bluish and ugly. It was beginning to look fat and sausage-like compared to her other fingers.

She couldn't cut the tapes off even with her right hand ... but Derek could cut it off for her. He even had a knife.

She stretched up and directed her gaze toward the group of boys who were kicking a football around at the edge of the playground. Derek was among them, but he wasn't doing much except walking about. He was hanging on the edge of the group too, as if he felt a little bit like she did.

She stood up and walked toward him, staying on the outer edge of the area, close to the fence where the big trees grew. She stared at the back of his head, the way she did when she wanted to get his attention, wanted to bring him to her without calling his name. They had made that up between themselves last year, when they had noticed it worked.

She stopped against the fence and waited, and for a time it seemed that today it wouldn't work. Then Derek turned and looked her way. She motioned to him.

He came toward her, walking as if he weren't sure he even wanted to talk to her. He wasn't smiling. She angled toward him, staying near the fence, where the teachers and other kids couldn't see exactly what he was doing when he used his pocket knife to cut the ring off her finger.

Derek stopped fifteen feet away. "What," he said in a blunt and not very friendly voice, and she remembered she had killed his brother, somehow, though they said she hadn't.

I didn't mean to, Derek, she wanted to say, but her voice said instead, "I need your knife."

His curiosity aroused, he came closer. "What for?"

She held out her left hand. "This ring. I put too much tape on it, and now I can't get it off."

He looked at her hand, at the puffy finger that now was darker than the rest. "Gosh," he said. "How come you do a thing like that?" He reached into his pocket and pulled out his little knife and dug the one blade out.

It had a sharp point, though the blade was no longer than an inch and three-fourths. The white adhesive tape was a dirty knot now around the ring on the back of her finger. The stone pressed against the underneath of her finger and palm. Derek began to saw on the knot of tape. *Nononono ... don't ... don't ...*

She heard the whisper, harsh over her shoulder, and she jerked her head to look behind her just as Derek jerked his up to stare at her.

"What?" he demanded. Then he looked at her hand again, more closely. "Did I cut you?"

There was no one behind her. There never was. But her eyes searched for the dark thing, the shadowy thing like a human figure. The big tree threw a dim, partial shade down as the sun gleamed dully from behind a layer of thin, high clouds, and the shade deepened beneath the tree. She searched for the dark thing there. Then the whisper was at her shoulder again, not clear this time, but as if it spoke to her from behind an invisible wall, the words a collection of whispered sound from which she caught only a word now and then.

Mmmmm ... kill ... killll ... Derrrr ... ek ... "No! No!" She cried out, jerking her hand away from Derek, whirling, trying to see this thing that had begun to plague her life. But there was nothing, *nothing,* as if it could blend in with the day, with the natural shadows around it, if it wanted to.

"What's the matter with you?" Derek cried, alarmed, backing away from her a step at a time.

A sharp blow stung her cheek and the side of her head, and at first she thought Derek had hit her. She cried out and reached up to put both hands on her cheek. She stared at Derek, tears blurring the oval of his face so that he began to look—*unreal.*

Then she realized he was too far away to have struck her, and he would never have done such a thing. Kenny used to grab both of them and bang their heads together until they cried, and once he had slapped her, so she knew the slap was from a human hand. Yet there was no one to have done it.

"What happened?" Derek asked, and she couldn't see his face, she could only hear his voice, and there was caution and distance in it. He seemed to be farther away, backing away. Yet at the same time he seemed larger and nearer.

He was no longer Derek, he was the dark thing, the thing that whispered at her shoulder. Greta too was backing away, her hands tight against her hurting face, and then she pushed into the wire of the tall, chain-link fence, and through her blurred tears she saw that Derek had turned and was running away, back to his friends.

The slap struck again and again on the side of her head and face, and the angry whisper was like the hissing of a snake. Greta screamed out in pain and fear, but her voice was smothered as if a large hand had closed over her nose and mouth. She couldn't breathe, she couldn't see. The pain in her head was deep and total and she felt helpless, beaten down, and she didn't know why. What had she done? "I won't, I won't," she mumbled through her tears, "I won't kill Derek."

Then she was alone. It was gone, whatever it was that had hovered over her, hating and hurting.

Her tears became a flood of misery and loneliness, and she sat on the ground against the fence weeping.

The bell rang, and it was time to go in. Greta straightened and wiped her eyes. Her ear hurt. She put her hand to it and felt something wet and sticky on her face beneath her ear. She drew her hand down and looked at it.

Blood.

Blood trickling from her ear.

CHAPTER 11

GRETA STOOD in the bathroom at home with the door locked and looked at her ear in the mirror. The blood had dried and looked like an ugly brown crust in her ear. She used the washcloth and cleaned out the brown stuff. She felt a little dizzy and sick to her stomach. After recess she had wanted to tell her teacher she was sick, that she wanted her mother. But she said nothing, knowing that in another hour school would be out and she could go home. She didn't even mind going into the house alone, because she needed to clean her ear and look at it. She didn't want anyone to know, not even her mother. Especially her mother. Because she didn't know what to tell her. If she told her there was something that followed behind her, something that wanted her to kill, her mother would put her away in a terrible place. That was what people did to crazy people, even little kids.

The bright lights over the mirror glared down onto the top of her head and her face, leaving no shadows. From beyond the locked bathroom door she could hear the television voices all the way from the family room, because she had turned it on the first thing. She didn't want the silence in the house. She didn't want to hear whispers in the silence, or see part of the shadows in the hall moving, gathering to follow behind her as if the shadows had become something else, horrible, too horrible to show its face. She had turned on lights everywhere, so the increasing clouds of the sky no longer mattered so much.

She scrubbed her face with the washcloth and saw there was a dirty spot left, a shadow of some kind on her right cheek. The blood in her ear was gone, but her cheek was discolored. From beyond the door came laughter, so unreal, from the television. That was canned laughter, Stephanie had said with contempt. And just as well, she'd said, because no half-witted person would ever laugh at those inane comedy shows, say nothing about someone with an ounce of intelligence. Canned laughter? Greta visualized someone opening a can and laughter exploding from it. She had wanted to ask Stephanie how they got the laughter in a can, but knew in her heart that if she did ask, Stephanie would give her one of those how-stupid-can-you-get looks and not even bother to answer. There were some things she had learned not to ask Stephanie.

The dirty spot on her cheek wasn't going away. Then she realized it wasn't dirty, it was bluish, almost purple. It was bruised.

She had to cover it up. And she had to hurry before Stephanie got home. Stephanie would demand to know how she had hurt her face, who had hit her, and Greta couldn't tell. She dared not tell. Terrible things would happen if she did.

She saw her chin and lower lip tremble, and felt she was going to cry again, but she didn't dare do that either. Stephanie would be home in a few minutes, and she had to hurry.

She let herself out into the hall cautiously, looking toward the end where it opened into the small foyer and where all the outer doors were. She could almost see Stephanie whirling her car into the driveway and coming to a sudden stop three inches from the garage doors the way she always did, and then coming on into the house and toward the bedroom with her armload of books.

Greta listened, but there was nothing beyond the voices on the television. Running, she went across the hall to Stephanie's room and opened the door. Stephanie never kept her makeup or perfume in the bathroom, not since the time when Greta experimented with it three years ago, when it was new even to Stephanie.

Going into Stephanie's room was one of the worst things she could have done. But she had to borrow her makeup. Just a little bit of it. Even as she crossed the threshold though, she felt as if she were a burglar.

It was a pretty room, cream and burgundy, with draperies at each side of the two windows, drawn back, and cream lace curtains covering the windows and holding out daylight as effectively as the white blinds in Greta's room. She had never crossed the threshold since the last decoration of Stephanie's room because her sister had given her orders not to. Greta didn't know why Stephanie didn't want her in there. She didn't care if Stephanie came into her room.

She tiptoed across the soft carpet to the dressing table. A bench with a ruffled seat was pushed in beneath the table. Three-way mirrors gave her three visions of her face as she approached, showing her three Gretas who were about to steal something for the first time in her life.

She stopped and almost turned back. Then she saw the bruise on her face and thought of the questions her mother would ask and the looks she would get from Stephanie. If it was only her dad, she wouldn't have to worry. He didn't look at her much at all, and right now she was glad.

She drew her gaze down from the reflections of her face and went on to the vanity table and began opening drawers. She saw arrangements of bottles and trinkets and all kinds of things that would have been fascinating another time, all neatly put in little metal boxes or plastic things to keep them separated into groups. Stephanie was so neat. When Greta picked up an item she laid it back carefully, because she knew Stephanie would see instantly if anything had been touched.

The second drawer she opened held the makeup. Lipsticks, eye shadows, mascara, not only black and brown but blue and green too. Pencils of all colors were in another little box, and at first Greta wondered why Stephanie was keeping her colored pencils here instead of in her desk, and then she remembered that sometimes Stephanie used the pencil on her eyelids, though Stephanie mostly didn't wear makeup at all that was noticeable. When a girlfriend came over to spend the night, they fixed each other up. And once, Greta remembered, they had come out laughing and looking like clowns, and Stephanie was so different that evening. Of course they had gone back to her room right away and cleaned it off, but still, she was different, more like the other girls on the bus who giggled and whispered together.

Whispered.

Greta stared at her reflections, scarcely seeing herself. The whisper over her shoulder was like the whispers of the girls on the bus.

It was a girl then, she knew suddenly and positively. And yet ... there was something more. Something far worse than any girl could ever have been.

She heard a car on the street that seemed to be turning into the driveway, and she hurriedly grabbed one of the little bottles of cream makeup. The powder would fall off, something within her said. She needed makeup to cover, the kind Stephanie used when she had an outbreak of pimples.

With the tiny bottle clutched in her hand she hurried back into the hall, then remembered she hadn't closed Stephanie's door, and turned back to pull it shut. She heard a door open somewhere at the back of the house and knew it had to be the door leading to the garage. Stephanie was coming in.

She ran into the bathroom and locked the door. The television sounds softened, as if someone had turned it down. Greta hurriedly opened the bottle of makeup, put a few drops into the palm of her right hand, her good hand, and smeared it on her cheek. It was awkward working with only one hand, with nothing to hold her hair back, but her finger had begun to hurt, and she instinctively kept her hand closed to hide the ring. She wished now she had never seen the ring.

There was something about it. Like it had taken on a life of its own and was closing in around her finger and would close tighter and tighter until it cut her finger off.

The color of the makeup didn't blend in very well with her skin. It was darker than she was, and now she looked again as if she had a dirty cheek, or one cheek that was tanned a lot darker than the other. She had to hurry and put makeup on her other cheek too, so difficult, so awkward.

Greta heard no footsteps in the hall, but suddenly there was a knock on the door. She cried out softly in alarm and almost dropped the bottle of makeup on the bathroom carpet. A couple of drops fell from the open end of the bottle, but they fell on Greta's foot.

"Greta, you there?" Stephanie called through the door.

"Yes!"

"Well, hurry, will you? I've got to get ready. I'm going out tonight."

Greta heard Stephanie go into her room and close the door. She waited another minute, holding her breath, listening for the explosion that meant Stephanie had found out Greta took something from her. But there was silence now. Even the sound of the television was so soft its sounds hardly reached Greta.

Greta poured more of the makeup into her hand and began to smear it all over her face, into her hairline, over her nose, over the other cheek. She began to look mostly one color, and the bruise was hidden.

She capped the bottle and put it into the pocket of her jeans. She finished smoothing the makeup, then washed her hand carefully. With the washcloth she cleaned the makeup out of her hair. When Stephanie pounded on the door again, Greta was ready to leave the bathroom. She turned out the bright lights over the mirror, leaving on only the dimmer ceiling light so Stephanie could not see her well. She ducked her head as she went past Stephanie.

In her own room she tucked the bottle of makeup into her own drawer of trinkets, into the center of the pile of stuff that not even she remembered well. Some of it was years old, and some of it new. Stephanie would never find the hidden makeup there.

She went out to the patio and looked across at Derek's house. Lights were on in the kitchen. She couldn't see the windows through the trees, but she saw the pale glow of the lights on part of the back patio that was much like her own. Two weeks ago she would have run across the two yards and gone into the house, and Aunt Alyne would have given her something to eat or drink. But today she turned back to her own house and went in to watch television.

Clare came home within a few minutes, and Stephanie came out and began to help her cook dinner. When Phillip came he brought his paper and sat down in his leather recliner and put his feet up and opened the newspaper.

Greta watched television blindly. When the news came on, she watched it with the same intensity, as if she were taking it all in. She went back to the bathroom when she was called to dinner and looked at her face in the mirror, and was pleased. She'd had all sorts of horrible visions of herself when she stared at the television, of the makeup streaking, of it sinking into her skin and leaving the bruise funny looking on the side of her face. But it was hidden beneath the tan of her makeup.

As she took her place at the table she felt Stephanie's eyes on her. She looked up. Stephanie was staring. Their mother and dad were getting ready to eat, each taking chairs across from each other just as they always had, with Stephanie and Greta in between.

Greta pulled her eyes back to the food on the table. There were four baked potatoes, one of them smaller than the others. There was a bowl of salad and a bubbly pot of dark beans, baked, vegetarian style. She saw this was Stephanie's dinner. There were muffins and cupcakes on the counter. Three times a week they ate Stephanie's way, and the other four times Stephanie sat with a pained look on her face as they had chicken or fish, while Stephanie ate her vegetables. Greta also saw a bowl of broccoli, which she hated. She heard herself whining a question, which didn't matter at all to her tonight, but helped, she hoped, to get Stephanie's mind off her face.

"Why can't we have corn on the cob on our save-the-animals night?"

But Stephanie said, "What's that on your face?"

"Would you like salad or not?" Phillip was asking Greta. Greta shook her head, keeping her eyes down. She didn't feel like she would be able to swallow anything, much less something as uncooked as salad.

"Are we having pudding for dessert?" she asked, the whine still in her voice. "Can I have my dessert now?" They were all looking at her now.

"What's she got on her face?" Phillip asked. "I didn't know Greta tanned like that."

Stephanie stood up and leaned over the table, got Greta by the chin and tilted her head to one side. Her fingers pressed into the sore side of Greta's cheek, and Greta had to bite her lower lip to keep from yelling.

"That's makeup! Look, Mom."

Stephanie turned Greta loose and sat back in her chair. Greta glanced swiftly at her mother and was surprised and relieved to see a half-smile on Clare's face.

"So she's been experimenting. She's nine years old, after all. You got into my makeup, Stephanie, when you were five, and had it all over your stomach as well as your face."

Stephanie's lips tightened. Greta knew she didn't like for Mom to make references to Stephanie's babyhood or early childhood when she did childish things. "Then somebody ought to tell her," Stephanie snapped, "that when you put makeup on your face, you have to put it on your neck too!"

"Didn't you say you have to be over to the gym at seven for band practice, Stephanie? You don't have much time."

Stephanie began to eat. Greta had self-consciously clasped her bad left hand to her neck. She slowly lowered the hand. She wasn't able to eat much, but she knew if she didn't at least pretend, there would be more questions and more attention focused on her. She ate with only one hand, which for her was an awkward process. She had always used two hands, which Stephanie criticized sometimes. When the dessert came she was glad it was the muffins so she needed only one hand. And she was relieved when the meal ended.

Stephanie got up, ready to leave. Then as if she had suddenly remembered, she looked again at Greta.

"Where did you get it?" she asked. "It had better not be mine!"

. . .

ALYNE STARED through the darkness of her room and thought about taking a sleeping pill. She used them only rarely. For the first nights after Kenny died and sleep had not come to her, she took the pills, and as a result she slept as if she too had died. For about four hours. Then she was awake again, but groggily, dizzily, as if her head were connected to her body by a thin, weak thread.

She had found a way to accept this change, this loss of her firstborn, without losing all ability to function. In her mind she put him in his room asleep, just as William and Derek were in theirs. During the day she saw him at school, going on with his life so that she could go on with hers.

Ross slept in his bed beside hers. They spent no more time together now than they had before the tragedy. His work called him and he went, and it helped him, she knew. His life had not been filled with the boys as hers had been. His was filled with his work, the factory, the workers.

She heard a car buzz into the driveway next door. Stephanie's car. It was small and had that quick, small-car sound. She drove it as if it had no brakes. The car door slammed. The small amount of added light in the room, a faint glow brought in from the car lights beyond the narrow strip of citrus trees, blinked out, and the room was softly black again. Alyne turned to her side, her back toward Ross in his over-sized twin bed, and let her gaze linger on the room. The furniture gradually formed lines and shapes. The lamp shade on the chest across the room looked ghostly white, a pale blob on the bulky dark of the chest. If she had been Derek's age, or even William's, she could have made a monster out of the chest and the lamp shade.

She closed her eyes, and after a moment they didn't insist on flying open. She felt relaxation creep over her body, like soft hands massaging her, as if her bones were melting.

She was small again, and she was looking up at someone. She wanted to grow up and look like her, she was so pretty with her long, straight, red hair. She watched as the girl drew a blue ribbon up under the long hair, pulled it against the sides of her face, flung her hair back with a toss of her head, and tied the ribbon on top in a perfect bow.

The girl moved away from her as if in a dream, drifting more than walking, floating gracefully. She went from an area of darkness into the light of a strange world, and from a distance Alyne followed. The girl disappeared into an area filled with trees, shrubs, green things growing, and Alyne got down on her knees and slipped beneath it. She saw the side of a building, white in the shadows, and the legs of a man. The girl with the swinging skirt was standing in front of him. From her hiding place she saw the man reach down and pull up the white skirt with the blue rosebuds. She saw the white thigh of the girl and her white panties. The man's hand caressed the white panties, and then they both moved, and went up steps she hadn't seen before and through a door.

Alyne was hiding then beneath something that let in only a small amount of light. She was shrinking into the darkness, frozen by a terrible fear. Something hung down around her, all the way to the floor, except for one corner. Through the corner she could see a man's legs, and the legs of the girl, and she could hear her crying, crying. Alyne the child wept too, and the tears from her eyes made the scene vague and misty, but still she could see they were struggling. There were loud sounds, slaps and cries, and then words spoken, screamed. You'll be sorry ... you'll be sorry ...

"You'll be sorry ..."

Alyne snapped awake, staring at a graying room, the words ringing in her head, fading away to memory. She sat up and looked around. Dawn was breaking, the light in the room a strange faded gray. She had been asleep a long time apparently, and then had dreamed. But the dream was too vivid to be only a dream.

"You'll be sorry ... "

She sat up on the side of the bed, her feet hanging down. It was very early, but she had gotten up early in the past and gone outside to watch the sun rise. She reached for her slippers, and when she straightened it seemed the world had grown dark again. For the first time she looked at the clock on her side of the bed, and the numerals read 3:21.

She blinked at the room in disbelief, feeling for a moment as if she were losing her mind. Then she realized the dream had still been with her, and the gray light in the room had been only a continuation of the gray and shadowed light wherever she had been in the dream.

She lay down, thinking, trying to find features about that gray world to identify it. A very small space, with a triangle of light in front of her. A table? With a cloth hanging down all around except for that one area?

How odd. How strange that she should dream of being a child again, of seeing the girl who had worn the dress, the material that was pulled out of the well. If one of her children had started dreaming this dream, she would have told him it came from not knowing, that the body, the bones in the well, had triggered something in his imagination, and he was trying to make sense of it.

She pulled the covers up over her head, but the words kept going through her mind.

"You'll be sorry ..."

Whom had the girl been talking to? Who was the man beating her?

GRETA ROSE SLOWLY from her bed, sliding out from beneath her covers. A cone of pale light from the small lamp glowed on her bare feet as she passed within its range and then out of it. She went to the closet door and opened it and stood staring within. The dark form moved at her back, becoming compact and thicker, like tendrils of fog drawing in and creating a body. It undulated in the still air, slender, tall, black shadows drawn together. Like a figure wearing a black cape that covered its head and its feet. The whisper came, sibilant, soft, issuing like air, like a hiss in the night ... *kill* ... *go* ... *steeeeph* ... *ph* ... *phanie* ... Greta turned woodenly and crossed the room to the other door and opened it. For a long moment she stood staring into the hall as she had stared into the closet. The dark figure moved behind her, its hissing voice almost silent in the quiet house.

... go ... Steeeeph ... go ...

Greta walked out into the hall and turned left. She stopped again and stood staring straight ahead, her chest falling and rising in long, deep breaths. The black figure wavered as if blown by a draft, and moved against her, and she shivered, the movement going over her entire body. The whisper hissed behind her ear.

... Kill ... kill ... Stephanie ... pet ... pet ... his pet ...

Greta moved, stepped over to the closed door of Stephanie's room and put her hand on the knob. She drew it back quickly, as if it had shocked her. The black figure behind her leaned over her shoulders.

... open ... door ... his pet ... petpetpet ... kill Stephanie ...

Greta put her hand on the doorknob again and though the shudder ran the full length of her body, she did not draw her hand back.

... Kill

Greta turned the knob.

THE DOOR KNOB WAS TURNING, making a soft sound of movement.

Stephanie looked up. The light from the head of her bed fell across the book in her hands. She watched the door begin to open, slowly, and chills ran down her arms. The book fell from her fingers and tumbled off her lap with a soft sound.

Greta stood in the doorway, her eyes round and staring straight ahead, her lips parted as if she were finding it hard to get her breath. There was no expression on her perfect face.

Behind her something moved. It towered over her, seeming to bend slightly forward, dark and thick, a body that was not a body, that had no definite form, with edges that drifted into the unlighted hall and blended with the shadows there. It was moving, with a slight undulation, as if it were blown by a silent wind. It had the form of shoulders and a head that was large and without a neck. There were no eyes, and yet it seemed to Stephanie that eyes stared, glared toward her. She felt the malevolence, the power.

She screamed, screamed, pulling away, scrambling across her bed backward, falling to her knees on the floor.

Greta jerked physically and blinked her eyes, and she too began screaming, her voice high-pitched and wild, as if she were no longer human at this moment, but something out of the dark, windy, cold netherworld.

And the black thing behind her faded, drifting back into the hall and mingling totally with the shadows there.

CHAPTER 12

Clare was moving before she was fully awake. She ran without reaching for her robe, and her thin, full-skirted gown whipped around her legs. At the door she struggled for a moment against Phillip. She felt his hand shove her back so that he could go unimpeded. She followed him into the shadowed hall and heard him mutter, "Where's the goddamned light switch?"

She reached for it and the hall became a pathway of light. Phillip was already in Stephanie's room before Clare reached the door. She paused on the threshold. The screams had stopped and were in part replaced by terrible sobbing. She recognized Stephanie's voice, though she had never heard such absolute terror or anguish from her daughter before. She saw Greta standing back to the left inside Stephanie's room, and the older girl was crumpled into a pile of dejection on the floor between her bed and the wall. Phillip ran around the foot of the bed and knelt on the floor, pulling Stephanie into his arms.

Clare stood in the doorway trying to understand the situation. Greta looked scared to death, white and shaking, but she was silent. Her large blue eyes stared at Phillip and Stephanie.

The reading light on Stephanie's bed burned softly, hardly enough light to read by. Clare saw the open book, half covered by blankets. She assessed the situation and guessed that Greta must have come into her sister's room for some reason, and it had simply scared Stephanie. Yet Stephanie's cries were out of reason for such a simple occurrence.

Clare drew Greta to her, and felt the child cold and trembling. Clare hugged her. Greta seemed stiff and unyielding, as if her emotion of fear prevented her from feeling anything else.

"What happened?" she asked, but got no answer from Greta. She saw the little girl was still staring across the room.

Phillip pulled Stephanie up and held her tightly in his arms. One hand brushed the dark hair off her forehead, and then clasped between them her fluttering, shaking hands. He repeated Clare's question over and over.

"What happened? What happened? What's wrong?"

Stephanie seemed hysterical. Tears rolled down her cheeks and into the corners of her open mouth. Her eyes glistened through the tears and kept darting, darting as if she weren't aware that Phillip had come, or that Clare and Greta stood in the corner of the room. Clare moved away from Greta when it seemed her older child needed her more, and went to bend over Phillip and Stephanie. She pulled a tissue from the small box on the shelf of Stephanie's bed, and used it to blot the tears that swelled from her eyes.

Gradually, Stephanie calmed down. She seemed to realize that she was not alone. Her sobs ceased to silent jerks of her throat and she managed a faint smile at her dad. She leaned into his arms, her head bowed.

Clare drew back.

With her arm guiding Greta, she walked her back across the hall to her room and tucked her into bed.

"What happened, Greta?" she asked, sitting on the side of the bed.

Greta's lower lip trembled, but no word came from her mouth. Clare saw the right side of her face looked dark. She rubbed it and Greta twisted away, her face crumpling. For a moment Clare was afraid Greta too would dissolve into hysterics. Stephanie had always been a somewhat flighty and very sensitive child, but she had never witnessed this kind of behavior from her before. Maybe Phillip would find out what was wrong. Stephanie had been terrified, there was no doubt of it. And though she was sensitive and highly strung, she was not a coward. She didn't find spooks where none existed. Even as a small child, monsters for her were not fearful things but something to be petted and loved.

"Were you going to Stephanie's room for something, Greta?"

Greta's lips trembled again, then she whispered, "I don't remember."

"You don't remember. How can that be?"

"I just ... I just ... woke up there. Stephanie's scream woke me up and scared me."

Clare's eyes sought out familiar objects in the room, as if that would help the growing connection in her mind. She looked at the teddy bed, filled almost to overflowing. She saw the desk beneath the window, a small white writing desk that had a matching chair, and on top of the desk bookends in the shapes of frogs holding a half dozen of Greta's favorite story books. "Black Beauty" was one of the books. It had been Clare's.

But her thoughts had gone back to the night when Greta's scream had brought them all out into the night, when Greta had been standing over the crumpled body of Kenny. Again, Clare could hear Greta's crying, "I've killed Kenny. I've killed Kenny." And later when she was asked why she had gone into the yard at three o'clock in the morning, she had said, "I don't remember. I woke up there."

Greta was walking in her sleep.

Clare tucked the blankets closer around Greta's shoulders, covering her neck, putting the soft blanket up against Greta's cheeks, as if by enclosing her within the blanket she would in some way protect her from whatever was happening. She saw one cheek was darker than the other, as if makeup had rubbed away on one side. Or, she thought, it might be shadows created by the light. Yet, that wasn't logical either. The lamp was on the side of the darkened cheek.

"Greta, did you hurt yourself?"

"No," Greta said swiftly, and turned her cheek so that it was hidden under the satin binding of the blanket. She added softly, "I'm sorry I went into Stephanie's room."

Clare nodded. "I'll tell her." Though it seemed strange that Stephanie should become so wildly frightened, so hysterical just because her sister had opened her door unexpectedly.

Clare closed Greta's door and went back across the hall. Stephanie was still sitting on the floor with Phillip's arms around her. Her head now was on his shoulder. Her sobs had stopped.

Suddenly suspicious, Clare picked up the book Stephanie had been reading. She looked at the title. Another animal book. Nothing about ghosts or murderers or anything that might have had Stephanie on edge to start with. Clare folded the book and laid it on Stephanie's pillow. She went around the bed and sat down.

"It seems Greta was sleepwalking," she said. "This is only the second time in her life that such a thing has happened, that I know of. I don't know why it's happening, unless ..." She stopped. Stephanie shouldn't be hearing her thoughts on the matter at this time, she decided.

Phillip had been rocking her back and forth as if she were a baby, but now he stopped.

Stephanie pulled back from him and looked up at her mother. "Sleepwalking," she repeated, but Clare saw something else in her eyes, a continuation of the terror of the screams.

Clare got up. In her bathroom she had some mild sedatives and she said, "I'll bring you something to relax you."

"No," Phillip said, his voice harsh. "Don't play doctor, Clare. She'll be all right. Come on, kitten, get into bed. Try to sleep."

Clare stood in the middle of the room, feeling as if she had been scolded, as if she had intended to give her child something poisonous. She wanted to be helpful, but didn't know how. Not with Stephanie. Not with Phillip.

"Do you want to talk about it?" she asked Stephanie.

Phillip answered for Stephanie again. "No, she doesn't."

No, Clare thought, she wouldn't. She was that much like Phillip. She would talk about everything in the world besides her own emotions, Clare now thought, surprised she had never really noticed before. She talked of world cruelties, of hunger, of terrible things that people did to people and to animals. But did she ever really talk about how she felt about anything other than that? There had never been a steady boyfriend, so there was no lovesick girl wanting to discuss broken hearts, or even sex. There had never been trouble in school, so there was nothing to talk about there. What it was that had so frightened Stephanie tonight would probably never be put into words. Tomorrow morning she would get up acting as she always did.

Clare slept little the rest of the short night. A couple of times she dozed enough to have odd, featureless dreams in which she felt a terrible anxiety. When she woke to see the edges of sunlight slanting into the room, and saw the alarm would go off in another three minutes, she sat up with her heart pounding and a new dread in her. The dread of the day coming. She shut off the alarm and went into the bathroom to get ready for the day.

Later, when Stephanie came to the kitchen, she was subdued, more quiet than usual, and there were faint touches of blue beneath her eyes, as if she hadn't slept well. Phillip came in soon afterward and kissed

Stephanie's cheek and said, "Good morning, kitten," but he didn't ask how she was. Clare understood him well enough to know that it wasn't that he didn't care, but that he had to feel everything was right and normal. Nothing, nothing could ever be wrong with Stephanie, his favorite person in the entire world.

"Did you sleep?" Clare asked Stephanie.

Stephanie nodded, but it seemed to Clare that she deliberately kept her head down, her shining dark brown hair falling across her cheek, hiding whatever might be revealed in her eyes. Stephanie would probably hate any sign of weakness in herself, Clare thought. She had grown up believing that she would somehow help to set the world straight, and to admit that somewhere within her lurked a weakness would be humiliating, devastating to her.

Clare saw that Greta was not up and ready for school, so she went into the bedroom wing to get her. She heard Phillip and Stephanie talking, but it wasn't about last night. It had something to do with school and with work. Clare heard Stephanie mention the name of a teacher. Their voices might have been a recording of any conversation from any morning.

THEY WERE GONE, and Clare was alone. She had never liked being alone in the house. She had used to wonder how Alyne could stand it, seeing her husband off to work and her kids off to school and then spending the day so contentedly alone. She kept busy, she'd told Clare more than once, as if suggesting that if Clare did the same she wouldn't notice that she was alone. "Besides," Alyne had said, "I'm not alone. You live on one side of me and Papa lives on the other. And I go shopping." But if that kind of life was suited to Alyne, it only pointed up the difference between Clare and her sister.

They had always been quite close. When they were younger Clare had worshipped her older sister. Alyne had almost taken the place of their mother when they were left motherless. She never knew, Clare was sure, how Clare began to look to her for answers. But that hadn't made them very much alike.

As soon as Greta was three years old, Clare decided she had to get a job. Before that she'd been involved in taking courses at the local college. She'd tried the arts first. Ceramics, painting, needlework, sculpting, and all she'd gotten out of it was a couple of flirtations with the instructors. Then she'd gotten serious and turned to refreshing her typing, bookkeeping, and everything else she could take in the short term courses offered by the college. When she had decided she had to get out of the house, have her own spending money, and feel young again if possible, she'd gone for a job. She had worked as a hostess in a restaurant, but the hours had been too awkward and interfered with her duties at home. She truly loved her husband and daughters and didn't want to spend that much time away from them. So then she'd joined a stenographic group in which she was sent to various jobs part-time. That hadn't lasted long because the jobs were routine and boring and didn't pay enough. After that she was a checker in a supermarket four hours a day. But they had wanted her to work weekends, and she could see herself losing touch with Phillip. She was also missing out on all the fun of things to do with the family on the weekend, the picnics, the weekend trips they sometimes got to take.

Her next job was the one she had now. The hours were from eleven in the morning until four or five, depending on the worker who came on after her and whether her children had allowed her to get away. It was an easy job as receptionist for an automotive repair place with the name of Car Hospice. The owner's wife came in sometimes and relieved her, so that on odd days she could leave and go shopping and otherwise just mess around. Phillip never knew exactly what her hours were, and didn't seem too interested in finding out. He didn't expect her to use what money she earned for the household expenses, so she spent it to suit herself. Once, when she was feeling especially left out of his affections, she had accepted the attentions of a man who brought his car in regularly for servicing. Their affair had lasted only three months, for her at least. He still stopped by, and she could see that look in his eyes that said he was in love with her. As Stephanie would have said, if she had known, "It's only sexual desire unsatisfied. It will pass." Clare wanted sometimes to tell him that, yet an unfulfilled need within her kept her from telling him finally and definitely that it was ended. She needed someone's love. If she couldn't have Phillip's, his would do.

She realized she was walking the floor, and she decided to get her jacket and leave. She checked the front door and found it locked. With her suit jacket over her arm she went out the patio door, leaving it unlocked. She usually locked her back door, but Alyne was just across the yard, and no one had ever gone uninvited into her house that she was aware of. Certainly if they had, they hadn't taken anything.

She stood on the patio looking toward Alyne's house, and a sense of duty called her. She checked her watch. She didn't go to work for another two hours, and it took only twenty minutes to drive to the job.

She stepped off the patio, her high heels sinking into the grass, and walked through it to the house next door. Her heels clicked on the stone of Alyne's patio, and she saw her reflection in the long panes of glass. A not-too-thin blond, she thought she looked fatter than usual. Her hair caught what little light the cloudy day provided in a nice way. She was wearing it in a loose, curly style now, slightly past her shoulders. If her hips and bust hadn't been quite so well developed, she would have looked like a teenager in the glass. At least, she thought it might be possible.

She realized she had stopped and was touching her hair. Beyond the glass Alyne became visible, a pale ghost in a shapeless morning duster, her slightly darker hair pulled back from her face, her face pale without makeup.

She looked so enervated, so sad, and Clare felt guilty for having paused to consider something as trivial as her appearance. Here Alyne was in mourning, her own appearance neglected.

The door slid open, and Alyne mustered a smile. "Come in, Clare. Aren't you working this morning?"

Clare remembered that none of her family knew her precise hours at work. It had simply been easier to let them think she had a regular nine to five, so they wouldn't question where she was going. "I have a few hours off," she answered, which wasn't exactly a lie, she thought.

She went into Alyne's kitchen and looked around. No matter what she did to her own house, it didn't have the sparkle and attractiveness of Alyne's. Once, when she had mentioned that fact, Alyne had said, "Well, I work at it. You don't. But your decorations are great, I think." That was nice of her, but it wasn't true. Clare was always adding things, taking away things, changing when the mood struck her, and still there was something not quite decorated about it. She had even talked about hiring a professional decorator, but decided that took more money than she had.

They sat at the table with coffee and a plate of coffee cakes cut into small pieces. Some had pecans on top, some were iced with a thin, white icing. They discussed the weather and the family and Clare watched the hands of the clock on the wall move slowly, slowly. These visits with her big sister were becoming farther and farther apart. It was easier to just run by and say hello, how are you, than it was to sit and visit. She didn't know what to say about Kenny. It was something she didn't want to think about.

"That one of us could be gone, just doesn't seem possible, Alyne. How are you coping?"

Alyne gave her a direct look, and it was a moment before she answered. "You just keep living," she said. "The boys need me. Even Papa needs me, whether he knows it or not."

"Speaking of Papa, I guess I should stop by to see him too." Clare rose, took her jacket off the back of the chair and put it on. "It looks like I should have brought my umbrella."

Alyne followed her to the door. "Before you leave, Clare, I want to ask you something."

Clare looked back, debating in her mind whether to get her umbrella now or wait until she was back from Papa's. If she went after it now she'd have to backtrack, and she'd probably change her mind entirely about Papa and go on without seeing him. And, she remembered, she hadn't seen him since the funeral.

"Do you remember ever seeing a girl when you were little? You must have been three. A girl with long red hair? And the dress I remember ... or seem to remember ... was mostly white, with the little blue rosebuds, and it had either a full circle skirt or a full gathered skirt. Do you remember seeing anyone like that?"

"When I was three? You're not talking about the girl whose bones were found in the well!"

Alyne's lips parted and her eyes strayed past Clare and toward the old orchard. Clare followed her gaze, but there were no signs now of the activity that had been there when the search was going on. The grass had sprung back to shape and was beginning to green from the fall rains. The police ropes had been removed.

"Yes, I think I am," Alyne said. "I've been having these strange dreams. In them I'm little and I'm following her. I lose sight of her sometimes, and when I see her again she's standing near a white wall and she's with a man. He's fondling her. Then I dreamed that I was hiding, and I was terrified, and I could hear her screaming. She said, 'You'll be sorry.' She was being beaten."

A sudden dark depression slipped down upon Clare's mind and, for an instant, she could see herself hiding in a place with no light, and the terror her sister had claimed she'd felt in her dream was Clare's. For just an instant she saw the hiding place, small, confined, yet with a feeling that she would easily be found, a feeling of exposure to something worse than she had ever dreamed. She blinked and the feeling receded. Suddenly she had to get away. She didn't want to hear this stuff. She forced a laugh. It sounded more like a bark.

"Alyne, it's anxiety. That's all. Your subconscious is trying to make sense of your feelings." She could almost hear Stephanie in the positive tone of her voice, that tone that said here, here, you're going to be all right. It's just your imagination, and for a moment she didn't like herself. But she realized it was a form of self-protection and of trying to help her sister at the same time. "It's something you'll just have to try to forget about, Alyne. They're never going to find out who that was or how she died. It *is* weird," she admitted, "that we lived here at the time and all this time since and didn't know anything about it."

"I think I knew," Alyne said, her eyes looking off into the dark trees of the orchard. "I'm beginning to think I knew her."

Clare shook her head. "It's doubtful. If you had, you wouldn't have waited this long to remember. After all, you were five that summer. My memory is very clear starting at age four or so. I remember exactly what we did the summer I was five. You, Mama, Papa, and I took that trip to Yellowstone, remember?"

Alyne smiled. "Yes, I remember. But of course, I was seven by then. It was a great trip, wasn't it?"

"We had a great family," Clare said. "While Mama lived. Well, Alyne, I gotta go. See you."

She decided to follow the alley. There she'd have to walk in dirt, but it was hard-packed. The grass was beginning to look damp. A light rain had begun to fall, but rather than run back to her house for an umbrella, she hurried on, walking fast, down the alley and into the protection of the big trees in Papa's yard. She envied him these old trees. When she was a child the lot where her house now stood had been more of the orchard. All of the trees had been taken out except the strip left between her yard and Alyne's. She and Phillip had planted a few more, but they were not very tall. They had one mimosa in the backyard that spread low limbs over a quite large area, and in the summer it was lovely with its big, open, fluffy flowers. But her yard looked bare compared to Alyne's.

She spent a couple of minutes talking to Anne, then went into the parlor where her father sat in his chair. His head was back, his eyes closed. She paused, looking at him, seeing his cheeks more sunken, a bluish look to his skin. Age had seemed to move heavily upon him these past few days since she had seen him.

She thought of leaving without disturbing him. Anne would tell him she had been here. But when she moved, he opened his eyes.

There was a brief look of gladness on his face. He reached out a hand toward her, and she went to him, put her hand in his and leaned down to kiss his forehead. "Papa," she said. "Were you sleeping?"

"No, of course not. Who sleeps at this time of day?" She sat down, and for a carefully timed ten minutes she encouraged him to talk. He was in one of his gripy moods today, complaining about the newspaper being battered and the sun not shining. He gripped his cane between his knees, his hands knotted on the top.

"You still have your job?"

"Yes."

"Well, I suppose by this time your husband and daughters are used to coming home and finding you gone. You should try to be more like your sister in that way, Clare. Are you sure you take good care of your family?"

"Well, Papa, let's put it this way. My family is self-sufficient. I'm there to direct the cooking of the dinner, and don't you worry, my husband never has to cook his own supper!" She got up, laughing, and kissed him again and saw the features of his face soften. He had never been able to get very aggravated with her, and she knew it. She had known when she was still small enough to cuddle on his lap that he would forgive her anything. All she had to do was smile at him and cuddle against him and he melted.

He caught her hand and clung to it. "Is Stephanie all right?"

"She's fine, Papa."

She saw the worry in his face and knew it was because of Kenny. But there was nothing she could do. His eyebrows were heavy and white and hung low over his deep-set eyes. His cheeks quivered just slightly, as if a nerve had been traumatized. He gazed past her in much the same way Alyne had done.

"Have her come see me," he said.

"Yes, I will. I'll tell her this evening."

He nodded. "Tell her to come over then."

"Yes, I will."

His head was leaned back again, his eyes closed when she left the room. For some reason leaving his house was like escaping from a cage, and the relief she felt in being out in the open, with the rain growing heavier on her hair, was like breathing again after a very long time of being smothered. She had never felt that way before.

• • •

Stephanie was unable to concentrate. For the first time in her life she'd be reading a paragraph and find that her mind had wandered and she hadn't absorbed one word. She let her head droop over her books, the print a dark blur on the white page, her mind wandering back to last night and the fear that had been borne in her. She saw Greta, in her memory, coming into her room, the door opening so slowly, so silently, as if it were being pushed by a draft. And behind Greta, hovering over her ...

Today, her logical mind tried and tried to make sense of it. Even to see it again. She had never been into such metaphysical things as astrology, even though she had read it and giggled over it with her friends. It was something to have fun with, just as a good ghost story was something she occasionally enjoyed. But her perception of reality had never wavered. Now she found herself wondering how many dimensions there were that the human eye couldn't see. And what was this thing that had walked—no, *floated*—behind Greta last night?

And she had heard a sound from it, a faint hissing, like a whisper, and it had sounded like *kill ... Stephanie.*

Had she been looking at the killer of Kenny?

After school she slipped away from her friends. She didn't want to go home, and yet she thought of Greta there alone. Greta, her little sister, so vulnerable, so unaware.

She had to hurry home to see that Greta was all right. She had to somehow determine what this was that had been guiding Greta last night, and how to destroy it, or at least understand it.

She drove her car faster than usual, but she took care to stop at each signal and each stop sign, though when she saw a street clear she had a nervous urge to hurry on through.

Would Greta be home alone, or would she be over at Aunt Alyne's? Before Kenny's death, Greta would have been with Derek, playing, their voices loud and happy. Since Kenny's death ... nothing had been right.

Or had it started before that? Had it started when the body in the well had been discovered?

She was relieved when she reached the back door to hear the television going. It was not as loud as it had been last night, which meant Greta was probably watching it.

Stephanie went into the kitchen and put her things down on the end of the counter. She could see into the family room. Greta was lying on the floor watching cartoons. The draperies were drawn, and the room was shadowed and half dark without any light, except from the open doorway to the kitchen.

Stephanie stood in the doorway looking at her sister. She looked so pretty, her shining, pale hair hanging to the floor beside her cupped chin, her profile visible, a perfect curve of forehead and little nose.

"Why aren't you out playing with Derek?" Stephanie asked, and Greta made a small sound, a half-squeak, and jerked her head round to stare at Stephanie. When she saw who it was she visibly relaxed.

"It's raining," she said, and turned her face back to the television.

"Not very hard. It never stopped you before from playing with Derek."

Greta shrugged.

Stephanie gathered up her books from the cabinet and took them to the bedroom. She noticed the shadows in the hall, as she never had before. She felt a coldness and turned on the light and looked at the thermostat. It was set on seventy, and she turned it up a couple of degrees. She heard the furnace come on, a soft sound of air moving through the pipes beneath the house. In her bedroom she put her books on her desk, then changed her clothes, getting into comfortable old jeans and a warm sweat shirt.

She remembered the makeup and opened her vanity drawer. The empty spot was easily detected. Greta hadn't even tried to push the rest of the stuff together to make it look as if nothing was missing.

A touch of cold fury made her feel more normal. Greta knew not to get into her things. It had been a real problem when Greta was three, four, and five years old. Mama hadn't made her stay out of Stephanie's room the way she was supposed to, and Stephanie was always having to take things back away from her nosy little sister. Why had her room always been so provocative to Greta? Strange kid. In Stephanie's less generous moments she was tempted to call her a snoop, at best, and a little thief, at worst.

She went back to the family room and straight across to Greta and got her by the shoulders, sat her up, and shook her.

"What did you do with my new bottle of makeup, Greta?"

Even in the shadows of the room she could see that Greta had used some of it again. It was smeared darkly on one cheek. Stephanie released her long enough to reach over and turn on a table lamp. The makeup was all the more noticeable on Greta's face.

"You really have a lot of nerve, Greta. Borrowing my makeup and trying it out is one thing, but keeping it is downright dishonest! Now tell me what you did with it or shall I go to your room and look through all your things?"

Greta stared at her, as if she were afraid. There was none of the old defiance that had met Stephanie's complaints before, none of the little sneaky giggles and grins as when Greta and Derek deliberately did something to tee Stephanie off. Stephanie grasped Greta's chin and turned her face so she could see the cheek better. Greta began making a whimpering sound, her fingers digging at Stephanie's hand.

Stephanie stared.

There was something dark red in Greta's ear, oozing out, making a tiny rivulet down the side of her cheek. Slowly, so slowly. Dark ... red.

Blood.

"Greta," Stephanie cried. "What happened to your ear?"

"Nothing." Greta tried to twist away. Her fingers pulled at Stephanie's and tears formed pearl-like drops in the corners of her eyes and, like the blood, oozed out, slowly, trailing down her cheeks. And it seemed to Stephanie the tears were tainted red too.

Leukemia?

"Greta, are you sick?" She'd seen children with blood trickling from ears, nose, eyes before. In the hospital where she was a volunteer one day a week during her summer vacation, she'd seen the leukemia victims, and she had been horrified to see that little innocent children could be so afflicted. "Greta?" And she had been so horrible to Greta sometimes! Even though Greta had asked for it, she shouldn't have stooped to a level of complaining or trying to make her sorry. *"Greta?"*

Greta was still twisting away, trying to keep her face hidden, putting her hands up to cover her face. And it was by that act that Stephanie saw her swollen and discolored finger.

"Oh my Jesus!" Stephanie exclaimed and grabbed at Greta's hand. Greta jerked it away and put it behind her back.

"What's wrong with you?" Stephanie cried, beginning to feel as if whatever it was Greta was trying to hide, it was not an illness but something she had done, a result of something she knew was wrong. "What are you trying to hide from me, Greta? Now let me see your finger!" Stephanie gave strong blunt emphasis to each word, in the voice of the most severe teacher, and she felt Greta go limp in her arms. The little girl slumped with her head down, sobbing.

Stephanie forced her left hand straight and saw there was something tied tightly around the ring finger. It was a lump of dirty adhesive tape used to make a large ring smaller.

"Greta, where'd you get this ring?" Then she remembered she had glimpsed it before, but she'd forgotten it. "Good Jesus, Greta, why don't you take it off?"

She turned Greta's hand over, and slivers of red light shot from the square stone in the ornate gold setting. Stephanie gasped. It was the most beautiful stone she had ever seen, deep red on the surface, with lights emanating from the depths that made it look like a brilliant diamond that was overlaid with rubies or garnets, or a layer of luminescent blood.

"It's beautiful," she said. "But you've got to get it off your finger or you'll ... *lose your finger ...*"

The end of the sentence trailed off in her mind as her eyes were drawn up and behind Greta. Something was forming there. She knew with a sinking terror in her chest that what she had seen last night was not any part of her imagination or an illusion or a hallucination. She could see it now as a thin, wavering vapor, no heavier than tendrils of fog rising from wet grass on a cool morning. She saw it rising from a point behind Greta, as if in some way it came from her. Yet it was removed from her, and Greta seemed unaware that it was there. When she pulled her hand away from Stephanie and Stephanie let it go, Greta simply put her head down into her hands sobbing. She did not know of the thing forming in the still air behind her, and Stephanie wanted to cry out and warn her, but her throat, her chest, her diaphragm seemed paralyzed. She could not move.

She watched it thicken and enlarge, and in part of her terrorized mind she realized she was seeing something that science would never recognize, and suddenly she felt abandoned and lost, and thrown back into the darkness of ignorance, because what she was seeing made a lie of so many things science had proclaimed as truth. If they did not know of this, how could they be sure of anything?

Greta raised her head and looked at her, and Stephanie realized she was beginning to make sounds of fear, strangled cries, like a victim of a nightmare. She almost fell backward as Greta jerked up and looked around. The dark thing, the creation, the ectoplasm, black and undulating now, with deeply glowing spots where eyes might have been, hung long and quavering in the room behind Greta.

Greta gave one long, high-pitched scream and clawed her way to her feet. Then Stephanie found herself running too ... with Greta ... toward the front of the house ... toward escape ...

And behind them, visible even as Stephanie ran, so that she knew it was there, the evil ectoplasm followed, into the darkened front hall where it blended and became lost. Stephanie wrenched open the front door and she and Greta stumbled out into the waning, misty day.

Something struck Stephanie and she sensed herself falling. She twisted her body to catch herself with one hand on the wet grass, and as she fell she looked up and she wondered what it was and why did it hate her? It was there, coming for her, against her, not Greta, but her. And at last she knew too what had killed Kenny.

But *why?*

CHAPTER 13

FROM THE WINDOW in his front door Milton could see part of the porch of Alyne's house and all of the porch of Clare's. He had been hovering in his dark hall, looking through a light area he had found in the stained glass of the door, since the school bus had come and let out the little blond girl and her two male cousins. He had watched the girl go down the walk alone to her house and go around to the back and go inside. This morning he had watched her and her mother come out onto the small front porch. Clare had then waited on the porch while the little girl, Greta, he thought her name was, had gone down the walk to stand in front of Alyne's house and wait there for the bus. He had noticed a difference in her behavior. In the behavior of all of them. They didn't horse around anymore like kids usually do. It was as if the death of the oldest boy had forever subdued the others.

But he wasn't interested in the other children. He was interested only in Greta. This evening he had seen the older girl come spinning home in her car, and then go into the house. He had stayed at the door. The children were alone in the house across the street. One of them was a teenager, medium size, with dark hair. He had never been close enough to see what color her eyes were, but he imagined they were brown, or perhaps green.

Her name was Stephanie, and she seemed more a companion of her dad than her mother or sister. Milton had observed that many times as she was growing up Stephanie went alone in the car with her father. This sort of thing had started when the child was so young she stood up in the seat, against her father, her elbow on his shoulder. They must not have gone very far, down to the store for something probably, because they were never gone very long. Much of the time the girl would come back carrying something, a toy or a bag of candy. Later when the other child was born, the older one still went with her father, and the little blond girl with her mother, or not at all. Alyne kept her a lot, and she had grown to this age being an almost constant companion of the youngest of Alyne's boys, Derek.

Milton's observations over the years were made casually, not even on a regular basis. Mostly because he'd be working in his yard and happen to see those things. But now he was watching, deliberately watching the girl, Greta.

He had seen something, he was sure. And then he had become not so sure because what he had seen had been put aside in his mind as non-existent, as connected with that old horror, as part of the shadows in his mother's room.

He had foreseen his mother's death. That day she sat at her dressing table examining the ring, talking about it. The things she had told him that day seemed too a part of the dream-like unreality of that horror. Her exact words were lost now in the distance of time, but their import had returned to haunt him. She had laughed and spoken lightly, a joke to her. But a fascinating joke. "... magic properties, you know. It's very valuable, but it's very dangerous ... it takes over the souls of all who are near, and it changes lives." And he could recall her laughing and saying clearly, "Maybe it will change mine. I could do with a change." He remembered hurt feelings because he thought he'd pleased her, except for the one thing. He had been a good son, and he thought she was happy most of the time. After all, didn't she go on her trips several times a year? And didn't he work to make life easy and pleasant for her when she was home? He knew, as he looked at her that day, as she admired the ring, that she was marked for death. Soon.

The scene in his memory changed. He had come home early that day, although he had told the police he hadn't. But that day he knew it had happened, and he climbed the stairs slowly. And he had seen it that day, in the shadows of the room, where the blood was fresh and hot and had that strange odor. He had seen the ghost-like substance, like a shadow, except it was not on the floor, not stretched to one side, thrown by the thin light at the window. It was upright in the room, detached, so that he couldn't tell exactly what it was or who it belonged to. But he had seen it that day, with its feet in the blood.

So now he watched Greta. Because he had seen it again, darker, larger, thicker, more fully formed. But he had seen it only the one time. Now, as he stared at the little girl until her image blurred, going to school this morning, coming home this afternoon, there was nothing. There seemed to be nothing. Yet he knew it was there, just as he had known his mother was marked for death.

He had kept watching the door. He wasn't sure why he watched the front door, because the family used the door at the back of the house most of the time. And he knew that chances were, as the day waned, as the mist grew heavier and tendrils of white fog began drifting through the orchard trees, no one would come out the front door. Still, he watched. The parents were not home yet. The inside of the house was growing dark. At the back a light had come on after the older girl had gotten home, and now it fell in a pale, dispersing cone onto the driveway.

He was watching when the front door flew open and the two girls came running out onto the porch. He saw the older girl fall, as if she had been pushed, and he saw the smaller girl fall too, but as if she were throwing herself onto her sister.

It was there, fully formed now, like someone dressed in black. It moved effortlessly, with a side-to-side undulation, a miasmic horror that hovered over the fallen girl. He saw the child, Greta, push herself to her feet, and he heard her scream, undulating in the air like the body of the thing that had thrown them in front of it.

The older girl lay still, her legs sprawled, her arms outward and bent at the elbow, her neck and head awkwardly sideways as if her neck were broken.

Before he thought of the consequences of what he was doing, Milton wrenched open his door and went running across the street. Within a few feet of the girls he stopped, remembering the dark substance, the thing that seemed to have come out of the darkness of hell. He stopped, his eyes searching the shadows beneath the porch and around the corners of the house. He looked into the black tunnel of the hall and knew it could be there, watching, seeing him as he had seen it. He began to back toward his own yard. Then he turned and ran.

SERGEANT CONRAD DONALLY had just driven into his carport and turned off the motor. From the seat beside him he was gathering up papers that he had brought home to go over tonight, when he heard the tone of Mutt's bark change. It became frantic, as if he were leaping at the fence on the other side of the yard.

Conrad got out of his car and stood up, turning his head, his eyes going to the shadowed full-length porch of Jonah Pattison's house across the road. Then he heard the scream. It sounded almost inhuman, far away, reaching him only in the pauses between Mutt's excited barks.

Conrad threw the sheaf of papers back into the seat of his car and ran. He reached his driveway just in time to see Milton dash from the street to the sidewalk outside the hedge that surrounded his yard on the front and sides. The short, round figure of the man blended into the shadows of the hedge and was gone. Conrad hesitated. Then he realized Milton had been running back from across the street, from Clare's house.

He heard the screaming, going on and on, mingling with the barking of Mutt and of other dogs farther away. Then he saw people coming out of Alyne's house, hesitantly, as if they were reliving a nightmare. He saw Alyne and her sons, William and Derek.

Conrad began to run down the middle of the street, swerving over to the sidewalk on the other side, past the end of the citrus grove that stretched to the sidewalk between the yards of Alyne and Clare's houses. Then he saw the little girl Greta, standing just off the small front porch. A moment later he saw the other girl.

At first it looked like she was rising up, slowly, from the ground. The street light at the corner began to flicker on, its light growing brighter and shadows forming more densely because of it. Darkness seemed to be descending like a lid upon the earth, shutting out all light except the struggling globe on the pole down in the middle of the block. The figure of the one child was plain, in her light-colored shirt, but the figure rising off the ground was dark. Black. A substance made of night and fear and something beyond the world of light.

Conrad realized it was not the girl. She still lay on the ground, sprawled like a broken doll. He ran, his mind placing the third figure he had seen back with the mysteries that were never solved, with the puzzle of the girl in the well, of the missing ring, of bodies dug up from secret graves.

He dropped to his knees beside the prostrate figure on the ground and lifted her wrist. It was limp. He felt for a pulse and found none. He tried again at her throat, feeling for signs of a heartbeat. He realized that Greta had stopped screaming. Alyne had reached her and was holding her. Greta's face pressed against her aunt, but she was crying something between sobs, and Conrad caught the words with only a part of his mind.

"I killed her ... I killed Stephanie ..."

But Conrad turned his head and looked toward the house across the road. The tall hedges blocked part of the view of the lower areas of the porch. The windows were partly visible, the glass in the door visible from this point. There were no lights, but Conrad knew Milton was watching from somewhere in those dark rooms.

He looked over at William, who stood several yards behind Alyne, his dark eyes fastened to Stephanie.

"Why don't you go call an ambulance," Conrad suggested. "Dial 911."

William hurried away, around to the back of Clare's house.

Conrad resisted an urge to straighten the girl's arms and legs, to try to make her more comfortable. He stood up and looked down. It wasn't often he was the first policeman on the scene of a death, and he felt a slight rush of panic. He forced it away by moving, stepping up onto the porch and reaching inside the door for the light switch. Light bloomed out from the fixture on the porch, covering the girl on the ground. He could see her eyes now, wide open, staring up, and what little hope he'd had was gone.

Someone was coming down the sidewalk. He heard fast steps, heels clicking, and something else making sharp stabbing taps against the concrete.

Two figures came out of the shadows into the light. Jonah Pattison and Miss Reade. The woman came on, hurriedly, her face a mask of white horror. Jonah slowed. Halfway across the lawn he stopped to lean heavily on his cane. Then instead of coming on to join the group close to the girl on the ground, he went instead to the corner of the house. And there he leaned, his hands on the handle of his cane, his head down. It was a picture of such despair that Conrad could not bear to look at him, and he knew instinctively that Jonah would not want to be seen. Conrad turned his back, and bent to examine Stephanie.

Blood ran out her ear, a thin stream down her cheek and onto her neck, where it had slowly come to a stop, clotting there.

Conrad looked up. "Why don't you take the children into the house?" he asked Alyne. "I'll stay here. And if you don't mind, would you call the station?"

"She's not dead," Alyne cried.

"Death hasn't been determined."

A car on the street slowed, then stopped against the curb. Phillip Shepley came running from it, leaving the door open. Before Conrad could stop him he had fallen on his knees at Stephanie's side and had gathered her into his arms. Conrad put out his hand, started to tell Philip not to move her. But then he stopped. How could he know a father's feelings at a time like this? Nothing he could have said would have stopped Phillip, Conrad knew. He had to pick her up, hold her, beg her to speak to him, to tell him she was all right. He was rocking her like a baby when Clare came driving her car just into the driveway before stopping.

Clare came to stand in white-faced silence just within reach of her husband and daughter. She made no effort to take Greta from Alyne. Then Alyne reached for Clare, and with her arm around Clare's waist they went toward the back of the house.

Conrad was relieved to hear the whine of the ambulance, and behind it the warning of a patrol car with its cat-like squall. The blessing of 911, Conrad thought.

MILTON WATCHED FROM HIS YARD, coming out of his house as darkness fell to look through the gate, standing back where the street light would not touch him, back far enough that he could not even feel the eyes of the police officer. Sometimes he looked into the darkness of the yard behind him and thought he saw it there, the black entity, the other being. He cringed both from the real and the unreal, and as the darkness increased, he at last went into his house and locked the door and stood there, feeling safer, watching through the glass.

Why had he run across the street? What had he thought he was going to do, save the two children from the thing they ran from? The darkness in the unlighted hall? The shadows that moved like fog? What had he thought he was going to do?

And now he wondered, had he been seen? Only seconds after he had reached his own yard he had looked back and seen Conrad in the street, going toward the house where the girls were. Even now he could hear the barking of Conrad's dog, sporadic, with long pauses between barks.

In the light across the way he could see only the figures of men moving about. It was a repeat of the death of the boy, where a spotlight from one of the police cars or the ambulance shined out over the grass. The ambulance hadn't taken the girl away yet. What were they waiting for?

But as he asked the question in his mind, the rear doors of the ambulance snapped shut and the two attendants hurried to the front, got in and drove away, the siren rising to a piercing ring that swept through the evening ahead of them. The two police cars lingered. One man in uniform sat in the front seat with the door open. Another car, plain gray, had brought men without uniforms, and they were standing on the lawn at the side of the house talking to the old gentleman, Jonah Pattison, and to the boy William. But within minutes they were going to their car. Slowly, all the cars were leaving, in one case being replaced by a van whose door also had the city police emblem. Milton blinked. His breath was short, his chest tight. He felt smothered for air. He pulled back from the glass in the door, seeing Conrad Donally's eyes come his way, linger, and stare. Milton pressed against the wall. He had been seen. He knew that now. Conrad was coming across the street.

Milton's stare went past the tall man coming toward his house, and searched into the dark places of the house across the street where he had seen the black phantom, the deadly thing that was causing the deaths of the children. Would it stop with the children? It had looked toward his house. He had not seen its eyes, the direction of its attention, but he had felt it, sensed it, as surely as if a message had come from it to him. Was it searching him out now as he stood in the darkness of his house? His chest grew so tight he felt he would smother, and he opened his mouth to breathe. It was almost a relief to see Conrad coming up his walk, coming through spots of darkness, beneath the midnight obscurity of the trees, Conrad himself like the dark thing now, appearing, disappearing. Milton heard his footsteps on the porch.

The knock came on the door, and then the old-fashioned doorbell clanged a hoarse, metallic warning in the back of the house.

Milton wanted to turn on the porch light, but he was afraid. What if the thing were drawn to light? Like some medieval insect?

The knock came again, and Milton realized he'd been standing too long, contemplating his own actions and the results, the possible repercussions. He had to turn on a light somewhere. He couldn't live in the dark forever, not even to protect himself. But he could turn on the small table lamp down the hall, the light that made only a dim glow in the hallway and could scarcely be seen from beyond the door.

He turned it on and then walked through the lighted hallway, feeling as exposed as if he were in the middle of the street.

"Good evening, Sergeant Donally," Milton said, hearing his voice only a little raspy. His eyes searched into the yard beyond Conrad, and he almost reached out to jerk him inside the door before it followed him.

"Milton," Conrad said. "I need to know what you saw across the street."

"The girl who was taken away ... is she going to be all right?"

"No. I think they'll find her dead. It looks like she fell and struck her head on the walk. I think maybe you saw what happened. Was she pushed or did she just fall?"

Milton put his hands into his pockets to keep from wringing them together like a nervous woman. He tried always to remember his hands, knowing he had effeminate characteristics. He knew he was suspect because he had never married, and it would make him furious if he'd let it. For that reason he stayed mostly to himself, but when he was out with people, he tried always to remember his hands. Keep your hands in your pockets, Milton, he could hear his mother say. You have the mannerisms of a queer.

"I saw ... I saw the two girls come out onto the porch, running. The one girl ... Stephanie ... seemed to be pulling the little one along by the hand. At the edge of the porch she ..." was pushed. Or struck in some way, somehow, by the black wraith, the materialization that seemed to be wedged in between the girls, or was somehow attached to the younger girl now. Though it hadn't been that way originally. In the beginning. Pushed. Shoved. Struck. Killed. He didn't know. He was more in danger, as each hour passed, he knew that. It was the only thing he knew positively. Without a doubt in his mind.

"Milton?"

Milton heard his name spoken and realized he was staring open-mouthed at the stained glass in the door and reliving the scene across the street. He closed his mouth, licked his lips. He couldn't tell Conrad about the thing. It was part of the secrets of the past, and to say anything at all would be to incriminate himself.

"She fell," he stated finally.

There was silence in the hall for awhile. Far beyond the walls came a single bark from Conrad's dog next door.

Conrad asked, "Do you have any idea why they were running?"

"Why don't you ask the little girl, Greta? She was a participant. I was only an observer."

"She's understandably in shock. She seems to be terrified. She seems to think she's killed her sister herself. Did she push the older girl? Were they fighting?"

"I don't think so. I don't know. They were running. The older girl was in front. She fell off the porch. That's all I saw."

"Had you gone all the way over there?"

"No."

"Why not?"

"I don't know. People were coming. What could I have done?"

"Where were you when the girls came out of the house?"

"I was ... I don't remember where I was. Maybe here in the house."

"But you were watching?"

"I just ... happened to be watching."

Conrad turned and put his hand on the doorknob, and Milton felt an urge to pull him back. He didn't want to be alone. And yet he wanted to hide, away from everyone. He watched as Conrad stepped out onto the porch and said good night, and then pulled the door shut behind him.

Milton lunged toward the door and locked it. But would the lock keep it out when it found him? When it remembered where he was?

CLARE WANTED TO COMFORT PHILLIP. The hours went slowly by and the night deepened, and Greta was asleep in her bed finally. Alyne had gone home, and Anne Reade had taken Papa back to his own house. For awhile this evening they had all been together, in the house where it didn't seem possible that Stephanie's voice was gone forever.

She was alone now with Phillip, and he still sat with his head resting in his hands. She put her arms around his shoulders and her cheek against his, but he was stiff and unyielding.

"Please, Clare," he said, and she was shocked at the coldness in his voice. "Just go on to bed. I'd like to be alone for awhile."

Clare drew away and knew as she went down the hall to the bedrooms that she would never again feel so alone in the world. To feel more alone would be to join her daughter and her nephew in death.

She went into the private bathroom and ran water that steamed into the tub, and then she lay down in it and closed her eyes. Odd, she thought, how one keeps doing the things one did before. Like a bath, dress, undress, eat, sleep. How automatic the movements. The ticking of a clock eased time on, one minute, two, an hour, two hours. Stephanie had been taken away at six o'clock, seven hours ago, and the time had moved on, and was still moving on; but something vital had gone out of their lives. She hadn't really known how to sympathize with Alyne. She hadn't known what it was like to lose someone you had nurtured and loved and, eventually, perhaps even become jealous of when they became so different from yourself and usurped your place in your husband's life. But never, never had she wanted to lose Stephanie in this way. She had looked forward to sending her away to college, but not this—never this.

She wept, but it didn't help. The water grew colder and finally she got out, dried her softened skin, and put on her gown. Her hopes of seeing that Phillip had come to bed drifted away in the cloud of depression that was growing deeper within her, as if the substance that had helped her to withstand pain were leaving her open and vulnerable to more pain than she had ever imagined possible.

She stood for awhile in the empty bedroom staring at the bed, then she went down the hall to Stephanie's room and turned on the light. She looked at the room, at books on the desk and on the bed. The books on the bed were school books that had been brought home today. Stephanie had been such a good student. Always straight A's, never anything else. She'd had such ambitions to help the world to become a better place in which to live.

She had been a volunteer hospital worker, and one afternoon each weekend she had worked at the animal shelter, though sometimes she came home crying in the early days because she couldn't bring all the animals home. When she had first learned that so many of the animals were killed and cremated, she had been in a depression for several days. Clare had heard her crying at night.

But it was Phillip who'd gone in to comfort her. "You don't know what to say to her," he told Clare after she had tried to comfort her.

She had said. "Death is not always the worst thing, Stephanie." And Stephanie had looked at her in horror. Clare had stumbled on, saying, "Well, Stephanie, think what life on this earth would be like without death. Think what life itself would be like, the disease, the inability to get well. Death is ... is a saving, in a way."

And Phillip had heard and looked at her with anger, and told her he would talk to Stephanie. That was the last time Clare had made an attempt to discuss anything serious with her daughter. They didn't understand each other, and Clare had felt the rift between them widening.

She sank down on the floor and laid her head on Stephanie's bed. She could smell the floral cologne Stephanie had used. And she wanted to weep and scream and protest the losing of this young life, but she could only hurt, hurt so much she felt she wouldn't be able to stand it.

GRETA WAS SOMEONE ELSE. She didn't know who she was or where she was. She could only feel the pain in her head. The world was black around her, but it was moving. She knew it was moving. Then she knew something more, as if she were becoming aware, as if she were waking from a deep sleep. She knew she was being carried. She opened her eyes and saw dark things moving above, and beyond the dark things was light. Then she was not being carried. She was being dropped and was falling, falling, and she could feel rough sides crushing her, as if the thing she were falling into was a tube, or a well whose narrow sides scraped her skin. She tried to scream and couldn't. She kept falling, falling ...

She woke sitting upright in her bed, gasping for breath. The room was dark, except for a dim light at the window. She stared at it and felt the solid bed beneath her. She wasn't falling into the well. She had only been dreaming.

For a moment she hadn't even remembered who she was. It hadn't been her falling in her dream, it had been someone else. Or she had been someone else, as if she remembered another life.

She crawled out of bed and felt her way to the post at the foot, and then she stood, searching the darkness for a familiar object. Gradually she saw the dark edge of the dresser and the paler cloth that covered the top. She went toward it, as if she were crossing an unknown sea, her hands reaching. She found the dresser and the lamp, and pressed the button.

And suddenly, as the light came on, she remembered.

Stephanie was dead. She had killed her. She had heard the voice telling her to kill, and then Stephanie had died. Just as Kenny had died.

She stood gripping the edge of the dresser with both hands, and then her reflection in the mirror grew in her awareness. There was something dark in her ear, a small dark red thing like a bead. She put her hand up and touched it, and it burst and broke loose and trickled down her cheek. The blood again. And her head felt heavy on one side, heavy and aching.

She went back to her bed and pulled a tissue from the box on the headboard shelf and put it to her ear. She got back into bed and lay on her side, the tissue knotted between her ear and the pillow. She was tired. So tired.

They hadn't taken her away and put her in jail. They hadn't even listened to her. Not this time.

CHAPTER 14

THE MEDICAL REPORT on the cause of death of Stephanie Shepley was much the same as the report on Kenny Kerwin. Simply, blood vessels had burst in the brain, causing instantaneous death. The death of Kenny had seemed to be from a blow to the head, but a weapon had never been found. There'd been a faint bruise on his cheek and a spot of bloody, broken skin in the edge of his hair on the forehead. The external damage did not justify the internal. It was the same with Stephanie. It was as if, Sam said, you had picked up an egg and shaken it so hard it had exploded internally, without doing more than leaving a few hairline cracks in the shell.

With Stephanie, the death blow was caused from falling off the porch and striking her head on the edge of the cement walk. Or so it would seem. With her there had been a small skull fracture. But still the internal causes of death were the same, and Conrad had wondered if there might be a weakness in the vessels and arteries of the brain. Sam Preston, the coroner, whose word was not the last in these cases, had told him there was no sign of a weak blood vessel, but it might be he missed seeing it. The weakness could have been at the very spot of bursting, but there had been no ballooning, no obvious thinning. If there had been, there would have been a history of pain. And yet, there wasn't always. The blood vessels could burst and death would take the victim without ever a complaint of any kind. Two ostensively healthy brains had exploded, as if they had suffered severe beatings.

Conrad sat at his desk, his feet crossed at the ankles on top of papers that were strewn across the desk. Beneath his legs, stretched out full length, lay Mutt, snoring faintly at times, but opening his eyes and perking his ears at Conrad's slightest movement.

Conrad stared at the calendar over his desk. Several days had passed since Stephanie's death. The autopsy had been completed, the body released, the funeral over. It was a repeat of Kenny's funeral, with even more kids turning out, it seemed, solemn, dressed in suits and dresses, with white gloves and carloads of flowers. The obituary had requested that memorials should go to the animal shelter, and so Conrad had opened a collection with a hundred dollars of his own money, and then passed the hat down at the station and turned in quite a nice donation in Stephanie's name.

But there was something that kept bothering Conrad. It was strictly of his own making. The department had nothing to do with the information he had collected. As far as the department was concerned, there had been two recent accidental deaths in the same family at almost the same address, and they had nothing to do with anything else. Certainly not the Crossover murder or the remains in the well.

The Crossover murder and the case of the body in the well were both closed. The jewelry had been returned to Milton Crossover, and that ended it. The department had filed away the missing ring with the rest. How could it ever be found now? Probably whoever did the killing and tossed the girl into the well had taken the ring. And there was nothing to investigate about the two recent deaths. They were coincidental.

But something was wrong, and Conrad felt it. He saw Milton Crossover's fear, and today he had seen Milton drive his car into the local lumberyard and haul away some pieces of lumber that stuck out the right back window. Tonight there were sounds of hammering from Milton's house.

But the thing that bothered him the most was what the department had called coincidental. Conrad didn't believe in coincidences. The two teenagers had died the same kind of deaths, and they were somehow tied in to the finding of the body in the well.

Yet no one was suspect. No one had been with Stephanie and Greta, no third person. There was no doubt that Stephanie had fallen. There was a witness. Greta had said the same thing she had said when her cousin died. "I killed."

And Conrad wondered, why did she think she had killed?

He wanted to talk to her, yet he hesitated to approach her and bring up the nights of the accidents. She seemed such a pitiful little person, coming out of the door each morning once again to wait for the school bus with her cousins. She stood apart from them, and he wondered if she now stood apart from everyone.

It was like her daddy had died too with Stephanie. Even when he came out of his office-den to eat with her and her mother he didn't say anything. Nor did her mother. The house was so quiet now. Greta had even stopped turning on the television.

Her first day back at school had been almost unbearable. Kids looked at her and whispered, and she'd heard them saying, "Her sister died. And her cousin died too." Even her friends hurried away from her. It was like she had forgotten how to play. Her head hurt, and her hand felt stiff. The ring tightened on her finger, and it was hard now to hold anything in her left hand.

No one had listened to her when she told them she'd killed Kenny and Stephanie. They said it wasn't true. But she remembered hearing the whisper in her ear. *Kill ... kill ...* And then they had died.

When the bus stopped in front of Derek's house, Greta was the first off. Without waiting for Derek or William, she walked on down the sidewalk toward her house, hoping her mama was home and she wouldn't have to go into the house by herself. Before, when she knew that Stephanie would soon be home, she hadn't minded. But today she didn't want to go in by herself. She was afraid.

"Bye, Greta," Derek called, and William repeated his words. She turned briefly and waved at them, and then she went on.

She saw that her mother's car was not in the driveway. The garage doors were shut, and she went to the small door at the side and looked in. It was empty, except for the things hanging on the walls, the curled hoses, the rakes and spades and things that were never used.

Greta closed the door and went on to the patio door and opened it. The family room looked frightening. The draperies were partly closed, and the shadows lurked in the corners and behind the furniture. The black thing that had run with her and Stephanie was here somewhere, hiding in the corner or behind the draperies or the furniture. It had been hiding since that day. But it was here, somewhere. Greta could feel it.

She backed away, closing the patio doors. She stood for awhile, looking toward the orchard and the place where she and Derek had found the well. She couldn't see it from here, and she didn't want to see it. The dark thing had come from there, she remembered. She had glimpsed it at her side that day when she and Derek had run to get away from Kenny.

She wandered out into the driveway and down toward the street. A car went by, and then another. But neither of them slowed, neither of them belonged to her mother.

She stood on the sidewalk looking down the street. Another car was coming, a light brown car like her mother's. She waited, hoping. Then she saw it was larger, longer than her mother's car, and a man was driving.

The man's face looked familiar. The car slowed, and pulled a U-turn in the street and parked at the curb beside her. She saw his face now, the sharp jaw, the mustache, and his eyes, brown and soft, like Stephanie's. Someone, she didn't remember who, had called Stephanie's eyes gentle. And that was the way with Sergeant Donally's eyes. She was glad to see him.

"Hello, Greta."

He got out of the car and leaned against the fender. She gazed up at him, aware that her lips had turned up at the edges for the first time in a long time.

"How are you today, Greta?"

"I'm okay."

He smiled. "You'd say that, no matter what, wouldn't you?"

She didn't understand. It was almost like talking with Stephanie again, with her feeling that what was being said was being spoken in a foreign language, like the people who had moved here from Vietnam. So she just looked up at him and waited.

He took something from his pocket and offered it to her, and she looked at it and hesitated. She saw it was a small sucker, orange, wrapped in clear paper. Mama had always said don't take candy from strangers, but Mr. Donally was not really a stranger. She took the sucker.

"Maybe you'd better keep it until you've had your dinner, suppose? We don't want to ruin your appetite."

"All right."

"Did you go to school today?"

"Yes."

"Did you learn something interesting?"

She looked at his toes. His black shoes were polished like her dad's, but it seemed an odd picture to imagine Sergeant Donally slapping a polishing cloth against the toes of his shoes the way her father did. Her father groomed himself very rigidly. She had stood only this morning in the bedroom doorway and watched him at the dresser in the bedroom he shared with Mama, hoping to get his attention as he put his tie on and fixed it very carefully. She had stood there lots of times before, though not recently, and watched him, and the look on his face had been different then. And then too he had talked to her. But this morning he hadn't seen her, not even when he turned and came out into the hall. She had stepped aside and said, "Daddy?" But he didn't hear her. That was the last she saw of him.

She had wanted to tell him she was sorry, that she missed Stephanie too, but he hadn't given her a chance. She looked up at Mr. Donnally's face and saw he was looking at her with that gentle look, except something was different now in his eyes. She blinked and took a step backward.

He leaned forward suddenly, got her by the chin and turned her so her cheek was toward him.

"Who hit you?" he asked, and his voice had changed too. It sounded rougher, deeper. She jerked back. His fingers slipped away from her chin.

"Nobody," she denied quickly, putting her hand up to her face. "Nobody hit me."

"That's quite a bruise you have there," he said, and leaned back against the car fender again, but the gentleness was gone from his face. "It must have hurt a lot. When did it happen?"

She opened her lips to speak, but had nothing to say. Then, "I don't remember."

"Try to think. You can tell me, you know."

He eased away from the car again and squatted in front of her, one knee up with his arm across it. She was now looking slightly down at him, and she could see his eyes sharp and searching on her face, on her cheek, on her ear. She put her hand up again, her finger into her ear. She felt the thin, crusty stuff that meant blood had oozed again and had dried in her ear. She held her hand over it.

"Did someone strike Kenny, Greta? Like they did you? Only harder, maybe, more times? Someone you don't want to tell me about?"

She took a step backward, then another. She stopped. A car was coming down the street, and she wanted to look and see if it was her mother or dad. Someone to rescue her from questions she didn't know the answers to.

"And your sister, Stephanie, was she running from someone? Had she been struck by someone, Greta?"

"I ... I," Greta said. "I think I did." She was going to cry, and she knew it because she could feel her face shrinking.

"I don't think you did," he said. "You're too small. The blows they received were too hard. You couldn't have done it. Who are you trying to protect, Greta?"

The tears came. Her face had puckered, shrunk like an apple left to wrinkle and dry up. She didn't know what to say to Mr. Donally. She wanted to tell him the truth.

"It's ... it's ... black, and it comes out of the ... the shadows. It came up out of the well. It followed me. It hurt me. It told me to kill. I don't know what it is."

A car stopped in the driveway, and a door slammed. Greta looked toward it and saw a blur of gray and a figure walking toward them. It was her mother.

"What's wrong?" Clare asked, and pulled Greta to her.

Sergeant Donally got to his feet.

"Go on to the house, Greta," Clare said, and her voice was angry. "Go to the car first, there's something on the seat for you."

Greta rubbed her good fist across her eyes to clear the blur away, then ran to the car. On the front seat was a package. She tore the sack open and found a new outfit for her Barbie doll, a beautiful evening dress and tiny little high-heeled gold slippers with matching bag, and underwear. Lacy bikini panties and a tiny bra. Greta clutched it to her and ran to the back door and into the house. She had been wanting this outfit for a long time, but her allowance just hadn't covered it. There were too many things she kept spending her allowance on. And sometimes she'd forget that she was going to save her money for this outfit and would find herself a quarter or fifty cents short. She went toward her bedroom smiling, removing the dress from the package even as she walked.

CLARE'S HEART was thundering behind her breast bone. She felt that he would be able to see it if he only looked. And the back of her neck felt as if her spine had been severed there.

"What was going on here? Why was my child crying?"

"And I would like to know a couple of things too, Clare," Sergeant

Donally said. "Who struck Greta? I hesitate to say slapped, because a mere slap doesn't make a bruise on a child's face like that one."

She was suddenly on the defensive and, worse, she hadn't the vaguest idea what he was talking about. "What?"

"The bruise on your daughter's face. Don't tell me you haven't seen it. It must have happened a few days ago, because it has that color of a bruise that's been there awhile."

"I ... Greta had no bruise this morning! And that doesn't explain to me why you had her crying. You may be a police detective, Conrad, and you may have a right to question suspects, but my nine-year-old daughter has not done anything to warrant her being questioned until she cries. What is it you want to know, anyway? Ask me or Phillip or Ross or Alyne. If there's anything you need to know that involves the family, we can tell you."

"Then tell me who in your family struck Greta. And how about Kenny? He received a severe blow to his head. It caused his death. We understood that only Greta was with him, and evidently she saw nothing, but was she the only one there? Maybe she came up later and found him. Maybe she'd been following someone? And what about Stephanie? Why was she running? And there is evidence that her cheek was bruised too, as if she'd been struck. Tell me the answers to that, Clare. I think I've been blinded simply because I felt I knew all of you. But the evidence is pointing at child abuse, Clare. Severe child abuse."

For a moment she found herself unable to talk, only to return the hard look from his eyes. She was stunned by his words, and felt that no matter what she said he wouldn't believe her. She began to shake her head. The fury she had felt was drifting away to a dark depression, a sudden plunge to hopelessness.

"You've got it all wrong, Conrad. Sergeant Donally. You're so wrong. There has never been any child abuse in this family. Never. We aren't like that. You've lived across the street from my father's house for five years now? Four? Don't you think you would have heard of something by now, if we were like that?"

"You can live right next door to a child abuse problem and not know it exists."

She looked around helplessly. She wanted to escape in the worst way, not only from the piercing eyes of the man who was looking for something that wasn't there, but from her own misery.

"Sergeant, you don't know what it's like to lose a child to death. I didn't know either, even though I thought I did when Kenny, my sister's child, died. He was my nephew after all, and I've known him all his life. He and Stephanie played together when they were toddlers. Not very well, but they were together. Kenny was always a sort of ... a sort of little bully, but his mother adored him. And I loved him too. And I thought I knew, but I didn't." She turned, but she couldn't go yet. Standing with her profile toward Conrad, she went on talking, saying things she had wanted to say to Phillip, but couldn't get through his shell of grief to so much as tell him she knew how he felt.

"I had wanted her to hurry and go away to college." She wouldn't tell this to her husband or to anyone in her family, and maybe, she thought, she shouldn't be telling Conrad, but she couldn't seem to quit talking. "I thought it would be better because, because, well, Stephanie was mature for her age, and she was very intelligent. She was going to graduate this semester, you know, even though she was only sixteen." *Because I felt like with Stephanie gone, Phillip and I would become closer again. I felt maybe he would talk to me again, instead of to Stephanie.* "But then she died, and now she's gone forever. And I never wanted it that way, Sergeant. Never."

"I'm very sorry."

She looked at him. "I can promise you, Stephanie, nor Kenny, nor Greta have ever been abused."

"Take a look at that cheek," he said, and she saw he was not convinced by her words.

She gave him a last look and turned away. She had stopped her car just into the entrance off the driveway, drawn to hurry to her child whom she had seen was crying. She got into the car, started it, and drove it forward slowly. She pressed the garage door opener and idled the car on into the garage as the door lifted. She pressed the button again and turned off the ignition. Her movements were automatic, her thoughts still with Donally and his conviction that her family was involved in child abuse. She wanted to feel angry and indignant again. She would rather have her heart pounding with fury than have this tired, sagging, hopeless feeling. This feeling of dark, deep terror, of things to come that were worse than the things that had happened.

Was this how Alyne had been feeling? Was this what caused the distant sad look in Alyne's eyes, the almost invisible frown of thoughtfulness that seemed stamped on her features now? Had Donally accused *her* of child abuse?

She removed the keys from the car and dropped them into a pocket of her purse. With the strap over her shoulder, she got her purchases from the back seat and went into the house. The kitchen was cool and shadowed, and she turned on the light. She glanced into the family room, but it was empty except for the furniture and the air of desolation. The first thing she saw was the bronzed baby shoes on the fireplace mantel. Stephanie's. By the time Greta was born, bronzing baby's first shoes was no longer especially interesting.

She turned on the lights as she went down the hall to the bedroom.

"Greta?"

"Huh?"

Clare went into Greta's bedroom and found her sitting on the floor dressing one of her dolls. She was working one of the slippers onto the doll's foot and didn't look up. She sat cross-legged, just the way Stephanie had when she was that age. At age eight Stephanie had shown little of the academic ability that she later possessed. She had been bright, but so was Greta. No trouble in school ever, not socially or with learning. Would Greta grow up to be like Stephanie? Or—a terrible thought came unbidden to Clare, increasing the sense of changed reality, of living now in a nightmare—would Greta grow up at all? Would her life end suddenly, soon, as Stephanie's had, as Kenny's had?

Clare sank to her knees at Greta's side, and Greta turned her blue eyes up in surprise, looking into Clare's face. The light in the room was not good. Clare squinted and looked at the cheek that was toward the glow of light that spread down from the lamp on the dresser. She saw no bruise.

"What was Sergeant Donally talking to you about, Greta?"

Greta ducked her head. Her fingers were nervous and flighty as they tried to fasten the buckle on the slipper. She shrugged. "I don't know."

"You were crying."

"I was crying because my sister died," Greta said clearly.

The phone rang. Clare jumped and felt her pulse speed. The phone had stopped ringing after Stephanie's funeral. All the teenagers who had called and the people from the animal shelter and various other organizations in which Stephanie was involved stopped calling. The phone had been deadly quiet for severed days.

"Who could that be?" Clare muttered as she got to her feet.

She went to the extension in the master bedroom.

"Clare," Phillip's voice said. "Clare, I'm not coming home tonight. I ..."

"What? Why?" Both her hands gripped the phone tightly, clinging.

"I have to get away, Clare. I hope you understand. I just can't come back there for awhile. I'm taking a week off."

"But where are you going?"

"I don't know. Just driving, I think. Somewhere."

"But why can't we go with you?"

There was a silence. She felt almost desperate to reach him, to make him take her and Greta too, to hang onto him, to not let him go. The sickness came up in her belly, in her stomach, the feeling of being abandoned, of being lost in a big and terrible world.

"Phillip," she cried, hearing her voice weak and wavering. "Phillip, take us with you."

"I can't, Clare. I have to get away alone."

The phone clicked and he was gone. She sat down on the bed. She almost fell onto it, with the phone held against her heart and her head hanging. But she couldn't just give up and let him go without them. Greta could miss a week of school. It would be better for her to get away now too than to try to go on as if everything were just as it always had been.

She punched out numbers on the phone rapidly and then waited through six rings. She realized she'd gotten a wrong number. The men's store where Phillip worked did not close until nine, and some of the clerks would be there. She broke the connection and dialed again, and the phone was answered on the first ring.

"I'd like to speak to Phillip, please."

"I'm sorry, Mr. Shepley hasn't been here all afternoon."

Clare felt as if she had received ice water in her face. Where had he been? Where had he called from? Was he already four hundred miles away?

She hung up the phone slowly and fell back on the bed, one arm covering her eyes. She would never see Phillip again. She knew that, as if the angel of death had whispered the words in her ear.

CHAPTER 15

CONRAD STOOD by his car for several minutes, his arms folded, looking toward Clare's house that was surrounded by privacy. On one side was the narrow strip of citrus trees, separating her yard from her sister's. He could see the area beyond the tree trunks where Kenny had died on the grass, where Greta had stood screaming hysterically. Alyne's house was as private as Clare's, with even less of the front yard open to the street. Although it didn't have hedges like Milton's house across the street, it did have plantings of evergreens with neat rock borders and a couple of trees that screened the front of the house.

Behind the two houses was the alley and the orchard that reached several hundred yards back to the homes and street on the north.

Kids played along the alley, in the yards, on the street. They rode bicycles on the sidewalks, although it was illegal. Only the older ones rode their bikes out on the street. He was in favor of the little ones staying in their driveways or on the sidewalks. There weren't so many pedestrians that anyone was in danger of being knocked down. In fact, the only people who used the sidewalks were the kids.

It was a pretty residential neighborhood, rural in flavor, with close families. Child abuse was one of the last things to associate with a neighborhood like this.

Yet, it was obvious. The child's cheek was badly bruised, and he thought he had detected a dark substance in her ear that might indicate dried blood. He was reminded of a case he'd checked on in the hospital.

A little boy, thin, skinny arms, reedy little legs, his head looking too big for his small neck, had been so badly beaten that his cheeks had looked like Greta's, only worse, and there had been dried blood in his ear. His arms and legs had been twisted, and the fingerprints of a large man's hand were visible in blue, just as the fingerprints were dark on Greta's face. It was difficult to see what size hand had struck her, whether it was a man's or a woman's, and he hadn't had a chance to get a really good look at it. But her attitude fell in with child abuse also. The tears, the denial.

And Clare's vehement denial.

Child abuse had not occurred to him before. Somehow, it was not even a possibility before. Kenny dead from a blow to the head, yet that had been minimized, the death attributed to a weak blood vessel in the brain. And Stephanie had fallen while running. The bruising of her face had been blamed on the fall. But Conrad could see now that he might have been all wrong. Stephanie could have been struck on the face just as Greta had been, as Kenny had been, and was running from her abuser when she fell.

He hesitated to call the station and report his suspicions. Years of training and experience urged him toward more definite proof that this was what was happening.

He left his car and walked back up the street. Voices of children came from somewhere behind Alyne's house, and Conrad strolled as if he were out taking an evening walk.

He saw Alyne's middle boy, a slightly chubby preteen, and two other boys. They had bicycles and, as Conrad watched, got on and started riding toward him down the driveway. Conrad waited.

Two of the boys looked familiar, but he didn't know their names and wasn't sure where they lived. They both spoke as they went by. He noticed they rode out onto the street and headed back west, going toward his car still parked in front of Clare's house. The third boy, William, stopped, resting one foot on the ground.

"Hello, Sergeant Donally."

"Hi, William. How're you?" he looked critically at the boy's face, but his smooth tanned skin was unflawed. The boy shrugged.

"I was just out riding with my friends."

"Who are they?"

"Dennis and Gary."

"Are they brothers?" How did one go about asking, hey, does your dad beat up on you and your cousins? Ross? Ross Kerwin? He was an executive somewhere who was hardly ever home. Your mother, Alyne? But no. This involved both families. And, in fact, seemed more to be in Clare's family. It involved, after all, her two daughters. And it was her nephew who had been out in the yard at three o'clock in the dark morning hours. So more than likely, whoever was responsible lived in Clare's house. Clare or her husband, Phillip.

"No, they're not brothers," William said. "They're just neighbors. I got to go. Mom said for me to be back by dark, and it's almost now. I was just going to ride down to the corner and back," he added as he pumped wildly away, standing up on the pedals, riding hard to catch up to his two cruising buddies.

Conrad turned and walked slowly back toward his car.

He sat a minute looking at Clare's house. Lights had been turned on in the back of the house and the flow out the windows had begun to contrast with the quickly deepening shadows. The neighborhood was settling down for another night.

He got in his car, made a U-turn in the quiet street, and drove slowly back to his own driveway, looking closely at Milton Crossover's house on his way past. It was dark. The yard seemed sunk in shadows, lightless areas beneath trees and shrubs and hedges. It was like Milton was letting nature close him in, away from the rest of the world.

Across the street from his own house was the large Pattison place, the old house like a jewel back in its setting of trees and smooth, carefully mown lawn. He'd been noticing more of what went on in the entire neighborhood, and he knew that Jonah had a gardener who came out weekly to mow and clip and trim. The woman who'd been his housekeeper for years came out daily to sweep the porches and steps and walks. Jonah, though, didn't come onto the porch to sit. It might be the weather, which had been cloudy and rainy, but only cool, not cold. Or it might be his health, faltering from the weight of burying two grandchildren in the span of two weeks.

There wasn't much visitation back and forth between the daughters and the old gentleman that he saw, but of course that probably was done during the day when he was gone, so he couldn't make anything out of that.

He knew now he was looking at the families across the street with different eyes, looking for any signs of ongoing child abuse. Or, perhaps it was wrong to think of it as ongoing. Maybe it was something new, something that had started recently.

He parked his car under the carport, got out, and locked it to the barking of Mutt, who had his nose through the slats of the fence.

Conrad spent a few minutes with Mutt, rubbing his ears and back, running the dog brush down over the wavy fur while Mutt wriggled in ecstasy. He opened a can of dog food and dumped it into Mutt's dish at the end of the cabinet and added a cup of dry food for crunching. Then he went to his desk, a piled area at the end of the kitchen.

He sat down, gathered the papers all into one pile, and began to separate.

Everything pertaining to the case across the street went into one pile. He reread the report on Stephanie and, as he had thought, the bruising was mentioned. But they were new, not old. If she had been struck by someone, it had happened just before she ran out of the house or as she ran out. It could have been that which caused her to fall. It could have been the bursting of the blood vessel that caused the fall. The ultimate cause of death was the same as for her cousin, a ruptured vessel in the brain, or, as it was stated in the report, massive brain hemorrhage.

He sat staring at the calendar hanging over the desk, and became so restless he felt like ants were crawling all over him. Mutt came up to have his head patted, then he lay down with a sigh on the round, braided rug that was exclusively Mutt's. But Conrad had to go. Although Milton wanted to withdraw from the world, Conrad couldn't let him. He was the only witness to the death of Stephanie, other than a little girl who was too afraid to talk.

He went out the back door, leaving Mutt in the yard looking puzzled. Instead of getting into the car, as Mutt seemed to expect, Conrad walked on past and down the driveway to the street. Behind him, Conrad heard one curious woof.

The street lights had come on. In Jonah's house there was a light in the left front, with the blinds drawn. In Alyne's house next door, the front was dark but, as with Clare's, light bloomed out into the darkening yard at the back.

There still were no lights at Milton's. It occurred to Conrad, as he went up the walk to the porch, that Milton might be alone in the world, with no one to check up on him occasionally. The man wasn't old, but he was acting very peculiar.

On the porch, which surrounded the front wing on three sides,

Conrad's way was lighted only by the pale blue ceiling of the porch, and what little light, those few gleams, that filtered in from the street lights beyond the trees. The place seemed deserted. It had that feel of a place that has been abandoned.

Conrad rang the doorbell and then knocked a couple of times on the front door with no hopes of being answered. He stepped off the porch and went back around the house to a gate in a wire fence and fumbled for the latch. At the rear of the driveway, deep in the shelter of some trees, was a one-car garage. Its white exterior looked ghostly in the dark.

Conrad got the gate open and went into Milton's backyard for the first time in his life. Spangles of light touched here and there like fireflies resting, but overhead there was no sky, no scudding clouds lighter than the shadows beneath. Overhead was the cover of tree limbs, thickly-leaved, hovering protectively over the house.

Conrad wished he'd brought his flashlight, but as he stood in the dark, his eyes adjusted and he could see the screen of the back porch as a darker area above the white paint of the house. He finally was able to see the screen door. But if it were locked, he'd be right where he'd been at the front.

Suddenly, startlingly, light blazed out at him. The bare bulb on the screened porch ceiling had come on, and he stood full within the light. Then, as he blinked, the back door of the house opened. Milton poked his head out.

"Good evening, Milton," Conrad said, feeling somewhat like an intruder.

"Conrad, is that you? What do you want?"

Milton stepped out onto the porch.

"Could I come in and talk to you awhile, Milton?"

Milton glanced behind, then shrugged. "Whatever I can say, I can say here on the porch, I guess."

Conrad came up the back steps and opened the screen door. The porch hadn't been swept in a long time. Debris, things that must have fallen off the trees and somehow got through the screen, were in tiny piles in the corners. Or perhaps it was just something that grew on a back porch over a long period of time.

Conrad was now standing where he could see into the kitchen. The light from the overhead bulb on the porch was like a torch blazing into the dark room, falling upon, oddly, a stack of lumber. Conrad's eyes went beyond the kitchen and saw a long hallway, and there, not lighted by the bulb on the porch but from a source somewhere else, a doorway was outlined. So Milton hadn't exactly been sitting in the dark, he'd been in a room where only a soft light had been turned on.

"What is it?" Milton said, his voice suggesting that he had very little time to waste. Conrad's eyes swept him and noted the man looked all right, no ill health or anything of that nature showing.

"I'd like you to tell me if you saw anyone else at all with the girl who was killed across the street the other day. You are the only witness and I apologize for bothering you, Milton, but I really need you to try to remember if you might have glimpsed someone back in the hallway or the entry of the house."

For a moment Milton was silent, then he said. "Killed? I thought it was decided that she died from the fall."

"There is evidence that she might have been struck on the face. Did you see anyone, or the shadow of anyone? The girls were said to be alone in the house, but were they?" Conrad made a mental note in his mind to check out the whereabouts of both Clare and Phillip, yet he knew what he would find. Both of them were on the road home. That would be their alibi, and it was true, provided one of them hadn't already reached home at the time of the incident.

He thought then that he saw Milton glance sideways, as if looking for something or someone. But Milton didn't turn his head.

"I didn't see anything," he said. "The two girls, like I told you, came running out of the house, leaving the door open. I didn't even look for anyone else. They were there, and I didn't look into the house. I didn't even go to their yard. I stopped in the middle of the road and came back to my own house."

"Why?"

Milton glared at Conrad through the light, his face partly shadowed, his nose looking long with the extension of the shadows, his eyes deep-set and dark and submerged in the shadows. Conrad could almost feel the intensity of the glare. Milton wanted him to go, so he could go back into the house and lock his door. And suddenly Conrad knew something about him.

He asked softly, "What are you afraid of, Milton?" Milton's eyes betrayed him. They glanced right and left, and he took a step closer to his kitchen door. The light fell more fully on his face, cancelling out the shadows. His features looked softer, rounder.

He answered the first question, as if the last one hadn't been asked. "I came back because I didn't know what else to do. I knew other people would come. The aunt, she doesn't go out to work, she's at home most of the time. The cousins, they're around, boys, you know, playing, riding bicycles. The housekeeper at the grandfather's, and Jonah himself. Somebody. They didn't need me."

The more he talked, the more Conrad became sure that the reasons Milton was giving were decoys. He had turned around and fled back to his house because he had been afraid. But why? The answer lay only with Milton.

"What were you afraid of, Milton?" Conrad asked again, trying to keep all criticism out of his voice. "It's important that you tell me."

Milton made an attempt at laughter. It sounded more like a barnyard fowl squawking. Then suddenly it was edged with anger.

"Look. Why am I being persecuted? Just because I was a witness to the falling? Don't I have any rights as a citizen? If this goes on, I'm going to have to see my lawyer."

Conrad motioned a shrug with his hands. "All right." He saw Milton's eyes search past him into the black backyard. "If you change your mind, you know where I live." Milton nodded. Conrad stepped back, and went down the porch steps and blended into the darkness.

MILTON STOOD on the threshold of his kitchen until he heard the squeak of the metal gate of the fenced backyard. He listened to it open and close, and then, because he didn't trust anyone, because Conrad could have opened and closed the gate just to make him think he had left and then slipped back to watch from the shadows, Milton waited and listened. He heard a soft wind rustling the leaves. And there was a movement in the grass near the edge of the porch that turned out to be one of his cats. It came softly up onto the step and meowed; and Milton, listening through the darkness even as he moved soundlessly to ease open the screen door for the cat, heard the crunch of a footstep out on the driveway. Conrad was leaving.

Milton hurried back into the kitchen, the cat going ahead of him to a dish in the corner. Milton turned out the porch light. He stood still again, but the only sound he heard was the cat eating its late supper out of the dish.

Milton went softly down the hall and into the lighted room. He closed the door. It was a small room, with one window. Boards had been nailed over the window from the top of the frame to the bottom. He had done that today, while hammering in the neighborhood, should it be heard, would not be especially noticed. He had brought in a comfortable chair and a cot with a pillow and blankets. Two of the cats were already here, one of them on a roll-top desk where the lid was up. He had found a bed on scattered papers. The other cat was on the cot, rolled up on the blanket folded at the foot of the bed. He had brought in their litter box, though it needed changing.

He sat in the chair and looked through the dim light of the desk lamp at the door; he wanted to nail boards across it, but had sense enough to know that he would be building his coffin if he did. Tomorrow he would work on the rest of the house. Today he had gotten only to this room and one other that had three windows. He had given them all the same treatment. First he had pulled the blinds, and then he had carefully straightened the curtains or, as in the case of the bigger corner room, the draperies. Closing them and arranging their pleats precisely. Mother would want it that way, though it didn't matter a goddamn what mother wanted. Nevertheless, he had fixed it just right, the hand of a woman, you might say, or a decorator. Then he had nailed the boards up, hiding the curtains, the blinds, the draperies, the windows.

Now, hearing a scratching at the door, he jerked up from his seat and stared at it. He felt so vulnerable, so terrified. Could it come in even where there were boards on the windows and locks on the doors?

Was it out there now scratching at the door, trying to disguise itself as a cat? Would he open the door to find a tall, bloated black gathering of something darker than any cloud he had ever seen, deeper than any shadow in the most stinking, damp cellar? Something that had the ability to create appendages from itself, arms that reached out, hands that killed?

From the other side of the door came a meow demanding entrance. Milton heard it sniffing, then it scratched again. It had located him and the other cats and it wanted in.

Milton unlocked the door and eased it open barely an inch. The cat's nose pushed into the opening, and behind the cat the back of the hall, hardly touched by the thin light escaping from the closed room, seemed to move, to begin taking form. Could it be there, in the darkness, a part of the darkness? Waiting to gather itself into a thing that would destroy? A thing with power such as he, a mere mortal, could never have?

He knew who it was. *It*, now, not she. Her femininity was gone, and gone with it the lure of her girlhood, the charm of soft skin, full, moist lips, smooth satin-like skin, curves of hip, waist, and breast that still he dreamed of after all these years. God how he had wanted her. He was willing to kill for her.

And she had been willing to kill for a ring.

But then something had happened. Her father? He knew her father was mean to her, and her mother was elsewhere, a whore someplace in Los Angeles or San Francisco. Sometimes she worked Las Vegas, the girl had told him, and he had seen the excitement in her eyes. She would be doing the same thing soon, if he didn't stop her, keep her for himself.

"You fool, Milton! She's only a child. Over my dead body, Milton, will you marry that little trollop, that ... piece, Milton!"

His mother's voice rang through the house, echoing as if from a deep cave, a hundred caves, and his first instinct was to cover both ears with his hands. He felt something digging at the toe of his shoe, trying to gain entrance to the room, and he lifted his foot to crush it, to kill it like a beetle that had gotten into the house. But then, as his foot came down on its head, he heard a tortured, twisted meow, and behind him the other cats leaped up nervously and began meowing. One of them jumped down from the desk and hid underneath the cot.

Milton realized he was trying to kill his own cat, and he reached down and pulled it through the narrow opening of the door, though it yeowled again and twisted in his hand and sunk all four sets of claws into his arm defensively. Milton muttered a curse and threw the cat. It struck on its side and when it got up, it had a twisted, crippled walk.

Sympathy and sorrow, bitter as gall, filled his chest and throat. He shut the door and went to the cat, who had crawled back under the cot. He pulled it out and sat with it on his lap, weeping over it, rubbing its fur, saying, "I'm sorry, Mike. I'm sorry, Mike. I'd never hurt you."

What had come over him? He was gentle with his cats ordinarily. Except of course when they needed punishment. Then he banished them from the house, though his hands convulsed to choke the life out of them. Because he knew he could kill, he banished them from the house on those days and nights when he felt this terrible urge to murder. When the past came back to haunt him.

And now it had come back, but not to haunt. To haunt was a nebulous thought, an idea not quite formed, a figure lost in mists and shadows, too fragile to create a body of itself. But this thing, which had come back from the well, had been brought up and, in some way, found the evil strength to become whole, had come back to kill.

And it was coming after him. Ultimately, he would be her victim.

Why me? He cried into the soft light of the room, in his mind, as he rubbed the relaxing body of his injured cat. Why me? I loved you. What happened wasn't my fault. Not my fault—not my fault—

He had seen her with bruises on her face and her body where she had been struck. He had seen purple fingerprints, made in fury on her arm. He had seen the subdued hatred in her eyes. And he had seen the love.

Come and live with me, I'll take care of you, I'll love you, I'll never hurt you.

Your mother won't even let me cross the threshold of her house anymore.

My mother won't be here forever.

Laughter. Your mother will bury you, Milton. She'll be here. Couldn't you go somewhere else to live?

Will you go with me?

Bowed head. My daddy. I don't want to leave my daddy.

That bastard? The way he treats you?

Bowed head, silence.

He loved her. Even apart from his lust for her young, moist body, he loved her.

I'll give you that ring, the one of Mother's that you love so much.

Give it to me now.

No, not now.

I'll do anything you want me to, if you will give it to me.

I can't. I have to put it back. It's hers. Not mine.

Why can't we have it all, Milton.

It all?

Yes, why not? The house, all the jewelry, everything.

But ... he knew, her thought reached him. It had reached him before. He had lain in his bed many times since he met Adriene and thought of going into his mother's room and, while she slept, putting a pillow over her head and holding it there. Her death would be silent. He couldn't bear loud noises like screams. He had heard her screams at him for too long. He only wanted her gone all the time, the way she was gone on her trips. Only forever. He wanted to think of her as living in Paris or Hong Kong, the way she often did for months at a time. Once, when he was a little boy, he had wanted her to stay with him all the time, but she hadn't. *Don't be a crybaby, Milton, you're seven years old. Mrs. So-and-so will be here with you. And later, Are you still sniffling, Milton? You're thirteen, for God's sake. Mrs. So-and-so will be here just as always. Then, I don't need her anymore, Mother, after all I'm seventeen now. Good, I'm glad you finally grew up capable of taking care of yourself.*

So he had begun to wish she'd stay away. Especially after Adriene came. What right had Mother to tell him he was a fool? For the first time in his life he felt like a man, and it was a feeling that he did not want to give up.

Yes, why not? But how, Adriene?

If you'll give me the ring, Milton, you won't have to worry about a thing. I'll do it while you're at work.

She had taken all the jewelry, and he hadn't seen or heard from her again. The police had come and questioned him, and questioned him, and made him prove that he was at work. And no one at work knew he'd left earlier than he'd said. Though it was a matter of minutes that put him at home during the murder because the murder had occurred late in the day, at the time he had left the office. The police said if the medical examiner had missed the timing by a few minutes, it would have put Milton at home at the time of the murder. Milton still felt the cold feel of the noose that almost pulled him in and accused him of murdering his own mother, a heinous crime. Only the fact of the stolen jewelry really saved him.

He didn't know where Adriene had gone. If he told the police about her, told the police that she had killed his mother for the jewelry, then he would have implicated himself.

All these years he had thought of her as following in her mother's footsteps, a whore in one of the big cities, a whore willing to commit a brutal murder for a few baubles.

And then the well had been opened. And the moment he saw the skull of that disjointed skeleton, so green-coated with slime, with moss-like stuff that darkened it, turned it almost black, the moment he saw that long, straight hair, so few strands of it left now, and coated and thickened like worms, he knew it was Adriene.

And worse, he now saw what had happened. On the very day of the murder of his mother, there had been another murder. Only no one had ever known of it. He had thought the girl had run away. She had only been leading him on, just as his mother had said, to get what she could out of him.

But she had been killed instead, and her body, with her stolen jewelry, thrown down the well. Or perhaps she had been thrown down the well first, where she died after her voice, crying out but enclosed by the pipe, went unheard by the people in the neighborhood.

She had been killed, and he thought he knew who killed her. But if he told the police, they would want to know how he knew. And then he would be tried for conspiracy to murder his mother.

They had brought her up from the well, and as if her soul had rotted entirely and become formed of the black depths of the well, she had risen with her bones, with the ring she had lusted for, killed for, and she had risen to kill again.

He had wanted to tell Conrad. *I saw it.* I saw it coming out of the shadowed hallway with the girls, as if it were welded to them, between them, dark and evil and moving like a wind-blown cloud, a black cloud of almost human proportions, though taller than her physical body had been, stronger, perhaps, though her strength then had been sufficient to crush a woman's skull with three or four sharp blows. He had seen her form an arm, with a hand that looked large, as large as a man's, with long, undulating fingers, and he had seen it strike the head of the older girl, and she had been knocked off the porch, her body twisting in the air, her arms flailing helplessly. Then her head struck the edge of the walk. And she lay still. The other child was screaming, screaming, and he realized both of the girls had been screaming, but their sounds were not terribly loud. It was more like the choked, distorted screams of someone in a nightmare. Or the cry of an animal in distress.

He saw it. He thought he saw it.

What choice had he had but to return to his own house? Where else could he go? He knew she was here, in existence on this earth, pushed by some power he didn't understand. The ring? His mother had gushed all kinds of nonsense about the ring, about magical powers, some of them not good, his mother had said. *Why did you buy it?* Milton asked. And she had answered with a smile, *I like a challenge. This ring, the power in this ring, shall not defeat me. Besides, isn't it the most gorgeous thing you've ever seen? Look at the way those lights shoot out from its depths. The man who sold it to me seemed very eager to get rid of it. He said when those lights start leaping and become very bright, that is when it becomes most dangerous, that is when its powers touch everyone, especially the owner, of course, but it also reaches out to others in its neighborhood. That was his choice of words, not mine. Isn't it odd that he used that word, that description? In its "neighborhood." But of course those poor ignorant people who sell things on street corners—and I had a feeling this was a stolen jewel—those ignorant fools believe in all kinds of superstitions and magical properties.*

So who is the ignorant fool, now, Mother?

He realized he hadn't locked his door. He put the cat down, and it limped off beneath the cot to hide in the deepest shadows, while Milton locked the door and then put the desk chair beneath the knob.

Then he sat in his chair staring at the door.

She—it—had become a solid form. A black creation of darkness and slime and evil, and as a solid form, she would not be able to come through a locked door or a boarded window.

He willed it so. He could not pray. God did not exist for him. But he could strengthen his will against hers—its—in an effort to protect himself.

Because he knew that eventually, when she had finished there, she would come for him.

He could hear the wind now, crying through the treetops. He could hear the wailing of something beyond the wind, apart from the wind, the shrill song of death.

CHAPTER 16

The house had never seemed so cold and lonely. Lights burned in the hallways, in the family room, in the kitchen. Everywhere Greta wandered she left lights on. She had eaten alone, finally, getting a cold hot dog from the refrigerator and a bun out of the bread box, and then she'd stuck it in the microwave. But she had turned the microwave too high and the wienie had gotten small and hard, and the bun was hard too. She ate it anyway, chewing and chewing and chewing. She walked as she ate, going into the empty family room where her daddy's chair sat cold and empty, where the couch that had been Stephanie's favorite place looked abandoned. Her own spot on the fluffy rug on the floor was cold-looking too. Mama's chair, close to Daddy's, was empty, like arms held out but not filled.

She had gone then into the bedroom where she'd been hearing sounds of sobbing. Although her mother hadn't answered her knock, she'd gone in anyway.

Clare was lying across the bed, on her back, with one arm over her face.

"Mama? What's wrong?" Stephanie's dead, Kenny's dead. It wasn't as if Greta hadn't heard her mother crying before this. But it was dark outside now and had been for a long time, and Daddy hadn't come home. Had he had a wreck? Greta had heard the phone ring hours ago.

Clare did not lift her head.

"Your daddy's not coming home, Greta," she said, and her mouth sounded full of something so that she could hardly talk.

"Not coming home! But why? Is he sick? Did he have a car wreck?"

Clare made a half-laugh sound of contempt. "That would indicate that he couldn't help not coming home, and your father isn't that caring of us, Greta. He wants to get away. He has taken a week off and he's leaving. But he'll never be back. I know he will never be back. I'll never see him again."

Her mother turned onto her stomach, her head buried in her arms against the bed, and wept hard. Terrible sobs that shook her all over. The worst sounds Greta had ever heard in her life. Greta began to cry too. She went around to the other side of the bed, got as close to her mother's head as she could without crawling up onto the bed, and began to pat her arm and shoulder.

"Mama. Mama. Please, Mama. I'm here, Mama."

"Oh, God," Clare screamed, twisting as if to rid herself of Greta's touch. "Just go on, Greta. Go to your room. Just ... go."

Greta backed away. Something cold touched her arm, and she turned. It was the television. Its blank screen reflected the light, and against the light by the bed, her own reflection appeared as a curved and hideous figure, her face distorted, looking ugly as a witch.

She cried out softly and ran from the room and into the hall. Then she remembered she hadn't closed her mother's door, so she went back and closed it.

After that she wandered the house. She went at last to the big television in the family room and was going to turn it on, but again, as she approached it, she saw something moving in the glass. She stopped and stepped backward, until the face was just a solid gray with only a bright eye, the reflection of the light.

She looked for the remote control device that always lay on the table by her daddy's chair, but there were also a lot of magazines and newspapers, and she couldn't find it.

She turned away and, moving in silence, she went to the refrigerator to get a bottle of milk.

She remembered the cat. Snowball hadn't been around the house much lately, and she wondered where she was. She went to the back door, opened it and called. A white thing separated from the darkness by the shed and came through the light rain to the patio. It was Snowball, and she rubbed her long hair against Greta's ankle and purred loudly, and Greta was so glad to see her. But when she reached down to pick up the cat, it arched its back, hissed, and then ran back into the darkness of the shed.

Greta stood still, feeling as if she had been abandoned by everyone. All her people were gone. Her sister was dead, her daddy had left home. Mama had closed herself into her bedroom and was crying, and Derek didn't want to play anymore. Her cat didn't like her; and then she thought. The cat. It had not been spitting at her. It had never spit at her in all its life. Its blue eyes had been looking behind her, into the kitchen. It was something in the house she was afraid of.

Greta stared straight ahead into the darkness and the rainy night, and longed to start walking and keep walking, right across the wet grass and into the shed with Snowball. There they would cuddle together, and they would love each other and comfort each other, and Snowball would protect her, and she would protect Snowball.

But the cat's world was not her world. She had to go back into the house, her house, and she was afraid to look behind her. She turned slowly.

It was there behind her again, and she glimpsed the edges of it as she turned, and kept turning. Rough, raw edges of black, as if she wore a shroud or a cape, something that stayed always behind her, fastening around her neck, hanging at her back.

She whirled like a dervish, crying in fear and frustration, trying to see it fully, to escape from it, as if to confront it would help her escape. She fell exhausted on the kitchen floor and sat with her head hanging down.

The sounds of the house and the world outside became exaggerated. She heard the soft click-clock of the cuckoo clock that hung on the wall in the family room. A car went by on the street, a soft sound, tires squishing as if the rain had grown heavier, and then she became aware of the rain, sliding like velvet down the windows, and the wind, crying, wailing, so softly, a kind of dark, horrible music, rhythmic weeping, a terrible sound that ground into Greta's heart and soul. And finally, there was the sibilant message coming at her shoulder. *ssswhmmsss ... killll ... kill ... Clarrrrrr ...* Greta jerked up and whirled, trying to see her tormentor, screaming in terrible anguish, "No! No! No!"

She ran down the hall, into the shadows, and against the front outside. She whirled again, her back against the door.

It was in front of her now, a tall and slender black figure that seemed bent forward slightly in the middle so that its head came down toward her. And there were arms now, and large hands, like a man's hands, and just for an instant it seemed she could see its eyes. Then a sharp pain in her hand drew her attention downward, and she sank to the floor. Red and blue and green fire shot from the ring, thin, streaming, piercing the air, reaching toward her face.

And she knew. It was the ring. Somehow, it had something to do with the black thing.

She got to her feet and ran down the bedroom hall to the bathroom and the whisper became a sound that filled her head and the hall, roaring as if she were in a huge, dark cave, echoing back at her, coming in hisses and commands, one word laid down over the next so that she understood only the gist of what was being said to her.

Kill ... kill ... kill ... Clare ... kill ... pets ... pets ... killl pets ... Clare ...

Greta fell into the bathroom and locked the door, and then realized she had shut herself into a room without light. She leaned her cheek against the door and breathed heavily for a moment and then she stood up and screamed, "NOOO!"

The blow came to her face without warning, without expectation. She felt the sharp slap of the hand across her face. She felt her neck give and her head strike the door. She heard the crack of the wood. And for an instant, what seemed like only an instant, she was in a world of vivid color that was pain, colors like the fire in the ring. She was surrounded by it. She was it, color, pain. That was all she was.

She heard a pounding on the door and a voice calling, "Greta! Greta!" Over and over.

At last she realized it was her mother calling, and she reached out and felt the doorknob and turned it.

Her mother stood outlined against the pale light in the hall. She reached forward.

"Greta! Greta, what is it?"

The bright lights of the bathroom came on, and from the corner of her eyes Greta saw the lacy, foggy edges of the black thing as it faded away. She wrapped her arms around her mother's thin waist and hung on for dear life.

CLARE STARED into the bright white of the bathroom, feeling as if something had just disintegrated in front of her eyes. Greta was squeezing her so tightly she could hardly breathe, and her mind had been on Greta, and what was wrong with her, and whatever it was she had seen hadn't really registered with her. But something had been there, like a piece of the darkness in the center of the bathroom that was slower to be replaced by light.

She blinked a couple of times, and sat down on the vanity stool and held Greta's head against hers, rubbing her forehead as she wept, brushing the hair with her hand. She'd been thinking only of her own unhappiness, she realized, and her little daughter, all she had left, had been pushed out.

"I'm sorry, I'm sorry, baby," she murmured in Greta's ear. "We'll make it, you'll see. Now, hush crying."

She pushed Greta back in preparation to washing her face with warm water, which she knew sometimes helped calm a case of nerves, or whatever Greta had. And she saw the red abrasion on Greta's forehead. The skin wasn't quite cut through, but it was an angry looking place about the size of a half-dollar. She remembered then hearing the cracking sound, as if a board somewhere in the house had split.

She looked around and saw the indentation on the panel of the door. It had caved in and looked as if someone had struck it with a fist—or fallen against it, striking her head. Or had struck her head against it deliberately, again and again.

She got up. "Greta."

Greta blinked up at her through tears, her chest jerking in a sob.

Clare put her fingers on the caved-in area of the door. It was the right height. Greta had struck her head against it, like a soul in torment, she thought, her daughter was beating her own head against the door.

"Greta, why did you do this?"

Greta stared at the broken spot of wood. She began shaking her head, and then she looked over each shoulder, as if she expected to look there for help. Yet the look in her eyes was of fear.

"I'm not going to punish you, Greta, I just want to know why you feel you need to beat your own head against the door. And you hurt yourself, you know."

Clare touched Greta's forehead, where discoloration was rapidly occurring. The skin looked more broken than it had, and blood was dark just beneath the skin. Then she saw in the bright light the bruise on the right cheek. She saw prints of a large finger, and the fresh, bright pink as if she had just recently been struck. Now she saw what Sergeant Donally had been talking about, and she gasped in shock.

"Greta! Who did this?"

She sank to her knees in front of Greta, so that her face was lower than Greta's, and held her by the shoulders. Greta's lips moved as if she would tell, yet nothing was said.

"Greta, you can tell me. You must tell me. If you don't, Sergeant

Donally will tell the state child service people, and put in his police report that you have been abused by me or your daddy, and they will come and take you away from me. You must tell me, Greta. It's more important than anything you have ever done in your life."

Greta had been in the bathroom alone with the door locked, and she had butted her own head against the wood so hard it had broken the thin panel. So was it possible that Greta had slapped herself? No, no, it just wasn't conceivable. The hand print looked larger. The one fingerprint that was still outlined in white was large, the size of a man's hand.

Greta, still not speaking, was holding her hand out, between them, pushing away from Clare as she did so. Her eyes were lowered. As Clare searched her face, Greta was looking down at her hand. Clare felt like spanking her. No matter how she urged Greta to talk, Greta was paying attention only to her hand.

Then the piercing of light brought Clare's eyes down. She saw cupped in Greta's palm something dark red that flashed a rainbow of light, thin little arrows of light, reflecting the bright light in the ceiling above and the long tube of lighting over the vanity and wash basins.

Clare sat back a little and Greta turned her hand, and the lights stopped. Clare could see now it was a jewel, a dark red diamond-cut jewel set in filigree yellow gold. It looked like a man's ring.

"Where did you get *that?*"

"Help me take it off, Mama," Greta pleaded. "It's hurting me. And there's something black that belongs to it and that keeps whispering over my shoulder for me to k-kill."

Clare's gaze leaped to Greta's face. "What? What? That's crazy, Greta!"

"But it does, Mama. And *it* did, when I wouldn't, *it* killed Kenny and Stephanie. And it hit me, Mama." She put her hand to her right cheek, and Clare saw the back of her left hand as she raised it too to touch the abrasion on her forehead. "It hit me and pushed my head against the door. It gets mad at me. It hates me. It hates all of us. It came out of the well, Mama, with the ring. Derek got the ring on his fish hook and then gave it to me. I put this tape around the back of it to make it fit, and when they brought up the skeleton out of the well, the black thing came too, except part of it came up with the ring. I know it did. I saw it. It ran at my side, like a shadow, and then it got thicker and blacker, and it got mean and it killed Kenny ..."

She stopped, looking into the distance, her eyes glazed as if she were trying to remember.

"I don't know," she said. "Maybe it was just Stephanie it killed. But Mama, now it even wants me to kill you."

A cold, terrible chill trailed along Clare's spine and up into the back of her hair and covered her scalp. She looked into Greta's eyes and saw their pure sky blue, with depths like the pearly eyes of a doll. Such innocence, such guile. And such lies.

Clare couldn't help pulling back from her. She got to her feet, went to the wash basin, and turned the water on and let it run until it grew pleasantly warm. Then she got a washcloth from the drawer and wet it, wrung it out, and turned toward Greta.

The little girl was still staring up at her, so trustingly, as if her mother could fix everything. Clare was torn suddenly between wanting to live up to the expectation in those eyes, or doing as Phillip had done and running away. But were those eyes as innocent as they looked? How could she come up with such a story? And now Clare was wondering even more strongly if Greta had bruised her own cheek as she had struck her head against the door. And she came up with an affirmative answer. But it was something she was not qualified to handle. Greta would have to be taken to a psychiatrist. Tomorrow she'd make an appointment.

She washed Greta's face, getting her hair wet as she pushed it back from her forehead with the washcloth.

"Greta," she said as gently as she could, bending over the child, "Have you ... hurt yourself anywhere else?" She chose her words carefully. She didn't want to incite another of the crazy stories about something black coming out of the well along with the skeleton. She wondered, as she slowly undressed Greta, if she could talk her out of such nonsense. It was all tied to the deaths somehow, she supposed, in Greta's mind. The death of Kenny, of Stephanie, and even of the girl in the well, whose death seemed to have started it all. Or at least the discovery of her body had started it all. For Greta. For all of them, it now seemed.

Mama, now it even wants me to kill you.

Had Greta killed Kenny and Stephanie?

The thought hadn't even entered her mind until now. It seemed impossible that Greta could have. Even the police had said so after Greta wept that she had killed Kenny. The police had assured her she hadn't. But Clare knew that Greta thought so, and now she wondered—*Did she?*

Mama, now it even wants me to kill you.

Clare shuddered with the long, cold chills that swept down over her body like a covering of ice. She could no longer look Greta in the eyes.

The child stood before her, naked, like a child nymph, perfect, no blemish except for the small brown mole on her shoulder that had been there since she was a baby. Clare turned her, looking at her all over, seeing no bruise except on her face.

She ran water into the tub, poured in a portion of bubble bath, and then told Greta to get in. She put down into the water a couple of the floating toys that Greta used to like, and left the room. She heard Greta call.

"Mama?"

Clare stopped, feeling as if she were deserting her child, yet hearing those words, coming so guilelessly from Greta's lips, *Mama, now it even wants me to kill you.*

She was afraid of her own little girl.

And that was ridiculous, she told herself.

Through the door she called, "I'll be back in a few minutes, Greta. Wash yourself. I'll bring ... clothes."

She stood in the hall thinking. They would leave. Why not? She had a checking account of her own with quite a bit of money in it, and she had credit cards. If Phillip could leave, so could they.

She went to her bedroom and brought down a suitcase from the top shelf of the closet and began folding in clothes. The yellow suit that just never wrinkled, thanks to polyester. It looked like cotton knit, but wore like the jewel it was. White blouse, yellow floral blouse, underwear, stockings. They would go south, out of the rain, into the sunshine. She put in summer slacks and shorts and more little tops. She threw in a pair of sandals, and a pair of dress shoes, just in case. They'd swing through Las Vegas and see if they could find Phillip. He always headed for the casinos, whether he was happy or unhappy. It was something that distracted him. When he was up, he won. When he was down, it pulled him up just to play.

She snapped the case shut and wheeled it out into the hall.

She knocked on the bathroom door. "Are you all right, Greta?" she called.

"I'm through, Mama.'"

"Dry off then. I'll bring clothes in a minute."

"Okay."

In Greta's room, Clare filled a small suitcase with jeans and shirts and dressier pants and skirts and a pile of shorts, tops, and underwear. She put in one pair of sandals. Arizona, here we come. Or maybe even Disney World in Florida. Why not? They'd drive, and drive, and drive.

Mama, now it even wants me to kill you.

The psychiatrist? She'd forgotten all about that. Already, she had forgotten about it. She paused. Would the trip be just as therapeutic? If the trip didn't work, they could see a doctor when they got back. But for now, both of them needed to get away.

She heard Greta calling. The sound was far away and eerie. *Ma-ma, Ma-ma.*

It was almost as if her little daughter were wheedling, holding out her hand and saying, Come, Mama, I have to kill you.

For just a moment Clare almost ran. Her thoughts flashed next door to Alyne; she knew that Alyne would take care of Greta. Alyne would take over just as she had when Greta was a baby and Clare needed someone to babysit. Alyne would take care of Greta. Clare could run, take her suitcase, and drive away, forever.

Yet she crouched over the dresser drawer, frozen. And then her hands picked up a pair of pants and a shirt, and she straightened and went down the hall to the bathroom, her body jerking forward like a puppet. At the bathroom door she paused and took a long breath.

Greta was calling, more frantically now, her voice tearful. "Ma-ma! *Mama!*"

Clare opened the door.

From the tub, water around her waist, Greta stared at her. Tears hung on her lower lashes, two round, tiny glimmering pearls. Greta blinked and they rolled down her cheeks and were gone in the dying bubbles of the bath.

For just a moment Greta's mouth drew into a thin, flat line, as her chin pushed up in a hundred wrinkles like a raisin.

"You didn't answer," she accused.

"I was in your room getting some things for you to put on."

"But you could have answered."

"Greta, just get out, okay? Don't criticize me."

"I wasn't criticizing you. I just thought you'd gone off and left me, the way Daddy did."

"I ..." Clare clicked her teeth shut. Why let a kid put her on the defensive like this? "He went away and left me, Greta, not you. He'll be back."

"Then he'll be back to you too. When's he coming back?"

"When he feels better."

Clare dried Greta's white little body and dropped the towel on the floor, something she ordinarily never would have done. Any other time she would carefully hang it up. But tonight suddenly she was in a terrible hurry. She was becoming more and more aware of the stillness of the house, of the quality of something being in the house that did not belong there. She wanted away, *away*.

She began helping Greta into underwear and jeans. Greta drew back in surprise.

"Where are my pajamas?"

"We're not going to bed, Greta. We're going to leave too."

Greta's eyes grew round. The place on her forehead was an angry red now, with tiny lines in its center like a cracked egg. A lump had puffed up. Her right cheek looked swollen and blue, with purplish spots, and the fingerprint that had been edged in white had now turned red.

Clare paused long enough after Greta was dressed to spray the abrased forehead with Mediquik. Greta squinted her eyes and twisted her face away.

"That doesn't hurt," Clare said.

"Does too."

"It says right here on the can that it does not sting."

"Well."

"Let's go."

"Where're we going?"

Clare stopped in the hall. Greta stood a few feet away looking at the suitcase sitting on its little wheels. Clare reached back inside the bathroom and shut off the light. She looked at her watch.

"We should tell Papa we're going. He can tell Alyne. It's not quite his bedtime." She got Greta by the hand. "Come on, we'll go over to your grandfather first and tell him we're going to be away for a few days."

They went out the back door and into the shadowed backyard. Clare stopped. In order to get to Papa's house by going the back way, they would have to go within yards of the well. It had been filled in and covered again, but it was there, in the darkness beneath the orchard trees, and she didn't want to go past it.

Rain was falling lightly, and she used it as an excuse to Greta.

"We forgot the umbrella."

They went back into the kitchen, and Clare closed and locked the door. "We might as well go out the front. The umbrellas are there, and there's more light."

They weren't alone, she suddenly felt, and wondered with a terrible arrow of hope in her heart if Phillip had come into the house. She looked around at the brightly lighted kitchen, looking for signs of Phillip—his gloves or hat on the table by the door toward the garage. His keys on the hook. There was nothing. She saw Greta, standing inches behind her, and she was shivering. Automatically, Clare reached into the coat closet and brought out a raincoat and helped Greta into it.

She went into the front hall and looked toward the bedrooms. The hall light was still burning, her suitcase still sat on its little wheels. The silence in the house shouted that Phillip had not come home, and she began to realize that her feeling of not being alone was not a good feeling. The fear began turning to ice on her skin.

Mama, now it even wants me to kill you.

She looked at Greta and found her staring up at her quizzically, asking in silence what she was doing. Those blue eyes, big and pale in the dim light of the hall, unnerved her.

She took Greta's hand and pulled her toward the front door.

Mama, now it even wants me to kill you.

It was like a whisper at her shoulder, sibilant, virulent, deadly.

CHAPTER 17

THEY HAD REACHED the sidewalk where the street light shone down on black pavement and turned it to shining onyx in the night, before Clare realized she had forgotten an umbrella after all. But she wasn't going back just for an umbrella. Her hair didn't matter. Nothing mattered but getting away. Now she felt that whatever had been in the house was a terrifying thing, and as she glanced back at the house repeatedly, she shrank inwardly from it, from whatever was within it, or had been within it. As if it were no longer her home, no longer the house she had helped build.

She suddenly remembered their suitcases. She had left them in the house too.

She dreaded going back into it even for the suitcases, their clothes. But she had to. If she bought new things, it would take away money needed for other expenses.

Greta hurried along slightly behind her, pulled by Clare. The sound of her sneakers squishing on the damp sidewalk made Clare feel she was being followed by the uninvited quality in her house, as if it had come out of the house with them and was trailing them on the sidewalk. She cast swift looks behind, as they passed beneath the street light at the corner of Jonah's yard and then went up the dark driveway to his house, but she saw nothing—only the glistening street, dark in the night, and the houses with muted lights in the windows. Across the street from her father's house was Sergeant Donally's house, with a chain-link fence around the front yard, and a dim light showing in one window as if it came from somewhere deeper in the house. The house next door to it, in front of Alyne's, was lost within its trees, shrubs, and hedges. Clare looked at the tall hedges and found them intimidating, as if they hid the worst of her nightmares.

She readjusted Greta's hand in hers. Like a limp rag, it was slipping away, a damp little boneless appendage. She dropped it.

"Hurry, Greta. Grandfather will be asleep if we don't hurry." She felt Greta clutch her skirt, as if she were three years old again.

She cut across the grass to the walk and ran up the steps to the porch. A light in the parlor made a patchwork triangle of dim yellow against the dark underside of the porch.

"Papa's still up," she murmured aloud.

She tried the doorknob and found it locked. Papa never used to lock his doors. But perhaps Anne Reade had locked up before she went upstairs to her room.

She knocked and waited. She heard Greta's teeth chattering and felt her hand pulling on her skirt. Clare reached down and pried Greta's fingers loose and then held the soft little hand in hers again. Footsteps in the hall barely preceded the opening of the door. Anne's round face looked out.

"My goodness," she said, pulling the door open. "You surprised me, Clare. What on earth are you doing out on a rainy night like this? And not even a scarf on your hair!"

"The rain is very light. It doesn't matter." Clare put her free hand up to her hair and felt dampness. "It's good to be here," she said as she entered the hall, and meant it. Coming home was a comfort tonight. "I have a notion to stay." She tried a laugh that failed.

"Well, you're welcome, I'm sure. Hello, Greta. Your papa is in the parlor, Clare, just go right on in. He's sitting alert, wondering who could be knocking on his door on a dark and rainy night." Anne laughed. "I'll bring you two urchins a cup of hot chocolate each. Greta is shivering."

"Thanks. We'd love it."

Clare went into the parlor and saw Papa sitting forward in his chair, his elbows on the chair arms. His cane lay on the cluttered table at the side of his chair where lamplight threw the shadow of its crooked handle against the floor. There, on the carpet, it looked like a coiled serpent.

"Clare! What are you doing out? And not even a hat on your head. What's the problem?"

She kissed him on the forehead and almost said, No problem, but that wasn't true and she didn't feel like pretending. She sat down in a chair to his left and asked him how he was.

He began to tell her he was fine, as fine as a man his age could be, as his eyes found Greta and ran the length of her from head to toe. He paused as if taking a breath and said, "What's that child wearing?"

Clare looked at Greta as if seeing her for the first time. The raincoat was wide at the shoulders and hung to her ankles, dragging the floor in back. It was black, not dark blue, as Greta's coat was, and Clare realized she had put Stephanie's coat on Greta. But she didn't say so. Her papa, she knew, would tell her to take it off.

Then Jonah was saying, "That's Stephanie's coat, isn't it? Get it off that child!" He picked up his cane and pointed it, and its tip quivered not far from Greta's chest. His voice quivered when he repeated the command. "Get it off!"

Greta stared at him, unmoving. Clare got up and quickly pulled the damp, silky raincoat off Greta and folded it, smoothing it out, and laid it on the love seat. When Papa got in a temper about something, the best thing to do was obey as swiftly as possible and then pretend nothing had happened.

"Is your cold better, Papa?"

"What cold? I don't have a cold."

Clare sat down again and motioned silently for Greta to sit too. She backed up until her knees came against another chair, and then she hefted herself backward into it. Goosebumps stood out on her arms.

Papa sat with the cane across his knees now, one hand gripping the handle as if it were a weapon. And in a way it was his weapon, Clare thought. He had used it ever since Derek was born to intimidate the children, the two little ones, the ones he had bluntly told Clare and Alyne they did not need. Yet Clare had never really believed in her heart that he had meant it. He was not especially a child lover, but he didn't hate children either. He had sounded like a severe father at times, but he had always been a good and even gentle father. She had grown up adoring him. More, she thought, than Alyne had. She felt now like asking him if she could move home.

"Phillip left, Papa," she said. She hadn't meant to tell him that. It slipped out, and she was glad it had. She sighed.

"Left? Walked out on you and the child?"

"He said he wanted to get away for a week. He'd only taken off a week from work."

"Then he'll be back. Don't worry, Clare. But this was a bad time to go off and leave you. Phillip has always cared for his family, though. He'll be back."

He cared for Stephanie, Clare almost said aloud. "I came over to tell you Greta and I are going away too."

"Were are you going?"

"I don't know. Someplace where the sun is shining. Mexico or Arizona or Southern California. Maybe even Florida. We might even take a cruise."

Papa said nothing. Clare noticed his eyes were turning to the right and seemed to be staring at Greta. But Greta was doing nothing wrong. She was sitting on the edge of her chair, her legs hanging down primly. She wasn't even kicking her feet.

"You're taking the child with you," Papa said.

She wished he'd call her by name. "Yes, of course. I'm taking Greta."

In the silence she heard his fingernails clicking against the handle of the cane. He was staring straight ahead now, at the wall.

"Well, Papa," Clare rose and kissed his forehead again. "Take care."

He nodded. "And you be careful, Clare."

They went out, Greta's hand in hers. At the door she saw Anne coming with the hot chocolate.

"Oh, I'm sorry. I forgot, Anne."

Anne hesitated only a moment. "That's fine. Why don't you just take the cups with you? You can bring them back another time."

Clare took the cups of hot chocolate. She hadn't eaten more than a few bites all day long. And Greta had had no dinner that she knew of. The hot drink smelled delicious. She put one of the cups in Greta's hand and cautioned her not to spill it.

"We'll be gone a few days, Anne. We're taking a little vacation."

"Have a good time, and don't worry about the cups. As you know, the cupboards are full and these two won't be missed."

Clare went out onto the porch to find the rain had grown heavier. A sip of hot chocolate trailed into her stomach and warmed her, lifting her spirits.

"Let's run, Greta. Can you carry your cup and run without spilling it?"

"Yes."

They went down the steps and ran out into the rain.

Jonah stood at the window, the blinds raised, and watched the two figures jog down the walk to the sidewalk and then turn right. Bareheaded both of them, he thought, but his eyes were on the little one. There was something about her, something not right. It was almost as if his eyes could see a dark twin, larger, taller, running at her back. As they went out of sight beyond the tree trunks at the corner of his yard, he saw three figures, dark and without definite shape, three figures gliding smoothly away.

He wanted to reach out and pull Clare back safely away. But frowning, he lowered the blinds instead. When he turned, he saw that the folded raincoat was still on the love seat. His little girl's raincoat. Stephanie's.

He sat down in his chair just as Anne came in with a cup of hot chocolate. She moved with ease and quickness, which pleased him, and made him feel as if he weren't surrounded by old age and impending illnesses. Her face, always managing to be cheerful, even made him forget for a moment that his two grandchildren were dead. Gone. An old man needed heirs. It made life worthwhile. Ultimately, it was all that counted, to know that what you had worked for in your lifetime was going into your family. Anne had said to him, "You still have three grandchildren, Jonah," in one of her serious moments. "I know that you loved Kenny and Stephanie very much, but you do have William, Derek, and Greta."

She didn't understand. No one understood. He couldn't help his partialities. He knew he had them. When his own daughters were born he was too busy to notice the first one. She was a little creature who took up his wife's time at night. But the second child took hold of his heart. And then with the grandchildren, the firstborn, Stephanie, had been the special one and he had known he would never have another grandchild like Stephanie. But when Kenny came along, he was the perfect grandson. The children born after that were like little strangers.

He knew his partialities, and lately a thought had been recurring in his mind. He was being punished for something. His loved ones were dying. Greta had said she killed them, and he thought, perhaps she did, perhaps she did.

He put his head back against his chair and closed his eyes, and Anne took it as a dismissal and left the room. It was what he wanted. He needed to be alone. His thoughts went with Clare, willing her to return to his house, to his care, where she would be safe. Wishing her to be a little girl again, like her own child, Greta.

And knowing it could never be.

Clare shook rain off her hair, and Greta laughed.

"You look just like old Buster, Mama, shaking your head like that. When old Buster gets wet, he shakes all over."

Clare smiled. The door stood open behind them, and a couple of raindrops glistened on the wallpaper of the entrance hall. She put her hand on Greta's head and ruffled her hair. "Your hair is a little wet too, punkin. Drink up if you have any chocolate left in your cup. And we'd better go back to the coat closet and get our own raincoats. Oh ... I forgot ..."

Clare put her hand to her mouth, and Greta said, "That's okay, Mama. Grandfather will take care of it."

"Yes, sure. Let's get on the road, Greta, or we'll have to get a motel right here in our own town, and that wouldn't be any fun, would it?"

"No."

She felt almost happy as she followed her mother down the hall to the kitchen. It was almost like it used to be, although she was aware of a dull pain in her forehead and her finger hurt. Her mama had forgotten to take the ring off her finger, but later, when they were in a motel, she'd remind her again. Now she wanted to hurry away, as her mama wanted to.

... ssssnn ... oowww ... now, do it now, kill her noww ...

Greta stopped, terror curling in her stomach like thousands of worms, crawling out in every direction toward her skin, into her hair and spine, paralyzing her. She wanted to scream NO! but even her breath was paralyzed. She watched her mother moving on down the hall toward the kitchen, and she saw the black cape hanging in the air between them. She tried to scream, to warn Clare to run, run for her life.

CLARE TURNED at the choking sound. It hadn't sounded like Greta, but it had to have been. Greta stood in the hall, halfway back toward the door, the cup in her hand dangling and chocolate dripping out of it onto the carpet. She stood with her mouth twisted and open, her eyes huge and round. The terror was almost an aura around her, it was so visible. Clare felt it reaching her own body, her own awareness, slowly, strangely; something she didn't understand. She had come back into the house without the feeling she'd had when she left it. It was no longer filled with a sense of something alien. It was her house, where her suitcases were. She would get her things and Greta's, and leave.

The hall light was so dim she could hardly see Greta. It was as if a dark veil had grown between them, a screen behind which Greta was slowly disappearing. With a cold dread Clare realized that something was forming in the hall between them. Her eyes focused on this nearer quality, this black substance in the air, and she remembered something Greta had told her, as if her words were being spoken again.

... a black thing ... came out of the well ... it hates all of us ... it keeps whispering over my shoulder for me to kill ...

It was forming before Clare's eyes. Behind it Greta was gone, smothered by the black, thin cloak of its body. Clare could see the rounding of a head and, deep within the head, two pinpoints of light that blazed in hatred at her. She saw a tall figure wearing something dark, like a cape that covered it head to toe. The outlines were as real now as anything in front of her. Clare whirled, her movement in slow motion, as if she were stuck in a dream from which she could not escape. She tried to run, but she felt it coming closer to her, and she smelled it, dank, cold, putrid, like flesh rotting deep in a well, closed into perpetual black, darker than any night. She smelled its virulence and knew this was the thing that she had sensed in her house before they had gone to Papa's. She tried to run, and she felt her head explode with pain as something struck her. Her arms flailed out, reaching for the wall for support. But it never came.

SHE WAS SMALL, looking up at the girl tying something around her long hair. It was a pretty blue ribbon, the prettiest she had ever seen. The girl had a smooth, curved cheek that tapered down from the bones on each side of her eyes. She saw the face clearly and knew she had seen it many times before. She wanted to grow up to be like Adriene, pretty Adriene. She finished tying the ribbon and then she floated through the air toward a door and opened it and ran out, her skirts leaping around her legs. At the road, a gravel road, she stopped and looked all around. Alyne followed her, and Adriene pointed a finger at her and frowned and shook her head, and Alyne the child pulled back, disappointment sharp as barbs in her dream. Adriene walked down the road and looked behind her again, and then she ran. Alyne knew where she was going, and she followed. She could feel the tickle of leaves against her face as she spied on Adriene. She saw Adriene's legs, all the way to her panties, as the man pulled up her skirt. She saw the man kissing Adriene, and she saw the man's face, round, boyish, with hair light against the red of Adriene's.

The scene changed. She was hiding again, and fear coated her all over like water, as if she were submerged in its liquid form. She could hear the crying, the voice screaming, *"You'll be sorry ... you'll be sorry ..."*

Alyne woke, cold and shaking. She had thrown off her blanket and lay in the chilly air of the bedroom without cover. For a few minutes she didn't move. In his bed Ross slept quietly, his breathing deep and even.

But they weren't alone. Someone else was in the room. Or the dream had been so vivid a portion of it remained with her, making her feel as if the girl Adriene were here too, a physical body in the room.

Alyne stirred, reaching down for the blanket. Why was she having these dreams, these same dreams? At times she knew they were memories, surfacing while she slept, and yet at other times she wasn't so sure. If she had known the girl, why was it nobody else in the family had?

The man's face in the dream—a young Milton Crossover? She should go over and talk to him about it. Tomorrow?

The room was almost dark. The bedroom door stood open a few inches, she saw, and a thin line of light trailed in from the hall night light. And then she saw the figure standing at the foot of the bed.

Her heart lurched in terrible fear, almost coming into her throat to choke her. She lay with her head awkwardly up, staring at the figure.

Then she saw it was a child.

"Derek?" she asked softly.

There was no answer.

Alyne sat up and turned on the lamp on the table between the beds. She stared in astonishment at her niece, looking so tiny at the foot of the bed, her eyes round and focused blankly on a point of the wall above Alyne's head. Dozens of questions struggled for expression in Alyne's mind at once. What was she doing here? How did she get in? What was wrong with her?

Ross grunted, stirred, muttered a curse under his breath. Ross was not a pleasant person to wake when he was sleeping. He always came up with a frown and a muttered curse, so different from the wide-awake Ross. Alyne could remember laughing at him and saying, "If I'd known you were such a bear when you were asleep, I wouldn't have married you, Ross." That might be one point in living together before marriage, she had thought then, something Papa would have disowned her for. She could just hear him saying something like, *"I know you're female and you can't help that, but you don't have to be a fool too."* In fact, hadn't he said that to her more than once?

So many strange things going through her mind, while at the foot of her bed, little Greta stood as if she were in shock. Her face looked pale on one side and very dark and bruised on the other. Her fair hair hung down in long curls over each cheek, partially hiding them.

"Greta?" Alyne said aloud. "How did you get in?"

"What the hell is going on?" Ross grumbled, turning over in bed. "Turn out the damned light, Alyne. What time is it? Damn, I just got to bed, it seems ..." He was up on his elbow, and his words cut off as he stared at Greta.

"Mama?"

Alyne looked toward the door and saw William, standing back in the soft shadows of the hall. His voice had been quizzical and timid. He stood in rumpled pajamas, his dark brown hair tousled. Alyne turned her face toward him, but at last she began to move, knowing now that something terrible had happened. Where were Clare and Phillip?

"William," Ross said, getting up and picking up his robe from somewhere on the floor. "What are you doing up? What's she doing here? What's wrong?"

"I don't know, Dad," William said, and his voice sounded strained and frightened. He came into the bedroom, his pajamas looking too small. "I heard old Buster bark, and then whine, like he knew somebody who was out in the backyard. I got up and saw Greta at the patio doors. Just standing there, like this. Like she's standing now. I opened the door and she came in. She didn't say a word."

Alyne got Greta by the shoulders. "Greta? Are you awake?"

Ross asked, "What happened to her face?"

"Did she fall down today, William?"

William had backed up to stand in the doorway. He looked as if he'd like to leave. "Not that I know of." Alyne guided Greta toward the master bathroom. She turned on the bright overhead lights and felt oddly chilled and frightened at the look in the child's eyes. She was either walking in her sleep, as she must have been doing the night Kenny died, or she was in shock from something she had seen. Yet she hadn't been to bed. She was dressed in jeans. They were damp, as if she'd been out in the rain for a long time.

She was just about to wash Greta's face with cold water when suddenly she knew she must go find Clare and Phillip. The urgency pulled at her. She wanted to be doing a dozen things at a time, but going to Clare now was most urgent.

"William," she called, and her son came to the bathroom door. She pushed the dry washcloth into his hands. "Wash her face, William. I'm going over to Clare's."

In the bedroom she grabbed a robe and wrapped it around her. "Ross, you'd better call a doctor. Something is wrong with Greta."

"Who is her doctor?"

"I don't know. Call ours."

"Will it do any good? Isn't the idea now to go to the clinic at night or over to the hospital emergency room?"

"I don't know!" Alyne half-screamed in frustration. "I'm going over to Clare's."

"I'm going with you. We can see about doctors later. The kid looks to me like she's still asleep. She probably just got up and walked out of her bedroom, out of the house, and over to ours. Her folks probably don't even know she's gone."

"She isn't dressed for bed, Ross."

"Mom!" William cried frantically. "Mom! Dad! There's blood on Greta's hands!"

Alyne rushed back into the bathroom. William was holding Greta's fingers out to the light, and something reddish stained their tips. On the heel of her left hand was a damp red stain that when wiped off, looked brownish on the cloth. Alyne saw the large ring, turned inward, taped on the back to make it fit, and saw that Greta's finger looked swollen, but she paid no attention to it. Kids would do these things, she knew. She'd had a ring from a boy once and taped it so it would fit. She'd worn it about three months before he decided he wanted it back. Other fleeting, useless thoughts swept through her mind, like dreams, pieces of dreams—the swinging skirt, so pretty, swinging out into a full circle as its wearer whirled, just to please herself. A white skirt with blue rosebuds. For a moment it seemed she heard laughter.

She took the washcloth and rinsed it out and began washing Greta's face, trying to be gentle on the bruised area, the discolored skin where redness circled one eye, and a deep blue had settled into the thin skin beneath her eye.

"That's a hand print, Mama," William said. "Somebody hit Greta. It was a big hand, see."

Greta began to whimper. The distant, vacant look left her eyes and one of disorientation and fear took its place. Her trembling hands reached out for Alyne. "Mama," she said.

Alyne stroked her hair. "You're all right, Greta. You're here with me, Aunt Alyne. William found you at the back door. You're all right, dear. Were you asleep?"

"Where'd you get the blood on ..."

Alyne poked William in the ribs with her elbow. William shrugged. But Greta seemed not to have heard him. Her whimpers were turning to sobs. She clutched Alyne.

"Mama," she said again. "Help ... Mama."

Alyne straightened. She saw then that Ross was not with them. Sometime during the past few minutes he had slipped out. And she had to go too. Now again she felt the strong need, the urgency to get to her sister.

"William, stay with her. I'll be right back. Take her into the kitchen and get her something to drink. Something hot."

Alyne hurried out, her house slippers gathering moisture in their soft toes.

The lights were on in Clare's house. The front hall light spilled across the walk and the lawn, and Alyne saw as she crossed the lawn that the door stood open.

When she reached the threshold, she heard Ross's voice, and by his one-sided conversation she knew he was calling the police. She slowed, trembling so hard her teeth chattered. What would she find in this house? A family massacre? Phillip dead? Clare?

Ross was coming down the hall. When he saw her he stopped in silence for an instant, as if she had startled him. Then he came on, got her by the arm, and turned her back toward the door.

"There's no reason for you to go in there."

"Are they ... ?"

"Phillip isn't in the house. I don't know where he is. It's Clare. There's no doubt she's dead. She may have been dead for quite awhile because she's ... cool."

Alyne pushed past him, while he grabbed at her again and almost ripped her sleeve away. "Don't go in there!"

"That's my sister!" Alyne screamed. "She's my sister, for God's sake!"

She ran into the bedroom hall. Clare was lying crumpled on the floor, as Kenny had lain on the grass and Stephanie with her head on the walk, and for a moment Alyne didn't feel she would be able to stand it. She sank to her knees beside Clare and saw her blue eyes, round and staring, so much like Greta's at this moment, with a blankness within them that said their depth, their soul, was gone. The light that had been Clare had slipped away and would never be here anymore for Alyne.

She heard the keening cry, but it seemed as if it came from a netherworld where all the mourners of all the dead ones had gone, where they now stood on the banks of a muddy river that ran swift and deadly, taking the souls away forever. She heard the keening and felt the pain, and she was reduced to those sensations of hearing and hurting in her heart, so that she felt as if she drifted in a world foreign to earth, where a person was made only of pain.

SOMEONE TOUCHED HER SHOULDER, and she turned and saw it was the red-haired girl. She was smiling down at her, but the smile wasn't kind or pleasant. It was teasing. Alyne got up and followed her. She saw the white skirt whirl and stand out almost like an umbrella, with the girl's long, tanned legs looking so pretty. She saw the rosebuds and the white panties the girl was wearing. She saw the tiny edging of lace around the legs of the panties. Then she was following her across a gravel road. The girl turned and pointed her finger at Alyne, and Alyne the little child shrank back, and sat down in the gravel and dirt of the road and began to sift the dirt between her fingers. When she found a pebble she threw it. She threw a pile of pebbles toward where the girl had disappeared. Into the green bushes.

She got up and slipped quietly on across the road, and then went down on her belly beneath the green bushes, and she saw the girl again, standing on a porch. She was opening a door, and then she slid through the opening and was gone.

Alyne followed. She climbed high steps to a porch, so high she had to use her hands to pull herself up. And then she was at the door and looking into a strange dark hall. She saw a staircase leading up and the white skirt of the girl as she disappeared at the top of the stairs. Alyne slipped through the door and followed.

"ALYNE."

The hand was on her shoulder and Alyne jerked back, and both scenes swam for a moment before her eyes. Her sister, on the floor, staring upward, her mouth drooping open with drops of blood gathered there, blood smeared down her cheek as if a small hand had tried to brush it away, blood jelling in her ear, and the smear there too. And yet it seemed she was still in the shadowed, strange hallway, where the staircase rose on the left, dark posts against a dark wall rising into a dark balcony.

"Alyne."

The voice wasn't Ross's, it was Conrad's. She heard sirens now, drifting off, winding down from a single wail, as both police cars and an ambulance stopped at the house.

"I don't know what happened to her," Alyne said, weeping silently, the tears rolling out of her eyes as if she had no control whatsoever, as if all her pain, her grief for Kenny, Stephanie, and Clare, were in some way mixed with the girl in the circle skirt, as if all of it had finally laid its cold and deadly hand on her.

"I'll take her home," Ross said.

"You'll be available?"

"Yes. I'll just get my wife to bed. She can't tell you a thing I can't, and I would just like to let her rest."

Rest. Just let her rest. How could she ever rest when something was tearing at her heart, her memories? It was as if she could turn all these deaths around and make of them only nightmares, if the other would just come true in her mind.

She didn't argue with Ross. She depended on him, knew she could depend on him. When anything went wrong in the family, Ross could become the dominant individual he was at times. With Kenny, Ross had just gone on back to work, and she had understood his need; but now he had turned and was going to help her. She could give in and know that the children would be taken care of, and the police too. Whatever the police wanted.

Who was killing the family? What was killing the family?

Ross took her into the bedroom and made her get into bed, and then he brought her a glass of water and one of the sleeping pills that were so seldom used.

Even when she was alone, even with her head covered, she could see the lights at Clare's house. She knew when the ambulance left, and she thought of her father. At last she thought of her father.

She threw back the cover and fumbled through the darkness where only stray lights from the cars at Clare's penetrated the drawn blinds. She finally found her robe and pulled it on, feeling as if her fingers had become thick and clumsy like sausages, and looped the sash at the waist. She went out into the hall and heard voices in the living room.

Men, two voices, talking to Ross. One of the men was Conrad. His voice had a softer, deeper quality than Ross's or the other man's. It reminded her of her papa's voice, gentle, but capable of being very stern, very strict. Only with Clare had he been totally gentle. Then, only a bit less so with Kenny and Stephanie. Stephanie had come first, Grandfather's little doll he had called her, and Alyne could remember seeing him walk along the alley with the hand of that tiny girl in this. The two of them, so slowly, the toddler and the grandfather. How his eyes had glowed with his love.

And now she had to get to him. Clare, the light of his life. Would he be able to survive this? Could she bear to lose him too? Would she lose all her loved ones? Would Derek and William and Ross and Greta be taken too? Did it have something to do with her—so long ago—going where she was not supposed to go? Following a girl no one knew? It was as if the girl in the well had only been a figment of her dreams, of her imagination, and in her bringing forth of that girl again, she was causing the deaths of all her family. Where was the beginning and the ending of reality? Where did the dreams end and reality start?

Memories ... not dreams.

Memories.

She slipped silently away from the front hall and went through the family room to the sliding glass doors. The night was cool, and the air seemed to penetrate the velour of her robe and turn it damp and cold.

Old Buster came up and sniffed at her ankles, and she realized she was barefoot. He started to follow her down the alley, but she sent him back.

The gravel in the alley poked into the tender soles of her feet, so she walked on the grassy verges, going beneath the black shadows of the trees, feeling her way along the fence behind her papa's yard. She found the gate and let herself through.

Light and dark filled the backyard, with only a small piercing of the light where the trees filtered the street light down at the corner of the front yard. Yet even in the almost total dark along the wall, Alyne could see the other figure.

At first she thought someone was walking toward her, or away from her, along the rear walk, but there was no sound, no footsteps. Then she saw more clearly the outline of the white skirt, the white shoulders, and the shadowed area in the back where the girl's long hair fell almost to her waist.

Sound came to her. A fine little tune, almost a song, wordless, with little form. It was the girl, going along the walk, singing, her voice young and fine and happy.

Alyne stood still. She was not dreaming, not now. And she was not seeing a ghost.

She had stood here once long ago, and she had seen the girl in the white dress go along this walk and had heard her singing.

But now, as if she were a ghostly illusion after all, the girl was gone. The darkness of the backyard was broken only by the spots of light that came through the trees. There was no white-dressed figure.

CHAPTER 18

ALYNE WENT UP onto the porch and into the kitchen. She could see a light burning in the hall, but the house was quiet, so quiet it might have been empty. Then she heard the murmur of Anne's voice somewhere.

She knocked on the inner door and called out, "Anne."

The answer came a moment later. "Alyne? Come on up, please."

She hurried down the hall and up the front stairs. The door to the old master bedroom at the front of the second floor stood open. Her father stood by the window dressed in trousers and shirt with suspenders. He was in his stocking feet. His face looked as if someone had drained all the blood away.

Anne was in a kind of puffy night cap and a robe, and would have looked comical if Alyne could have seen humor in anything. Anne grasped her arm.

"I'm so glad you came, Alyne. It's terrible, what has happened. But I can't see what good it would do for your father to go to the hospital now. She won't even be there, will she? Clare, I mean. Her body. Ross came over and told us she is dead too, and your father insists on going to the hospital."

"I'm going. That's my baby girl. Nobody is going to stop me. Will you hand me my coat, Alyne. This woman is trying to keep me from getting my own coat."

"Papa," Alyne said, putting her hand on his arm. "Why don't we just go downstairs and talk? I don't think they're taking her to the hospital, Papa. She ... her body was already cold. I think she'd been dead an hour or two. Longer, maybe. I don't know how long it takes for a body to turn cold, but ..."

"A body! That's my little girl, not a *body!*"

His jaw quivered and shook, and his shoulders heaved and were more bowed than ever. Alyne wanted to clasp him in her arms and weep with him, allow him to weep on her shoulder, but she knew he never would.

"Anne, would you make us some coffee? Make it strong, please. Ross gave me a pill to make me sleep, and it's made me a little dizzy. I'm going to stay with Papa. We'll go downstairs and sit and talk. You might call Ross for me too, please, and tell him where I am. Tell him to watch the children. But of course I know he will."

EVERY LIGHT in the house was on. The body had been taken away, but a few of the police lingered, one of them yawning, looking around in such a haphazard fashion that Conrad knew he was going to pull out soon too. And tomorrow, or as soon as the medical examiner's report came in, there would be a report filed that would close the case, just as there had been with Stephanie Shepley and Kenny Kerwin and, of course, the unknown girl in the well.

"Nothing here," the detective said to Conrad. "You'll find it's the same thing as with the other two. She'll have a burst blood vessel in the brain, caused either by her fall or which precipitated the fall. She and the little kid were alone. I think I'll turn in."

Conrad didn't mind if they left. Outside the door was one of the officers who had responded to the call, and he would probably be leaving too.

"I'll take care of it," Conrad said. "I live just across the street. I want to talk to these people some more."

He was glad to be left alone. He wandered slowly through the house, seeing that it was neat and fashion pretty, with colors coordinated. Only the family room and bedrooms looked lived in. He saw the chair that obviously belonged to the man of the house. It was dark brown leather or soft plastic, a recliner, with its own table and lamp. Newspapers, both today's, had been laid on the table and were still folded. There was no sign that Phillip Shepley had come home tonight, or if he had, that he had done his usual evening thing of sitting in his chair and reading his paper.

Conrad went back to the bedroom section and into the master

bedroom. The bed had not been slept in, though the spread was rumpled. He looked into the closet and saw no signs that Phillip had packed a bag. The suitcase in the hall contained only a woman's clothes, presumably Clare Shepley's. The tag on the suitcase listed her name and address. In one of the other bedrooms he saw pictures and posters that indicated it had been Stephanie's room. Across the hall was a guest room, and the next room belonged to Greta. Here things had been brought out and were crammed into a small suitcase.

So Clare had been planning to leave, taking the little girl with her. But where was the husband?

He went back out into the hall and stood looking at the place where Clare's body had lain. There was no indication now that she had ever fallen here. Knocked down by a hand strong enough to burst a blood vessel in her brain? Or, as was believed by the other detectives, a natural weakness in the structure of the brain, the vessels, the arteries, causing the death first and then the fall. Like weak bones in elderly people causing falls.

He went down the hall shaking his head. There was a pattern forming that he didn't like. None of the three people who had died were alone, and each of them was in the company of only one other person at the time. Greta. Yet she herself was showing signs of the abuse. Her fear. The bruising on her face. There was one other possibility. Greta was protecting that third person. The man who struck the death blows.

Her daddy? Where was Phillip Shepley?

Before putting out a call to bring in Phillip Shepley, he needed to talk to the rest of the family, and especially to Greta.

He turned out the lights when he left the house and carefully locked the doors. His car was out front. He had driven over because he knew he might have to go on to the station. But he left it parked at the curb in front of Clare's house and walked next door to Alyne's. He was relieved to see lights were still burning. The porch light was on. The detectives who had been there ahead of him had already left, the taillights of their car disappearing down the street.

Conrad rang the doorbell and waited, standing beneath the bright bulb of the porch light, feeling exposed and vulnerable. Feeling as though someone or something was staring at him. His eyes were pulled toward the dark house across the street and to an upstairs window. Milton. Of course he would be awake, disturbed by the noise in the neighborhood in the thin hours of the morning, when night was its darkest. He made a mental note to ask Milton if he had been awake before the siren disturbed the area, if he might have seen something.

The door opened and Ross, a dark covering of beard beginning to show on his lower jaw, looked out at Conrad.

"I'm sorry to bother you again, Ross, but I need to get a few things straight."

Ross stood back and scratched his head. He looked ready to drop, not from fatigue but from confusion, perhaps, or simply emotional overload.

"I don't know what there is to get straight, but come on in."

"I needed to talk to Greta, mostly, but I suppose she's asleep by now."

"Yes, long ago. My wife went over to stay with her father, and so I just put the kid to bed in the spare room. I think she was asleep before her head hit the pillow."

"I didn't ask before. But where is the child's father?"

"Phillip." Ross led the way into a living room that didn't look any more used that it had two hours ago. He sat down on a chair and crossed his legs at the knees. His robe fell open to reveal the leg of blue and white plaid pajamas. He was barefoot, and the hair on his leg was as black as the stubble on his chin.

"Yes, Phillip Shepley."

"I don't know where he is. I hadn't even thought about him until one of the detectives asked me. He wasn't home, obviously."

"He isn't home now, let's say."

Ross's eyebrows lifted. "You mean you think he might have had something to do with Clare's death?"

"I think there are indications of abuse here. Greta, I noticed this evening, has a large bruise on her cheek. All three of the others, the ones who died, could have suffered the same kind of abuse."

"No," Ross said, disbelief in his voice. "No, you've got it all wrong. You're thinking Phillip would strike any of them? No, no way." He shook his head and turned sideways in his chair, still shaking his head. It was clear to Conrad the thought had never entered Ross's head before.

"Besides," Ross added. "My own boy, Kenny ..." Pain flitted across his face, causing him to pause, to frown, and to stare at the wall behind Conrad for a moment. Then he said, "I understand the police, the medical examiner, decided that he hadn't been struck on the head, that whatever abrasions he had could have been sustained when he fell. That a massive brain hemorrhage occurred. And that it was the same with Stephanie. And, I'd say, the same with Clare."

Conrad kept quiet, wondering what Ross would make of it, watching his face change, the frown fade, his eyes grow confused again. Then he looked at Conrad.

"What's happening to this family, Donally? That's too much of a coincidence. Who's next?"

"That's what I was thinking, Ross. No matter how it looks to the law or to the ME, the coincidence is there, and I'm not a believer in coincidences."

"I never was either. After awhile, when a pattern forms, there has to be a force at work. There's a force at work here, isn't there? But you're wrong when you think Phillip might be a closet abuser. Someone known only to the family."

"Maybe not even to all the family?" Conrad suggested.

Ross looked at him again. "You don't think I would have known it?"

"Are you around a lot?"

Ross turned in the chair again, crossing his legs in the other direction, almost squirming beneath the question. "Well, no, I'm not. But if anything like that had ever gone on, I'd have heard about it. These families, Alyne's and Clare's, have always been close. The kids have played together all their lives. I've seen Phillip's daughters at least once a week since the day they were born, and I can tell you he had two happy daughters until this thing ..." He paused, tapping the fingers of one hand against his knee, staring at the wall again. "Phillip worshipped Stephanie. He was knocked out of his tree at her death."

"But where is he tonight?"

Ross shook his head slowly. "I don't know. I guess I didn't even think of him in all the confusion."

"Greta didn't mention him?"

"She wasn't capable of mentioning anything. The doctor who examined her said she seemed to be in some form of mental shock, or block. He advised just putting her to bed."

Conrad got up. His watch indicated it was close to four o'clock, and the night was still very dark. There was nothing more that could be done tonight.

"I'll be back in the morning," he said. "To talk to Greta."

Ross got up and went with him to the door. Conrad heard the lock click behind him.

He stood under the shadows of the porch after the light was turned out, looking across the street. He still had the feeling that Milton was at one of his bedroom windows staring down at him. But he also had the feeling that Milton would not answer a knock on his door.

THEY HAD NOT GONE DOWNSTAIRS. Papa had remained at the window until his legs were trembling visibly, then he sat down on the chair by the window and leaned his head against its high back. Alyne sat on the cedar chest at the foot of the bed.

The furniture in the high-ceilinged bedroom was old and dark, the bed more than a hundred and fifty years old, its intricately carved headboard reaching ten feet up the wall. Matching pieces, chests, dressers, end tables were scattered about the room, giving it a heavy, dark, enclosed feeling. Alyne could remember the sense of comfort she'd had as a child when she was allowed to come into this room and climb the funny little steps into the high bed. Only a few times had that happened. Once, she recalled, during a thunderstorm. And another time after her baby sister was born, and her mother lay in this big, soft bed with the tiny new baby in her arms. Alyne had wanted to be there too, and her papa had lifted her up and put her into the middle of the bed, and that night the four of them had slept together, or had gone to sleep together. The next morning she had awakened in her own bed, and thereafter, because the baby had a bed of her own too, Alyne was convinced to go to sleep in her own bed.

Pictures adorned all of the tops of the chests, most of the tables, and even the dresser. Pictures of Clare when her hair was long and curly. She had looked enough like Greta to be her twin sister. Yet, oddly, Papa had favored not Greta but Stephanie. Pictures of Stephanie were here too, in ornate frames. Stephanie as a little girl with dark pigtails. Stephanie growing up. A large photograph of Kenny hung on the wall.

As Papa talked, going back to his days with her mother before either child was born, Alyne got up and wandered about the room looking at the pictures. She was looking for William, Derek and Greta, and finally found one in which they were part of a family gathering in which all of them, including Papa, had stood still for a picture taken by Anne. She remembered the day, Father's Day, last year.

"Anne framed that," Papa said. "She said I needed a family portrait."

Alyne thought of the picture in the album in which someone had been cut off, and for the first time she wondered about her mother's family.

"My mother, Papa. What kind of family did she have? In the old album that you gave to me, the one that was hers, it seems to start only with her marriage to you. Did she have any brothers or sisters?" Was the girl in the white dress with the blue rosebuds her sister? Yet, if she had been, wouldn't Papa have known her?

"Rebecca came out here from somewhere in the East. I've forgotten the name of the town now. She came to teach school, and in those days traveling cross country wasn't done as easily as it is now. There were trains and cars, of course, but it was war time and there was no air travel, and it took days to go from coast to coast. The big war was just ending when we got married, so we just went back once to see her people. Her mother had died when she was quite young, and her father married again. There was an older brother, but he was killed in the war. Actually, Rebecca came here to marry some young soldier. I guess it doesn't do any harm for you to know that now. She was a beautiful girl."

His eyes had found an early photograph of a blond girl, smiling, her face tilted to one side seductively, the way photographers used to pose their subjects. Her hair was pulled up into a forties' pompadour on top and hung long over her shoulders. She was wearing a blue suit with a white collar, and a tiny pillbox hat. She was pretty, but Alyne had never thought she or Clare had looked much like that picture, nor, for that matter, had the mother she remembered looked much like it. Mother, in her memory, had short, blondish hair, more light brown, cut in a pageboy that curled under just below her ears. She had been slightly plump and very comfortable to be hugged by.

Papa was saying, "She never had any sisters. She didn't really have a very big family, and there was nothing for her to want to go back to, since she wasn't particularly fond of the stepmother."

"What did she die of, Papa? What was wrong with her heart?"

"Who?"

He seemed to have left her. He was staring into the past, she felt, but not past her mother's part. He was looking toward a photograph of Clare, and his eyes looked old, as they never had before, as if the color had been just recently drained from them.

"My mother?"

His lips moved, but he was silent. Then he said, "Her death certificate is in the safe, if you want to see it."

"No, I just want to hear it from you."

He shook his head. "She sickened. That was all. She just sickened, the way people used to do sometimes. Still do, I reckon. The doctors don't know everything. They said it was her heart."

"She was happy, you know, Papa. She had a good life. Everything always went her way, pretty much."

"Your mother?" the question was sharp, his glance toward her like a sudden fling of a dart.

"No, Clare. Clare had a happy, secure life." Except for Phillip, she thought to herself. Clare had come to her a few times talking about how Phillip didn't seem to know she existed anymore.

Phillip.

It was the first time she had thought of him. But Papa had picked up on her statement about Clare and was talking. Clare when she was a toddler, Clare when she started to school. Clare.

She didn't want to interrupt him. Let him talk, and then let him sleep. This was what she had wanted. She wanted her father to have someone who would listen, who would encourage him to talk out his feelings about Clare, who was still his baby. But Alyne's thoughts were on Phillip now. What had Phillip been doing when Greta left the house after Clare's death? Where was Phillip?

Jonah allowed Alyne to help him into bed, for the first time in his life, and Alyne made sure the covers were just right, and the room darkened as he liked it. At the door she looked back, but said nothing. Then she slipped out of the room and went quietly through the halls, down the stairs, and out the back door.

The east was turning deep rose, and a gray, dim light was beginning to infiltrate the shadows of night. She was not sleepy. She felt as if she would never be sleepy again.

She went down the alley and across the back lawn to the patio doors. Ross had left them unlocked. She stood for a moment on the patio looking toward Clare and Phillip's house, and then on impulse she crossed the lawn, ducked under the rows of citrus trees that separated the two lawns, and went to the garage.

Clare's car was still in the driveway, but Phillip's was not there, and it was not in the garage.

Puzzled, she returned to her own house and checked on Ross and the kids. They each seemed to be sleeping soundly. In his own bed, Ross seemed not to have moved since he stretched out on his back.

Greta was in the guest room, her light hair against the blue of the pillowcase. The room was inordinately dark, as if dawn weren't bursting in the east, as if the window weren't uncovered. The corner beyond the bed especially seemed filled with a black nothingness, a depth of night lingering, and Alyne stared at it, a feeling rising in her that it was more than shadow. The uneasiness was turning to fear, irrational, unexplainable.

She almost withdrew from the room, telling herself it was nerves, but she felt as if she were leaving Greta close to a danger that had no name, a terrible danger from which she would not be protected. Alyne slipped her hand inside the door, along the wall, and pushed the light switch.

The shadow in the corner seemed to linger, even with the ceiling light flooding the room in soft white, and for a moment Alyne felt she was looking at the shadow of someone who stood between the corner and the light. Someone who was tall and distorted by the light. She saw the bulge of a head on shoulders that dispersed under the light, and she saw appendages at the sides, like arms sticking stiffly away, but most of all was the horror of the hand-like clumps at the ends of the arms. Large, with fingers spread, moving, rising. Icy waves of warning and terrible fear broke out over Alyne, as if she had been plunged into a world that had never known warmth or light. A black voice of terror and darkness, perpetual ... endless ...

Death.

She was looking at death, and she knew it. At death at its worst, a death in which the body dies but something else lives on to suffer in torment for all of eternity.

She brushed her hand across her eyes and looked again, and saw the corner bare, the wallpaper of geometric pastels adorned with a painting of a mountain scene, and on the facing walls at the corner, two field scenes carved in wood by someone who'd had a booth at one of the arts and crafts shows. There was nothing else in the corner.

But the sensation of intense fear lingered in her like the shadows of night lingered in the yard outside the window. She had felt the danger of something that had been outside herself.

Greta suddenly began moving. Her hands went up to her head, and her head turned back and forth on the pillow. The ceiling light was waking her, and Alyne reached back to turn it out before the waking was complete, but then Greta began to cry.

"Mama. Mama. No, no, no."

Her head tossed, and Alyne went to the bed and looked down at her, and then was stunned by what she saw. Greta's cheek was dark blue with purple in the area beneath her eye, as if she'd suffered a severe blow from a large hand. The child was whimpering and sobbing, the words now only mumbled and incoherent.

Alyne sat down on the bed and drew her up into her arms and held her. Greta's sobs softened to deep, soft murmurs of anguish. She relaxed against Alyne's breasts, curling in against her like a kitten with its mother.

WHILE HIS HOUSE was still heavy with shadows, before the streaks of red sunlight had crossed his back porch, Milton began to build. He carried lumber from the meager pile in the kitchen and nailed the front door shut, the boards fitted so closely together that not even a ray of light could have passed it. He nailed the boards over the stained glass in the door, over the jambs and onto the walls. When he had finished with the door, he went into the unheated, closed room that was the parlor, unused all these years since his mother's death, and proceeded to nail boards over all the windows there, the curtains plastered beneath the boards. He was sealing himself into a lightless world, a place where no one could enter. Still, he was terrified, and he wondered if she would be able to find him anyway. He looked around for other substances that would protect him, and at last remembered the books on the occult that his mother had kept in her bedroom.

He paused in the darkened parlor, where only a pale filter of light made its way through the top of an east window where the board had been nailed an inch too low, and considered fully the occult. Thirty-three years ago he thought his mother a little flaky because of her beliefs, her willingness to believe in anything. But now ... now he wondered if she had been wiser than he.

He didn't want to go up to her bedroom, but he would. He would if he had to. But later, after he had finished the sealing of his house. Last night there had been another murder across the street. He had been awakened by the sirens, and he had gone to an upstairs window and watched as a body was taken away on a stretcher.

Tonight there would be another murder. They were coming more and more often, and there would be no survivors. The police were helpless against this killer. He couldn't turn to them for protection. Even if they weren't helpless against this killer, he couldn't turn to them for protection. He had to protect himself.

He went to his pile of lumber in the kitchen and found there were only two boards left. He'd have to go back outside, where he had found some old half-rotten boards in a stack beside the shed. He had bought them years ago and the reason was long forgotten. But they were there, and the cats hunted among them and found such tidbits as chipmunks and mice and even a few snakes.

In his kitchen he remembered he had not fed his cats. They came to him meowing around his feet, and he squelched his first impulse to kick them away. Didn't they feel the urgency? Didn't they realize he had other, more important things to do? But they were only cats after all, and he bent and stroked the fur of the one he had injured, and then he got a sack of dry feed out of the bottom cabinet door and dumped a bunch of it into the communal pan. He didn't have time to put water or milk on it, and he didn't have time to open meat for them. He kicked the cabinet door shut and hurried out of the house for more boards, before it became too late for boards to help.

He was stooped over the wood pile, stacking boards onto his arms, when the voice spoke.

Milton stifled a scream, dropped one of the boards on his toe, and gasped at the pain. He looked over his shoulder and saw no one.

"Getting ready to build something, Milton?" Conrad Donally's voice asked.

Milton's first explosion of fear turned to anger, to terrible fury at being disturbed again on his own property. He looked, and finally found his neighbor with his head above the vines on the fence that divided their property.

"I'm very busy, Donally," Milton said, and readjusted the boards on his arms. His toe still hurt, and he wondered if he would lose the toenail. He had done that once when he was a boy, and remembered still the dreadful appearance of the nail before it came off, and the awful pain. It had oozed pus and blood out from beneath the nail, as the nail seemed to thicken and rise. Miraculously, after the old nail came off, a fresh, pink new one was there underneath.

"What are you building, Milton? Shelves or something?"

Had his neighbor always been this nosy, or was it the policeman coming out in him? Milton wondered irritably if he'd ever be rid of Donally. Why did he have to have a policeman next door? Having anyone next door was bad enough, but this was getting to be far worse than a nuisance.

He kept his lips pressed thinly together and did not answer.

"I need to talk to you again, Milton. Shall I come over, or can you answer the questions I have to ask now, over the fence?"

He had been given a choice. If he didn't stay and talk, Donally would come over. The boards were getting heavy in his arms.

"Just let me lay these on the porch," Milton said in resignment. "Though I can't imagine what you'd have to ask me. I don't know anything about what's going on across the road."

"How'd you know that was what I wanted to ask?"

Milton didn't answer. He reached the steps to the porch and struggled to open the door with one hand while hanging onto the stack of boards with the other. Fortunately, the boards were quite short. In fact, some of them might be too short for some of the windows, but he'd make them do somehow, even if he had to nail one board to the end of the other.

The hand came past his shoulder and pulled the door open, and for an instant Milton was so startled his heart came into his throat and he almost dropped his load. Then he saw it was a man's hand, and hair grew on the wrist. A glance over his shoulder showed him Conrad Donally, smiling a little as if he were enjoying some private joke, and Milton knew the tall, rangy man had vaulted the fence.

"Here," Conrad said, helping himself to part of the boards in Milton's arm. "Let me give you a hand. Where do you want this stuff?"

Milton started to tell him to just leave it on the porch, but before he could finish his instructions, Conrad had already gone into the kitchen. He put the boards down on the floor with the two that remained from the last pile. Milton saw him looking down the hall. The front door, with the boards, was visible in the gloomy light.

Milton dropped his load and brushed the debris off his shirt. Cleaning house, or trying to keep a clean house, was no longer an issue. He just wished that Conrad would go away and leave him alone. He wished he had the guts to tell him.

"What's wrong with your cat, Milton?" Conrad asked. "It's limping. Looks to me like its shoulder is out of place."

"I don't know what's wrong with it. Jumped off of something and hurt itself, I guess."

"You need to take it to a vet."

Milton didn't answer. He stood in the middle of his cluttered kitchen and waited for Conrad to ask his questions and leave.

Conrad pulled out a chair from the kitchen table and sat down, one leg up and resting ankle on knee. He took a notebook from his pocket and leaned back in the chair. Milton stared at him, at his audacity at coming into his house uninvited and now making himself at home. In another minute he'd be asking for coffee.

"You're up early, Milton," Conrad said.

Milton's jaw quivered with the pressure of teeth against teeth. "I always rise early," he said, and didn't add that he'd actually never gone to bed. He hadn't been to bed in three nights. He had closed himself into the office, the small, tight room where the window was tightly boarded, where he could watch the door, where his cats could stay with him.

"You're boarding up your house, Milton," Conrad said, easily, casually, looking relaxed as he read something in his notebook. "I see you've got your front door covered, and I've been hearing you pounding over here. Are you covering all the windows? Or only the ones on the first floor?"

"I—I—I—don't think that's any of your business, Conrad. What other questions did you want to ask me? I don't know anything about what happened across the road last night. I can't tell you a thing. I was here in my house."

"How'd you know anything happened?"

"I—I—" His spluttering was caused more from anger and indignation than from the fear that trembled always just beneath his skin. He was amazed that his hands were steady. But he clasped them at his sides in awful tension and felt the building of a tension headache. He cleared his throat and tried again. "I heard the siren. I was awakened by it." That was true. His neck had been hurting, twisted as it was. He had gone to sleep in his chair and the siren had been like a gunshot to his brain.

"So then you watched what was going on? From your bedroom window?"

"I might have. I checked, certainly, to see what had happened, but all I saw were the police cars, the ambulance, and the stretcher being taken away."

"Yet you haven't asked me who died last night."

Milton pressed his lips together. Then he blurted, "It doesn't matter who. They'll all go, one by one."

Conrad lifted his head and looked hard at Milton, and Milton realized he had said the wrong thing.

"Why do you say that, Milton?"

Milton shrugged. "It's looking that way, that's all. I can't tell you anything, Conrad. I've told you all I know."

"Let's go back to the killing of Stephanie. You ran across the road.

Think again, Milton, did you see anyone else, a third person? Back in the hall, perhaps?"

"No. No one. I didn't go close enough. I just saw the girls in the yard. I mean when they came out of the house."

"You saw Stephanie fall."

"I ... yes. She just kind of pitched off the porch and fell to the grass and the walk. The other girl got down beside her. They were both screaming. I didn't see anyone else."

"Yet you came home and started boarding up your house right away. You went to the lumberyard the next day and bought several feet of one-by-sixes from four to five feet long. You saw something that made you afraid, didn't you, Milton?"

Milton felt his cheeks quivering. But he had to get rid of Conrad in a way that wouldn't bring him back. He had to think of something.

"I'm going away. I'm going to be gone for several months, and that's why I'm boarding the house. I'm thinking I ought to get out and see the world before it's too late for me. After all, I'm sixty-seven now, and I've not been off the place in all my life except to go to work and back for a number of years. So I decided it's time for me to get away."

"Why are you boarding the house on the inside? A couple of boards across the outside would have been sufficient. And you wouldn't even have had to do that. You could have just told me to keep an eye on your place and I would have, gladly, for free. I'll be glad to feed your cats while you're gone. Anything you need."

Milton glanced away and said nothing. He shifted his feet and wished Conrad would go. But he was beginning to feel that Conrad was here for something that hadn't been disclosed yet.

"What I really want to ask you, Milton," Conrad finally said, "is about the murder of your mother."

Milton jerked his head back to stare at Conrad. He couldn't tell now if the dark eyes were friendly or hostile. They were steady and waiting. Waiting to trap him.

"What ... what about it? That was a long time ago, Donally."

"But you don't forget things like that, do you? According to my records, your mother was killed quite late in the day. Four o'clock or so. Is that correct?"

Milton's trembling beneath the skin was coming to the surface. The nervousness covered him, made him feel short of breath. He was afraid, for just a moment, that he was going to lose control, go into a panic of nervousness and have to be put away. And then just for a moment the thought of being put away in a nice safe mental institution seemed welcome. But he was here, in this house, where it had happened, and it was across the road and coming closer with each day.

"Four o'clock," he repeated.

"You didn't get off work until five, correct?"

"Yes, that was checked at the time. It must be on the records. I was at work when the murder occurred."

"Tell me what happened when you came home."

"Don't you have the report on that too? I can't talk about this anymore!" Milton's voice quavered.

"We need to talk about it, Milton," Conrad said softly. "Sometimes distance helps to remember."

"I don't know what!" Milton half-screamed. "And what difference does it make now?"

"It's still an unsolved case, Milton. And there are strange threads of these present deaths that seem to lead always back to that one. And also, from what can now be determined, there was another murder in this neighborhood on what might have been that same day. Did you find someone you knew, a girl, here in the house when you got home that day? Did you kill her, Milton, then under cover of darkness, carry her body across the road and to the old well? The best place in the world to hide a body you didn't want found? Did you also put your mother's jewelry there to throw the police off?"

Milton was shaking hard all over. His hands shook, and he put them into his pockets to hide them. The loose skin on his jaw and neck shook and quavered like the neck of a turkey, and he could feel it, and he saw that Conrad Donally noticed. He wanted to scream, it wasn't like that! But he dared not say anything.

"Who was the girl, Milton?" Conrad asked in that same soft, deceptively gentle voice. "Was her name Adriene?"

Milton's mouth fell open. He snapped it shut, and it made a reptilian sound in the silent room. He couldn't control the shaking, but he had to defend himself. He licked lips as rough and dry as sandpaper. "Where'd you get that name?" He tried to laugh. After all these years, how strange it was to hear her name spoken. "I—I—" I didn't know anyone around here would remember her. He had almost said it. God help him, he had almost hanged himself.

Conrad said nothing. He was watching Milton with those dark, steady eyes, waiting. The pencil poised over the notebook was steady.

Milton said, "I didn't kill my mother. I was at work. I had witnesses. I didn't kill ... anyone. Not that girl, not anyone."

"Adriene?"

"I don't know. I never saw that girl. I don't know who you're talking about."

Now that he'd said it, the trembling eased. Milton was able to turn away and open the kitchen screen door for a cat that wanted out.

Conrad got to his feet, folded the notebook, and put it away. He patted Milton on the shoulder.

"Don't leave for that trip around the world yet, Milton. We might need to talk to you again."

And Milton knew by the sound of his voice, the almost teasing quality, that Conrad hadn't believed a word he'd said.

CHAPTER 19

GRETA WOKE and looked around her at the strange room. Here there were lace curtains at the windows, with dark green side draperies. The wall-paper was squares and triangles and soft colors, and the furniture was dark and glossy. It wasn't her room.

She sat up and the previous night flashed before her mind in little pieces, like parts of a dream. The only thing she remembered clearly was that she had left her house to get help for her mother.

Her mother was dead. She sat still, frozen in a cold world, alone. They were all gone. Stephanie, Mama, and Daddy, too. Her room was gone.

Somewhere in the house voices mingled, distant, quiet. Greta looked around again. There were two doors in the room and both of them were closed.

She got out of bed and opened the door across the room and saw a dark closet with clothes hanging in plastic bags, as if they had been put away for the season, the way her mama always did summer or winter clothes.

She turned toward the other door just as it opened. Derek stood there, looking at her. She had seen him look first at the bed, and now his eyes were on her, and they seemed the eyes of a stranger. It was another time when they had played together, another whole lifetime. Now she was here in his house because she didn't have a family of her own anymore.

I want to go home.

As if he had read her mind, he said, "You're going to live with us, now. Maybe even after they find Uncle Phillip. The police are looking for him, did you know that? They want him to come home."

Greta shook her head. No, she didn't know that.

"Mama told me to come and see if you were awake," Derek said. He was already dressed in jeans and a knit shirt with long sleeves. "You've been sleeping a long time. It's almost noon now. Come on."

She hung back. She didn't want to go to his kitchen, to be with his father and mother and brother. She didn't belong here.

"I have to go home," she said.

"You can't go home. Nobody's there. Come on."

"I have to wash my face and put my clothes on."

She looked around, but saw none of her clothes. Then, on the floor she saw a small overnight case. On its lid it said *Going to Grandma's,* which struck her as being odd now, since she didn't have a grandma and never had had one. But it was her case, and she had pleaded and begged to be able to buy it, even though her mother and Stephanie argued against it. *Going to Grandma's* had something about it that seemed really great, really fantastic, at that time, when she was only six years old. Who had gotten this old case down and put clothes in it for her?

She went to it and bent to open it. Jeans and shirts and underclothes erupted from it.

"I don't even have a grandma," she said to Derek.

"I know," Derek said. "But I do."

"I know that." Greta busied herself getting clothes for the day out of the bag. "I know you do. I remember you going to see her."

"And Grandpa too."

"Well, I have a grandpa."

"Not a grandpa, a grandfather," Derek emphasized, nudging the case with his toe. "But he's my grandfather too. He's not like Grandma and Grandpa. They're more fun."

"I know." Greta had heard all about Derek's trips across country to spend a week with his dad's parents. They'd done all kinds of things. Gone to amusement parks and horseback riding and boating and fishing. But then Derek liked to fish. Greta sighed. She felt like she wanted to lie down and crawl back under the bed into the dark and close her eyes, and then maybe God would take her to be with her mama.

But maybe her mama wasn't dead. She remembered now, an ambulance had come. She had heard its siren, and they had come for her mama.

She remembered now how she had sat beside her mama in the hall, holding her head, wiping from her ear the blood that gathered there like the setting on the ring Derek had given her. Like the blood had gathered in her own ear. And she hadn't died.

"I have to hurry," she said, pulling the jeans on before she got to the bathroom. "I'm going to the hospital to see my mother. She's not dead. She was just resting."

She rushed into the bathroom in the hall, the pink and brown bathroom where Aunt Alyne had sent her and Derek many times to wash mud or other gunk off themselves. Where Aunt Alyne had even put them both into the bathtub with a lot of bubbles, back before they got too big to bathe together. She looked for a toothbrush and saw only three, Derek's, William's, and, she guessed, Kenny's. None was hers. She pushed Derek aside and rushed back to her *Going to Grandma's* case and found a toothbrush and a small tube of paste and hurried back to the bathroom. Derek was standing in the door, and she had to push him aside again. He said nothing, which wasn't like Derek. She glanced sideways at him.

With her mouth foaming from toothpaste she said, "Go away. I got to get dressed so I can go see my mama."

"What's wrong with your face?" he asked, instead of going away.

She paused, the back of her right hand going briefly to her cheek. In the mirror she could see that although the center of her cheek looked better, the outer edges had a greenish look, mixed with deep purple under her eye. But the blood had stopped draining from her ear, and the dull pain in the side of her head had stopped. She finished brushing her teeth without answering him.

He was still there, so she turned her back to him, pulled the top of her pajamas off, and pulled on the knit top she had grabbed out of the overnight case.

Then she saw that she had pulled her jeans on over the bottom of her pajamas, so she had to pull them off and then, with her back still to Derek, pull her pajama bottoms off. She was still wearing her panties. She had put them on after her bath last night. And then she had dressed, she remembered. Where had she gotten the pajamas? Whose pajamas were they?

She held them up and looked at them, and as if Derek saw them for the first time too, he grabbed them away from her.

"What're you doing wearing my pajamas?"

"I don't know." She didn't like it any better than he did, and she frowned at him to let him know that.

She remembered now. Uncle Ross had put her to bed. He was the one who must have put her into Derek's pajamas.

But now that Derek was gone, taking his pajamas away, Greta turned back to the bathroom and the cubicle where the toilet was. She hurried, only half doing her job. After that, she washed her face and was reaching for a towel when someone handed her one. She looked through the veil of water that fell off her eyebrows. But at first, her very first glimpse, showed a large, dark bulk in the doorway, and her fear became so intense that she felt a trickle of pee-pee between her legs. She held herself tightly, knees together.

"What's wrong?" William asked, and Greta felt like hugging him around his plump waist. It was only William, only William. She dried her face.

He reached out and touched her cheek gently. "Did you fall?"

She nodded. It was the best explanation she could have thought of. "I fell," she said, and knew that it would be her answer from now on when she was asked about it. It was the only truth she knew. The bad thing, the thing that struck and killed, the thing made of night and darkness and odors of deep wells and slime and things that grew in deep, dark places, was not real. She was old enough and smart enough to know that. Monsters did not exist. Things didn't really hide in corners or follow behind you and whisper in your ear to kill, kill the people who made up your real world. There were no monsters like that.

So now she wondered ... what kind of monster lived in her mind?

And she was more and more afraid all the time, when she let herself think of the dark thing she saw and the whispers she heard. Because monsters weren't real. Her mother had told her that, and her mother knew.

Derek came back. He was a head shorter than William, and it was like looking at two people who weren't related at all. William's hair a pretty, dark brown, rich and thick, like Stephanie's had been, and Derek's like her own. No color, unless the sunlight made it glisten.

"I've got to go now," Greta said, running a hairbrush down over her long, tangled curls once, twice, and then putting the brush on the counter. "I'm going to the hospital to see my mother."

The two boys looked at each other pointedly, a silent message passing between them. Greta felt left out in a way that made her want to cry. She felt her chin pucker and she pushed it hard up against her teeth.

"Sergeant Donally's here," William said. "He wants to talk to you."

She didn't want to see Sergeant Donally. He had accused her of being beaten by someone in her family, and she was afraid of him.

"I don't want to."

Derek said, "You got to. He's the police. If you don't, he'll take you to jail and keep you."

William hit Derek on the shoulder, a gentle poke that had a threat behind it. "Shut up, Derek. That's not true." As if he understood how frightening that threat was, he put an arm around Greta's shoulders and walked with her down the hall, in a way forcing her along when she didn't want to go at all.

"But you do have to talk to him, Greta. It's important. You have to tell him everything about last night, just like you did the other times."

"What other times!"

"You know—Kenny and Stephanie."

"But Mama's not dead!" Greta cried, her voice shrill and carrying. She stopped, refused to take another step. "The ambulance came and took her to the hospital. I heard it! I'm going there. No one can stop me from going there! I'm going to my mama!"

Alyne came into the hall and gathered Greta into her arms, crooning soft sounds of comfort into her ear. Greta wrapped both arms around her aunt's waist, but it was like hugging and being hugged by a stranger now. This was not her mother, this was Derek's mother. She wanted her own, and she sobbed out her need, over and over.

Through her tears she saw that someone else had come into the hallway and was bending down so his face was close to hers. He was holding something red and small toward her. The light glistened on the clear paper it was wrapped in. A sucker. Sergeant Donally again. His eyes looked soft and kind, like the eyes of a dog. Brown and deep and loving in the ways of a dog who knew you and liked you, loved you. Like old Buster.

Greta's tears stopped. The sobs that had shook her body melted away and left her with only small shudders going compulsively through her body at times.

"Maybe you'd like to go on out and eat some breakfast first," Conrad Donally said. "I can talk to your aunt first. When you feel like you're ready to talk to me, you can come on in. Okay?"

"Okay."

"William," Aunt Alyne said, "help Greta with breakfast."

"What'll I give her?"

"Whatever she likes. This time. Either cereal or something sweet if you want to. Look in the bin and see what's there. She likes glazed doughnuts. You can get some out of the freezer and stick them in the microwave for a few seconds."

"Hey!" Derek said his voice eager. "Can I have one too?"

"Sure, all of you. Go on now."

They went down the hall toward the kitchen. The paper on the sucker crinkled as Greta tucked it into her pocket. Sergeant Donally was kind of nice, she decided. She wished her daddy was more like him.

"DOUGHNUTS ARE a special treat at our house," Alyne explained to Conrad as they went into the seldom-used front room and sat down. "If I'd let them, the kids wouldn't eat anything else. So I keep them frozen and they're brought out only on Sundays or some other special days."

"Everybody has some kind of sweet treat they have a weakness for, I guess. I'm a chocolate buff. Has your husband gone to work?"

"He had to go in for awhile. Ross almost lives at the office sometimes. You'd think the place wouldn't run without him. But he said he'd be back shortly after noon, if he could get here. He didn't get much sleep last night."

"No. I kept him up for awhile myself. And I need to ask you some questions you might not want to hear also, Alyne, but please understand that I don't like to ask them any better than you like to hear them."

Alarms went off in her, a system of alert that had been staying on the verge of erupting since all this had started happening. She felt as if she were being suspected of something. The way the police had acted, even in the death of Stephanie, which so clearly was caused by her fall and her striking her head on the hard surface of the walk, it was almost as if they suspected the whole family of some sort of conspiracy to murder. Yet they hadn't come back. Only Conrad had come back.

She didn't encourage him to ask whatever question he was so sure she wouldn't like. She stared at him and waited. He seemed to be handling his notebook too much, as if he were fumbling, as if he didn't know where to start. Then he looked up. His eyes were soft and sympathetic, but determined.

"Have you noticed the big bruise on your niece's cheek?"

Alyne frowned, feeling the pull of it between her brows. Whatever she had expected, it wasn't this. "What?"

"You haven't noticed? How could you help not seeing it?"

Alyne glanced toward the hall. She had forgotten. Of course she had noticed the discoloration of Greta's cheek, but in all the other happenings it had simply been put aside. Greta was, after all, safe. "Papa needed me," Alyne explained. "And Clare was ... Clare was ... hurt. There were so many other things."

"She has a large bruise on her cheek, a bad one. It was there yesterday afternoon. I talked to her while she was waiting for her parents to come home."

"What did she say?"

"Denial, which is typical. Nothing that made sense. And you know that the death blows both to Kenny and Stephanie could have been caused from a very hard punch on the head. A slap, if the hand were large enough and it was done more than once. I'm sorry to bring this up, but there's a pattern here, Alyne."

"What ... pattern?"

"Clare's death last night was possibly caused by the same thing as the others. A burst blood vessel in the brain. So far there has been no real sign of any of them having less than normal blood vessels, so it looks in all cases like it might have been a beating death, with the concussion on Stephanie an added factor. Caused by the fall."

"Kenny ..." Alyne said, her thoughts going back to him lying on the grass, at age fourteen as angelic looking as he'd been at four. Dead, her baby boy, her firstborn. At that time she'd been told he'd died simply of a brain hemorrhage, which was, in a way, easier to accept.

"Kenny was hit by someone? That wasn't what I was told."

"I know that, Alyne. These facts are just becoming more plain because, you see, every one of them died from the burst blood vessels. Massive hemorrhaging. That was the ultimate cause of death. But what caused it to burst? Since there was no other cause showing up clearly, it was assumed a genetic weakness lurked somewhere there. But there's a pattern growing. In each of the reports I read of a bruise on the face. A bruise that in some cases no one but the ME would have seen. It was written down in one short sentence. Hematoma of the right cheek."

He paused, looking steadily into her eyes, and she knew he wanted her to hear what he had said and draw certain conclusions from it. She blinked, confused, hurting, the deaths all brought to her freshly, where she was now unprotected by the shock that surrounds a family death. "You mean ... someone who's left-handed ... ?"

"It kind of looks that way. I hadn't thought of that part myself until last night. I noticed that the bruise on Greta's face is on the right cheek. And the bruises on all the others, including Clare's last night, were on the right cheek. So it must have been someone with a left hand?"

"Unless they stood behind, struck from behind."

He nodded.

"Exactly. An abuser will often attack from behind. The sneak approach, especially on children. The child isn't doing exactly as the abuser wants the child to do, even though the child probably doesn't even know the abuser is near, and wham, he hits her. And he hits her so hard it knocks her down, and not only causes a dark bruise on her face but causes her ear to bleed."

"But ... Greta. If she ..."

"Why didn't she die too? Maybe there's something to the weak blood vessel theory and Greta is stronger. But the question I have to ask, Alyne, is, Who's doing it? I think I've ruled out you and your husband. Neither of you would have been in the house the night Stephanie was killed, or last night when Clare was killed. Kenny was out in the yard when it happened."

She whispered the answer he was seeking. "Phillip."

He said nothing for awhile as wave after wave of stunned disbelief went through her mind.

"Do you know where he is?" Conrad asked.

"No. Isn't he ... I don't know. Of course I knew he evidently wasn't at home last night ... Clare was alone ... in the house, I mean."

"Greta?"

"Oh, she ... she was there. She came here. William let her in. You know about that. But no one was in the house with Clare. But none of us really thought about Phillip, I guess. With all the other ... the thing ... the death of Clare ..."

She felt hot tears burn behind her eyelids. Oh, God, no, not now, she prayed. She couldn't break down now, when everyone was expecting her to be ready for whatever was needed. She turned her head away and forced the tears back.

"I spent the night—after the ambulance took Clare's body away—with my father. He's very broken about all this, as you might expect. Papa has always had favorites, and each of them has been taken."

"I'm sorry. I know at his age it's something he might not find easy to survive."

"No. They were all he lived for. Visits from Kenny, Stephanie, and Clare. All I can do now is try to make up for his losses. So I stayed the rest of the night with him and encouraged him to talk. He likes to relive old times, especially about the children when they were young." A tear ran down her cheek, a tear for her papa, and she brushed it away with one finger.

"I need to talk to you about Phillip, though, Alyne. Has he been abusive toward any of his family or anyone else?"

She almost laughed. She tried. "Phillip?"

"Then you don't know."

"I know he was a little like Papa, he had favorites too. It was as if Phillip worshipped Stephanie from the day she was born. So if you're thinking he might have struck her, then you're way off track. No way. Absolutely no way."

"That you know of."

She shook her head. "Seeing Phillip in that light makes me think I've lived next door to a stranger all our married lives. He and Clare were married before Ross and I were, you know. A year earlier. They built their house first, even though Papa had already given me this lot. We got married and built this house the year Stephanie was born. So I was right here and saw Phillip every day. He was even worse than Papa about spoiling Stephanie. No, he would never strike her. And certainly not my son. Why would he?"

"And Greta?"

She stared at him.

"Someone did, Alyne. Someone she won't talk about. She just makes up preposterous stories. Or won't talk at all. And that's the way a child will act when he's questioned about abuse from someone he loves. He'll deny it almost every time. At other times, even when there's no love, he's apt to deny it out of fear. So I haven't decided yet exactly which it is with Greta."

"You have to ask her about all these things?"

"I'm sorry. I do. It's the only way we'll get an answer about these deaths. She was the only one there in every case, the only witness except one."

"Who?"

"Milton, across the road, saw Stephanie and Greta come running out of the house. He saw her stumble and fall."

"Then he must have told you if someone else was there."

"He didn't see anyone."

Alyne pressed her hand over her eyes for an instant. "I don't understand."

"Neither do I, and it bothers me."

"But we can't ..." can't help you, she was going to say, when she was interrupted by the kids coming into the living room. She saw signs of doughnut crumbs at the corners of Greta and Derek's mouths, and motioned them near and cleaned it off with a tissue from her pocket. She had learned to carry tissues around with her whenever possible from the time Kenny was a baby. Perhaps even before that, when Stephanie was a baby, though there were many hands to see that Stephanie stayed in tip-top shape. They were a close and loving family. How could the police suspect any member of abuse? It just wasn't feasible. It was contradictory to everything they stood for, to all the years they had lived here. In her own childhood home there hadn't even been a spanking. She couldn't ever remember being spanked. She wished she had told Conrad that. He had her on the defensive, and there was a feeling of anger behind the confusion, a growing anger.

Conrad put out his hand and Greta went to him. He lifted her to sit on his knee.

"Did you enjoy that doughnut?"

She nodded.

"Did you drink a glass of milk with it?"

She nodded again.

Derek and William stood watching and listening, and Alyne motioned them out of the room. "Why don't you boys go make your beds, clean up your rooms."

"I did," William said.

"Then go out and ride your bikes or something. Sergeant Donally wants to ask Greta some questions."

"Can't we stay?" Derek asked.

"Maybe we can help," William said.

Conrad nodded at Alyne. "It's all right if they stay. Maybe they remember something that Greta has forgotten."

Greta sat on his knee awkwardly and finally slid down, but she stayed between his knees, one hand on his leg. He held her wrist loosely. Her hand drooped down like a flower, fingers curled under.

"Where's your daddy, Greta?"

"He left."

There was a moment of silence in the room. Alyne saw Conrad glance swiftly at her and then back at her niece.

"Where did he go?"

"I don't know. Mama said he might have gone to Las Vegas. He likes to go to Las Vegas. Does he know Mama is sick and in the hospital? Does he know that I need him to come home?"

ALYNE STARED AT GRETA. She seemed surrounded by strange, pale, darting, yet almost invisible lights. Reds, greens, blues. They rose from her, or somewhere near her, and shot into the air like Fourth of July fireworks exploding, going silently out into the dark night and exploding again. The noise in Alyne's ears was a low drumming, so that she had lost all sense of whatever was being said, of the conversations among the two boys, Greta, and Conrad. She wondered if they couldn't see the darting lights, the brilliant, silent, deadly lights.

Then she realized the lights were being played out against a darkening background, as if a fog had gathered in that corner of the room behind the boys, behind Greta and Conrad.

... kill ... kill ... pppp ... ppp ... pets ... killll ... aaa ... Alyne ...

It was a whisper, and it seemed to be coming from Greta, from the sharp, thin, darting lights, from the darkening in the corner of the room. But no one was paying attention to it. Conrad acted as if he didn't see it, and Derek and William seemed oblivious to the danger so close to them. Only Greta finally, slowly, turned her head.

CHAPTER 20

ALYNE GOT up and murmured an excuse to leave the room. She had begun to feel as if her heart were bursting. She went into the kitchen and leaned over the sink for a few minutes, her eyes closed. She could still see the flashes of light, somewhere behind her eyes, and she wondered if she were getting a migraine headache. She had never had one, but she had read that sufferers of migraines sometimes saw flashes of light.

She drank a glass of water and then went to the half-bath off the utility room and got aspirins from the medicine cabinet. She took two.

"Alyne?"

It was Conrad, calling her from the kitchen. She answered and went to find him at the sliding doors, his hand on the handle ready to slide it open.

"Thanks for letting me talk to the kids. Greta will be all right. She might not understand that her mother is dead until she sees her again, and I wish I could help you with that, but I wouldn't know how."

"Was she able to help you?"

"No, except it seems that her mother received a phone call from her dad right after they went into the house yesterday evening, and he was already gone somewhere. She said her mother then decided that they would take a vacation too, and they were getting ready to leave when it happened. She became quite vague about that. Couldn't remember, she said."

Alyne nodded. "I'm sure she doesn't. It's better that way maybe."

"The poor kid must have sat with her mother for hours before she came over here." Conrad opened the door. "If you need me just yell."

His smile was warm and sympathetic, and she felt the corner of her lips tremble in response.

"We'll find Phillip."

"Thank you, Conrad."

She watched him go across the patio and out of sight around the corner of the house. She went to the stove, poured another cup of coffee, and sat down. The doughnuts the kids had taken from the freezer were still on the table, the box half empty now, the doughnuts no longer frozen. Alyne picked one up, felt its sticky glaze in her fingers, decided she didn't have an appetite for it, and put it back into the box. From the paper napkin holder in the middle of the table, she got a napkin and wiped the stickiness off her fingers.

The kids came into the kitchen, Greta trailing as if she were a stranger in the house, a bit timid and holding back.

"What are we going to do today, Mom?" William asked.

Alyne shook her head. She chose her words carefully, remembering that Greta was in the room. Greta, looking small and lost, was dressed in blue jeans and knit shirt that emphasized her thin, shapeless body. Her thick, curly hair was in disarray. She'd have to brush Greta's hair, Alyne thought in the back of her mind as she tried to answer William.

"Just ... nothing much." She hadn't been doing much, she thought, since the day Kenny died—no, longer than that. She hadn't been holding to her old routine since the day the kids opened the well. They had to wait now and see if anything definite came from the autopsy report, but she didn't want to say that in front of Greta. And then, when the body was released, she, at least, maybe Ross, and Phillip, if he had come home by then, had to go make funeral arrangements.

Greta edged nearer, putting her elbow on the table. "Aunt Alyne," she said.

"Yes, Greta."

"Will you take me to see my mother?"

Alyne looked into the small, pleading face and almost burst into tears. She motioned the boys away.

"William, Derek, go out and play. I want to talk to Greta."

Derek asked, "Can't Greta come out and play too?"

"Why can't I go on to school?" William asked. "I could ride my bike. It won't matter that I've missed a couple of classes."

"No. I don't want you riding your bike on Walnut Street. It's too dangerous."

"I could take the back streets."

"William, tomorrow you can go back to school. Right now, go ride your bike in the alley. You too, Derek."

"Can't Greta ... ?"

"She can come out as soon as I've talked to her," Alyne said, her patience growing thin. Why did kids have to make life so much more difficult at times? "Go!"

The boys went out and Alyne motioned Greta to come to her. Greta backed up against her knees, her head down. Alyne brushed her hair back with her hand.

"There's a hairbrush in the washroom. Let's go in there to talk, Greta, okay?"

"Okay."

They moved to the small room with the shower, the wash basin and the stool, and Alyne sat on the stool in front of Greta and began brushing her hair. Greta's head hung low, her eyes seemingly toward the floor. She was no longer asking to be taken to her mother. Alyne brushed the curls around her fingers, slowly, carefully. Once she had wanted a little girl with hair like Greta's, and now it looked as if she had one. She hadn't wanted it to be this way, and of course Phillip might take her away somewhere and Alyne would never see her grow up. But she doubted he would. He would probably say it was better for Greta to stay here, with Alyne, Ross, and the boys, and he would be right.

"She's dead, isn't she, Aunt Alyne?" Greta asked faintly.

"Yes, baby, she is. But I'm her sister, and she knows I'll be here for you, sweetheart, all your life. You're not alone."

"Isn't my daddy coming home either?"

"Of course he will."

Alyne brushed the hair back behind Greta's ears, and then she saw the dark bruising around the edges of Greta's cheek, reaching into her hairline on the right side, and the deep, blue-green, purplish darkness beneath her right eye. With Greta's face in her hands, Alyne forced Greta to look into her eyes.

"Somebody hit you on the face and the head, didn't they Greta? Just like Sergeant Donally thought."

A frown flickered on and off Greta's face, her eyes darted back and forth between Alyne's, as if she were searching for something there, as if she were trying to make up her mind about something.

She whispered, "It got mad at me when I wouldn't kill Derek and it hit me. And it told me to kill Stephanie, and Kenny, and then Mama. It told me to kill Mama."

A long, hard chill passed over Alyne's body. Suddenly she felt as if someone were behind her in the tiny bathroom, in the corner, watching her with piercing, evil eyes. She cast a swift glance over her shoulder and saw the wastebasket in the corner, and the small tri-cornered knick-knack shelf with the what-nots it held. Little glass and wood figurines stood on the shelf, special woodwork Kenny had made in woodworking class. The corner seemed darker than usual, but no one was there. Of course there wouldn't have been. Greta was having mental problems, and no wonder, with all she'd been through lately.

"You've been hearing voices?"

"Whispers. It whispers to me and tells me to kill."

Alyne's face turned cold. She remembered the whisper she had heard in the living room. It had seemed to come from Greta, from Greta's own lips.

This was something she wouldn't be able to handle alone. What could she do? Call Ross at work and ask him to come home? Move on her own and make an appointment for Greta to see a psychiatrist? Wait for Phillip?

She had to think. To talk to someone. She wished Clare were here to help her. Here for her to help Clare, for them both to help Greta. One more day wouldn't hurt. One more day, just to give her time to think.

She took Greta's hands in hers and felt the bulk of something tied tightly around her finger. She dropped Greta's right hand and concentrated on the left.

"Good Lord, Greta. Your finger is swollen and blue. What have you got tied around it?" It looked like dirty tape, a lump of it on her ring finger. She almost smiled. She could remember making rings out of all sorts of things, wires, ribbons, especially the soft copper wires that were so flexible. "You got it too tight, sweetheart."

"Mama was going to take it off, and she forgot." Alyne picked at the tape, loosened one end of it and pulled a piece loose. She turned Greta's hand and darting lights shot upward, as if they had been freed, thin, swift arrows of light, blues, greens, red, yellows, white lights like soundless shots through a dark night. It was the strange lights she had seen earlier in the living room that seemed to surround Greta. They had been coming from the ring, from the gem in the setting of gold. Greta must have turned her hand so the light struck the gem just right, and the shards of light had been released. It was beautiful, one of the most beautiful gems Alyne had ever seen.

Greta was saying something about Derek finding it, fishing it up, and giving it to her. Alyne stared at the ring. She had seen it before. A long, long time ago. She had seen this ring.

Suddenly the whole world seemed to drop away, and there was nothing but the dark greenish-red gem in its marvelous setting of gold.

She had crept closer so she could see what the man was showing Adriene. Alyne could hear her making a sound like a cooing, as if she were very happy about something. Alyne wanted to see too, but she knew if she crawled out from beneath the bushes they would be mad. Adriene had already made her go back across the road. She had pointed her finger and told Alyne to go home; but Alyne had waited, and then she had followed. She knew Adriene was going to meet the man again, the man who lifted her skirts and played with her legs, the man who pulled her against him and held her with his arms so tight around Adriene's body, while Adriene laughed and twisted. Sometimes the man kissed Adriene. Alyne had gotten close enough one day to see the kiss. The man's face was hidden against Adriene's, and when Adriene pulled away she looked very glad, very pleased, yet she ran from him, then stopped so that he caught up with her, and then she ran again, and they went around the back of the house and into the trees and bushes, and Alyne couldn't find them. She had to go home, she knew, or her mother and papa would know she had gone and would make her sit on the old chair in the parlor for a long, long time. They called it punishment. Mama's punishment, but Papa went along with it. He hadn't let Alyne disobey her mother's punishment. She didn't want to sit on the chair.

Then she heard them talking, the man and Adriene, and something flashed in the light and Alyne caught a glimpse of it. A red ring. Lights flashed up from it when Adriene turned it. "Ooooh, sugar," she whispered, cooing, and Alyne, on her hands and knees, strained forward to see the ring. They weren't looking at her, at where she crouched beneath the green bushes.

"You can have it," he said. "If you'll do it, you can have it, forever and ever. And you can have me too."

Adriene was nodding. There was no smile on her face now. Nodding, nodding. Her chin looked soft and round, and her lips were pink and full and not smiling. "All right," she said, in a whisper. Adriene always spoke in a whisper. Almost always. Adriene was so pretty. So pretty. With her long, red hair hanging straight to her waist, and her white skin with the pale little freckles, with her strange, dark eyes that were green, not blue like her mama's and not brown like her papa's. She wanted to grow up to look like Adriene, and she had told her mama that, and her mama said, with a snort, "Fat chance of that!" as if there were something wrong with looking like Adriene.

The scene changed. Adriene was going down the sidewalk instead of walking in the road. She kept looking all around, as if she were looking for someone. But there was no one, not even a car on the road, or a woman on the porch across the road. Adriene walked down the sidewalk, going so fast that Alyne couldn't keep up. She sat down under cover of a bush, the way she always did when Adriene told her to stay home, and waited. It was a long time before Alyne saw a glimpse of the pretty dress Adriene always wore. It was a white dress with a full circle skirt that Adriene would hold for Alyne to see as she whirled around. The white dress had little blue rosebuds that were raised. Flocked, her mama had said. The dress had been made by Mama, and Adriene thought it was the prettiest dress in the world, and so did Alyne. It was the only dress Adriene had. So now she knew, just by the glimpse of white, that Adriene had crossed the road after all and was going to the house where the man lived.

Alyne got up and ran, crossing the road and going in beneath the bushes there to crouch down again. What was Adriene doing? She wasn't going around to the side of the house like she always did before. She was going to the porch and climbing the steps. But she was climbing slowly and walking softly and looking all around.

Alyne watched her, saw her go around the porch to the front and then open the door. She stood for a long time in the open doorway, and then she pushed the door shut and was swallowed by the house.

Alyne ran across the grass and up the porch steps at the front. Adriene had climbed the steps at the side. But Alyne's feet were bare, and her steps on the board porch were silent. She went to the door, that strange door with the pretty glass in all colors, like the colors that had come from the ring, and found that it wasn't quite closed.

The room she stepped into was like a hall, like the entry at home, except it was longer, narrower, and darker. She stood trembling, ready to call for Adriene. But there was a lady living here, and Adriene had gone into the house without knocking, and Alyne needed to be with her now, in this strange house, with the dark in the hall and on the stairway. Where was Adriene? Where was the lady who lived here?

Then, in the dark above, Alyne caught another glimpse of white. The corner of Adriene's pretty skirt, that swung when she moved, that sometimes moved and formed pleats even when Adriene stood still.

Adriene, where are you going?

She had only whispered the words, and Adriene didn't hear. Then she followed. With her hand on the banister, higher than her head, she went up the stairs.

She stood in a hall that went in three directions, and she saw Adriene nowhere. The hall was dark too, just like down below. And it was scary, and she wished she had minded Adriene and stayed at home where it was not so scary. Then she heard voices. A voice.

"Adriene! Well, hello, dear. What are you doing here at this time of day?"

Adriene did not answer, but Alyne heard a footstep, dull, muffled on the bedroom rug. Alyne knew Adriene had gone into the bedroom without being asked, and it was just like Mama said about Adriene. Adriene was ... headstrong? Adriene was ... bad?

"What are you doing?" the voice of the lady screamed and then her voice rose higher, without words, into a thin terrible scream that filled the house and Alyne's head and made her ears hurt.

Alyne flung her hands over her ears, but still she heard the other sounds, the thud, thud, thud of something hard beating against something softer, and she heard the sounds of the scream die away and change to a terrible gurgle. She heard grunting too, as the beating kept on, on, on.

Alyne ran. She wanted to run away and hide, but she ran to the bedroom door instead and stopped, her own scream of horror silent in her throat.

The lady lay on the floor, and her head was mushy and red and stuff spilled out of her broken skull. Blood was everywhere, and in its puddle, her toes touching the lady's robe, stood Adriene. On the floor by the lady's head lay a black stick with a claw at the end, and Alyne knew it was a poker from the fireplace downstairs.

Adriene didn't see Alyne. She was opening a drawer, taking something from it. She was smiling, looking at the thing in her hand. Lights flashed from it, blue, green, red ... and Alyne knew it was the ring.

But all she could see was Adriene, with her pretty dress ruined by the blood, even though she had lifted the skirt and tied it around her waist. Alyne watched her stand and rub the blood off her legs with the lady's new scarf that she took off the dresser. She wiped blood off her legs, her feet, her arms, her face. Alyne turned and ran, her bare feet silent in the hall and on the stairs.

SHE WAS HIDING. This time it was not a bush, but something that drooped all around her to the floor. On one side the cloth hung off the floor several inches, so that she could see the legs of the man and of Adriene.

She was holding her hands over her ears, and she was crying, but no one heard her. She could hear beating again, a hard something striking a softer something, the thud, thud, and the cursing of the man and the crying of Adriene. Their feet and legs tangled together, and Adriene's white skirt swung and danced, jerking this way and that as the man beat her.

Goddam you to hell, you worthless slut! It was a black day that you were born.

You're no goddamn better yourself! I hate you! I hate you, you dirty old man!

You killed ... you murdered an old woman for this ... a ring?

No—no! ... I hate you ... I didn't!

There's blood. Blood on you, blood on the stone. Here, keep it ... and be damned ... damned to hell ... you'll burn for eternity ...

No! I didn't! He ... he did ... he! He gave it to me ...

There's blood on your hands, damn you to hell ... you'll burn ... burn for eternity ... take this pitiful stone and be damned ...

Through her tears, beneath the edge of the tablecloth, beyond the legs of the table under which Alyne was hiding, she saw Adriene fall. Her face had been ravaged, the skin torn away by the rough, hard hand against it. Blood ran from her ears and mouth and eyes. She had stopped crying. Her head hung backward. Her eyes, staring open, looked at Alyne underneath the table, through the blood.

But Adriene didn't see her.

The arms, the hands, reached down and picked Adriene off the floor, and heavy footsteps crossed the room and a door slammed.

Somewhere in the house someone else sobbed.

It was a lonely, terrible sound.

Alyne buried her face in her lap and wrapped her arms around her head so she couldn't hear anymore.

• • •

ALYNE STAGGERED to her feet and looked around. She was in her own kitchen, no longer the child, the vulnerable tender child, but for a moment she stood confused, trying to separate the dark underneath a kitchen table with a heavy cloth that hung crooked to the floor from this shining, bright place. The feeling of terrible doom remained with her, the shock of what she knew now was a memory, but which was as immediate and as vivid as a vision, now difficult to separate from the present, as if death were imminent again. And again, and again, as if history were repeating itself and would go on repeating itself as long as any of them lived. And with the memory had come a strange and terrible anger. She had been lied to. Lied to. She wasn't the only one in the family who remembered Adriene. She knew that now and shook with an odd illness, a terrible sensation of having been blind, of having been blinded, perhaps, by further things that had not yet reached her memory and perhaps never would.

She hadn't seen the face of the man, but she knew who he was.

She went out the sliding doors. The sounds of the neighborhood reached her ears but were like something on a screen, apart from her. She heard the sounds of her own children, her two surviving sons, as they worked on the other side of the garage on bicycles. She heard a dog barking farther down the street, and somewhere a lawn mower was humming. Cars moved slowly along the street, one not slowly. It honked and sped up, passing. Her mind clicked off a fact, though it did not touch her raging emotions. Forty-five miles an hour. No passing zone.

She reached the alley and began to run. Shade hovered over her in large cool shadows like scabs on her flesh. The warmth of the sun was left behind when she entered her papa's backyard.

She went in without knocking. Anne Reade heard her and met her in the hall, her first smile fading into a puzzled grimace as she stared at Alyne's face.

"Where is he?" Alyne demanded.

Anne motioned toward the front of the house. "He—uh—uh—"

Alyne nodded and went on toward the parlor. She pushed open the door so hard it struck the wall. Her father was sitting in his chair, his hands folded on the top of his cane. The room was silent. The television had not been turned on. His head drooped over his hands, over his cane, as if he were sitting with his eyes closed. When he heard her the huge, old head lifted.

For the first time, she noticed the size of his hands. She had always thought of him as being a giant, and she knew now she had always been a little bit afraid of him. But she had never known why.

She stopped halfway between him and the door. His eyes found her and widened, and then gradually narrowed until they became as hard and piercing as the blue lights that shot from the ring, like slivers of ice, of shattered glass.

"Why did you let me live, Papa?"

His eyebrows lowered until they were a white bar across his brow, hovering over his eyes, almost hiding them. His mouth thinned and pressed tight, and he didn't waver in his stare. It was as hard as the gem, and as cold.

She said it again.

"Why did you let me live?"

CHAPTER 21

SHE REMEMBERED. As his eyes flickered, just a barest changing of light that she would never have seen had she not been so sensitive to his every nuance, she remembered.

As he carried Adriene out the back door, she had slipped from beneath the kitchen table and run, run toward the front of the house, for the stairway and up. On the stairs she had found her baby sister, Clare, huddling in the dark turn of the stairs. Huddling and weeping softly, almost silently, a tiny girl scared of the sounds she was hearing. Alyne went on up the stairs, on and on, down a long dark tunnel that was never to end, never, never. The farther she went the closer she came to the other sound in the house, the terrible, anguished sobbing of her mother.

"WHAT ARE YOU TALKING ABOUT?" Papa demanded, his voice strict and harsh and cold, the way it always could be when he was angry with her. A tone within his voice said she was crazy, she was imagining things again. She was a foolish girl.

"Adriene. She was my sister, wasn't she, Papa? Mine and Clare's sister?"

"Nonsense!" His cane thumped suddenly against the floor, a hard gunshot sound that made her jump. He got to his feet and stood tall in front of his chair, not more than six feet from her. He looked down upon her from beneath his heavy, lowered, shaggy eyebrows.

"You know, and you know it well, your mother and I were married one year before you were born. Who is this Adriene? What kind of madness have you got in your mind, Alyne?"

"No, no." She shook her head back and forth, back and forth. "You're not going to make me think I'm crazy, Papa, or that I'm dreaming this up just because that poor—poor ..." She remembered the murder that she had seen, the first one, the cold-blooded, deliberate killing of a woman for her ring, her little pouch of jewels. At least the second murder was one of passion. At least it had that absolution within it.

But now she wavered. It was true, Adriene could not have been her mother's child. Adriene had been fifteen years old, and her own mother was too young to have been Adriene's mother.

"Then who was she, Papa? Don't tell me there was no such person. I remember her. I followed her when I was a child! I saw my mother making that pretty white dress with the blue rosebuds, the dress with the circle skirt. I saw it! I saw Adriene meeting some man who—who fondled her, who pulled up her skirt and caressed her skin." She saw his face grow white, and his jowls began to quiver. His eyes lost their harsh sting. Yet he did not lessen his stare. She could almost feel the terrible strength it was taking for him to hold his station in front of her, to avoid weakening. Yet she could see it all, as if she felt it within herself.

"I saw her, Papa, go into that house across the road. I followed her up the stairs and into the bedroom. I heard Mrs. Crossover talking to her before I heard the poker strike Mrs. Crossover's head. When I looked into the room, Adriene was cleaning blood off herself. She had tied her skirt around her waist in a bundle to keep it from being splattered, and she had taken Mrs. Crossover's jewelry, and she was looking at the ring. The ring."

Jonah swallowed. His shoulders sagged, infinitesimally, but she saw it. His eyes never left her. "I think you should go to a doctor, Alyne. Your imagination has gone wild, ever since the bones were found. I knew—I knew ..." He thumped his cane against the floor again, but this time she did not jump. "I knew they should have left that well alone! I told you not to allow that to happen! I told you children to stay away from that well! It was dangerous, and had always been dangerous. It was a blight on the land and should have been filled in long ago. Had I still owned it myself, it would have been filled in. But the owner, that newcomer, didn't want it touched."

"It would have been filled in," Alyne said, "and the body of Adriene would have been buried forever, wouldn't it, Papa?"

"I know nothing about this Adriene person! Why do you keep talking to me of her!"

"STOP LYING TO ME!" Alyne screamed, for the first time in her life raising her voice to her father. She expected his hand against her face, although never before had he struck her or even struck out at her. But even now, he didn't raise his hand against her. She began to weep, and his face blurred before her eyes.

"I have loved you, Papa. I have always loved you, and I wanted your love, Papa. But you never loved me. Why? Was it because I knew you killed Adriene? Was it because you knew that I knew your secret?"

He raised his cane and pointed the trembling end at the door.

"Go. Get out of my house. You're no daughter of mine."

"Who was Adriene, Papa? At least tell me who she was."

"Go! Never again darken my door. Go!"

He was only a tall, dark shadow in front of her tear-filled eyes. She could see his white hair and his white face, and the closed and buttoned shirt that was dark, like his trousers. She could see the cane wavering, its end pointed at the door, like a very long finger extended from his hand.

She turned, and something in the doorway moved, stepping aside, and she knew it was Anne. But Anne said nothing as Alyne passed her.

She went through the house, her hands reaching out to touch the wall for balance, to guide her in her blinded leaving of her father's house.

She stumbled down the back steps and along the rear walk to the heavy plank gate in the brick wall. Her hand tangled in the vines as she felt for the latch. She was sobbing now, her grief coming up in throes of hurt and loneliness. She could hardly see where she was going.

When she reached the alley, she forced her sobs down and closed her eyes against the rush of tears, so that by the time she reached her house, she could see again, although the tears kept coming, against her will, throwing up a wall between her and the world.

How foolishly secure she had been all the years between childhood and two weeks ago! How could she have lived under such a cloud, buried so deep in her memory?

She went to the telephone in the kitchen and called Conrad's home phone number. She got his answering machine. For a moment she listened to the silence on the line as she wondered what to do. Should she call the police station instead? No, she couldn't do that. Talking to Conrad was like talking to a friend, a relative. Talking to him at the police station would be like talking to the world. She had to tell him, but in her own way.

"This is Alyne, Conrad. I remember the girl. In the well. Her name. I remember Adriene. I don't know who she was, but I remember following her around when I was little. I adored her. I wanted to look like her when I grew up. I can remember my mother telling me I had a fat chance of growing up to look like Adriene."

She drew a deep sigh. The wall in front of her, with the note pad and the pencil, blurred, became colors of pale yellow against the wallpaper of pastels. The pad was like a hole in the wall, and the pencil a miniature walking cane.

"I saw her ... just after the killing of Mrs. Crossover. I didn't see her actually kill the lady, but I saw her with the blood on her, and with the ring. I heard the killing. I saw ... I saw Adriene herself being killed. She ..."

She was killed by my father.

She couldn't say it.

Wasn't it enough, after all these years, just to have the girl identified? One name was better than none. Now they could bury her with a name. She wouldn't have to be Jane Doe.

And the mystery of Mrs. Crossover's murder was ended now.

Adriene had killed her.

For jewelry. For a ring.

You killed her for the ring?

She heard her papa's voice as if he were in the room. *You killed her for the ring?*

The horror in that voice, the disbelief, the disappointment was as if he were talking to Alyne, it was so piercing and hurt so deeply that she was shaking again.

Who was Adriene?

Would she ever know?

She needed to know. She needed desperately to know, and the only person who could tell her was Papa.

She hung up the phone and went through the house. She went out onto the stoop and looked across the road at the Crossover house, and her eyes were drawn to the figure that moved across the porch. For just a moment he paused, turned and looked at her, and recognition exploded. Milton!

How could she have forgotten him?

It was he who had loved Adriene. It was he who had known her, who had told her to kill his mother. She remembered now the words, and knew what it meant. *Do it while I'm gone, Adriene, and I'll give you the ring. Do it ...*

He was staring at her, as if he had read her mind, as if he knew now that she had been there, more than once. As if he remembered the day he had helped Adriene drive her away when she had slipped up on them making love in the bushes behind Mrs. Crossover's house. She could hear Adriene laughing as Milton chased her away. She could even hear the laughter of Milton as he went back to Adriene and heard his voice asking, "Will she tell?" And Adriene had assured him that no, no, Alyne would never tell.

Alyne stepped back into the house and closed the door. Milton had not killed his mother, but he had persuaded Adriene to do it for him. In all the years that he had been alone, had he not wondered where Adriene had gone?

She stood in the hall and felt as if she were being observed behind the glass panels in the door. She pulled the blind down and turned.

There was a darkness in the hall she had never seen before. Her eyes had blurred again, so that it seemed as if a large, black wall had closed off the hall, closed off her escape to the bright kitchen. Then she saw that someone, a small figure, stood between her and the dark and shadowy filling of the hall. Greta.

Alyne started to speak to Greta. Her eyes cleared as if a hand had brushed across them and lifted the veil of tears and showed her something that drew down over her with the most intense cold, the most terrible sense of doom, of fear. Blue, red, green shards of light were shooting silently from Greta—no, not Greta, but from the ring on Greta's hand. The lights were the slivers of ice from another world, another dimension, from a reality that pulled Alyne toward it, something she did not want to know about or be faced by. The lights seemed to be arching toward her, and she saw that Greta was coming closer, and now she could see Greta's eyes. They were staring. They did not see her.

Killl ... killl ... kill Papa's pet ... kill ... Al ... yne ...

The voice, the whispers, as piercing as the lights, seemed to be coming from Greta, but Greta's lips were not moving.

Then Alyne's eyes were drawn behind Greta to the dark thing in the hall, the shadow of blackness that was not just a shadow, but something forming. Like a whirlwind that moved within itself, she saw bright points where eyes might have been, and within the swirling darkness she saw the black forming of a shoulder, an arm, a hand.

The hand was large, like Papa's hand had been, that day when she huddled under the table. She had seen his hand, a hand like this one coming toward her, strike Adriene's head such a blow that her neck had snapped as her head jerked sideways. She had seen ... and heard ... and felt ...

She tried to scream and couldn't, but then she heard screaming, somewhere in the house, as if it were coming from above. Her mother, screaming, crying, sobbing, sobbing, sobbing ...

JONAH HAD COME out onto the porch and stood looking, his stare glazed and blending present with past. The road in front of his house might have been dirt and gravel again, and the figure in his memory, the jaunty and saucy bounce of the full white skirt with the silly little flowers as she walked along. She was always bouncing along, hadn't she been? Twisting and wriggling and bouncing. A slut, like her mother. A killer, as it turned out. He had known that first time he saw her when she got off the train, that first time since she was three years old, that she was not the child he had left. She was like her mother now, a slut, a no-good, sent to ruin his life again.

He would not allow it. He would straighten her out. And he had pitted his will against hers and had punished her in every way he knew, and it had done no good.

Bad seed.

He should have known never to marry that woman in the first place, but he had, and for a moment he saw the little girl who had been born, a tiny, freckled, red-haired beauty even then, and something in his heart reminded him that he had loved her too. More than ... *he* had.

He stared toward the Crossover house, but it was as dark and shrouded as his own, the vegetation grown heavy and tangled over the years, never pruned back quite enough. Milton had hidden there. Hidden. But Jonah knew. It was Milton who had made Adriene the murderess.

It was Milton.

The cries came as if from the past. The cries of a woman and of a child. He could almost hear Adriene's screams again. *You'll be sorry ... you'll be sorry ...* and he could hear the woman's scream dying away, but the cries of the child were stronger, tortured, animalistic.

They weren't from the past, they were real. They were next door. Jonah began to run. With his cane out for balance, he went down the steps, cursing in silence the stiffness of his legs, the old-age awkwardness, the frailty he had tried to pretend he did not have.

He reached the sidewalk and ran hobbling, as if his ankles were chained together. He saw his grandsons, William and Derek, come around the corner of the house, their eyes large and frightened. They stopped and waited for him. The cries within the house went on and on, and Jonah knew it was the child, Greta, although the voice might have been the screaming cry of any wild thing in the forest, of a dying bird or a wounded animal.

He swung his cane when he reached the boys and shouted, "Get out of my way! Why are you just standing here?" His voice choked on breathlessness as he went up the three steps to the porch.

He reached the door and wrenched it open. The cries of Greta filled the house, filled his head and his being, and finally became a mere part of himself and no longer heard.

He stopped and stared.

Alyne lay on the floor, her body twisted as if it had been broken. She looked much the same as Adriene had on that last day, that day when past and present came together and sealed forever his doom.

He whirled, waving his cane in front of him. And then he turned back. He stared again. Blue and red lights shot out at him like a snake flicking its tongue, flicking in derision. Greta's hands were up at the sides of her head as if to ward off a striking hand, and her palms were toward him.

She was wearing the ring on her left hand.

He stepped toward her and reached out and got her by the wrist and jerked her forward. She fell to her knees, but he held on to her hand and tore at the ring on her finger. Her screams changed to a whimper as if she were coming awake, and then to gasps of pain as he forcibly twisted the ring off her finger.

He dropped her, and with the ring in his hand he whirled again toward the door and went out. The boys, white faces like blobs on a painting, stepped back for him.

He raised his head and looked across at the Crossover house. Milton Crossover was standing on the sidewalk looking across the road. Jonah started toward him, and Milton turned and ran, awkwardly, like an old woman who had grown too fat around the torso. Like a scared rabbit, he threw looks over his shoulder as Jonah hastened his walk.

Milton disappeared into the wildness of his yard, and Jonah heard a door slam before he had reached the sidewalk.

Jonah climbed the steps to the front door, shouting.

"Open up, Milton! I've got something for you! Open up, Milton. I've come to get you, Milton!"

He found the front door locked, and he raised his cane and pounded on the stained glass oval in the door and the glass shattered and fell around his feet. Beyond the hole was a lace curtain and boards nailed across the door.

Shouting in anger, Jonah went around the porch and came to another door, a solid wood door. It was locked. In silence now he went down the steps at the end of the porch and around the house, sliding open the latch of the gate at the backyard. He followed the path to the screened back porch and went up. The door had not been latched. Milton had been in a hurry when he had run into the house, and Jonah smiled wryly.

He crossed the porch, striking with his cane every step, so that Milton would not think he had escaped. He reached the back door and slammed the curved handle of the cane into the glass without even trying the knob. The glass shattered, just as the stained glass at the front had. Jonah knocked it away with his cane, and reached in and turned the knob.

He stepped into the kitchen. A cat ran and hid in the corner between cabinet and wall.

"Milton!"

His call echoed back at him faintly, as if he faced into a cave. He saw the lack of light and the boards over the windows. Only the door had been left unboarded.

"Milton!" Jonah shouted as he crossed the kitchen and entered the long, dark hall toward the boarded front door. "Milton! I've come to tell you I know you killed your mother!"

He saw in the shadows at the foot of the stairs a movement, and from faraway in his past came a spurt of energy, of youth, of anger and determination. Before Milton could escape up the stairs, Jonah lunged forward and grabbed him. Milton sank to the bottom step of the stairs, crouching, one arm up as if to protect himself.

Jonah held the ring between his finger and thumb and put it inches in front of Milton's eyes.

"Here's the ring, Milton. The ring you promised my little Adriene, if she would help you kill your mother. Do you want the ring, Milton? Was it worth it? You dirty little bastard! You're the one who killed her. You!"

"No! No, take it away! I don't want it!"

"It was your greed, Milton, your evil ways that killed my child, my

Adriene. You killed all of them, my daughters, my grandchildren! It's you who are going to pay, Milton!"

Milton's hand reached out. Jonah, in his fevered mind, saw the reach as if it were intended for the ring, and he let it fall to the floor.

He released Milton, and as the ring rolled he brought the head of his cane down upon it. The cane struck the stone, but only glanced off, and the ring rolled again, circling. Milton screamed.

Jonah's eyes fell upon Milton and saw he was looking behind, in the hall, that something there had caused his face to twist in terror and he was struggling to get away, like an insect trying frantically to crawl back into a crack of the stairway.

Jonah turned.

For just an instant he saw her, a little three-year-old girl crying at the door as he left, her hair the color of a new copper penny, her eyes veiled by a covering of tears, and her voice pleading, *Daddy, don't go, Daddy, don't leave me.*

For just a moment he saw her, and then he was blinded. The darkness of the hall, the moving hall, swept down upon him. He felt the pain in his head and knew he was feeling the pain he had inflicted upon her so many, many times, and knew too he was feeling the pain that at the end had been hers, his Adriene's, and Kenny's, Stephanie's, Clare's, and Alyne's.

You'll be sorry ... sorry ... sorry ...

Daddy, don't go, Daddy, don't leave me ... Daddy ... Daddy ... Daddy ...

EPILOGUE

THE FILES WERE CLOSED on an unsolved mystery. Conrad sat at his desk and looked at the wall with the calendar and a few reminders thumbtacked to the bulletin board, and thought of the case. Milton Crossover was in jail for the murder of Jonah Pattison. The old man had gone to the Crossover house for some reason that Conrad had not been able to determine, and Milton had beaten him to death with his own cane. Milton, who had been reduced to a babbling idiot, it seemed, told a garbled story that made no sense whatsoever. The killer, he said, was Adriene Pattison, the girl whose body was found in the well. Adriene had also murdered his mother, and although he had known about it all these years, he hadn't told anyone. The girl had disappeared, and he had been afraid to tell, he said, because he knew the girl's father, Jonah Pattison, had killed her, although he hadn't guessed, ever, what he had done with her body.

Milton sat huddled in a corner of his jail cell, staring at something in the opposite corner. She was there, he said, watching him, waiting for the moment to kill him too. She had killed all of the Pattison family, the grandson, the granddaughter, Clare, and Alyne.

Milton was at this time awaiting transfer to the State Psychiatric Hospital to be examined. At this point it didn't look as if he would have to stand trial. The man had gone mad.

And yet Conrad wondered, and that was why he had marked his own file on the case as unsolved.

The rest of them would survive, he supposed, saddened by the losses, but somehow more calm now, as if the storm had passed. The psychic storm: Phillip had returned, and the last Conrad saw of Greta, she was in his arms. Phillip took her away with him, the two of them into the sunrise, more or less, after the funerals of Clare and Alyne and Jonah. A For Sale sign had been posted in the front yard of their house, and in the yard of the Pattison house. Just yesterday Conrad had talked to Ross and his two boys, and Ross said he was thinking of selling out too and taking the boys higher into the mountains where they would have land with a stream of water and plenty of trout.

The old Crossover place was empty now too, and Milton's cats had moved across the fence into Conrad's yard and were getting along fairly well with Mutt. This morning Conrad had even seen one of them, the crippled one, sleeping curled up against Mutt's stomach. These were two who a month ago had played chase, with no humor in it.

The ring Milton had reported missing had been found. On the floor beneath the bloodied body of Jonah. It had been given to Milton after it was cleaned of blood.

Milton was right in that the mysterious girl, Adriene, was Jonah Pattison's daughter. Records showed an early marriage to a Gladys Araby, of Reno, Nevada, and the birth of a daughter, Adriene, a few months later. There was then a divorce granted to Jonah and Gladys when Adriene was three years old. Several years later, after Jonah had returned home to live on his father's farm, he had married the mother of Alyne and Clare. If Milton could be believed, and in this instance Conrad supposed he could, the daughter, Adriene, had come to live with Jonah, his wife, and two young daughters thirty-three years ago, in the summer. She was fifteen and very mature, and Milton had fallen in love with her. She was also very wild and heartless, and she had murdered his mother. After her disappearance he hadn't said anything because he was afraid to.

Conrad remembered the times he had gone to Jonah to ask him about the girl, and Jonah had denied knowing her. And Conrad was left to wonder exactly how much of the heartlessness was born into the girl and how much was put there by the heartlessness of others.

It was the ring, Milton said. It had powers. Adriene had coveted it, and it had turned her into what she became.

Milton babbled incoherently at times, making no sense. After years of silence, now he clung to Conrad when they talked, begging Conrad to believe him.

Conrad closed the open file in front of him, his own personal file on a case close to him, important to him, and went outside. The cats gathered meowing around his feet, and Mutt stood back wagging his tail. The sun had gone down and the backyard was sheltering deep shadows beneath the trees and shrubs.

Conrad poured dry cat food into a pan and the cats dived in. In Mutt's dish he poured dry dog food. They would all eat the proper food for awhile, then they would switch plates and eat one another's food. He didn't suppose it mattered. A little more protein in the cat food was the only difference he knew of.

From the pantry he brought two cans of meat and a can opener to add their favorite treat to the dry food. He was opening the cans when he saw a light flicker on next door.

He stopped and stared through the trees at the slivered light in the upstairs window of the Crossover house, an odd feeling of fear passing through him. The house was locked. He had locked it himself. Milton had boarded all the downstairs windows and doors except the back door, yet someone was in the upper bedroom. The bedroom that had belonged to Milton's mother.

The blinds there were only half drawn, and a figure passed by the dimly lighted window, head down, as if it were looking for something. And it seemed to Conrad that he saw femininity in the shape of the head and upper body, and long hair that flowed forward over the shoulders.

Behind him the animals made small eating noises, and the light in the house went out.

The house was dark again. And as Conrad stared at it, he wondered if he had really seen a light, and a girl with long hair, a girl who had been searching for something.

OTHER NOVELS BY RUBY JEAN

1974 The House that Samael Built
1974 Seventh All Hallows' Eve
1974 House at River's Bend
1975 The Girl Who Didn't Die
1978 Child of Satan's House
1978 Satan's Sister
1978 Dark Angel
1982 Hear the Children Cry
1982 Such a Good Baby
1983 The Lake
1983 MaMa
1985 Home Sweet Home
1985 Best Friends
1986 Wait and See
1987 Annabelle
1987 Chain Letter
1988 Smoke
1988 House of Illusions
1988 Jump Rope
1989 Pendulum
1989 Death Stone

OTHER NOVELS BY RUBY JEAN

1990 Vampire Child
1990 Lost and Found
1990 Victoria
1991Celia
1991 Baby Dolly
1992 The Reckoning
1993 The Living Evil
1994 The Haunting
1995 Night Thunder
Pending Bear Hollow Charlie
Pending Cry of the Soul
Pending Pride of Bella Terra
Pending Animal Backtalk

www.ingramcontent.com/pod-product-compliance
Lightning Source LLC
Chambersburg PA
CBHW020609310726
48979CB00008B/1407/J
* 9 7 8 1 9 5 1 5 8 0 4 0 7 *

Every step took him closer to the terror he had started feeling the minute he heard Gwendolyn was missing. With the boys gathered at the bunkhouse, and Mr. Preston and Hagar at their own house, and the police car gone, Rufus walked away, as if he was just strolling. But he had a purpose in mind.

Gwendolyn, a runaway? That was what the police had suggested. "Did she have any reason to run away?" they had asked, and for a moment, there had been stunned silence. No one felt like answering the question. It was too preposterous. Of course she didn't have a reason to run away. What would it have been?

They had looked at the ponds, all of the boys, organized by Vance.

"Five of you go to pond one, and five to pond two ..."

Rufus had wandered along behind them, following for awhile the boys who had gone to check out the first pond, and then the boys at pond two, on and on, through all seven ponds. There were arguments, too, about that. Why would she go out in the rain to fall into a pond that she would have been able to swim through on any day? Or night. Of course it was possible to drown in one of the ponds, but not Gwen, not here, not in the rain. It didn't make sense.

Finally the boys had given up and gone back to the bunkhouse. The day was fading, and they were wet, cold, and confused. Mr. Preston had driven his pickup over the whole place, following each little trail, going into small groves of trees, around each pond, along the pasture fence. Rufus had ridden part of the time with him, and had heard Mr. Preston say, "She's not here. Why would she be out here in the rain? But, she's got to be here. She wouldn't run away. Why would she run away? The gates haven't been opened. The keys are on the wall in the office."

She could have taken a key. But the keys were still there, except for the ones in the care of the boys who were responsible for the gates today.

Where is she?

Rufus had heard the cry from Mr. Preston, and from others, so that as he walked in the silence of the evening, he kept on hearing it.

She was here, somewhere, a terrible premonition told him. She was here, somewhere, and he was afraid that one of the boys knew where she was.

Marsh.

He had watched Marsh during the search, had seen that look on his face, the same look that had been there after the dog's death. He had seen it, and he was sick inside. Where is she, Marsh? He had wanted to ask, but hadn't.

He stopped and looked at the sky. The buzzards would tell him where she was. He knew all he had to do was wait until they started circling.

He saw a crow and heard its caw, caw, and then, sliding silently through the air was one buzzard, then another. They were moving in, large, dark birds, nature's revolting but necessary scavengers.

He watched them circle, their heads lowering, their silent, gliding flights bringing them closer to the ground. They were coming down near the edge of the woods, down below the hollow near pond three. So close? No more than a quarter of a mile from the main house.

Rufus began to walk fast, going back over his tracks, then turning right, he headed away from the path he had taken, and went toward the small tract of woodland. It was here the boys cut wood for the big old fireplace in the living room of the bunkhouse. The fireplace was used only for special occasions, Thanksgiving, Christmas, a winter birthday.

Shadows filled the hollow, but through the trees, he could see the ground was almost as neat as the mowed area around the buildings. On the other side of the woods, though, nearer the ponds and the paths, was a pile of brush.

Rufus went toward it.

He stopped at the edge of the brush, dreading his next move. She was here. The buzzards had told him. They were still overhead, still circling, waiting for him to go away.

He bent down and began moving the cut limbs and dried leaves. The white hand lay palm up on the dark grass, the fingers curled. She was still wearing the small birthstone ring she had gotten for her last birthday, and which she had shown him so proudly.

Look, Rufus, what my dad gave me. And see the diamonds, one on each side. Look, Rufus.

Her face was turned toward him. Empty holes where her lovely blue eyes had been seemed to stare at him, mutely questioning this horror that had happened to her. Her mouth hung open, her lips pale and white, as if she had been drained of blood.

Rufus fell to his knees. "Oh, God, Gwen, oh Gwendolyn, oh God, Marsh, *Marsh*." He had hoped, prayed, he was wrong. That he wouldn't find her—that it wasn't Gwendolyn that drew the buzzards. He had prayed, he knew now, without knowing he prayed.

He turned away, tears hot beneath his eyelids. Two thin drops squeezed out. Tears had not come to his eyes in so long, he no longer knew how to cry. He needed the relief, but it didn't come.

Marsh ...

He had to protect Marsh.

Marsh didn't know what he was doing. The calf, the dog, and now the girl? The eyes—Rufus didn't understand—why was he removing the eyes? He had to be using a knife. Marsh with a knife? Where had he gotten it? Why? Would the psychiatrist say it had something to do with the ax attack on Marsh when he was hardly more than a baby?

It was his fault for letting Marsh leave the bunkhouse.

He had fallen asleep. He had meant to stay awake and listen to any movement Marsh might make through the night. But he had failed. It was as much his fault as it was Marsh's. Something was haywire in the boy's brain, but it wasn't his fault, not the boy's fault. Blame those faraway parents, blame anybody but Marsh.

Rufus took off his raincoat and put it over the girl's body. When he pushed the brush away he saw she was dressed only in those little shorty things he'd seen in catalogs. So she had come out at night?

It didn't make sense.

Could Marsh have gotten into the house and taken her out?

Without anyone knowing?

No, it didn't make sense.

But here she was, and only Rufus knew. And Marsh.

He would have to bury her, somehow. It would be better to let everyone think she had run away. Better than letting Marsh suffer for something he couldn't be blamed for—something he didn't know was wrong?

Yes, he knew. Surely he knew.

Marsh, oh, Marsh, what have you done?

He straightened, leaving her covered with his raincoat. The deed was done. It would have to be hidden. What good would come of having Marsh punished? Taken away and put behind bars?

From now on, he would watch Marsh, every minute through the night. He would spend his nights in the chair. The future ...

There was no future.

Only tomorrow, and another tomorrow if they were so granted.

And tonight.

Tonight he would bring a shovel from the barn and dig a grave in the soft soil of the woodland, and bury her deeply enough the buzzards would go away. Later tonight.

Lights were coming on in the houses when he approached the barn. Twilight would soon turn to darkness. He walked toward the bunkhouse with a heavy, slow tread, feeling his life and energy draining away step by step.

BABETTE SAW THE GATES TO BOYS' Farm. The man had driven slowly, talking, telling her about his family. Three daughters, and four granddaughters and Babette reminded him of them. He had told her about his wife dying, and how far away his daughters lived, all of them married to men who were from other states. "Met them in college," he said. Sometimes he went to visit them, but he didn't feel like intruding on their lives or going to live with them permanently, so he had gotten himself a job selling cameras, and he pointed out the cases in the back seat. The job took up his time, but kept him on the road a lot, and he had gotten tired of listening to the radio. Did she know the kind of music that was being played these days? Well, he supposed she did, but she was young. His music wasn't played much anymore. And he got tired of listening to news. All of it bad, it seemed. Where was she going?

She had finally told him Boys' Farm. Her aunt lived there, she said, worked there, and she was going to see her.

He knew where it was, he had passed it a few times.

On the way he had wanted to eat, and asked if she was hungry. A hamburger, he said, a Coke and fries—fast food. So they had stopped, and it seemed they spent an hour. He was in no hurry, and she had stopped being afraid of him. He was a grandpa, he told her. She was far hungrier than she had realized.

When he stopped on the side street by Boys' Farm, the high, closed gate just yards away, he asked, "Does your aunt know you're coming?"

"Oh, yes," she said. "Thank you for the ride. And everything."

She got out and stood watching him, wanting him to go. Behind her the long buildings just beyond the fence looked weathered and deserted, and she hoped they stayed that way until the man was gone. Lights in the windows at one end of a long building looked like jack-o'-lantern eyes, yellow and hooded, with the blinds drawn.

At this moment she was glad it was still raining. There was no one out, that she could see. Trees beyond the gates hid parts of more buildings, most of them white, like regular houses. She glanced back and then looked again at the grandfather, realizing at that moment that she didn't even know his name.

"Why don't I drive you on up to the house?" he asked through the open passenger window.

She shook her head, and cast a glance over her shoulder. She saw a woman come out onto the narrow porch of the long, low building with the lighted windows.

"There she is," Babette said hurriedly. "There's my aunt."

The man nodded, waved, and drove away. Babette watched the window shut as the car turned and pulled onto the street leading to the highway.

Babette looked toward the woman and saw she was still on the porch of the long building to the right of the entrance building by the big gates. She seemed to be looking north, but Babette couldn't see her features. Was the woman watching her? Dusk had settled beneath the overhang of the roof, and the woman was a shadow without identification except for the round, grandmotherly shape of her body and the dress she wore.

Babette looked around, suddenly frantic for someplace to pretend she had been going to, any place other than those big gates, and those buildings behind the high fences. If the woman went back into the house and told someone there was a visitor, Babette wouldn't stand a chance of getting to Paddy. Someone would come out to see who she was, and the police would be called—and Miss Thornton—and she'd be taken away. And if she told them to please protect Paddy from his mother, and why, they would only think she was being hysterical. She couldn't say, "My mother thinks my brother is a vampire, and she's going to kill him."

She couldn't.

She saw a house across the road, a white farmhouse, at the end of a driveway, sheltered in a grove of trees. She started toward it. The woman would think she had been let out on this side of the highway, and she was visiting someone at the farmhouse.

She went to the edge of the highway and stood waiting for traffic to pass. Before she started across, she looked back at the porch. The woman was gone.

Babette saw to her right, along the tall fence, a row of mesquite, like a hedge, a green camouflage.

She ran toward the trees along the fence of Boys' Farm.

. . .

Rufus sat in his place at the dinner table unable to eat. The boys were quiet tonight, sharing little of the banter and joviality that usually went on. Always quiet, Marsh sat on Rufus's right. Rufus could see his big hands as they tore a bun in half, then tore each half, and kept tearing the bread until it was in bits. Then the boy's big, smooth hands, bigger than his own, picked up the bits of bread and wadded them into a round, hard ball of dough.

Marsh had come to the farm ten years ago with this habit. But in the years since, he had eaten heartily and grown, and had seemed to be happy and well.

The authorities had wanted to take him away after a few months on the farm and institutionalize him. Rufus had persuaded them not to. "He's all right," he had told Mary Bolinger. "He's going to be just fine here." He had tried so hard to persuade them to leave the boy.

He saw now that he had made a terrible mistake.

After dinner he sat on the porch, waiting, his fingers drumming on the wooden arms of the rocking chair. He watched the night darken, and then he saw the clouds thin and the moon come out full and bright.

He waited until all the boys had gone into the bunkhouse and were in bed. All evening Marsh had sat on the porch, in front of Rufus, leaning against a post, his legs swinging. All evening he hadn't spoken a word, and Rufus had said nothing. A few of the other boys had sat with them awhile, and a conversation about baseball had come up.

But it was with relief and dread combined that Rufus waited to be alone. He waited for the sounds of settling in for the night to cease, and the bunkhouse lights to go out.

Then he went to his room and took his rifle down from the top of the closet. It had been a long time since it was used. A few years ago he had enjoyed keeping it in shape with a little target practice in one of the back fields. But it had been three or four years since the rifle had even been cleaned.

He checked the bore and found it still looked fairly clean. He snapped the barrel in place and loaded it from the little box of bullets tucked in the corner of the top shelf.

When he left his room, the rifle was under his arm, the muzzle pointed toward the ground.

Tonight he had to bury Gwen, the little girl he had rocked on his knee when she was only a baby. He wondered if he could bury her, if he could put her body into a hole and cover it with dirt. He wondered if he could ever go back to that wooded lot.

He had to stop Marsh before he killed again.

He walked across the park-like area between the bunkhouse and the barns. A light from the horse's stall spread like a lacy fan out into the paddock. Shadowed upon it was a long, thin figure standing next to the huge shadow of the horse. Orion. Rufus had watched him cross the yard toward the barn, a small, quick figure going to stay with the horse.

Rufus paused. The shovels were in the barn. Could he take one without Orion knowing? The shed room containing the shovels, rakes, and hoes, was on the side of the barn opposite the horse stall. There should be no problem.

Rufus swung to the left, keeping to the shadows as much as he could, the light of the moon seeming like filtered sun in contrast to the darkness of last night with its clouds and rain.

He passed within reach of the rusted old combine and the picnic table beneath the maple tree. He went toward the barn, under cover of the tall trees.

The shovel. The grave ...

He wouldn't allow himself to think of it.

It was something he had to do.

And then he had to stop Marsh.

"Rufus."

Rufus almost dropped the rifle. The voice came out of the darkness and trees to his right. It was a man's voice, but he didn't recognize it.

He blinked and saw the pale outline of a man's face. The figure moved, separated from a black tree trunk, and became the familiar shape of Mr. Preston.

"I see you've got your rifle, Rufus." Martin said.

"Uh—yeah, I thought I'd best get it out."

Martin Preston stepped into the scattered moonlight at the edge of the tree so that his face, head and shoulders were dotted with light. Rufus watched him lift his head and look off toward the big gate.

"I'll walk along with you, Rufus. Out for a walk, or going down to the cattle pastures?"

"Uh—just thought I'd walk around a bit."

Rufus angled toward the string of ponds, away from the grove of trees where the child's body lay. For a few yards they walked in silence. Rufus started shaking so hard that the rifle rattled against the little stud at the side of his boot. He lifted it, cradling it in his arm, the muzzle pointed forward and slightly downward. With his finger on the safety catch, he snapped it off.

"Her mother ran away too, Rufus," Martin said.

"Eh?" Rufus thought at first he hadn't heard Mr. Preston right.

"I never told you," Martin Preston said, walking at Rufus's side, hands still in his pockets. "I never told anyone. She ran away from me and the babies, said she wanted some excitement out of life. She was a beautiful woman. Gwendolyn took after her. Hagar isn't like that, she's more like me. Daily life was always good enough for me, and seems to be for Hagar. Life and animals, and the people around home. But Gwen is different. I could see that, though Gwen didn't know I could. Hagar came to me a short time ago, a few days, and wanted to talk about Gwen—but I wasn't ready to take a real good look at what I felt might be trouble someday."

Rufus didn't know what to say. He could see the little girl, her hand thrown out, palm toward the sky. He could see her face, and the holes where her eyes had been. He felt he was going to collapse, his legs giving out beneath him.

But he had to keep on walking. To keep on listening. Mr. Preston wanted to talk.

Rufus had to listen. And say nothing.

"Her mother had been restless for a long time. After each of the girls was born, she was interested in them for a little while. But maybe she was too young to be a mother. She was twenty-three when Gwen was born. Maybe for her, it was too young."

Rufus nodded. They walked through moonlight, strolling more and more slowly toward the bright surface of the pond. On the grass at the edge of the pond sat the ducks, settled for the night, their heads tucked under their wings. Rufus looked at them without feeling. For the first time in the lives of these fowl he had so enjoyed watching, he wasn't really seeing them. He had a sudden memory of Marsh holding one of the baby ducks in his hands, making a soft, cooing sound of pleasure. He had held the little duck so gently. Those big hands that had turned into killers ...

"She filed for divorce ... she had been gone two months. And then one night I was watching the late news and there was a report of a traffic accident. A man and a woman traveling at a high rate of speed had gone off the road, overturned several times, and were both killed. It was my wife."

Rufus had never known that. He knew Mrs. Preston was dead. That was all. He had never even wondered about it much. Lots of folks die when they're still young. There had been too much other stuff to keep his mind occupied over the years since he met Martin Preston and his two little girls.

"So when I saw that Gwen was growing up to look like and act like her mother, I knew the time would come when she would leave, too. I just didn't think it would be so soon. I still saw her as my baby, you know."

"You—uh—you think she ran away then," Rufus said, hearing his voice unfamiliar in its huskiness.

"I have to think that. It *can't* be anything else. If I have to lose her it has to be that, Rufus. At least she's somewhere out there—and I'll find her if I can."

It was better that way, Rufus saw. Burying the girl would be the most humane thing to do after all. It was better that Mr. Preston think his little girl was still alive somewhere in the world than for him to know the truth.

"We'll go ahead and open the gates tomorrow. The farm has to go on."

He walked on and Martin kept step with him, silent now.

The moon rose higher in the sky. They stopped and looked at its trail across the surface of pond two, and then Rufus turned back toward the bunkhouse.

He had known, in the depths of his heart, that he couldn't bury the child anyway. Not without a casket, not without the protection of at least that. He didn't know what to do.

In the middle of the moonlit compound he separated from Martin and went back to the porch of the bunkhouse.

He climbed the steps, his legs trembling with weariness. He sat down in the rocking chair, leaned back with a sigh, and laid the rifle across his legs.

The chair squeaked softly as he rocked. Tomorrow, as Mr. Preston had said, the gates would be opened, and the Saturday crowd would come in. And none of them would know that within the last week two children had died here, one of them—and perhaps both, he now thought—mysteriously. So too had a dog been violently killed, and a calf mutilated—and one of the children.

There was a pattern, it seemed to Rufus. Something in the back of his mind was trying to get his attention, like a portion of a dream that would mean something if only he could understand. But then it was gone, and he could only lean his head back, close his eyes, and listen to every movement around him.

Tonight he would not sleep. Tonight, but later, he had to make himself attend to the burial. He had to keep thinking that choice was best for them all.

Or tomorrow night—

Tonight he must stay awake.

If Marsh came onto the porch tonight, Rufus would know.

THE ROCKING of his chair stopped. The night grew still, traffic stopped, even the barking of a distant dog silenced. In the deep quiet, Rufus half heard the mooing of the cow far over in her pasture, and the sound reached him like a great moan of despair and loneliness. It ran over his skin like a warning.

He snapped alert. He hadn't gone to sleep, yet he had dozed, sitting upright in the chair, his head back against the wood slats. But behind him there had been a movement. Not a sound, just a feeling.

Someone was behind him.

Just standing there.

He could feel it.

A rush of chills covered his body, and he whirled.

The boy was standing within arm's reach behind his chair. Rufus could see the ghostly outline of his face, and nothing else. He clambered to his feet, and the rifle fell to the floor with a loud clang.

Marsh? ... not *Marsh*.

"Here," Rufus said, a rush of anger flooding into his fear. "Here," he said again. "What are you doing out here?" It was the new boy, he saw. Patrick. He saw the boy stoop and pick up the rifle and hand it toward him, the stock first, as if someone had taught him the proper way to hand a gun to another person. Rufus took it, his hands still shaking, the fury blending with fear, his heart pounding.

"I just got up to go to the bathroom," the boy said.

"Well, go on, it's not out here!"

The boy turned and went back into the hall, and Rufus sat down in the rocking chair, his hands gripping the rifle between his knees. He was already sorry he had barked at the boy. The kid had probably seen him through the open doorway, and had wondered what he was doing on the porch at this hour.

Well, tomorrow he would tell Patrick he was sorry.

Then something popped into his mind. He was seeing the boy again, a shadowy but dimly visible image. The boy hadn't been wearing pajamas. He had been wearing his jeans.

Rufus sat forward in his chair frowning. Then he shook his head and leaned back again.

No, he must have been wrong.

CHAPTER 26

KETTI MINGLED with the crowd of families entering the open main gates to Boys' Farm. Though she walked behind a family of five—mother, father, and three children—she felt exposed. No one knows I'm here, she told herself for the hundredth time. No one would ever recognize me.

She hardly recognized herself. For the first time in her life, her hair was short. After she had cut and dyed it, she had gone to a beauty parlor several blocks away, where she was certain not to meet anyone she knew, and had it professionally shaped. Her reflection in windows she passed revealed a woman she'd never seen. Thinner from her days in jail, days of terrible trauma and the decision she'd come to accept, days when she had trouble forcing food down to keep up the strength she knew she would need.

It's for Babette, she kept telling herself. It's to make very sure that Babette will live.

She wouldn't allow herself to think about the moment when it would happen. The knife was wrapped in a dish towel and carried in a brown sack at her side. Anyone looking at her would think she carried her lunch.

She paid her entry fee at the window, and went through the small, open gates in the breezeway, past the open door of the gift shop, and the soft drink dispenser.

At the end of the breezeway, porches with benches ran along the sides of the buildings. Ahead of her, families were walking toward picnic tables, children were running toward a pond where ducks and geese and a couple of swans paddled in clear, glassy water. Kids were beginning to climb onto the antique machinery that spotted the grassy park. Some families, she saw, were down at the barns, looking at birds in pens, chickens, pheasants.

She went down the steps, looking toward a long building to her right that had a full-length porch facing the slope of the park, the barn, and the ponds.

She knew, in her heart, he was here somewhere. Or he had been, not long ago. She saw someone sitting on a rocking chair. A man. He was too distant for his features to be clear, but he looked like he might be quite old. As she watched, a boy came out of a door and onto the porch. But it wasn't Paddy.

The boy was watching her, she could see, probably because she was staring at the bunkhouse. She turned away. She must remember to act very casual, like a guest. Someone who had come to spend a pleasant day, that was all.

Clutching her brown bag close, she went back to the porch of the entry building and bought a can of Coke. Sipping as she walked, she followed the families toward the ponds to watch the ducks.

The sun was growing hot. She could see steam rising from somewhere beyond the trees that edged part of the pond, and she went toward it. To her right, she noticed, was a big barn, a sprawling structure that seemed to have a lot of pens and sheds. It was surrounded by big trees. Families were going to the pens, looking at the animals, reaching through the wire to stroke animals' heads or feed them from the bags of packaged grain purchased at the entrance.

Ketti watched, making sure she smiled, so she wouldn't stand out as different. She stood at a fence and looked in at three cute goats.

She walked on around the fences of the barn and looked over a board fence at a beautiful black horse standing in a stall. A young girl with hair almost as dark as the horse's coat was brushing the horse, paying no attention to the people who watched over the fence. She reminded Ketti of Babette. They were enough alike to be sisters.

Ketti pulled away and headed toward the barn, going down a kind of open pathway between fences. In the shadows beneath the overhang of the barn roof, she saw a door.

She was alone for a moment.

She went to the door and turned the wooden latch. The door swung open and she stepped into a darkened inner hall. Rooms off the corridor were shadowed and dim, the only light coming from the corridor or cracks in the walls. Farm equipment of various kinds filled the rooms, harnesses were on the walls, along with saddles. It was quiet in the middle section of the barn.

She went back out to the corridor and followed it to a lighter area in the center. To her right was an open area of pens with animals eating and resting. It was a roofed area, and no people had come into the pathway between the pens. In one was a cow with a calf so young it was still wobbly on its feet, and Ketti suspected this was an area in which the public was not invited. This was a private part of the barn, and it would be a safe place for her to hide later.

To her left was a room that held loose hay. Beyond the hay, she saw when she looked cautiously around the corner, was a manger and beyond that a horse stall. The beautiful black horse had been taken out now, and beyond the open end of the stall she saw the young girl who reminded her heartbreakingly of Babette as she walked the horse in the half sun of the open area of the paddock.

Ketti moved quickly and quietly back through the barn. She would mingle with the people until time for the gates to close, then she would come back to the barn to hide. She hadn't seen Paddy yet—Patrick, as she must think of him now, because she knew in her heart that Paddy had been gone from her, and from himself, for a long, long time.

She must let him see her, come near her. She must lure him into the barn, where it was quiet and dark. She pulled her paper sack tightly under her arm. A terrible nervousness came up her spine and spread across her shoulders and into her jaws. Her teeth began to click together faintly, and she felt colder than she ever had in her life. It was the cold of Danny, and of Billy—she wondered how many other deaths Patrick must have caused—and the forewarning of her own death, so soon to come now. Of course she must die. She would not be able to live after killing the body that had been her son. She was afraid ... so afraid, so filled with terror because she knew deep down that she would not succeed.

Babette came into the outer groups of people, picnickers at a table beneath a big tree not far from one of the ponds. Two little kids were wading in the shallow edge of the pond, and a baby sat on a quilt near the picnic table. Babette paused near another tree, her arm brushing its trunk, and saw the couple on the picnic benches glance at her.

She had safely entered the public area of Boys' Farm.

She went on, walking casually as she felt any visitor would, though her heart beat fast and hard. She felt conspicuous, even though she saw she wasn't the only lone stroller. Many people wandered the paths or sat alone at tables or benches, or stood at the ponds feeding the water fowl.

She was tired, so she sat down, her back against another tree trunk, closer to the gates, to the long bunkhouse she had seen yesterday when she first arrived at the gates of the farm.

She had spent the morning walking the fence that surrounded the farm, and found it tall and barbed at the top, impossible to climb. In a way, it was like a prison fence, she guessed, though she knew the wires were to protect all within. She walked miles, it seemed, with nothing but fields and trees on her left and the tall fence on her right. Through the wires of the fence she could see pastures with cattle, horses, goats, and sheep. She could see pasture fences, all of them miniature in comparison to the big outer fence. She saw ponds like small lakes surrounded by lacy mesquite. She could see open ponds, with paths, and swimming areas in the distance, and people. The people seemed to come out with the sunshine.

Last night she had seen she would not be able to get inside the fence, and she had found a clump of mesquite close to the wire and had huddled there, sleepless most of the night, hearing sounds she'd never heard before. Things moved in the leaves, in the air. Traffic was a comfortable drone, familiar but even that had faded, leaving her in the dark, with the drizzling rain, and finally moonlight. That she had slept at all amazed her when she opened her eyes to see sunlight. She had stood up and looked around, her sense of accomplishment overwhelming, bringing to her face a half-smile.

She had survived.

And she had found a way in. A hole under the fence, back where the fence took a sharp angle to the west. To her surprise, the tall fence ended, and the barbed top was gone. The fence was still higher than her head, six feet tall perhaps, but she could manage the climb. But after she had walked a few hundred yards looking for an easy place to go over, she had found the ravine, and at its bottom, the fence didn't quite reach the ground. Something else had burrowed under there many times in the past, it seemed, so that a bare little tunnel went under the fence. Her body barely fit in it, and without too much strain, she crawled through.

She strolled the grounds. The farm was even more beautiful than it had looked from the outside. Big trees dotted the grassy, rolling land that stretched from the ponds past big barns, sheds and pens to the bunkhouse. Over to her right, she saw a row of white houses with their own little yards. She strolled, trying to look as casual as the others. Kids ran, climbed on the machinery, hung on boards of a stockade fence connected to the barn. Boys that looked as if they might live here went around in twos and threes, sometimes stopping to talk to the families or the kids.

But somewhere around here was her mother. Somewhere among the crowd, a woman with dark, short hair, was carrying a knife.

Where would she have gone?

Had she not arrived yet?

Or had she been here and already gone, leaving Paddy dead somewhere, and no one aware of it.

Babette moved across the sunny park toward the building by the gates. She was thirsty, but not hungry, never hungry. Her package of bread and jar of peanut butter had not been touched. She felt in her pocket for two of the quarters and stood for several minutes near the Coke machine, her fingers tightly clutching the coins. Dads came to the machine with their kids, getting cans of pop. She told herself she was waiting because the machines were in use, though in her heart she knew she was afraid to spend what money she had.

But if she had a can in her hand, wouldn't she look as if she belonged to the crowd that had paid its way through the gate?

She slipped the quarters into the slot before she could think too much about it. Then, with the opened can of Coke, she sat down on one of the benches and watched the boys, looking for one among them.

Long after the Coke can was empty and had grown warm in her hands, she got up from the bench and went down to the barns and strolled the sandy, hard-packed paths that led from pen to pen. The sun had dropped low in the west, and there were fewer people looking at the animals. Babette had moved among them for hours without seeing a familiar face—not Ketti, not Patrick. At times she felt she had come to an alien world, that neither Paddy nor their mother had ever been here.

She watched a group of boys come with feed for the pigs and wished she dared ask one of them if he knew Paddy.

People were leaving through the breezeway that led to the steps and gates in front. Near the big entrance gate was another gate that opened and let out a red pickup, and then closed behind it. Two boys at the gates looked like Paddy. Both were blond. She went toward them, but stopped beneath a tree. If she went too far out into the open she would be expected to leave with the crowd.

She saw groups of families over beyond the ponds, and she went toward them, walking as if she were going to join one of them. As soon as she was behind the mesquite at the edge of pond two, she ran under cover of the shrub-like trees toward the pastures, where she would not be seen. Where she could safely stay until dark and find her brother.

KETTI POSITIONED herself in the barn so she could see the bunkhouse. She had spent most of the afternoon in the barn, watching. The chores had started, and she remembered from her youth how animal feedings were handled. The boys would be around with buckets of grain or pitchforks of hay. And among them, somewhere, she might find Patrick.

A small boy with dark hair went into a wire pen with a bucket of grain, pulling the door's wooden latch into place. "Chick, chick, chick," he clucked to the pheasants as they came to him.

Ketti watched as he poured the grain into feeders and then went out to a hydrant to get a bucket of water for the waterers. Three little children clung to the wire and watched him, silent and awed. Their parents stood nearby.

Ketti almost didn't see the boy coming down the path. She glanced at him, and then stared. Patrick. Shadows covered his face as he walked beneath the deepening shade of a tree. His eyes looked hollow—lifeless—in that first startled moment of recognition.

Then he was staring at her, and she saw the pale gray, that odd lightness that had replaced the soft blue of Paddy's eyes.

She felt penned by his eyes, trapped against the shadowed door of the corridor in which she knew Patrick had recognized her. He was not fifteen feet away, and other people wandered the path—the two young parents, the children who had watched the feeding of the pheasants, the boy with the feed bucket and others. Yet she felt as if she was in a frightening world alone with this person—this non-person—she must kill.

She had wanted this confrontation, yet now she was terrified.

Then Patrick was moving on, casually going out of sight.

With her back pressed to the rough board wall, she hid. Through the open end of the corridor she had a narrow view of part of the path and the dark trunk of a tree. Two children ran by, in her view for only a second. Maybe she had only thought he recognized her. Maybe he had stopped and stared because she was staring at him. She had planned to call him to her, to get him away from the crowd, to ...

But she couldn't.

In the end, she couldn't, and hadn't she known, perhaps, that she would never be able to kill him?

Yet if she didn't, he would kill Babette—she had to remember that.

She edged down the central corridor into the darker areas of the barn. She pulled the knife out and let the paper bag fall to her feet. She stood with her back against the wall, around the corner from the corridor, and listened for footsteps on the board floor. Beyond the wall at her back she heard animal sounds, shuffling, eating, and the voices of people. A man called, "Come on, kids, it's time to go."

"Wait just a minute, Daddy, he's going to feed the goats. The little baby goats."

Their voices sounded light and happy, a stark contrast to the truth of her world, her feelings. She wanted to cry. Why couldn't her life have been like that ... three sons, one daughter ... Edward ... a day at a park, or zoo, or farm like this.

He was there, suddenly, his face at the corner by hers.

She had heard no sound, no approaching steps.

Her hand jabbed into her pocket for the small plastic bag of *Wolfsbane*, and found nothing. She had lost it. Dear Lord, where had she lost it? When she rested for a few minutes on the hay? When she leaned down in the corridor to tie her shoe?

She was unprotected. She had to get away.

Escape ...

Get to Babette—take her away—run once again from this being that had once been her baby boy.

She jerked back and started running, stumbling over the hay, her breath caught in her throat and chest. Something dark and swift flew over her, and she whirled and felt her feet tangle in the hay. She felt his hand grip her wrist and press, and heard the cracking of her own thin bones. The pain shot up her arm and she gasped. Her fingers released the handle of the knife. She twisted away from him and tried to get to her feet, but felt herself being thrown back again, pushed into the hay. His face above hers was a pale and featureless blur, his eyes as empty as holes. She saw ... wings ... wings growing from his body, and his mouth had fangs. It was the terrible creature she had seen over his bed that night so long ago ... when Paddy was only five ...

She could no longer separate her son from the winged creature. They became one, and her fear distorted what she saw. She tried to scream, but heard only a gurgle in her throat. And it was then that she realized she had already been slashed, that her throat had been laid open. She could smell the warm, metallic scent of her own blood, and she saw it sprinkle his face like freckles. Then he was opening his mouth and lowering his face.

And she lost sight and feeling.

MARK FORD LAY in the recliner on the patio at the back of his house. Light from the kitchen made a slight, almost sickly contrast to the dwindling light of day, passing over his feet and fading away on the potted plants at the edge of the patio.

The kids were still in the wading pool probably with chattering teeth, he thought, but he was reluctant to tell them to call it a day and come on in. It had been a great day, the kind that came too seldom. He had been off work for two days now, and was just about to get so used to it that he would never want to go back to the dark side of life, the killings, the drugs.

He heard the phone ring, but it was a distant sound that had nothing to do with him. On his days off, he was seldom called back to the station, and their friends and family were always taken care of by Janice.

When she called him, he felt surprise, irritation, and then curiosity.

"For you," she said again, looking out the patio doors, the light creating a halo of brightness around her blond hair. "It must be fairly important. It's someone from the station."

On Saturday evening, the second day of a three-day weekend?

He got up, feeling a little stiff from lounging so long on his spine. "Better come on in, kids," he said, pausing at the door. "You'll be turning blue the next thing you know."

"Aw, Daddy ..."

"I'll pull the plug on that thing when I get back if you're not out of it."

"Okay, Daddy, just a minute."

Mark gave his wife a light kiss on the cheek as he passed by her. He saw the kitchen phone was dangling at the end of its cord, but he passed it by and went to his office.

"Hey, Ford," said the familiar voice of a fellow detective. "I know you're real glad to hear my voice, but we finally got some news on that guy in Washington that you were interested in a few days ago."

"Justin Skein? The boy's dad?"

"Yeah. They found him. I thought you'd want to know."

"Sure. Where is he?"

"He's dead, that's where. They found him in the woods, behind his house under some brush. But the strange thing is, he was covered by a leather jacket that had a furred vampire bat and the word 'vampire' on the back—like a cult or gang jacket. You know the kind. And there was something else. His eyes had been cut out of his head. He'd been dead about ten days."

Mark frowned at the wall in front of him, seeing again the dead calf, its eyes removed. He didn't realize he hadn't answered Detective Johnson until he heard him ask, "You still there?"

"Yeah, I'm here. Was there anything else?"

"Not much. No one in the area seemed to know anything about a vampire gang or club. They said Skein had lived there for about seven years, and had been a good enough citizen. He had a woman living with him, and until recently, a son. The son had gone to school, with ordinary records. There had never been any trouble."

"What about the woman?"

"Nothing. But I've got a hunch she's hit the road. She probably got mad at him. Pretty damned mad, if you ask me. Killing him wasn't enough."

"You think she's the killer?"

"Well, that, or it's a cult killing. Anyway, I thought you'd want to know. I knew you were wanting to find the kid's dad so you could send him home. But that's it. I guess the boy is a permanent at Boy's Farm, if they've got room for him." After they hung up, he sat down at his desk and stared at the calendar on the wall.

A calf with its eyes removed. A man with his eyes removed. A leather jacket with a vampire, a cult thing?

A retarded boy calling another a "bad boy."

He leaned forward, dialed the station number, and asked for Detective Johnson.

"You didn't tell me how Skein was killed," Mark said.

"Well, maybe that's because I didn't have anything to tell. The report from there simply said he was found dead. I guess the ordinary way, shot or stabbed. Maybe, if it was done by the woman, he was poisoned."

Mark Ford hung up the phone again. Or no visible means, he thought, just as there had been no visible means on the calf, only a strange lack of blood in the body. And its eyes had been removed.

He looked up Martin Preston's number at Boys' Farm and dialed it, not exactly sure what he was going to talk to the man about. Just before the phone rang, he hung up. He sat frowning at the back of his hand as it rested on the phone.

He would have to talk to the boy, Patrick. The father had been dead for over a week, ten days, so that meant the boy must have some information about it. *He went away*, he remembered the boy saying to him. His old man had gone away. Left.

Yet there was something wrong. And Patrick, was tied to it.

Tomorrow would do. He could drive out tomorrow and talk to the boy.

He started to leave the office, yet a feeling of urgency drew him back to the phone. He felt puzzled, thoughtful, as if the answer was behind a curtain in his mind. One phone call, tonight.

A girl answered on the first ring, and said, "Hello?" Not "Boys' Farm," as he had expected. This had to be one of Martin Preston's daughters.

"This is Detective Mark Ford. Is Martin Preston available?"

"Have you found Gwen?" she asked quickly, her voice anxious and rising.

"Gwen?" Was he supposed to know someone named Gwen? He couldn't place the name.

"My sister," the girl said, her voice dropping, becoming soft and faraway. Then she added, "My dad isn't here. He went to look for her, I think, though he didn't say."

"Your sister was expected home at a certain time and didn't come?"

"My sister ran away, the police think, night before last."

"I hadn't heard about this. Would the county police have the information?"

"Yes, I guess so."

"Tell me about her."

"She was only eleven. But she looked older. She had blond hair and blue eyes. She didn't take anything. Daddy's been looking for her everywhere."

"You don't think she ran away." It was a feeling he had, more of the puzzled blackness in the back of his mind.

"Why would she?" the girl cried, and he could hear a throatiness in her voice, as if she was holding back tears. "Dad thinks she might have, because he said our mother did, and Gwen was a lot like her. And she knew where the keys are. The keys to the gates. But none of them is missing".

He heard the doorbell ring, and his wife went down the hall. A moment later, the two kids were squealing and greeting Grandma and Grandpa, and Janice called, "Company, Mark."

He had to go. His wife's parents had driven from the other side of town to have dinner and spend Saturday evening with them. The case of the missing girl was in the hands of the county police since Boys' Farm was outside the city limits.

"I'm sorry about your sister," he said. "I called to talk to your father about one of the boys. I'll be in touch tomorrow—"he started to say, and then he remembered that tomorrow was Sunday, and he haul promised Janice they would go to church, and then on a picnic with friends. One more day, he supposed, would solve nothing that couldn't be solved the day after. "I'll call back Monday."

He hung up the phone, listened for a moment to the voices of the kids, still loud and eager. In the back of his mind the puzzle squirmed, broken pieces fitting together on their own.

And in the middle of it was the missing child, thought to have run away through locked gates.

He knew as he went back to the family room to join the guests that he would not be waiting until Monday to talk to Martin Preston.

CHAPTER 27

BABETTE SAT on the bank of the pond looking into the clear water. Beneath the surface she could see the green tops of plants undulating in the still water as though there was a slow current somewhere in the depths. Air from the pond's surface rose to chill her arms, and she put on her wind-breaker. She saw her reflection in the glassy surface of the pond, a triangular face framed by a fringe of dark hair. Her bangs had grown since she had last really looked at herself in a mirror, and now they reached almost to her eyebrows. She put up a hand and pushed them back, but they fell forward again. She thought of Narcissus looking into the water, and falling in love with his image.

She sat still, her small sack of food on the ground beside her. She had finally eaten a slice of bread with peanut butter, using a little stick to dig it out. She had tried her fingers first, and they still felt gummy even though she had washed them in the pond.

The sounds of the day were changing. The voices of the children and other visitors were gone, and in their place she heard frogs beginning to peep from ponds farther away, and the sounds of chickens and ducks clucking and quacking to be fed. She wanted to look for Ketti, and for Paddy, but if she walked across the park now, she would be seen—a guest who hadn't left, they would think, and would escort her to the gates before they closed for the night. Maybe they had closed already. She had heard cars starting and moving away, soft droning sounds in the distance, rising over the sloping land. She heard the put-put of a tractor somewhere back on the farm and then it stopped, and the evening grew more quiet. Twilight was slipping rapidly toward darkness.

In the stillness came the splash of water, not far from where she sat. A fish, she thought. But the soft splashing continued, and then she saw a boy's hands reaching into the water not ten feet away from her, on the other side of the clump of mesquite under which she was hiding.

She leaned forward slowly, cautiously, to catch a glimpse of his face. She saw blond hair as he leaned down to wash. His hands covered his face, and she stared. Paddy? The hair was like his—not light blond, the way it was three years ago, but dark blond, a soft, golden brown frosted with sun-bleached lightness. *Paddy?*

She wanted to call out his name, but didn't dare. It might not be Paddy, it might be any of the other dozen blond young boys she had seen today, boys that she thought at first glance were her brother.

He took his hands away from his face, and she saw the vaguely familiar features, the soft lips, the firm cheeks, the high forehead.

"Paddy!"

His head jerked toward her, and he stared a cold, hard stare that she thought meant only that he was startled at seeing her here. In that first moment his eyes looked oddly empty, as if he had no eyes. The deep chill that moved over her was denied, pushed beneath her delight in finding her brother at last. Not harmed, but well, alive. Safe.

"Oh, Paddy!" She began crawling toward him beneath the mesquite branches. She saw that the front of his shirt was wet from the water he had used to wash his face, arms, and hands.

"Babette," he said, and smiled faintly.

She could see his eyes better now, but there was something odd about them, and against her will, she was remembering what her mother had said. His eyes had changed, at age five. They had been blue, a soft, light blue, but they changed to gray. He was no longer my son, Paddy. He was the other—*thing*, Ketti had said.

She shivered in her windbreaker. It was the cool air off the water, she told herself, and hugged her arms against her stomach, tucking her hands in beneath the jacket.

"I've looked all day for you, Paddy."

He seemed not to hear what she'd said. His eyes were slightly narrowed, as if he was suspicious of her, withdrawn from her. She felt the lack of friendliness, the absence of the brother and sister relationship they used to have. A deep loneliness settled in her. Weren't they going to be close anymore?

"What are you doing here?" he asked.

"I've—I've been trying to find you—I—"

"You're supposed to leave at six o'clock, didn't you know? They locked the gates at six."

"Paddy, I have to talk to you. Did you know our mama came here today? And she was looking for you, too."

He stared at her, and she began to feel that he was scared, as she was. That they needed to stick together. She wanted to reach out and touch him, to reassure herself, but the chills kept her hands beneath her jacket.

"She's—she's—she thinks terrible things about you, Paddy. Her mind just isn't right anymore. I had to come—I've run away from the foster home where I was living, and I can't let anyone see me or they'll take me somewhere and lock me up. They do runaways, you know."

She gave him a chance to answer, to ask about their mother, but he only stared at her. Shadows seemed to be deepening all around him, taking him away from her, his face growing darker, his eyes deep holes. Once again they were looking empty and soulless, and she couldn't bear to look at him. She let her gaze drop to his hands. She saw something dark beneath his fingernails. He seemed to see it too, now, for he began digging at it.

"She even dyed her hair, Paddy, and cut it short. I went home, and I saw where she had. Then I came out here, yesterday evening, but I didn't have the money to come through the gate, so I crawled under the fence at the back of the farm."

He said nothing.

She heard a loud cry from somewhere up by the barns. She shuddered.

"Peacock," he said. "They make that noise."

"Oh. Paddy—what are we going to do? You haven't seen Mama, have you?"

"I haven't seen her."

For a moment he gave his attention to cleaning his fingernails. She watched him dip his hands into the water again and wash away whatever it was that darkened his nails.

"I know she's coming to find you. I just know it."

"If they see you," he said, "they'll make you leave. Or Mr. Preston will call that Child Services lady and they'll take you back, like you said, and put you where you can't get out. So I have to hide you."

"I slept under the mesquite last night. Paddy, I was thinking. We can go together. Why don't we go together? I know where to get out. Come with me, Paddy. Together maybe we can get back to your dad, and he'll let me live with you, too."

"Naw."

"Why not?" She felt frantic with anxiety. She reached over and clutched his sleeve. The thought hadn't really come to her until now, but it seemed the only solution. "Mama doesn't want us now, Paddy. She thinks you—you're—she thinks you killed Danny and Billy. She's gone crazy, Paddy. And if we run away together, it will help her too, because she'll have to go back to work, and maybe in time she'll be better. Come with me, Paddy. There are a lot of farms and woods and places we could hide."

He shrugged slightly, pulling his sleeve away from her hand. "Look," he said. "Maybe you're right. Yeah, we can do that."

"Oh, Paddy! Come on, hurry." She stood up.

"No, we can't do it that way. I tell you what. You wait for me in the barn, and I'll come out after everyone's asleep. If I'm not there for supper, they'll find us before dark. But if we wait until midnight, we'd have hours and hours before they found out I was gone."

She squatted, some of the fear coming back. She wanted to leave now, both of them. "In the barn?"

"Sure. It's dark and safe. It's a big place, with lots of rooms and passages, and I can take you there. Come on. Wait, let me see if anyone's around."

He stooped and went out under the hedge of mesquite, calling to her, "Okay it's safe. Nobody's in sight. They've all gone in for supper now. Hurry. I have to go, too."

The chills had come back, shaking her whole body, causing her teeth to chatter faintly. She tightened her jaws until her teeth began to ache.

Away from the mesquite, with no guests roaming the area, she felt exposed, as if the dark windows of the houses beyond the trees could see her, and were watching her. Dusk was falling rapidly now. Paddy went ahead of her, walking fast, keeping to the edge of the mesquite. At the end of the pond he glanced back only to see that she was close, then he ran to the shelter of the tall shade trees that grew between the upper end of the second pond and the lower parts of the barn lot.

At the corner of the barn, near a pen built with two sides of board fence, a barn side and a wall, he stopped and took her arm.

"In here," he whispered. "There's a long hall."

They passed by the pen where three goats munched hay. They raised their pointed faces with the little beards, and looked at them. They looked oddly contented, it seemed to Babette, but a little weird. She wasn't afraid of them ... yet she was afraid.

She hesitated at the door Paddy opened. Beyond it she saw darkness, and smelled a dusty, musty, hay-like odor, and smothery blackness.

"It's not as dark as it looks," he said softly in her ear. "When you get in there you'll see that light comes through the cracks. You'll be all right. I'll be back at midnight."

She stepped up into the barn, and the door closed. She stood with her back against the wall, her hands feeling the rough boards.

Midnight was so far away.

MARTIN STOPPED the pickup at the gate, got out, and took his keys out of his pocket. A tall light near the gate outlined the hood of his old, red pickup. He could hear a faint buzz from the light as he unlocked the gate.

He had driven into the small town to the east where the kids went to school, and had talked to three girls he had heard Gwendolyn mention. None of them had heard from her.

He had driven the highway, as slowly as he could, pulling over when a car wanted him out of the way, as if he might find his child walking in the grass at the side of the road.

He felt drained with weariness and hopelessness. Where was she? His baby, his little girl.

During the day he had walked the farm, looking. Why did he keep going back to the ponds? It was as if he would see her reflection in the water. His baby, tucked safely into a basket and set to drift on the ponds.

He had gone again to the sheriff, but there was nothing. They had put out a missing child report, the sheriff's people told him, and they were on the alert for the girl, not only here, but everywhere. She had become one of the thousands of missing children.

He drove through the gates, got out and locked them again, and put the keys into his pocket. He drove to his usual parking place under the trees.

Hagar was still up, or else she had left lights on all over the house, it seemed. For the first time, he wondered if she had been afraid of being alone in the house.

But the house was quiet. The hall lights were on, and that was all he saw, even though it had seemed as if every light was burning. He went into the bedroom hall and saw that her door was standing open.

She was asleep, her face softly outlined against her white pillow. He bent and kissed her cheek lightly before he went out into the hall.

Gwen's door was closed. He stood with his hand on the doorknob, hoping that a miracle had happened and Gwen had come home and was safe in her bed.

He opened the door. But the hall light shining across her bed showed it was the way she had left it, covers thrown back, the pillow still bearing her impression.

Empty.

MARSH LAY stiff and still in his bed, his eyes glued to the cot against the wall, to the figure that lay on it.

Marsh would not sleep, tonight. Last night he had meant to not sleep, but he had, without knowing. And when he woke, it was turning day, and time to get up. The strange boy, the bad boy, was in his own bed. Then, as now.

Marsh's eyes closed against his will, and he felt as if he was spinning off into a dark, safe, warm tunnel. He pulled his eyes open.

Movement somewhere. He could hear the soft sounds of a blanket, like the sounds of a mouse making its bed. He widened his eyes and stared toward the dark corner.

The boy was moving, at last. He was rising from his bed.

Marsh heard the sounds of his movements, of his bare feet on the floor as he slipped toward the porch.

The sounds made Marsh tremble. Fear held him, kept him safe in his bed.

The boy was gone, onto the porch, toward where?

Marsh moved. He had to follow. He couldn't lie trembling in his bed the way he had trembled in the dark so long ago.

Marsh got up. He had gone to bed with his jeans on, and like the boy, he went barefoot, going out into the cloakroom, instinctively knowing the way through the dark.

For just an instant, the other boy was a dark figure in the doorway. Then he stepped to one side and was gone.

Marsh hurried to the doorway, and saw that Rufus was sitting in the rocking chair, but he was sleeping. Marsh could hear the sounds of his breathing, the snork-snork of his faint snores.

And outside, going toward the barn, was the bad boy.

He was going to hurt Star Beauty.

Marsh followed him.

RUFUS JERKED AWAKE. For the first moment he was disoriented, his eyes blinking at the moonlight that turned the edge of the porch silver. It seemed brighter than he had ever seen moonlight, as if it was part of the distant dream that had been his world just a moment ago.

Something had awakened him. Now he knew where he was. He had settled on the porch, determined to stay awake, to make sure Marsh did not leave the bunkhouse.

The chair squeaked as he sat forward.

The figure was only a shadow in the moonlight before it slipped beneath the darkness of the trees. *Marsh.* Going toward the barns.

Rufus reached down and lifted the rifle from the floor beside his chair. His finger released the safety catch as he hurried down the steps.

CHAPTER 28

MARK LAY on his side of the bed, his arms under his head, staring at the ceiling. Light from the moon filtered through the trees and spread across his feet like lace. The ceiling light was an object to stare at while he pondered the puzzle of the boy, Patrick Skein; his mother, Ketti Graham; the two little brothers who had died in their sleep; the sister, Babette, that lost, scared fourteen-year-old who had been the main caretaker of the baby boy; the girl, Gwen, who at eleven was younger than she looked and who suddenly was missing; the calf with its eyes removed; and now the father of the boy, his eyes missing from his body ... The puzzle kept changing form, like a kaleidoscope. The pieces shifted, yet refused to come together.

Bad boy ...

Vampire ...

No, it was crazy.

Insane.

He had to get up. He couldn't lie still in a safe, comfortable bed while something he didn't understand was unfolding among a group of helpless people.

He had to get up and do something about it. Maybe if he took a drive, it would help. Maybe if he talked to Preston, it would help. Maybe he ought to just have a cup of coffee and think more about it. Sometimes a midnight cup of coffee helped him figure things out.

He sat up carefully, trying not to disturb Janice, and found himself reaching for the jeans he had taken off, instead of the robe he had meant to put on. He was pulling the jeans on when his wife turned over.

"Couldn't sleep?" she asked groggily.

"No. There's something I have to do before I can sleep. I may go out for awhile—to Boys' Farm. Something is going on, and I need to talk to Preston." He had told her part of it—the missing girl, the mother who had tried to kill her son, the calf with its eyes removed.

She drew a long breath. "Okay. Be careful."

In the hallway he pulled his keys out of his pocket and began walking faster. Now that he'd made a decision, he felt relief to a certain degree, and something new—an urgency to get on with it, as if suddenly he knew that nothing would wait until tomorrow. Before he left he thought to call Mr. Preston and ask him to meet him at the gate.

IT SEEMED to Babette that she had stood in one place for hours while around her, strange, faint noises went on—movements beyond the walls, bumps under the boards of the hall floor below her, rattles like leaves or old hay. Once she sneezed, a sound that seemed to echo through the vast darkness of the barn and, as if her own alien sound had frightened others, the barn became very quiet for a few minutes. She heard the pounding of her own heart in the silence, and felt the coldness of her fear throughout her body.

"Babette. "

It was a thin whisper, but it was Paddy, calling her, from down the long, dark corridor in the center of the barn.

She started toward him, toward the sound of her name, her hand touching the wall for guidance. "Paddy?" Her call to him was soft, yet it seemed to resonate in the barn. She heard the stirrings again, the bump of an animal against its stall. The horse? She could only guess. She listened intently, and got no answer.

"Paddy? Where are you?"

"Babette."

The whisper again, as if it came from far away, as if he was calling for help.

Thin tracks of moon light came in ahead of her, showing her a more open area, and the edge of something that might have been hay. The light looked like bars across the hay, thin and pale.

She went toward it.

Something silent and swift zipped over her head. She felt its movement, the stir of air. In the thin spots of moonlight she glimpsed its body, and saw a wide span of dark wings.

It was gone, and then suddenly it was returning, coming through the arrows of pale light swiftly, and it seemed she heard it now, a piercing, high-pitched sound, almost inaudible. With a small cry in her throat, she dropped to her hands and knees.

It skimmed over her head again, and she felt the current of air pull against her.

Her fingers touched something on the ground that was small and cool. A pouch. A small plastic bag of something. She could feel the cardboard label at the top of the bag. With her breath held, she picked it up. Herbs in the bag crinkled faintly in her fingers as she turned it, feeling, reading from memory.

Wolfsbane.

Protects you from vampires, Babette. *Mama!*

She almost cried it aloud. *Mama.* Mama was here. Had been here! She had dropped this little bag of herbs that she bought for protection.

Babette sat still. She slipped the bag into the hip pocket of her jeans and stared through the darkness around her.

Paddy had lied.

He said he hadn't seen Mama.

He had lied.

She had to get away from him, go for help, try to find Mama.

She reared up and ran, her head low, toward the hay and the open area of pale moonlight. She stumbled over something in the hay, and almost fell, catching herself on her hands. When she looked down, she saw a face staring blankly at her.

She rolled sideways, away from the person in the hay, and got to her hands and knees again. It was just a pale face, with dark blank holes for eyes and mouth, the features shadowy and hardly recognizable. Then as she steadied herself, she saw the face more clearly, the moonlight revealing the outline of nose, chin, and shadowed sockets where eyes should have been.

Mama.

Babette slowly pushed herself to her feet, her hand still touching the hay. In the moonlight she could see Ketti's throat—the open, raw wound, red against her white skin.

The shrill scream that echoed through the barn seemed to come from an animal, not herself. She heard the cracking of boards and the pounding of hooves as the horse tried to break out of its stall.

She turned, and turned again, desperately looking for a way out.

Mama ... Mama had been right... it was Paddy ... Paddy, the killer ...

Or ... Patrick, the vampire ...

Ketti was right. Her mother was right.

Babette whirled toward the horse stall, and the light of the moon beyond, toward safety and away from the horror that her brother had become. But he was there, standing between her and the dim light of outdoors, the horse stall behind him.

She couldn't see his face, only the shape of his head and shoulders. She heard the *whirr* of wings again, an almost silent, swift approach, and saw the winged creature light on Paddy's—Patrick's—shoulder so that in the shadows it now looked as if the boy himself was a winged vampire.

The horse had reared and was hammering at the boards of its stall. Beyond the horse, Babette saw someone else had entered the paddock. Another dark, shadowy figure was running, climbing over the stall gate.

With a cry, she ran toward that person, trying to dodge around Patrick.

She felt herself grabbed by a hand on her arm, and she was flung sideways. She fell, crashing into the stanchions. With her hands out, grasping for anything, she got hold of the boards and tried to pull herself free. If she could only get into the horse's stall, she would be safe ... safe with that other boy ... whoever he was.

But the hand that gripped her arm pulled her back slowly, and she saw moonlight glint on the knife blade as it flashed toward her. She pulled the *Wolfsbane* out of her pocket and held it up.

MARSH HEARD a strangled cry somewhere in the dark of the barn, beyond the empty horse stall. Star Beauty was gone. He could hear her hooves pounding the packed soil of her track at the far end of the paddock. The goat was running alongside her with small, quick movements, like a ghost in the shadows of the open paddock. But the bad boy was hurting something—or someone—in the dark of the barn.

A voice cried out, hoarse and low. Marsh went toward it, blinded by the darkness. Smells of hay and manure, old and gone to black dirt now, mixed with the scent of something else—something tangy and sickening.

It was a smell he remembered vaguely, a smell that once came from his own flesh. Blood. *Blood.*

He came up against the wood of the manger and stanchions, and crawled through. In the striped moonlight that lay beyond, he saw the dark movement of bodies in the hay. Something large and black with swift and hissing wings came at him and he felt the scrape of talons in his scalp.

He lunged forward, and felt something like the fabric of jeans beneath his hand. He closed on it, and found he had grasped an ankle. He jerked, putting all his strength behind the pull. In the pale streaks of light he saw the oval face turn toward him, teeth barred, a hand raising and a knife catching the light before it plunged into darkness again.

He didn't feel the tearing until the knife was pulled from his flesh. Blood squirted onto his shirt from the open wound in his shoulder.

With both hands he reached for the arm with the knife and felt slender bone and thin muscle. Pulling hard, he reared back and felt the boards of the stanchion give way as he tumbled out into the horse stall, the burden of the other body grunting over him.

Who had cried out? She was screaming now, her voice raised. *Hagar?*

With a cry of fury and fear in his throat, Marsh dragged the boy out into the stall and jerked him up, his hands around the soft throbbing neck. His eyes caught a glimpse of movement above him as dark wings swept down, the talons coming at his face. He twisted the boy's neck toward the talons as hard as he could.

Rufus heard the horse's scream blended with the bleat of goats and the restless stirrings of other animals. The paddock, spotted with moonlight and black shadows, revealed nothing. He heard the sound of the horse's hooves against cracking boards.

He ran forward, his rifle up.

As he reached the paddock fence, the horse broke free and pounded out into the open. The black body flashed briefly in the moonlight before it passed in front of Rufus, a wild flight from danger.

Beyond the broken stall gates, Rufus saw Marsh, a dark shadow moving at the edge of the moonlight.

He raised his rifle and aimed.

Tears blurred his eyes, and his hand began to shake so badly that he couldn't pull the trigger. There was no way he could save Marsh from the punishments that lay before him. But, he couldn't kill the boy. Just as at first he hadn't been able to bury Gwen's body, he now couldn't kill Marsh.

He lowered the rifle. But he had to stand up like a man and do what he had come to do. He *had* to kill Marsh.

He brought the rifle up again, aimed, and pulled the trigger, just as a hand grabbed his arm and shoved it upward. Rufus heard the bullet whine harmlessly off into space. He looked at the face beyond his shoulder.

The lawman. Ford.

Without a word, the detective ran to the paddock fence and leaped over it.

As Rufus's eyes cleared, he saw that the figure he'd thought was Marsh was actually two people fighting in the horse stall.

He heard footfalls and turned to see Mr. Preston running past him toward the paddock gate.

A girl's scream tore through the air, released, it seemed, from a trance of silent fear.

Hagar?

Rufus dropped the rifle and ran.

The light in the horse stall came on, and Rufus saw before him a white-faced girl who he at first thought was Hagar. Then he realized that if Hagar was about she would be trying to calm Star Beauty. He had not seen this girl before.

Marsh knelt over someone on the ground, with Mark Ford and Mr. Preston looking on. His hands were still on the boy's neck. The boy's head hung awkwardly to one side, and it was obvious that he could not be alive.

EPILOGUE

Babette sat on the fence watching Hagar ride Star Beauty around the paddock. Orion stood near her, his arms folded across the top board.

Behind her, Babette heard the contented cluck of hens. Tomorrow was visitors' day, and the boys were getting ready, grooming the animals, choosing the chickens and roosters that would be penned for viewing.

Racing season was growing near, and Orion had decided to give Star Beauty her chance. She would be entered in her first race, the Futurity. She was three years old now, and ready to race.

A year had passed since Babette slipped beneath the farm fence, since she had stumbled onto her mother's body. Since Patrick had been killed by Marsh. Since the body of Hagar's little sister, Gwendolyn, had been uncovered by Rufus.

Patrick was now known to be the killer, of not only Gwendolyn, but his own mother, father and stepmother—and also Rex, as Babette knew in the dark, secret places of her mind. But all the things Ketti had believed of him were not known by anyone but Babette.

Babbette was finally happy with the Prestons, living on the farm, knowing she had a home and a family again. But at night, she lived the early part of her life over again, when Paddy was her little brother, innocent and sweet, before the other—whatever it was—had come to him.

At night she thought about a lot of things. She thought about Rufus and Marsh. At first Rufus had gone to jail for concealing Gwendolyn's death, but then Martin had hired a lawyer for him and he was released.

Marsh had not been taken away at all. The knife wounds had not been deep, and Marsh had spent only a few days in the hospital. He was their hero. He had saved Babette's life. She often saw the two of them on the bunkhouse porch, Rufus in his chair, Marsh petting the new pup.

At night she thought of everyone who had been a part of her life—even Rex, who had not really been a part of her life. Rex, whose picture hung on the wall of her new Dad's office.

Sometimes at night Babette saw a dark figure drifting through the moonlight, and she wondered—has Patrick in some way survived to come back to the farm? Was it the winged creature of darkness, the vampire that was part of him?

She had never told.

But she was afraid of the nights.

Between her breasts, in a locket, she carried a tiny portion of *Wolfsbane.* She would carry it all her life.

OTHER NOVELS BY RUBY JEAN

1974 The House that Samael Built
1974 Seventh All Hallows' Eve
1974 House at River's Bend
1975 The Girl Who Didn't Die
1978 Child of Satan's House
1978 Satan's Sister
1978 Dark Angel
1982 Hear the Children Cry
1982 Such a Good Baby
1983 The Lake
1983 MaMa
1985 Home Sweet Home
1985 Best Friends
1986 Wait and See
1987 Annabelle
1987 Chain Letter
1988 Smoke
1988 House of Illusions
1988 Jump Rope
1989 Pendulum
1989 Death Stone

OTHER NOVELS BY RUBY JEAN

1990 Vampire Child
1990 Lost and Found
1990 Victoria
1991 Celia
1991 Baby Dolly
1992 The Reckoning
1993 The Living Evil
1994 The Haunting
1995 Night Thunder
Pending Bear Hollow Charlie
Pending Cry of the Soul
Pending Pride of Bella Terra
Pending Animal Backtalk

www.ingramcontent.com/pod-product-compliance
Lightning Source LLC
Chambersburg PA
CBHW020609310726
48979CB00008B/1406/J

* 9 7 8 1 9 5 1 5 8 0 4 8 3 *